S0-CWQ-020

UNDER THE MOON

"With marshmallows?" Steve asked.

She handed him a mug of cocoa and flipped off the lights on the way to the porch, then led him to the swing. Strains of "Put Your Head on My Shoulder" wafted out the door as Rebecca curled both legs under her and sat sideways facing Steve.

"My older sister used to spoon with her beau on the front porch," he said, slipping his arm around her shoulder.

"What happened? Did he get the girl?"

They have four grown children and nine grandchildren," he said, his voice only a whisper. He gently rocked the swing back and forth.

"Did you ever do any serenading of your own?"

He tipped her face until her eyes met his, her skin warm against his fingertips. "I'm afraid I'd sound more like a frog than Prince Charming." His hand's firm, yet gentle, touch sent a warm shiver through her body. She moved closer, her face near enough to feel his breath against her ear.

"My dear Rebecca . . ." He slid his lips across her mouth, then tenderly nibbled her lower lip. The kiss started gently, then deepened. He drew her against his chest and gazed at her hungrily. "I'm glad I came tonight," he said between kisses.

"Me, too." Rebecca relaxed against his chest with a sigh of pleasure. It had been years since she'd felt like this. Romance. That's what this was. True romance . . .

IT'S NEVER TOO LATE FOR LOVE AND ROMANCE

JUST IN TIME (4188, $4.50/$5.50)
by Peggy Roberts

Constantly taking care of everyone around her has earned Remy Dupre the affectionate nickname "Ma." Then, with Remy's husband gone and oil discovered on her Louisiana farm, her sons and their wives decide it's time to take care of her. But Remy knows how to take care of herself. She starts by checking into a beauty spa, buying some classy new clothes and shoes, discovering an antique vase, and moving on to a fine plantation. Next, not one, but two men attempt to sweep her off her well-shod feet. The right man offers her the opportunity to love again.

LOVE AT LAST (4158, $4.50/$5.50)
by Garda Parker

Fifty, slim, and attractive, Gail Bricker still hadn't found the love of her life. Friends convince her to take an Adventure Tour during the summer vacation she enjoys as an English teacher. At a Cheyenne Indian school in need of teachers, Gail finds her calling. In rancher Slater Kincaid, she finds her match. Gail discovers that it's never too late to fall in love . . . for the very first time.

LOVE LESSONS (3959, $4.50/$5.50)
by Marian Oaks

After almost forty years of marriage, Carolyn Ames certainly hadn't been looking for a divorce. But the ink is barely dry, and here she is already living an exhilarating life as a single woman. First, she lands an exciting and challenging job. Now Jason, the handsome architect, offers her a fairy-tale romance. Carolyn doesn't care that her ultra-conservative neighbors gossip about her and Jason, but she is afraid to give up her independent life-style. She struggles with the balance while she learns to love again.

A KISS TO REMEMBER (4129, $4.50/$5.50)
by Helen Playfair

For the past ten years Lucia Morgan hasn't had time for love or romance. Since her husband's death, she has been raising her two sons, working at a dead-end office job, and designing boutique clothes to make ends meet. Then one night, Mitch Colton comes looking for his daughter, out late with one of her sons. The look in Mitch's eye brings back a host of long-forgotten feelings. When the kids come home and spoil the enchantment, Lucia wonders if she will get the chance to love again.

COME HOME TO LOVE (3930, $4.50/$5.50)
by Jane Bierce

Julia Delaine says good-bye to her skirt-chasing husband Phillip and hello to a whole new life. Julia capably rises to the challenges of her reawakened sexuality, the young man who comes courting, and her new position as the head of her local television station. Her new independence teaches Julia that maybe her time-tested values were right all along and maybe Phillip does belong in her life, with her new terms.

Available wherever paperbacks are sold, or order direct from the Publisher. Send cover price plus 50¢ per copy for mailing and handling to Penguin USA, P.O. Box 999, c/o Dept. 17109, Bergenfield, NJ 07621. Residents of New York and Tennessee must include sales tax. DO NOT SEND CASH.

OVER THE MOON
BETTY COTHRAN

ZEBRA BOOKS
KENSINGTON PUBLISHING CORP.

ZEBRA BOOKS are published by

Kensington Publishing Corp.
850 Third Avenue
New York, NY 10022

Copyright © 1994 by Betty Cothran

All rights reserved. No part of this book may be reproduced in any form or by any means without the prior written consent of the Publisher, excepting brief quotes used in reviews.

If you purchased this book without a cover, you should be aware that this book is stolen property. It was reported as "unsold and destroyed" to the Publisher and neither the Author nor the Publisher has received any payment for this "stripped book."

Zebra and the Z logo Reg. U.S. Pat. & TM Off.

First Printing: June, 1994

Printed in the United States of America

For my husband, Jack
First, last, and always

One

If it hadn't been Halloween, Rebecca Roswell would have believed that she had landed in the enchanting land of Oz. She resisted the urge to ask the towering scarecrow if he was in search of a brain. She cleared her throat and asked instead, "Are you all right?"

Beneath his floppy hat the scarecrow's angular features were covered in white make-up and streaked with soot. Long, lean fingers protruded from the cuffs of his oversized denim shirt stuffed with hay.

A fire truck screeched to a halt in front of the brick ranch house, jolting Rebecca to attention. She stared past the scarecrow to the melted pumpkin on the scorched kitchen counter. No flames. No smoke. It was obvious the fire was no longer a threat.

Out of the corner of her eye, she saw two young boys on their hands and knees—a pirate and a clown—mopping up water with dish towels.

"Captain?" A husky male voice shouted from the front door. "Where are you?"

"Back here in the kitchen, Mitch." Rebecca stepped into the hall and waved the firefighter to the back of the house. "Everything's under control." She couldn't resist adding, "thanks to the scarecrow."

Dressed in full fire regalia, her partner dragged in a thick hose and dropped it in the middle of the kitchen. "Well, I swear!"

Rebecca's explanation was cut short when the rest of the crew burst into the room. The small clown latched onto the scarecrow's thigh like a vise and wailed loud enough to rival the scream of the sirens blaring outside. She shook her head and gave Mitch an "okay" sign with her thumb and index finger to reassure him that things truly were under control.

Slowly, a smile twitched the corners of the scarecrow's mouth. Rebecca's answering grin sparked contagious laughter that engulfed the crew and turned the two little boys' wails to giggles.

The silver-haired firefighter's look of amusement was mirrored on the scarecrow's paint-smeared face, prompting Rebecca to sneak a good look at herself in the mirror. Her black rubber boots—topped by a yellow fireproof coat that hung way below the knees—dwarfed her petite frame. Short silver curls were captured under the black helmet that concealed most of her sweat-stained face. She looked more like a kid dressed up for Halloween than the captain of the Willow Ridge volunteer fire department.

The lanky scarecrow closed the distance between them. "Mrs. . . . ?"

"Roswell. Rebecca Roswell. Not much time for introductions earlier when you had your hands full." She extended a hand. "And you are?"

"Steve Jordan." He laughed and shook her hand firmly. "But I think it's fair to say my leg was more occupied than my hands." He nodded toward the tiny clown now seated on the floor giving the whole crew his undivided attention. "I appreciate your help, but my grandsons and I can clean things up before my daughter gets home." The deep resonance of his voice demanded attention and conjured up a warm feeling in Rebecca's well-hidden heart.

"Don't be silly," she cut him off. "It's my job. Besides, I've met your daughter, Melinda, and she's going to kill you if she comes home and finds this." A sweeping gesture took in the soggy mess in the kitchen. She stole a glance at the broad-shouldered man, then looked away when she realized he had caught her staring.

"I couldn't possibly expect you to—"

"Now, look here, I'm a Hallmark card kind of firefighter."

The scarecrow looked puzzled at her remark.

"You know," she said, and playfully winked,

"Willow Ridge cares enough to send the very best."

He didn't laugh, but instead flashed Rebecca a dazzling smile. His sense of humor might be lacking, but something about his dark, wide eyes and full lips made up for it. This man definitely evoked a response in her—first with his low, sexy voice and now with his five-alarm smile.

Rebecca shrugged her shoulders and started to take down the singed curtains above the burned counter. She deftly handed out a few brief orders, and things started to fall into place. Sensing that the costumed stranger was watching her, Rebecca tried to maintain some semblance of professionalism. She felt like a schoolgirl experiencing her first crush—one minute drawn to the object of her desire, the next pulling back, uncertain what she should do now.

"Can I help?" The little clown tugged at her sleeve. "Can I?" The scarecrow's youngest grandson had inched around the room until he stood next to Rebecca.

She unhooked her helmet strap and rubbed her chin. "Let's see . . . how old are you?"

"Eight!"

"Eight, huh? Why don't you see if you can open up some of the windows and get some air in here?" She pushed up the sash over the sink in the pretense of getting him started, but knew in her heart she needed the cool burst of air to clear her thoughts of the mystery man with the penetrating eyes. Who was this scarecrow? Rebecca thought she knew everyone in Willow Ridge.

"Me, too?" The pirate barely waited for a response before racing after his brother.

Rebecca turned and her eyes briefly met the scarecrow's, then she quickly retreated to the front room and peered out at the sidewalk spectators and curiosity seekers, most of them costumed trick-or-treaters.

A car pulled into the drive and Rebecca wasted no time in walking down the short path, past her own faded red Jeep, to meet the wide-eyed Melinda. "Nobody's hurt," Rebecca assured her. "The fire's out."

"Where are they—the boys?" As if on cue, the pirate and the clown appeared. Melinda hugged them both at once, checked them over to make sure they weren't hurt, then hugged them again when she was satisfied they were okay.

Rebecca could feel Steve's presence, even before she looked behind her and found him standing with his hands stuck deep in his pockets.

"Dad!" His daughter locked him in a bear-hug, then pushed him an arm's length away to get a good look at the scarecrow.

They're close, Rebecca decided, watching the handsome father and daughter. Melinda was immaculate, as always. Rebecca recognized a power suit when she saw one, and this woman was dressed for serious negotiation. She reminded Rebecca of a younger version of herself.

Thank goodness those days are over, she thought as she watched the two young boys vie for control of the conversation. Things had been hard enough for her when she was building her career, but at least she wasn't divorced with kids. A pang of something—regret, no, relief—filled Rebecca when she realized that that part of her life was over and done with.

Her gaze moved across the family and came to rest on Steve, as Melinda took the pirate's hand and demanded an explanation about the fire. "Jeremy, what happened?" Rebecca watched the scarecrow's eyes shift to the pavement.

"It was awesome, Mom. Jake stuck a gigantic candle in the jack-o-lantern, pushed it too close to the curtains and . . ." Jeremy threw out his arms and yelled, "Poof!"

"You know I didn't mean to." Tears pricked Jake's eyes as Steve patted his grandson's shoulder.

"Then Granddad ran over to the sink, grabbed the sprayer and started shooting water at the fire . . ." Jeremy held up his fingers like a pistol and made machine-gun noises, pretending to spray the group.

"And that was that," Steve finished.

Rebecca's gaze locked with his, and he quickly looked down and studied his feet again.

I wonder what lurks beneath that scarecrow's costume. Rebecca blushed at her inquisitive thoughts— thoughts she hadn't had in a long, long time. Maybe never.

"Dad, you've had quite a night. Go in and change out of those silly clothes and I'll talk with Mrs. . . . ?"

"Roswell," Rebecca chimed in as she watched Steve disappear through the door.

"I remember you, now. We met at a Chamber meeting a few months ago." Melinda smiled.

Rebecca nodded, then waved at Mitch pulling off in the fire truck. "I just need a few details for my report."

"Sure, no problem. Come on in for a cup of coffee. I can't put off seeing how *little* the damage really is." Melinda's shoulders drooped a fraction under the padded suit.

Jeremy pulled on Rebecca's sleeve. "Aren't you hot in that get-up?"

"To tell the truth, I am." She smiled at the boys as they watched her unhook the clamps on her jacket and stuff both gloves inside her pocket. Then she pulled off her helmet, raked her silver curls into place with her fingertips, and put the rest of her gear in the storage compartment of her Jeep.

"It's her!" Jeremy pointed at Rebecca.

"Who?" Jake asked.

"The balloon lady."

"No! Really?" Jake punched Jeremy's upper arm.

"Yep," Jeremy said, and returned the punch.

"Is not!"

"Ask her then," Jeremy yelled, almost in tears, "if you don't believe me."

"Boys!" Melinda's tone meant business. "That's enough!" She turned to Rebecca and apologized. "I'm terribly sorry, but you know how kids are."

Not really. Rebecca's experiences didn't include children. For nearly thirty years, she and her late husband had collected everything—fine works of art, expensive wines, loyal employees, and numerous companies. But children had never been a priority. Then it was too late.

"Jeremy's right." Rebecca joined the group as they moved into the house. "I am the balloon lady."

"See. I told you so." Jeremy poked Jake once in the chest with his index finger, then they both took off running to the kitchen.

Rebecca watched Melinda's smile fade as the young woman surveyed the fire's damage, first touching the ragged edges of the burnt wallpaper, then running her fingers along the deep hole in the counter. "I wonder how much all of this is going to cost me," she said to no one in particular. Her brow furrowed and tears glistened in her eyes.

Rebecca didn't try to force the upset woman into a conversation. It had been a long time since she herself had worried about the cost of anything, big or small. But it was a feeling one never forgot.

By the time Steve entered the room a short time later, the boys were sampling their Halloween loot and the women were sitting at the table with their coffee.

"That's an improvement, Dad," Melinda said, as Steve poured himself a cup and sat down.

I'll say. Rebecca boldly checked out his transformation. The scarecrow had changed into a soft flannel shirt and a pair of faded jeans

"What? Tired of the Wizard of Oz look so soon?" He laughed, then shifted his chair so that he faced Rebecca. "Mrs. Roswell, I want to thank you for helping us out. This place cleaned up pretty well, all things considered."

You clean up pretty well yourself. Rebecca openly looked him up and down, admiring his salt-and-pepper hair, his dark, dreamy eyes, and his taut, trim body, no longer hidden under the baggy scarecrow costume. She focused on his long, lean fingers—graceful, yet somehow rugged and strong at the same time. When she looked up at his eyes, she blushed to find Steve staring back at her with an equally appraising look. Outside, the fall air was crisp and cool. Inside, it was hot and getting hotter by the minute. She moved to the open window and took a deep breath.

"Has my daughter filled in all the details, Mrs. Roswell?"

"Please," she told him, "Mrs. Roswell was my mother-in-law. Call me Rebecca."

"She's the balloon lady, Granddad," interrupted Jeremy.

"What?" Steve stretched his long legs out in front of his chair and raised a questioning brow.

"I guess you could call me that." Rebecca hastened to explain. "I run a hot-air balloon business from my place just north of town."

"You don't say." His deep voice raised slightly, hinting at surprise.

"We cater to business execs from Atlanta and tourists going to the mountains," she added, wondering if he was genuinely interested or merely being polite.

"Well, I'll be. I never heard of a woman doing such a thing." Steve shook his head.

"A woman?" Rebecca barked at him, with every intention of biting.

"I only meant . . . I should have said I'm impressed that anyone—man *or* woman—has the nerve to go up in those things."

Quick save, she thought, accepting his off-hand apology at face value. "Come on out to my place, and I'll show you there's nothing to be afraid of."

"Afraid?" Before he could protest further, the boys started bickering about who had the most candy, and Steve squatted down to settle the issue.

Rebecca cautiously broached the subject again. "What about it?"

"What about what?"

She didn't give up easily. "What about letting me take you for a balloon ride? All of you."

The children's eyes lit up. Carbon copies of Steve's eyes, she thought.

"Yeah, Granddad. Can we? Please!" Jeremy pleaded.

"Please," echoed Jake.

She could tell that their outburst of enthusiasm made him uncomfortable. But why?

"Boys . . ." his voice was different, deeper. "Your mom would have a fit."

Startled by the change in his tone, Rebecca looked to his daughter for a clue.

Melinda answered Rebecca's questioning look with a shrug. "I'm not sure you two are old enough to fly without benefit of an airplane," she said, as she tousled Jake's hair, "especially without a bathroom on board."

"Mom!" The boys groaned in unison, and Steve's features eased a bit. "Please!" they begged.

The smartly dressed woman appealed to Rebecca, with a look that asked her to salvage the situation.

"I have an idea." Rebecca leveled her gaze at Steve. "There's no harm in the boys coming out to watch us inflate a balloon for someone else's ride, right?" She looked to Melinda for an answer.

"Sounds good to me." Melinda flashed a smile at her father.

"Now, that's a suggestion I can handle," Steve conceded.

"And then who knows what might happen." Rebecca leaned forward and tapped Steve on the arm. "Tomorrow, say ten-ish." It was more of a statement than a question.

Melinda took a towel from the drawer and began wiping up a puddle of water around the faucets. "I've got some work to catch up on, but Dad can do the honors."

Rebecca noticed Steve's reservation. "It's been a long night," she said, trying to give him an out. "See how you feel when you get up, and give me a ring in the morning, okay?" He appeared grateful for the reprieve.

She was tired. Bone tired. Rebecca wanted to be home in her bed surrounded by what she called country quiet—crickets, bullfrogs, and the distant hoot of her resident owl. Steve jumped up to hold her chair when she stood to leave.

"Jake. Jeremy. Don't you have something to say to Mrs. Roswell?" Melinda prompted a "thank-you" out of each of them. "It's not every day you have a lady firefighter come to your rescue. Is it, Dad?" she ribbed her father.

"Without a doubt, it's a first for me." That deep, resonant voice mesmerized Rebecca, almost causing her to miss what Steve was saying. She smiled, then made her way to her Jeep.

Rebecca's Jeep had survived many winters, but when she turned the key, no familiar growl answered her. Not even a click. Silence met each subsequent twist of the key. Dead battery. Rebecca could have kicked herself when she realized she'd left her storage compartment light on earlier. She had known the battery was on its last leg. Why hadn't she been more careful?

She trudged up the steps, angry and embarrassed, and knocked on the door for the second time tonight. Thankful that Melinda answered, Rebecca explained her dilemma and asked to use the phone to call a wrecker.

"I won't hear of it. We'll drive you home," Melinda insisted as her father joined them.

Steve smiled at Rebecca. "You might as well give up. Once my daughter sets her mind to something, it's history." He fished the keys out of a drawer. "You go ahead and get the boys to bed, Melinda, and I'll see Rebecca home."

Melinda laughed, but didn't protest. "You get the best end of that deal. I've got my work cut out for me after all the sugar those two have eaten."

Steve escorted Rebecca to a small-size pick-up truck and opened the passenger door for her. "I'm sure Melinda has some jumper cables around here somewhere." Steve slid into the driver's seat. "Want to try to jump start your Jeep?"

Rebecca shook her head. "I'm afraid the battery's a goner. Its days were numbered and it's way past time for a new one."

"Whatever you say. Which way?"

"Head up Main and just keep going," she directed. "I live in the old Smith place."

"Smith?" he asked. "I thought you said it was Roswell." The darkness enveloped them as they passed the city limits sign, a dilapidated filling station, and the old apple warehouse.

"The Smiths were the original owners. We bought it fourteen years ago this spring, and I moved up from Atlanta permanently five years ago . . . after my husband died."

"Five years is plenty of time to put down roots," he said.

"Not in a small town like Willow Ridge. You're a newcomer almost forever." She pointed out the turn-off, and Steve slowed the car to a crawl on her steep uphill graveled drive. "A house keeps its name here, even if the owner sells, moves, dies, or divorces."

"And I thought Atlanta had some crazy notions," he joked.

"People still refer to this as the Smith place, even though the last living relative died over a decade ago."

"How did you end up in Willow Ridge?" he asked, keeping his eyes on the unfamiliar road lined with large oaks.

"We had the balloon business for years as a tax write-off. Then after my husband's death, I decided I needed a change and this was it."

"Miss the city?"

After a moment's hesitation, she answered truthfully, "At first, but not now. Willow Ridge is home."

Turnabout was fair play. Rebecca was dying to find out more about the tall, dark man who was playing havoc with her emotions, dusty from years of being kept on a shelf. "Is our fair town going to be your new home, or are you just visiting?"

"I told myself I was coming to help Melinda with the boys." His voice hinted at more than his words were saying. "She's having a bit of trouble."

"Yeah, I heard about the divorce. It's too bad."

"You know?" Steve sounded surprised.

"Rule number one in a small town," Rebecca advised. "Everybody's business is *everybody's* business."

"I'll remember that for future reference." He parked in front of her Victorian cottage nestled between two weeping willows. Porch lights illuminated the immaculate white house fringed by intricate gingerbread and window boxes full of colorful pansies. His long, low whistle told her he was impressed. "Nice place you've got here."

He offered his hand to help her out of the car. Rebecca was surprised, but pleased. Men didn't do that anymore. It reminded her of debutante balls and coming-out parties—big skirts and big hair, stolen kisses in the garden, and being pinned by that special beau.

His hand was slightly rough to the touch and firm, not fleshy and smooth. She liked the way his fingers wrapped around hers and pulled her up effortlessly. She resisted the impulse to hang on longer after she was on her feet.

While she searched for her keys, Steve retrieved her things from the trunk.

"You don't have to walk me to the door," she protested half-heartedly. "It's been a long night."

"My mother always taught me to see a lady to the door." He smiled and offered her his arm again. "And now that I'm getting older and wiser, I realize she was usually right. Besides, except for the occasion of our meeting, I've enjoyed tonight."

"Me, too." Rebecca fumbled with her keys when they reached the beveled-glass door. "Call me in the morning if you're coming." She flipped on the foyer light.

"Do I detect a dislike for surprises?"

"On the contrary, I love surprises."

"I'll remember that," he promised.

It had been an eternity since she had met someone new—someone who might have remembered *Casablanca* before it became a classic, and Lucille Ball when she was a glamour girl. Someone her own age.

Rebecca lingered in the foyer and watched his tall, handsome silhouette in the moonlight as he walked back to the car. Her heart fluttered as the red taillights of Steve's car faded out of sight. Finally, she peeled off her clothes, had a quick shower, and crawled into bed.

Picking up a book off the nightstand, she started to read. Usually, she read a few pages and nodded off to sleep, but tonight her mind kept wandering back to the scarecrow, the loving grandfather and concerned father.

Tonight she would dream of something besides the characters in her romance novel.

Two

Steve pushed his half-buttoned flannel shirt into his jeans and stopped short when he caught his reflection in the full-length mirror on the bedroom door. He consciously pulled his shoulders back, sucked in his stomach, and loosened his belt another notch.

"Gotta get back into exercising," he mumbled after sizing up his physique. He hadn't exactly let himself go, but he had been less than regular with his running since moving in with his daughter. He'd spent most of his time listening to and being supportive of his only child's problems. And his grandchildren had grown into two active little people—full of non-stop curiosity with tons of energy to match.

He took another look at his reflection. He didn't usually bother this much with his appearance, but meeting Rebecca had made him think twice.

The petite woman had barreled into his life the night before with the impact of a hurricane. And she certainly looked to be in terrific shape, he thought, mentally conjuring up her lovely legs. Most tiny women appeared fragile, but not Rebecca Roswell. She looked strong and healthy, full of vitality.

He smiled, remembering. Her beautiful smudged face, her compelling eyes and those silver curls that begged to be touched. "Rebecca," he murmured, letting it roll off his tongue, tasting the sweet sense of something new and wonderful.

For the first time in months, he anticipated what the day offered instead of lingering over memories of what might have been if his wife Dolores had lived. Today he was looking forward to seeing Rebecca again, getting to know her better. But he wasn't looking forward to the prospect of going up in one of those darned balloons.

At the thought, his expression clouded. He shook his head, finished buttoning his shirt, grabbed his jacket, then walked down the hall to the kitchen.

"Jeremy. Jake. Front and center."

Each morning started with his marine sergeant routine. He wanted to do things differently than the way the boys' father had done. A concerted effort to change their daily practices seemed to help them adjust to his absence. The youngsters hopped up from the dining table and stood at attention in front of the refrigerator.

"Shoulders out, gut in," he bellowed, attacking their ticklish spots. Ribs were Jake's downfall, but just an approaching hand at Jeremy's underarm made him jump. "Shoes?"

"Old pair, sir!" Jeremy snapped back to attention, his worn sneakered heels knocking together.

Steve flipped his thumb up in response and continued his inspection. "Dungarees?"

This time the younger Jake answered. "Grungy ones, sir!"

Another thumbs up accompanied by a grin. "Breakfast?" he asked, after a second's hesitation and a glance at the messy table.

"Banana toast, sir!"

Steve wrinkled his nose on cue at the prospect of banana slivers embedded in crunchy peanut butter on top of browned toast. His stomach turned a bit, but he wasn't sure if it was the children's concoction that evoked the reaction, or the thought of the impending balloon adventure.

"Teeth brushed?"

"Aw, Granddad—" Jake started.

Before the usual complaints began, Steve cut them off and added, "Jackets?" He was learning. After several weeks with his grandsons, his grandfatherly tendencies to spoil them rotten had fallen by the wayside and his parental skills had kicked in . . . out of survival.

"Do we have to?" Jake pleaded.

Nodding, Steve said, "Affirmative. The faster you start, the faster we can get going to see Rebecca . . . ah, Mrs. Roswell."

Jake only managed a half-step forward before his older sibling jerked him back "Wait, not yet."

"Oh, right." Steve straightened into attention and gave them a grand salute with his right hand, "Dis—missed." The duo bolted to their respective rooms, frantically searching for their jackets. They met in the adjoining bathroom, then made a hit-and-miss attack on their teeth to placate their grandfather before rushing back downstairs.

After gathering up the dishes, Steve made himself a cup of coffee in the microwave and picked up a leftover piece of plain toast. Maybe this will help settle my stomach, he thought, attempting to soothe the swarm of butterflies in the pit of his abdomen.

Finally, they made their way to Rebecca's house. Steve wished he'd asked Melinda for directions again before she'd headed to work this morning, but subconsciously he knew each turn was as permanently etched in his memory as the features on Rebecca's face.

Before Steve could unbuckle his own seatbelt, the boys had popped theirs open, unlocked the door, and raced toward Rebecca's house. He followed quickly, determined to catch them before they took over the place or destroyed something.

Rebecca's home was even more beautiful in the

daylight. Everything was picture perfect—well thought out, symmetrical—but not stuffy or stiff. When she had talked about the place the night before, he could sense the affection in her voice. He liked it immediately—it was as warm and inviting as a cozy fire on a blustery day.

Rebecca greeted them on the porch. "Welcome to Riding the Wind, boys." She reached out and ceremoniously shook each boy's hand.

Steve's heart skipped like a smooth rock on a still lake when she took his hand and gave it a firm squeeze.

"I was delighted to get your call this morning . . ." She let the sentence trail off and grinned at him.

Her delicate hand felt silky to the touch. He didn't want to let go, but instead wanted to wrap his fingers through hers and absorb some of the confidence and strength Rebecca seemed to possess. After a moment, he grinned back, answering, "Wouldn't have missed it for the world."

Jake tugged at his grandfather's sleeve, forcing him to release Rebecca's fingers. "Where's the balloon?"

"Yeah, where is it?" Jeremy's eyes searched the area.

"Patience, boys. All good things come to those who wait." Steve patted each boy with what he hoped was a calming hand. He loved them, but disciplining grandsons was not the same as raising one's own children. Steve wanted things to go well today, wanted to impress Rebecca, wanted to get through the morning without incident—particularly where the balloon was concerned.

"Well, you won't have to wait much longer, guys. But I do have to ask your granddad one teensy little favor first, okay?"

Steve noticed the boys were enthralled with Rebecca—her voice full of laughter and her teasing green eyes held their attention.

She turned to Steve. "Do you mind?"

"Anything for a lady," he answered.

She raised her eyebrows and cocked her head in his direction. "Mama's rule, again?" Holding each boy by the hand, she moved down the porch steps, around the corner of the house, and straight out into the field without waiting for a response.

Steve answered anyway. "Well, she did raise me right, but I can't say that I remember if that was one of her dictates or not." He marveled at how well she responded to the boys and wondered if she had grandkids of her own. He also noticed that she looked as great from behind as she did from the front.

"How's your back?" she shouted at him over her shoulder.

"My back?" Steve asked cautiously.

The boys surged ahead of Rebecca, squealing in

delight, before Steve could assure her that he was in tip-top shape from years of working in the landscape business. He strained to see what was causing the commotion, his steps quickening.

"Meet the newest additions to the Roswell family and the proud mama, Casey." Rebecca squatted down in the field and showed the boys how to touch the three little Welsh Corgi puppies without hurting them or upsetting the tired, but protective mother.

"Oh, Granddad, look how little they are." Jake gently stroked their downy heads one at a time with his index finger. The young boy beamed when Rebecca nodded her approval at how carefully he was treating the newborn puppies.

"What do you know!" Steve joined the crouched circle, hovering over the tangle of puppy paws curled up next to their mother.

Rebecca straightened and left the boys to "ooh" and "aah" over the newborns. She motioned for Steve to join her a few feet from the group. "They're the reason my Jeep battery died on me last night at your house," she confessed.

"Pardon me?"

Rebecca leaned toward Steve and confided, "Before the fire call came in, I missed Casey and found her out here in labor. When I couldn't coax her to move to the house or even closer to the yard, I gave up and pulled the Jeep out here to shine my headlights on the poor girl while I did my best to help her along."

"Whew! You delivered them?" He gestured toward the puppies. The boys seemed content to watch them nurse for a while. "I'm impressed! I wouldn't have known what to do."

"Can't say I have any experience in the birthing department either. Luckily, my firefighter's training taught me what to do if the situation came up with people, so I just did what needed to be done and let nature take its course. Casey did all the work."

"Poor little thing, she must be worn out."

"That brings me to that small favor I mentioned earlier. I need some help getting Casey and her pups to the porch. I can't stand the thought of her spending one more night out here by herself."

"Uh, huh, and how many times did you trek out here in the middle of the night to check on them, Mrs. Roswell?" His teasing tone was full of admiration for her compassion.

"Okay, you caught me. I did spend more time out here than in my own bed last night. But Casey was tuckered out from her ordeal, and the little things can't do much more than wiggle yet. I just had to make sure nothing bothered them."

She walked to the boys, who were still amazed by the tiny bundles of fuzz snuggling around the warmth of their mama's tummy. "Boys, I need your help. Jeremy, how about running to the porch for me and bringing your granddad that wicker basket . . . and Jake, please go with him and bring the jar of dog treats from the top step." The children took off like greased lightning.

Steve welcomed a moment alone with Rebecca, although he felt a little awkward. The idea of getting to know someone new, someone besides Dolores—who knew his every thought practically before he did—was scary. Attempting to shape words into the semblance of a conversation was harder than any business course he'd ever taken or any landscape deal he'd ever made.

"It's . . ." he began, with Rebecca speaking at exactly the same moment.

Nervously, they both stopped. "I'm sorry," he said. He swallowed hard, his mouth dry.

"Me, too," she smiled. "What were you going to say?"

"Oh, it's nothing. You go ahead." His palms were sweating and he couldn't remember what inane remark he had been about to make in the first place. What in the world had ever possessed him to think he could do this again?

"I just wanted to say how lucky you are to have such great grandkids. They're really terrific."

Relieved to talk about something—anything—particularly something he liked and knew about, Steve blessed her for shifting the conversation to his grandsons. "They are the most precious kids I know," he said with an exaggerated wink. "Of course, they are the *only* kids I've known since my daughter left home for college."

"Spoken like a true grandfather."

"What's the old saying? 'I wouldn't take a nickel for either of them, but I wouldn't trade them for a million bucks.' Since moving in with Melinda, I've wanted to give them away a dozen times, especially when the cartoons run out on Saturday morning. Then there are times when I love them so much I could bust."

Rebecca touched him on the arm. "I think that's one of the nicest things I've ever heard a man say about his grandchildren."

A little embarrassed that he'd opened himself up to someone he hardly knew—not that he was prone to open up to anyone, not even Melinda—he abruptly changed his tone. "A *man?*"

"Touché," she said, with a deep bow. "I stand corrected. What I meant was that your sentiment was lovely. I think it's nice to find a man—or woman—who loves his grandchildren as much as you do."

Pleased at the compliment, Steve was more anxious than ever. He couldn't have been this nervous on his first date. But this was a first date, sort of. Maybe "outing" was a better word. Was she jittery, as well? He gave her a quick glance to see if her nerves seemed as shot as his and found a reassuring smile.

After all, this isn't an enemy camp, he thought. I'm supposed to be having fun, for goodness sake.

Dog treats in hand, the boys stood back while Rebecca carefully loaded the Corgi and her puppies into the basket. The job ended up being more difficult than she'd expected.

Casey proved to be a bit excited about being jostled around and separated from her offspring. Rebecca's initial attempt to place her in the basket backfired when the little mother promptly returned to her grassy post and growled at having been disturbed. Even her favorite treats wouldn't coerce the determined dog to budge.

"This favor has grown, I'm afraid," Rebecca said uneasily. "I've never seen her act this way."

"Mothers have a way of protecting their young at all costs. She's acting as naturally as any mom. We've just got to do it her way."

Finally, they hit on a plan that worked. Steve grabbed the pups while Rebecca tackled Casey. They loaded them simultaneously into the basket, and Casey finally seemed satisfied.

Rebecca wiped her forehead. "Whew! Nothing to it, right? Now all we have to do is carry them to the porch."

"We? That sounds optimistic." Steve moved closer to the basket, prompting a low growl from

Casey. "I'm not sure she and I have had enough time to get to know each other. From the sound of that growl, Casey agrees."

"Her bark is worse than her bite," Rebecca assured him.

"It's the bite part that bothers me." Steve hoisted the heavy basket up while Rebecca cajoled Casey with soothing words. Together they balanced the basket and walked to the porch where Steve deposited his load at the appointed spot near the window.

Rebecca reached down and adjusted the pillow in the basket. "The wind's not so bad here, and Casey can still have a good view of the yard."

Steve imagined her peeking out the window at all hours of the night to make sure Casey was taking good care of her pups. "The view from the window's not so bad either."

"Guilty as charged," she laughed.

After a round of lemonade, everyone followed Rebecca across the yard and into the barn. They passed under a hand-painted sign featuring a colorful balloon and the name "Riding the Wind" in bold, black letters. Inside, they came upon two tall men walking toward them. The elder man wore his hair braided, moccasins on his feet, carried what looked like a handmade leather-sleeved knife on his belt, and appeared to be full-blooded Native American. The other man was undeniably his father's son, but with lighter skin, shorter hair, and contemporary clothes.

"Here we are!" Steve noted the proud tone in Rebecca's voice. "This is Running Hawk and his son, Doug, the two best balloon engineers in the state of Georgia."

Jake was the first to speak. "Wow! Indians!"

"Boys!" Their grandfather gave them a warning look, hoping to forestall any additional comments before they offended the men. "Remember your manners."

"It's okay," the older man assured him, "we're genuine Indians and proud of it. It's a pleasure to meet you, Mr. Jordan."

Steve grasped the man's extended hand. "Steve, please."

"My friends call me Hawk."

The younger man walked toward Steve. "Don't worry about the kids. They'd be blind if they didn't notice, right?" He offered his hand, too. "I'm Doug."

"Doug? That's not an Indian name, is it?" Jeremy piped in.

Nothing was going to stop their curious comments.

The younger Indian crouched next to the two boys. "My whole name is Lightning Doug. My great-grandfather was named Lightning Hawk. So the Lightning part comes from him and it made my dad happy. But my mother was fond of the actor Kirk Douglas. So she named me after a movie star instead of an Indian. Go figure, huh?"

"Who?" Jake asked. Steve noticed that his grandson wrinkled his nose just as Melinda did when there was something she didn't understand. Dolores used to do that, too. It was nice to think about his wife without the stab of pain he usually felt. Being around his family had helped him as much, or more, than he'd helped them.

Hawk chuckled. "The kid doesn't even know who Kirk Douglas *is,* Doug." The elder Indian pushed his braid over his shoulder. "You're getting old, son, when the young don't know who you are talking about. I told you you would be as old as me some day."

"Aah, I'm crushed," Doug protested, but a wide smile remained on the young man's handsome face.

"Happens to the best of us." Rebecca chimed in. "Here, let me help you up, old man, so we can show these youngsters a thing or two about ballooning." She reached out and grabbed Doug's hand. He played along, moaning and groaning as though he were an old man barely able to make it out of bed in the morning.

"Wow!" the boys shouted as they exited the back of the barn and saw the incredible sight in the field beyond. Spread out over the ground was a breathtaking balloon with diagonal stripes of blue, white, and yellow. On its side lay the wicker basket connected to the massive sail with lines of rigging coiled between them.

But Steve wasn't thrilled by what he saw. His stomach lurched alarmingly. Swallowing hard to force the sickening sensation away, Steve told himself he couldn't let the boys see him this way. He wouldn't lose it, no matter how terrified he was of heights.

Before long, Jake was following Doug's every step and Jeremy was helping Hawk roll out the lines to the steel pins positioned around the field. "The boys approve, Steve. How about you?" Rebecca took his arm, and they walked slowly toward the basket.

Steve forced a smile to his lips, but his eyes remained glued to the basket. He had to say something. "It's a beauty, all right," he finally managed.

Did she notice his hands were trembling? He nervously stuck them in his pocket. Why had he come? Here he was, standing in the way of his grandkids having the time of their lives, and worrying if he was going to live through it.

The phone rang in the barn, and Steve was left alone with his thoughts and his fear. Fears, plural, if he counted them out one by one. Fear of flying. Fear of balloons. Fear of the balloons breaking loose. Fear of hitting a tree. Fear of being in a situation he couldn't control. Fear of heights.

Fear, period. Plain and simple.

Rebecca rejoined him. "I've got bad news and good news."

"What's that?" The sinking feeling in his stomach intensified.

"The bad news is, my client called and canceled out on me, but the good news is we're all set up so I can treat the boys to a balloon ride . . . if you think it's okay," she quickly added.

"Well, I don't know. Melinda wasn't expecting us to actually go up today. She might not like me making that decision for the boys." Panic was beginning to set in.

Rebecca shrugged. "It's your call." She peered at him with a knowing stare. "I understand."

She knows. She can see it in my face. I'm not good at lying. Never was. "I have a little problem with heights," he blurted out, on the one hand relieved to have it out in the open, on the other, embarrassed at having to admit such a thing.

"That explains it."

"Explains what?"

She took both of his hands in hers and tugged his clenched fists apart, loosening his vise-like grip. "Your fingers were turning blue."

Steve wiggled his fingers and smiled when he realized she wasn't surprised or upset by his confession.

"Happens all the time. You're not the only one to be taken aback by the gentle giant there."

"Gentle giant?"

"Yeah. You see how intimidating the balloon is because it's gigantic, but it's very gentle, calming really. I've never lost a client yet, and I'm happy to say I've never had one who didn't return for more."

"Glad to hear it," he responded skeptically, "but did any of them fear heights—all heights? I can't ride elevators, stay in high-rise hotels, or eat in those ritzy rotating restaurants Atlanta is famous for."

"I'm a certified pilot. I've done this literally hundreds of times, and so has my crew. I'll help you through it. What do you say?"

Before Steve could answer, Jeremy ran up behind him and rattled off a string of facts about balloons, compliments of Hawk. "We've just got to go up in one someday, Granddad. It's so cool!"

Rebecca shot Steve a questioning look, but didn't speak. Would she still respect him, he wondered, if he didn't at least give it a try?

He closed his eyes, tilted his head upward, took a deep breath and said, "Okay."

"Okay, what, Granddad?"

He had said it aloud once, now he just had to muster the courage to go through with it. "Okay, we can go up in the balloon today, if you like." The look of joy on his young grandson's face made the torture worth it. Seeing Rebecca's wide grin of approval, he almost forgot about the upcoming flight.

Rebecca gave Jeremy the go-ahead to tell Jake the good news, and asked him to pass along some instructions to Hawk. She turned to Steve and lightly touched his arm. "You're a good man, Steve Jordan."

"This better prove it for years to come," he said shakily.

"I'll walk you through it. Be right there by your side."

The thought of Rebecca by his side was comforting, though he could think of better places for them to be.

"Going up in a balloon is a piece of cake. Landing is a little trickier. So to make your virgin flight as painless as possible, we'll eliminate the landing part."

"That's a neat trick. How will you manage that?" He knew he sounded apprehensive.

"By tethering the balloon right here on the airstrip. We simply pile into the basket, take her up a hundred feet or so, and slowly bring her back down until you can step out of the basket safely."

"Then what?" He wanted to make sure there were no catches.

"Then nothing. Hawk and Doug pull the basket down and I roll out. We deflate the balloon while you guys watch from here. Sound good?"

"That last part about watching from here particularly appeals to me." He wanted to lighten up, but fear still nagged at the back of his mind, reminding him that no matter what happened he could break his fool neck even from a few feet up, much less a hundred. But a deal was a deal. He'd said he would try it, and he never went back on his word.

Rebecca pointed out all the parts of the basket to Steve and the boys, explaining what they could and couldn't touch, and how everything worked. "Each part must be approved by the Federal Aviation Administration: the basket, the hoses, the envelope—that's what the balloon part is technically called—right down to the thread it's sewn with and the kinds of stitches."

Steve knew she was going into such great detail for his benefit, and he was glad. It kept him one more minute away from flight. Or prolonged the agony.

Hawk and Doug attached the lines and spread them out to avoid tangles once the balloon inflated. Steve and the boys stepped back to let the crew do their work. Hawk held open the mouth of the envelope while Doug turned on a small fan to partially inflate the balloon with cold air.

"Once we blast the hot air into the balloon, the mouth tends to close up, sort of like the way we pucker our lips after biting a lemon. I'm going inside the balloon now to make a pre-flight check of all the lines and pulleys." Rebecca disappeared into the wavering bulk of nylon for barely a minute before exiting.

"Man, look at that!" Jake exclaimed, as they watched the top of the balloon protrude with air and inch off the ground in slow motion.

Doug and Hawk held down the basket as the balloon gradually filled, then billowed left and right as the shifting hot puffs hit their mark inside the giant. Out in the field, Rebecca positioned herself at the crown line, holding the top of the balloon steady with the attached rigging. She walked toward the basket as the crown rose higher and straightened above her. Then she got into the basket for her final check.

"Hands off," she commanded the crew, making it easy for her to rock the basket to gauge the feel of the balloon's pressure. Satisfied with the results, she called, "Hands on," and they grabbed the rising basket, now a foot off the ground, and pulled it down. "Ready for take-off," she yelled over the roar of the burner. "All aboard!"

Jake and Jeremy excitedly raced each other to the basket. Hawk helped them climb up and get settled. Steve put one foot in front of the other, but his steps felt as if lead weights were attached. Hawk gave him an arm to latch onto as he stepped into the basket and found a spot behind Rebecca.

He thrust his fingers through his thick hair, watching her make some last minute adjustments to the lines.

"You're doing great," she whispered, leaning close to his face, her breath warm against his cheek. "I'm right here."

The balloon shifted slightly as Rebecca shot a blast of hot air into the crown and they started their upward ascent. Since her hands were occupied with the controls, Steve grabbed the first thing he could get hold of from behind—her waist. Her muscles tensed, probably from surprise, then relaxed under his grip. But she never let on she knew how afraid he was.

"I'm gradually taking us up a foot or two at a time." She directed her explanation to Steve, since the boys were no longer interested in what she was doing, only in how high they were going and what they could see from their perch. "We're tethered to the ground, so we won't go left or right at all, except when the wind blows us a smidgen."

"Right," Steve answered, focusing straight down at Rebecca's hair.

"Steve, look outward. Find the horizon," Rebecca warned. "Looking down like that tends to make people woozy."

He immediately looked up and out, a little too quickly. He felt his knees buckle and the back of his neck prickle with goose bumps. His reflexes made him squeeze tighter.

"We'd both be a lot more comfortable if you loosened your grip a bit." She took one of his hands and placed it on the nearest rail, but left the other one in place.

For a moment, Steve's thoughts drifted from his fear to whether he should move or stay put. He decided he liked things just the way they were.

Rebecca's constant chatter about what she was doing kept him occupied until they stopped and she had nothing to do but periodically puff a little air into the crown to keep their altitude.

The boys asked a thousand questions about the balloon and all the sights for miles around. She patiently answered them and gave them little tidbits of information about the area and the Indians who used to live on the land. Steve was surprised at how easily she entertained the boys, whose attention span was short at best.

Steve realized he still had a firm grip on Rebecca's waist. He summoned all his strength and let go, grabbing the instrument console instead. Rebecca acknowledged his attempt to stand alone with a silent nod. She gave him a minute by himself, then moved to his side, picked up his hand, and put it on the blower control.

"What do you say we take this giant down?"

He nodded amidst groans from the boys. He

couldn't tell if being closer to the burner was warming him up, or if being closer to Rebecca was doing the trick. Either way, he was relieved to be
working his way toward solid ground.

"We're going to take it slow and easy, letting
her gently fall back at her own speed," she directed.
"Hawk and Doug are adjusting the rigging as we
go. We don't want to run them ragged, so we'll
puff a little air in once in a while just to give them
time to keep up with us." She kept her hand over
Steve's and shifted the blower on for a second, then
off. Before he knew it, they were making progress,
and the end was in sight. Once again, she'd managed to take his mind off crashing. She was an
amazing woman.

Back on the ground again, Hawk helped the boys
and Steve off, then tipped the basket down for Rebecca to roll out before the envelope began to col-
lapse. The three crew members spent the next ten
minutes securing lines, coiling up rigging, and de-
flating the balloon. Steve's legs felt like rubber—a
bit wobbly, but functioning. He directed the boys
to the nearest bathroom in the barn and found a
welcoming seat under a tree near the airstrip. Rebecca joined him when she'd finished.

"I hope you don't mind." She pushed a curl off
her forehead. "I told the boys they could have a
soda in the office and look at our photo collection
of balloon trips."

"Mind? I'm thrilled for the **chance** to get my legs back before I have to drive those two home." Steve leaned back on the tree trunk and shook his head incredulously. "You're terrific, you know. You fight fires, deliver puppies, win over two very particular grandchildren, maneuver a hot-air balloon as though it was nothing special." He paused. "And help me through one of the scariest fifteen minutes of my entire life. Is there anything you don't do?"

"Not much."

He couldn't tell if her candid answer was serious or not, until she burst out laughing.

"In all fairness, you made that flight yourself. I was just there for moral support."

With a sarcastic note, he said, "Right. Remember that tomorrow when you have black and blue marks where I held on for dear life."

"All in the line of duty." She gave him a lopsided salute.

Walking back through the barn, they found two empty soda bottles, but no boys. "They must have twisted Doug's arm into visiting Casey again. Let's see if I'm right," she suggested.

On the porch the boys were giving their undivided attention to the puppies.

Jeremy ran across the wooden planks to Rebecca's side, with Jake in his shadow. "Tell us about Africa, please. Did you really fly over elephants and giraffes?"

Steve gave her a quizzical look. "Africa?"

"Africa." Her voice had depth and confidence, and an underlying tone of humor. "I did have a life before Willow Ridge, too, you know." She mussed Jake's hair and added, "But that's a tale for another day."

"Promise?" Jake asked.

"You can count on it."

Africa, huh? This beautiful woman was full of surprises. No wonder she wasn't afraid of a little hot air. He could only imagine what adventures Rebecca had taken in her life. The thought intimidated him a bit, yet excited him at the same time.

And he was just as eager as his grandsons to hear about each and every one.

"Say your goodbyes to Casey and start working on those seatbelts, boys," Steve directed, hoping for a chance to say goodbye to Rebecca alone. "I can't thank you enough—"

"Not another word. Their faces thanked me plenty."

"But—" He couldn't find the right words to express how happy he felt—about the day, the boys, about her.

"No buts. We don't regret the things that we do, but the things that we don't do. Now you'll never regret not taking your grandsons up in their first flight . . . or doing it yourself."

Several steps from the porch, Steve turned and

gave a boyish grin. "Maybe that's one of those things Mama *should* have told me."

Waving goodbye, Rebecca added, "It's never too late."

Three

"I'll be home late tonight, Dad. I've got an important appointment," Melinda said as she helped the boys gather their things for school. "There's soup from the deli and some sandwich fixings for dinner."

Steve hesitated before responding. He watched his daughter try to fasten the top button of her skirt—unsuccessfully—once more. She'd gotten heavier almost overnight. Pretty soon she was going to need maternity clothes. "Oh, honey, I didn't realize you wanted me to take care of Jeremy and Jake tonight. I've got plans of my own."

There. He'd said it. Now all he had to do was sit back and wait for the inevitable fireworks.

"Again?" His daughter stopped searching the kitchen drawer for a safety pin. She gave her father a familiar look of chastisement and disappointment. "Well, if you can't be bothered with your own grandchildren, then I'll get a sitter to come in and take care of them."

"Melinda. Don't do this."

She was bringing out the big guns. Guilt and manipulation. Before he'd come to Willow Ridge, she'd managed just fine with the occasional sitter. He suspected she'd even worked her schedule so that she could be home with the boys more. But now she didn't have to because she had a live in baby-sitter at her beck and call. Or so she thought. Steve wondered if she had taken advantage of her husband the same way before the separation.

Melinda sighed—a long-suffering sound she had perfected. "It's short notice, but I suppose Rhonda can come over from next door and watch them a few hours while I work to make ends meet. You know how tough it's been since Joey left." She gave him a pitiful glance.

Steve recognized the look. He ought to. He'd seen it every time she'd wanted something from one of her parents since she'd been old enough to walk and talk. It worked, too. For years, he would give in to those soulful eyes that begged for bubble gum at the grocery store, a matinee on Sunday afternoon, and an extension of curfew in high school. And every time, his surrender had come after first saying "no."

But she was a grown woman now, with children of her own. Steve loved his grandchildren, but they were just that—grandchildren. Parenting them was Melinda's job, not his, whether she liked it or not.

He met her accusing eyes with a sense of determination. This time, her sorrowful expression didn't work. Steve followed the boys into the foyer and helped them find their rain gear without responding to Melinda's ploy to get her way.

Looking out the door, Steve checked for the school bus and noticed the burnished morning haze was lifting. The air was heavy and warm—at 75 degrees, unseasonably warm for early November. He knew it must be tough on Melinda being pregnant in this heat.

Melinda walked into the hallway to kiss the boys goodbye. "Love ya both," she told them as she pecked their cheeks and handed them lunch money.

There was a restless energy about Melinda's movements, her actions, even her voice. Steve didn't want to make matters worse for his daughter, but he knew she had to face up to her responsibilities and work out her own problems. He'd offer his support, of course, but he couldn't straighten out her life for her.

His younger grandson's singing brought him back to the matter at hand. "Grand-dad's got a da-ate . . . Grand-dad's got a da-ate."

Steve stiffened, momentarily disconcerted. "Now, Jake," he began, feeling his face grow warm. "I'm just having a late lunch with Mrs. Roswell, then we're going to the Chamber of Commerce meeting."

"That spells date in my book, too, Jake," Melinda mumbled.

Steve caught her thinly concealed accusation.

Jake continued his sing-song refrain. "Granddad's got a da-ate," but this time added, "with Mrs. Ros-well."

Jeremy gave Steve a sympathetic pat. "Ignore him, Granddad, he's a chump. Besides, he doesn't even *like* girls."

Melinda brusquely changed the subject. "Time to catch the bus." She opened the door and ushered the boys out, then followed them onto the porch.

"Save me a bedtime story, okay?" Steve directed his question to his grandchildren, ignoring Melinda's disapproving look as he pushed past her to the steps.

"Don't make promises you can't keep," she replied fiercely.

Without comment, Steve stared past his daughter to the confused faces of his grandsons. He didn't want to send them off to school feeling anger permeating the air. He resisted the impulse to react to his daughter's stinging remark. "Make it 7:30 sharp and we've got a date. What do you say, guys?"

"Can we read about Wilsey the dognapper?" Jake asked.

"No, that's for babies," Jeremy argued. "I want to read one of the astronaut books."

Steve promised to make time for both, and

waved the boys off as the bus pulled up to the curb.

He watched Melinda's features congeal into a scowl as she turned and entered the house without a word, grabbing her briefcase in the hall before searching the closet for her raincoat. When she couldn't readily put her hand on it, she dropped her briefcase onto the hardwood floor and angrily shoved the coats aside, one by one.

"Isn't that your raincoat on the sofa?" Steve laid a hand on her shoulder, but Melinda immediately shrugged it off. "What in the world is wrong with you, Melinda Jordan Camden? You are still my daughter, and I expect a modicum of respect from you, no matter what." He always used her full name when he was upset with her.

"I don't want to discuss this, Dad." She waved her hand in a dismissive gesture. "Besides, you are going to do what you please no matter what *I* think about things."

"Things? You mean Rebecca, don't you?"

She disregarded his direct question. "I'm just upset, that's all."

He gently took her by the shoulders and turned her so that she faced him. "Are you *this* upset about my friendship with Rebecca?"

Melinda shrugged his hands off again and turned back to the hall mirror, giving Steve a clear reflection of her face. "No," her voice thick with sarcasm, "I'm upset that they keep changing the taste of Coke and the color of Tab!"

Her inappropriate outburst made him uncomfortable. "Why do you keep doing that?"

"What?" She continued to stare at his reflection in the mirror behind her own, avoiding direct contact.

"Make everything so hard."

"You're a fine one to accuse *me* of that. After all, you're the one who's out day after day with practically a stranger, and a *woman* at that." She spat the word out as if it were dirty. "What would Mom say?" Melinda shook with rage as she broke eye contact and swept around to face him again.

Steve felt like a buck frozen in the headlights of a car. Surprised. Stunned. Blindsided. Angry. "How dare you ask such a thing? You have no right!"

"I have every right. She was my mother and your wife. One of us has apparently forgotten about her."

He wasn't up to this yet, but he had no choice. He knew Melinda was overprotective, but he'd had no idea how deep her resentment ran. "I've never forgotten your mother, Melinda. She was the most important person in my life, but she's gone." He breathed a long sigh of resignation. "And I can't do a thing to bring her back."

"But *dating?*" Another dirty word to Melinda.

She added hastily, "Mom would never have done that if you had di . . . passed away first."

"Died, Melinda. You can't even bring yourself to say the word. Your mother died and left me here alone to carry on." He sat down in the nearest chair, bent his head and studied his hands. In a second, he felt his daughter touch his shoulder in a comforting gesture. "I was so angry at her for doing that to me, then I hated myself for feeling that way. It wasn't her fault she died."

Steve lifted his head and searched his daughter's eyes for a glimpse of understanding.

"I'm sorry, Dad." Melinda clutched his hand. They were finally communicating in a way that they hadn't in months. Her tone sounded regretful. "It wasn't your fault Mom died, either. It's just so hard to see you with another woman."

"I'm not *with* anyone, Melinda. Rebecca and I are friends. I'd think you'd be happy for me. I know your mother would be."

Melinda set her chin in a stubborn line. "She would not. How can you say that?"

"I can say that because we discussed it before she died. She made me face the reality of her . . . leaving. She knew I'd be lonely. And I have been, more than you can imagine."

Melinda stared at her mother's photograph on the end table. "I never thought you . . . that she . . . that you two would talk about that."

"Your mother and I talked about everything."

Melinda reached over and lightly fingered the edge of the rosewood frame, touching her mother's smiling face in the photo. "I've been lonely, too, since Joey left."

He knew she was trying to understand what he was feeling. He also knew she missed her mother, but he couldn't stop himself from answering, "It's not the same."

"I know." Her voice sounded small.

"I'm not a kid, Melinda. I need friends my own age, people I can relate to. And as much as I love you and the boys, I'm not their father. They have a perfectly good father who loves them very much."

"Dad, don't start—" she cautioned.

"Okay, I'll try to keep my opinions about your marriage to myself, if you make a real effort to be civil to Rebecca and try to understand that I need friends, too. Deal?"

She tentatively nodded. "No promises, though."

"Melinda?"

"I'll try," she said slowly. "But that's the best I can do."

"That's all I ask." He knew it would take time.

Rebecca pulled off her helmet and handed it to her assigned partner Mitch as she guided the small red fire engine past the three cars that constituted the mid-morning rush.

"Thank goodness that call turned out to be nothing more than a small leaf fire." She downshifted to a crawl as they passed through town.

"Pull up to the cafe and I'll pick us up some lunch." Mitch stashed their helmets in the compartment behind the seat, then slid his red suspenders off. "There. That's more comfortable. You want fried chicken or the daily special?"

"I'll take the sure thing. Get me the chicken, okay?" She expertly maneuvered the fire truck into two parallel parking spaces in front of the Main Street Cafe.

Mitch jumped out of the passenger seat and climbed down the two steps to the street. "See you back at the station."

"It's so hot today. Are you sure you want to walk?" Even with the windows open, there wasn't a hint of breeze. Rebecca missed the crisp fall weather, the change of season.

"It's only a couple of blocks." Mitch patted his belly. "Besides, I'm getting the apple pie, so I need the exercise."

Rebecca waved goodbye and blew her damp, silver bangs off her forehead. The lack of wind had been good earlier when they were putting out the burning leaves, but now that the danger was over, she hoped for a little wind to cool her off.

She eased the fire truck into the street, then stopped again at the town's only traffic light. Waiting for the green signal, she noticed a figure jogging toward her on the far side of the street.

Who in his right mind would run in this heat? She shuffled in her seat to get a better look at the puffing man closing in on the fire engine.

"It's you!" she yelled to Steve. Rebecca checked the rearview mirror to make sure no one had pulled up behind her. "Want to race?"

Steve jogged in place on the sidewalk opposite Rebecca. "Sorry, I'm sticking to the speed limit," he joked. "Taking the truck for a spin?"

He looked good, she thought, even in loose gray sweats. For the last few weeks, she and Steve had spent many hours together. Each time, she became more acutely aware of what an attractive man he was—his wide, strong shoulders, his deep, dark eyes, his long, lean body, and a smile that overwhelmed his entire face. Her pulse raced at the sight of the man who had become a confidant and good friend.

"Lunch?" she invited through the open window. "Mitch is picking up chicken from the cafe. You're welcome to join us. We're eating at the station house."

"Love it," he answered, still jogging in place.

Lunch. Meetings. Long walks. Everything but an honest-to-goodness date. They'd both been careful not to push things too quickly, yet Rebecca knew that what she was feeling was more than simple friendship. But she still wasn't sure she wanted to complicate her life with a relationship. She *was* sure about one thing—she valued her friendship with this wonderful man.

Mitch walked out of the cafe, surprised to see Rebecca still sitting at the traffic light. "You didn't need to wait for me," he said, climbing into the fire engine. The aroma of fried chicken filled the cab. Then he saw Steve through her open window and smiled and winked at Rebecca. "Ohhhh," he drawled.

"Ohhhh, nothing." Rebecca swatted her glove at him. She turned to Steve. "Hop in and we'll go eat."

"Got to make it a mile today," Steve said, barely lifting his heels. "You two go on and I'll meet you there in—"

"An hour?" Mitch threw in.

Steve rolled his eyes. "Ha, ha, ha."

Rebecca poked her partner in his well-padded gut. "Maybe Mitch should join you."

"Me?" Mitch put on his best high-pitched voice. "Well, I never."

"Never will, either," Rebecca chided.

The light had changed several times during their conversation. A brown station wagon pulled up behind the fire engine, prompting Rebecca to put it into gear, but not before she waved, saying, "Work up an appetite." As they pulled away, she shot a warning glance at Mitch. "Not one word."

"I wouldn't think of it," he told her, not bothering to conceal his laughter.

She could feel the heat of a blush right up to the roots of her hair. Mitch knew her as well as anyone, and Mitch knew she liked Steve. Not just liked him, but *liked* him. She couldn't deny it because it was true.

Back at the station she and Mitch changed out of their gear and laid out the food. Rebecca scooped chunks of ice into Styrofoam cups, watching the opened garage doors for Steve. It wasn't long before he jogged in, breathing heavily and holding his side. Sliding onto the picnic bench, he propped his chin up with his hands, elbows on the table, and took one last ragged breath. "Gave it my best effort in front of the station to impress you. You are impressed, aren't you?"

"Absolutely." But mostly, she was impressed that he cared what she thought. When his breathing didn't quickly return to normal, she asked, "Are you all right?"

"Stitches," he managed to say between gasps. ". . . my side."

"Oh," she said, acutely aware of the tenuous situation. Should she pamper him? Feel sorry for him? Make light of his predicament? She was at a loss.

She forced a slow smile to her lips, but her eyes remained on his face.

"I admit it. I overdid it." He grabbed his side again.

"True," Rebecca told him with a soft laugh, relieved that he seemed to be recuperating. "Let's eat. Mitch, are you ready?" Her partner brought in the warmed rolls from the kitchen and joined them at the table.

"That's it? You're not going to rag me more than that?" Steve poured tea over a glassful of ice and took a swallow.

"Her?" Mitch started, but Rebecca shot him a look she hoped would scare a bee from his own hive. With a huge grin, he took a paper plate and handed one to Steve with a smug expression on his face. "Start off slower next time," Mitch advised, "and work your way up to a mile."

Rebecca flashed Steve a smile. "Think you learned your lesson?"

"Definitely."

As they ate, Mitch asked, "So Steve, what brought you to Willow Ridge?"

Rebecca could have kicked him. Mitch knew she didn't want him to pry. She'd made her opinion crystal clear.

Steve wiped his hands on a paper napkin, inched his wallet from his back pocket, and pulled out some photos. "I'm here because of them. This is my older grandson, Jeremy." He pointed. "Here's his younger brother, Jake." He passed the photos to Mitch, who shared them with Rebecca.

"And the good-looking couple? Your daughter and her husband, right?" Mitch asked as he hauled out his own wallet and pictures to show Steve.

She'd seen Mitch's family pictures a dozen times, but today the sight of them caused a tiny tug of envy to pull at Rebecca's heart. Family. Belonging. Things she didn't have or feel.

Mitch gathered up his garbage. "I'd better get out of here while the gettin's good. You never know when another call's gonna come in."

With that he was gone, and they were left alone.

"How do you feel now?" she asked.

"I am so sore," Steve told her, rubbing his aching shoulders with his cupped palms. "I can't believe how old I feel at this moment."

"You're in luck, Mr. Jordan. I have the perfect solution." Rebecca stood up and began massaging his shoulders before she thought about what she was doing.

"A perfect solution for old age?" he asked. "You'll be rich."

"Not for old age. For the soreness." Standing behind him, she pressed and prodded his muscles with her fingers. As he groaned, she worked out the kinks.

"This hurts too much to be perfect!" he complained with a smile.

She gently pinched his shoulder blades. "This isn't the solution I was referring to." Rebecca stopped ministering to his aches and sat down across from him on the other bench.

"No?" His voice was warm and friendly, matching the amicable look in his eyes.

"What I have in mind is even better than a massage. But it takes a while and involves special equipment."

He quirked his eyebrow and sputtered, "I'm afraid to ask, what *do* you have in mind?"

"It's a surprise. Come to my house at 7:30. I promise you won't regret it." Rebecca loved secrets, as long as she was the one in the know. "It's an alternative to that torturous exercise you call jogging."

He smiled. "Count me in."

Rebecca opened the French doors and stepped into the enclosed garden outside her bedroom. A brisk burst of cool air swept through the trees, ruffling what leaves still hung on the branches. She was thankful it was finally cooling off.

An eight-foot hedge shielded her private retreat from interfering eyes. She walked the short distance to the pool and gingerly tested the water tem-

perature with her right foot. Tossing her navy che-
nille robe over the back of a white wicker chair,
she slowly lowered herself into the whirlpool at the
end of the heated pool. The steamy, swirling water
surrounded her body as she slid in deeper, allowing
the tension to wash away with the bubbles.

When she was with Steve, her thoughts automatically turned to her feelings about this new man in
her life, but when she was alone she wondered if
she had lost her mind. Wasn't her life full enough
already?

They talked every day, and several times a week
they met for lunch. On the weekends, Steve took
the boys out to visit the puppies and see the hot-air
balloon. Their friendship was growing into something special. She felt hopeful and happy again for
the first time in years.

"Rebecca . . . Where are you? Rebecca?"

"Around back," she directed, then realized that
Steve didn't know his way through the maze of
hedges. She'd planted the tall, thick bushes to keep
people from wandering in unnoticed. Her privacy
was important to her, especially since the business
was located next to her house. And because she
lived alone. One could never be too careful these
days. "Just a minute."

Before she could step out of the pool, Steve had
found his way through the hedge and was standing
before her.

"Nobody's going to sneak up on you. Boy, would I have loved to see the landscapers get these huge shrubs in here. It must have cost a fortune."

Rebecca felt self-conscious, knee-deep in water, dripping wet, and with a brisk wind hardening her nipples through the thin jersey fabric of her lavender maillot. She hoped he wouldn't notice, but knew immediately from the crimson shade of his face that he had. She crossed her arms over her breasts and shivered from the cool bite in the autumn air.

The early November night was clear and crisp, brightened by an almost full moon. Indirect lighting along the brick path, and in the pool, lent the scene an iridescent quality. The tall, dense hedge resembled spires from a medieval castle. In the streaks of moonlight that filtered through the hedge, she could make out Steve's face smiling at her.

Rebecca slipped back into the warmth of the bubbling water. "What do you think?"

"Beautiful," he said, admiration in his voice.

She wondered if he meant her or her garden. The secret retreat was something to be proud of, to be sure. The heated lap pool and whirlpool were surrounded by patterned brick work lined with beds of petunias and patches of lush green mondo grass. Rebecca had designed this place as a private haven and now, for the first time ever, she wanted to share it with another human being.

Steve crouched next to the whirlpool and dipped his hand into the warm bubbles. "Perfect."

Rebecca's heart skipped a beat. Warmth crawled up her neck. Nestling deeper into the water to avoid his gaze, she welcomed the dim lighting. For a minute, her nerve disappeared.

What possessed me to invite Steve here?

She had to admit, if only to herself, that she wanted to share this place with him. And she wanted to be alone with him.

"This garden is wonderful," he complimented. "Who did it for you? They did a great job."

"Actually, I designed it myself, but I did have some help digging the hole for the pool."

Steve threw his head back and laughed a deep, robust laugh that made Rebecca happy she'd invited him. She splashed a little water his way, causing him to jump back to avoid wetting his jeans.

"Hey, unfair advantage." He moved to the edge, reached down and splashed her back, before jumping out of range again.

"Brave man, from way over there." Rebecca pointed her finger in his direction, then crooked it back and forth. "Come here and let's see how brave you really are."

"I'm not falling for that old trick." Steve moved

a step backward and challenged her with a boyish grin. "You can never get me from there."

"Never say 'never.' That's one of those words that always comes back to haunt you," she warned. "But I promise to be good and not splash you again."

"Can I trust you?" he asked solemnly.

"With your life," she promised.

In two long strides, he joined her at the edge of the pool and leaned dangerously close. Rebecca could feel his nearness, almost as if he were touching her. She wanted to reach out and stroke his cheek, trace the curve of his chin, and press her fingertips to his lips. But she maintained her composure and waited. She'd made the first move every step of the way in their relationship. Now it was his turn. If he felt what she felt, it was only a matter of time. If he didn't, then she'd keep her integrity and he'd be none the wiser.

"If you'd given me a hint that this—" he motioned to the pool "—was your surprise, I'd have brought my trunks. Then I could've joined you." He cupped his hand, scooped up some water, then watched it fall back into the whirlpool near Rebecca's shoulder.

She found herself warming, opening, receptive. Take it easy, she reminded herself. But her emotions were stirring. She had an overwhelming urge to take Steve's hand and pull it to her pounding chest. For the second time tonight, she felt her nipples strain against the thin fabric of her swimsuit. This time the wind wasn't to blame. This man was.

She moved against the rim of the whirlpool, pressing her body against the concrete, feeling the pounding rush of water from the jets against her abdomen. It only intensified the problem, rather than alleviating it. She lifted her body out of the water slightly, still pressed against the side nearest Steve.

He took her chin in one hand and tilted her face toward his. Then he took her hand and touched her moist palm to his lips, letting the droplets of water trickle down his face before gently brushing them away.

"I sure wish I could join you."

Rebecca now had the assurance she needed to make the next move. "Why don't you?" She didn't want to shock him, but neither did she want to pass up a golden opportunity.

"But my trunks—"

She knew it was a long shot, but she had to try. "Be brave, Steve. I dare you to jump in." She gave him a tempting stare.

"With my clothes on?"

She couldn't get a handle on which way he was leaning. His voice indicated nothing, at least nothing definite. She'd just have to fly on intuition and follow his lead. "Whatever suits you . . ." She left it hanging. Turning, she pushed off the wall with her feet and swam to the middle of the lap pool with long, steady strokes.

"You don't think I'll do it, do you?" He bent down, untied his saddle shoes, and kicked them off. Standing in his stockinged feet, he loosened his belt buckle and unsnapped the top button of his jeans.

She was surprised at his boldness, but she was thrilled by the thought that she—Rebecca Roswell—had a wonderful, handsome man flirting with her, dangerously flirting.

"Well, are you coming in or not?" she demanded on her return trip to his end, splashing water over the edge.

As the wave of water ran toward his shoes, he grabbed them up, tossed them on the nearby table, and said, "You asked for it now. Here I come." Without delay, he yanked off his socks, pulled his sweatshirt over his head, dropped his jeans, and dove into the pool.

He swam to her side and ducked her with one swift movement. "You deserved that, you little tease."

They laughed and played, racing and swimming laps, splashing around like teenagers. When they were both spent, they soaked in the whirlpool, allowing the hydrotherapy to soothe their bodies. For the first time, Rebecca felt shy, realizing how close they were . . . and the fact that Steve wore only his boxers underneath the churning water.

They were white boxer shorts that, once wet, clung to his muscular thighs. She couldn't take her eyes off them. Although nothing showed, it didn't stop her from looking.

Steve moved close and touched her hand under the bubbling water. "Rebecca, this has been terrific."

She closed her eyes and leaned back against the hot tub, letting the jets do their wonderful work. "For me, too," she whispered.

"Can I hide here again sometime?"

She opened her eyes and confronted his dark ones, only inches away. "That depends. You're welcome to hide here anytime." She gave him a secretive look. "Except if you've robbed a bank. Then you're on your own."

Steve chuckled and playfully pushed his arms out as if he were going to splash her again, but he didn't. "I've got to get going." He lifted himself out of the water and plopped down on the concrete rim, his boxers clinging to his body. She could see the darker color of his skin through the stark whiteness of his shorts.

Rebecca motioned to the stack of towels on one of the chairs. "Towel off before you catch cold. You can change in the room off the end of the patio if you like." She reluctantly swam laps to give him a chance to dry his long, lanky body in privacy, without benefit of her scrutinizing gaze.

He gathered up his pile of clothes, grabbed a

towel, and headed to the changing room to dress. Rebecca decided to stay in a few minutes longer. She switched off the jets and enjoyed the stillness of the night without the roar of the heater or filter motors.

In only a moment, Steve was back, fully dressed. "You're a sneak!"

"Me?"

"Yes, you. Guess what I found hanging on a peg in the changing room?"

"Oh, yeah. The swim trunks." She averted her eyes. "Sorry."

"You should be." He burst out laughing. "I've been hoodwinked."

Her mouth dropped open in surprise. He wasn't angry.

"You don't think we have to tell the boys about this, do you?" He squeezed the water out of his wet boxers, then wadded them up in his hand.

"It's our secret, just like this place," she assured him, her mind returning to the lack of shorts under his jeans.

"I'm having more fun than I've had in years," he confessed.

"Me, too." Rebecca found it hard to tear her eyes from his well-shaped posterior as he retreated from sight through the hedge and into the darkness.

Four

A middle-aged woman in pink curlers leaned over her grocery cart and snickered to the heavy-set shopper beside her. "She's pregnant?"

The second woman overtly rubbed her own stomach and joined in the laughter. "Well, it's not lasagna that's making those fancy suits tight as a tick!"

Rebecca tried to steer Steve out of earshot. She pushed their shopping cart farther down the aisle, only to get jammed behind a group of browsers. She wanted to buy the wine and get Steve out of there. But no such luck. The women worked their way right behind them. Maybe Steve wasn't paying attention.

"Did you hear her husband moved out?"

"Uh-huh. Joanie at the Beauty Barn told Lois, who told me after Wednesday night services."

"Fill me in, girl. You're holding back on me."

"I heard from reliable sources—" the curler woman began.

Rebecca's face burned with the heat of embarrassment. They were talking about someone she knew and something they knew nothing about. Somebody ought to tell them to shut up.

"Maybe it's not his," the woman continued.

"Oooh, you don't mean . . ."

"Maybe Melinda is only business-like in the board room."

"Or maybe, she does it *in* the board room." They launched into ribald laughter.

Steve stopped cold in mid-aisle and gripped the cart handle so tightly his knuckles turned white. "Melinda?" he asked Rebecca. "Are they talking about Melinda?"

Rebecca simply shook her head and touched his hand. "They're just busybodies. Ignore them."

His face turned as red as the bottle of Bloody Mary mix he had just picked up. "She's my *daughter*," he reminded her bluntly. "I can't possibly let these . . . these . . . women," he stammered, "talk about her that way."

At the sound of his angry voice, the two women turned and looked. So did all the other shoppers within hearing distance, not to mention the checkout clerk who had left his post to clear up the cart jam on Aisle Four.

The curler woman plunged on carelessly with her tirade, while her companion was openly embarrassed.

Steve left his cart and walked toward the women.

"You have no right to talk about Melinda that way."

"Excuse me? *Who are you?*"

"As if that mattered, I'm the father of the subject of your malicious gossip. And I demand an apology from you both."

By this time, half the Grocery Mart customers and a handful of the staff had congregated at the scene. Rebecca quickly side-stepped the network of carts and moved to Steve's side.

It was a standoff. The two gossips looked a bit nonplussed, but remained aloof. Steve stood glaring at them, his jaw jutting forward and his hands firmly planted on his hips.

Rebecca stepped between the women and Steve, filling the awkward silence with quiet but strong words. "You two spoke out of turn about something that was none of your business. You should be ashamed of yourselves."

They should have been ashamed. Any gracious adult would have apologized, but by the look on their faces, they weren't sorry at all. They were only sorry they'd been caught.

Rebecca decided that further confrontation would only make matters worse. "Let's get out of here and leave these two biddies to their gossip." She took Steve's arm and guided him through the growing crowd.

She sensed his emotion as a swift shadow of

embarrassment swept across his features. With each step, she felt his mood turn to raw anger at being publicly humiliated.

Steve stopped at the end of the aisle. "I have to set the record straight before I leave." He removed his arm from her grip before turning to face the women again. "You ladies got one thing right. Melinda is pregnant, and unfortunately, she and her husband are temporarily separated—*temporarily* being the operative word. We're praying for a healthy baby and a quick reconciliation."

The women stared at him without uttering a word, as if he were a raving lunatic.

Steve linked his arm through Rebecca's and started back up the aisle. "Oh," he added when he reached the middle of the crowd, "just so your facts are completely accurate when you repeat this at the Beauty Barn, Melinda's husband *is* the father of her baby." He strode through the door with Rebecca to a smattering of applause from the onlookers.

Oh Lord, Rebecca anguished. We need to get past this awful thing that just happened. We need a distraction to get Steve's mind off this mess. They climbed into her Jeep. "I'm sorry," she told him as she turned the ignition and pulled into Main Street. Both of them lapsed into an uncomfortable silence.

They drove the few miles to his daughter's house before he spoke. "You warned me."

Rebecca could still see his anger. It showed in his erect posture and squared shoulders. "About what?" She gave him a questioning glance out of the corner of her eye. She didn't know those two women, except in passing.

"You told me everybody knew everybody's business here, but I had *no* idea what you meant by that . . . until now. I can't believe those two had the nerve to say such things." He shifted in his seat, clutching the shoulder belt and pulling it away from his neck a couple of inches.

"Don't let it worry you." She tried to reassure him. "People don't listen to gossip like that."

He looked directly at her. "Yeah, right."

Finally, she pulled in front of Melinda's garage and shifted the gear into park, then faced Steve. "This doesn't happen that often. Don't hold it against the rest of Willow Ridge."

"You mean that wasn't the regular five o'clock floor show at the local Grocery Mart?"

Rebecca gave his hand a squeeze. She didn't want to make light of the situation, but neither did she want him to make too much out of those busybodies. She smiled and hoped it was contagious.

Steve opened his door and climbed down to the driveway.

Rebecca jumped out, and taking the steps two

at a time, beat Steve to the door. She grabbed the
knob and opened it for him with a flourish and a
deep bow.

"Rebecca, what are you doing? I thought that
was my job."

She wanted to get him out of this blue funk, and
if acting a little silly did the trick, then silly she
would be. "A wise man's mother always said to
walk one's date to the door, right?"

"I think she meant a *gentleman* was supposed
to walk a *lady* to the door, not vice-versa."

She leaned against the doorframe. "Can you say
that for sure? How do you know?"

"But tradition—"

His grandsons raced into the hall before he could
finish.

Rebecca's fire alarm beeper went off, putting an
end to their conversation. "That's me! Gotta go."
She quickly waved goodbye and returned to her
Jeep with a sigh of relief. If anyone can get him
into a good mood, the boys can, she thought as
she started toward the fire station.

The boys were fed and watching their favorite
video when Steve heard the back door slam. He
got up and walked into the kitchen to greet his
daughter. Melinda plunked her purse down on the

counter and unceremoniously dropped her briefcase onto the floor.

"Bad day, honey?"

She unbuttoned the top button of her tailored slacks. "My day? A bitch," she answered dully, kicking off her shoes and plopping into the nearest chair.

"Melinda," he scolded. "Watch your language. The boys might hear you."

For a second, her eyes clouded with what he mistook for shame. What came out was anger. "It's my house, Dad. I'm a grown woman and I'll curse if I want to."

She had a point, but since she'd put him in charge of the boys, it wasn't easy for Steve to turn his parenting habits off when she walked in the door. Why, just this evening he'd picked up toys, prepared dinner, fed the boys, given them baths, and had just settled into his chair with the daily newspaper when she'd gotten home.

Steve poured two glasses of tomato juice and wished for the Bloody Mary mix he'd left back at the store when the ruckus occurred.

"Sorry, Dad. I know you're right, but the boys can't hear a thing with the TV blaring, and I've really had a tough day. Nothing worked out right. I've been early or late all day, I busted completely out of my last pair of pantyhose, my feet hurt because these shoes are tight, and I'm still fighting with motion sickness every time I see a car."

He crossed the kitchen and kneaded her shoulders. "Why don't you put on your robe and slippers, then come back and have some dinner?" He popped her plate of leftovers into the microwave and punched it on.

"Sounds good." Still seated, Melinda leaned over to pick up her shoes, and the unmistakable sound of ripping material made her put her head in her hands. Tears filled her eyes as the microwave buzzed and the telephone rang. "You get dinner and I'll grab the phone." Melinda maneuvered out of her chair, left the shoes, and went down the hall to her bedroom to catch the phone.

When she returned, Steve knew something was terribly wrong. She sat down and propped both feet up in the chair across from her. Then she shoved her plate away and looked at him. "Tell me what happened."

"What happened when, honey?" Steve busied himself with the leftovers on the counter and played dumb.

"You know exactly when, Dad. Today. At the Grocery Mart. A friend just called and told me one version, but now I want to hear it from you. Please, Dad, tell me the truth."

She looked so tired. He hadn't been around her much when she was pregnant with the boys. It had been decades since he had been around anyone who was pregnant—not since his wife was expecting Melinda. He didn't remember the dark circles, the swollen ankles, the odd pallor. But then, he hadn't left his wife alone to care for two active children, work a full-time job, and go through a pregnancy by herself. Melinda was trying to do it all. And he couldn't imagine how she was going to manage.

Nothing on earth could have made Steve leave Dolores when she was expecting Melinda. Where was Joey—and why wasn't he here?

"Dad, I need to know."

He let out a long sigh, then related the events of the episode at the store. "Rebecca and I were picking up a couple of things at the Grocery Mart when we overheard two women talking."

"Rebecca?" she bristled. "I might have known she'd have something to do with this."

He knew her anger was misplaced, but Steve resented the way she jumped to the worst possible conclusion every time Rebecca came into the picture. "Yes, Rebecca. But you'll be happy to learn that she stood up for you and put those biddies in their place."

Melinda dropped her legs to the floor and pushed them back under the seat of her chair as she leaned forward. "I don't need that woman or anybody, for that matter, to stand up for me." She propelled the words in his direction and slammed her fist on the table.

Steve knew she was hurt. But she didn't have to take it out on his new friend. "Melinda Jordan Camden, I know you're mad as hell about this . . . situation you're in. I also know you are confused and frustrated. But we both know that your feelings toward Rebecca have nothing to do with what happened in the Grocery Mart, don't we?"

Melinda stared at him in disbelief. "You're right about one thing—I do have definite feelings about Rebecca and they aren't always pretty ones."

"What has Rebecca ever done to you, Melinda?"

She sat thinking. "She takes you away from me . . . and your grandchildren. They need you now more than ever since their father doesn't seem to have much time for them."

"Now, Melinda, we've had this argument before, and you know I don't believe those boys are being neglected by their father . . . or by me. If anything, they need more time with *you*." He hadn't planned to get into this tonight, but Melinda had pushed so hard that he couldn't sit back and ignore it one more time. "But that doesn't really answer my question. What has Rebecca done to make you so mad?"

"Dogs go mad," she corrected him. "People get angry."

"You know what I meant . . ."

She stood up and stretched her back, then got some more tomato juice from the refrigerator before sitting back down. "I don't like her."

"Why, Melinda? I'll ask you again. What has she done to you?"

"She's not my mother and I hate her for it." Her tone was as cold as the ice that hit his teeth as he drank the last of his own tomato juice. He put the glass down and wiped his mouth with a napkin from the pile on the table. He didn't know what to say. He'd known his daughter wasn't fond of Rebecca, but once again, he'd miscalculated the intensity of her feelings.

When he didn't respond, Melinda continued, "Don't ask me a question if you don't want an answer."

"What's happened to you, Melinda? You used to be gentle and kind. You cared for people. I thought you'd want me to be happy. What's happened?"

She stared at the napkin he was ripping to shreds. "I grew up."

He frowned in exasperation. "As far as I'm concerned, at this moment I don't believe you turned out so well." He stood up, pulled his coat off the hook, and left before he could say anything more.

Rebecca was startled when Steve knocked on the door. She'd snuggled up with a novel in her comfy overstuffed floral chair, cozy in her midnight blue silk pajamas. She saw Steve's face through the window and hurried to let him in.

He pulled his bomber jacket off and gave it to Rebecca. "Were you asleep?" He averted his eyes from her nightclothes, but not before she noticed his smile and the glimmer of appreciation in his eyes.

Rebecca felt self-conscious in the flimsy, sheer pajamas. "I splurged on the set last Valentine's Day after I'd spent the whole week ushering couples on champagne balloon rides. I didn't know anybody would see it."

Steve made no attempt to hide the fact that he was watching her. "I'm glad I saw it. You look gorgeous."

What she didn't confide to him was that she'd had no date that Valentine's Day, no one special in her life, so she'd bought the pajamas to make herself feel better. She didn't usually believe in buying herself out of a mood, but that time it had worked. Tonight, the admiration in Steve's eyes made her feel better than any purchase ever could. His open appraisal of her appearance filled her with a delicious inner excitement.

"I'm sorry it's so late." A tinge of red stained his cheeks.

She tapped the sofa next to where she sat down. "This is a twenty-four hour establishment. My door is always open to you." When he joined her on the cushioned seat, she couldn't miss his clean, citrus smell.

"Right now, twenty-four hours is about how long I want to sit here and hold your hand and talk about something . . . anything . . ."

Rebecca put her finger gently over his lips and promised, "Nothing heavy." She twisted her fingers through his hair and traced a line down his cheek to his firm jaw.

"Nothing serious," he added. "No Melinda."

"Not tonight," she assured him.

"No kids."

"It's a deal." She extended her hand and they ceremoniously shook on it.

Steve pulled her against his chest, slipped his arm around her, and sat quietly. After a while, he lifted her head and stared into her eyes. "Rebecca? Would you mind if we sat in the swing?"

"Mind? It would be lovely." She leaned forward and curled her fingers through his, pulling him to his feet. "Why don't I fix us a couple of mugs of hot chocolate first?"

"With marshmallows?" He followed her to her spacious kitchen.

"Is there any other way?"

Rebecca felt exposed in the glare of the fluorescent lights. The thin fabric of her silk pajamas shifted with her every movement. Reaching into the cabinets for hot chocolate fixings, the satiny material rubbed back and forth, causing her nipples to react to the stimulation.

When the cocoa was hot, she handed Steve his mug and flipped off the lights on the way to the porch. As a last thought, Rebecca grabbed a sweater from the hall closet and put on some music before joining him on the swing.

Steve blew into the hot liquid, scattering the marshmallows to the lip of the mug. "The boys taught me how to do that."

She wagged her finger at him and frowned.

"Oops," he said, "I forgot. I wasn't going to talk about the kids."

"Everybody's entitled to a slip-up once in a while."

Steve put both feet on the planks and pushed the swing, then lifted his legs and let the hand-carved wooden seat sway almost to a stop before giving it another shove. He hugged the mug with both hands, carefully sipping. "Are you warm enough?"

"Sure am." She thought she would be cold, but an unusual warmth from within made her flush with excitement at being so close to this strong, handsome man. "Excuse me a moment."

Rebecca left him in the swing and went inside. She turned up the volume on the compact disc player to compensate for the closed window.

Strains of "Put Your Head on My Shoulder" wafted out the door with her as she rejoined him on the porch. Rebecca curled both legs under her and sat sideways facing Steve, humming the old, familiar tune.

"There's nothing like a favorite song to make someone romantic," he said, reaching out to smooth the hair around her face. "My older sister used to spoon with her boyfriend on our rickety front porch," he told her, slipping his arm around her shoulder. "I'd spy on them through the bushes."

"You bad boy." She shifted until her shoulder fit under the crook of his arm, then laid her head on his chest. "Go on . . ."

"Dad wouldn't let us listen to music when he was home. We only had one radio, and he kept it tuned to the news and the fights. My sister's boyfriend would sing all these crazy songs to her when they were dating." Steve stopped the swing and set the empty mugs on the window ledge. "He had a lousy voice, but she loved every off-key word."

"What happened? Did he get the girl?"

"They're married with four grown children and nine grandchildren. My sister says those golden oldies still make her toes tingle and her heart swoon like a teenager's." He gently rocked the swing back and forth.

"Did you ever do any serenading of your own?"

He tipped her face until her eyes met his, her skin

warm against his fingertips. "Me? No. I sounded worse than Ross, my brother-in-law. More like a frog than Prince Charming."

"I used to love frogs as a kid." His hand's firm, yet gentle, touch sent a warm tingle through her body. She moved closer, her face near enough to feel his breath against her ear.

Steve whispered, "My dear Rebecca . . ." He slid his lips across her mouth, then tenderly nibbled her lower lip. The kiss started gently, then deepened, searching, in a private, intimate way. He drew her against his chest and gazed at her hungrily.

Rebecca wanted to crush herself against him, feel his hands explore her body. Her breasts threatened to expose her desire, her nipples forming hard little knots that pressed against the delicate silk of her pajamas. She could feel the heat of his body, even through his clothes.

"I'm glad I came here tonight," Steve murmured, then leaned back and gave the swing another push.

"Me, too." Rebecca relaxed on his chest with a sigh of pleasure. It had been years since she'd felt these twinges of . . . romance. That was it. *Romance.*

The CD had finished, but the evening was far from silent. Thousands of crickets and tree frogs provided a symphony of sound in the darkness. Small bats zig-zagged between the inky blackness and the security light near the end of her driveway. She nestled into his arms and closed her eyes.

Nothing else happened between them that night. But it was a beginning. Of what, Rebecca wasn't sure. She only knew he made her feel desirable and alive and wanted.

Later, alone in her bedroom, she slipped out of her pajamas and let them puddle on the floor. After she'd married, she'd started sleeping in the nude. When her husband died, she'd begun to wear pajamas once more. But tonight she had the urge to be naked again. She enjoyed the feel of her skin next to the fresh cotton sheets and remembered how wonderful it was to feel sexy and alluring. She switched off the lamp, then pulled the heavy patchwork quilt around her chin in the large feather bed.

Rebecca found herself thinking about Steve, dreaming about him, even fantasizing about what the next months might bring. She leaned out of bed and rapped the hard wooden floor three times for luck. Then, just to be sure, she did it again.

Five

"What do you say we make this short and sweet?" Mayor Oliver called the organizational meeting for the annual Willow Ridge Fund Raiser to order. "We've done this four years in a row, people, so it shouldn't take long." The portly man sat down at the head of the conference table.

A spindly woman with bluish-white hair stood up and addressed the mayor with a southern accent that would have made Scarlett blush. "Mr. Mayor, I took the liberty of typing out an agenda." She took one of the copies and passed the rest around to the others. "I prioritized the list, so we should start at the very top."

"Thank you, Flora." The mayor took one of the papers, glanced at it, then placed it face down on the table. "As I was saying, last year we did a fine job raising money to spruce up the park. I propose that we follow the same game plan this year, to raise enough funds to redo the courthouse grounds. What do you say, people?"

Rebecca wanted to get out of the meeting as

quickly as anyone, but she knew they needed a firmer plan to get things rolling. "Mark . . . Mayor, I believe I speak for everyone when I say we're happy with the results of last year's festival." Rebecca knew enough about small town politics not to step on any hierarchical toes. "But I think we need to work out a few details—just to make sure things go smoothly. Flora, why don't you tell us your ideas?"

With twenty years of business experience, Rebecca could handle things with one hand tied behind her back. But she wanted to put that part of her past behind her. She fought her innate urge to take over, trying instead to become a member of the group, not the lone leader.

As Flora drawled slowly through her agenda, Rebecca felt herself drifting away. Maybe she shouldn't have given Flora the floor. The woman could make an earthquake sound boring. She felt as if she were a young girl back in chemistry class counting the minutes until she could escape. Today, chemistry was again the culprit—the chemistry exploding between her and Steve.

Life had become complicated since Steve Jordan moved to Willow Ridge. One minute she was thankful to have a wonderful new friend, and the next she could swear she was in high school, fretting over what she should wear on a date. Dates! The mere thought of going through that particular brand of torture again was mind-boggling. So, she and Steve had called an unspoken avoidance of official "dates." They'd "gotten together" for coffee, dinner, a movie, but they'd kept it just between friends. But it *wasn't* just between friends, and they both knew it.

Flora's drawl broke into her consciousness. "Mrs. Roswell? What do you think?"

Rebecca sat up and nodded. Apparently, she'd managed to daydream her way through Flora's entire list. It was so easy these days to lose herself in thoughts of Steve. Nothing, not even boring Flora and her lists, could get her down.

"I'm sure you have everything under control." Rebecca hoped that her innocuous answer would suffice. But they were all looking at her, waiting for her to elaborate. She would have if she'd known what they were talking about, but she didn't. Instead, she simply smiled and tried to look confident.

Alice Anne broke the silence. "De-ar, we want to confirm that you are planning to have the festival at yo-ur little business, and that you will supervise the booth building. Is that cor-rect?" Alice Anne's accent was exaggerated more for attention than from her upbringing.

Rebecca kept her composure, even though the woman's voice and attitude irritated her as much as fingernails on a chalkboard. "Oh, I thought that was understood. I'm thrilled to host it again this year. Hawk and Doug have volunteered to supervise the building, so that detail is in good hands."

Twenty minutes later, Mayor Oliver closed the meeting with a rap of his gavel and made his way through the group to Rebecca. "Anything wrong? You seem preoccupied."

Rebecca stepped back away from the mayor. Mark was harmless, but he always stood too close for comfort. Rebecca could feel her private space being violated. Giving him the benefit of the doubt, she attributed it to his immense size and bulging belly. Mark leaned in when he spoke to her, so she had to pull her neck back to avoid having his bald head in her face. "Mark Oliver, you always did overreact."

"Well, why don't you let me take you to lunch and we'll talk about it," he persisted.

Ignoring his invitation, Rebecca stepped farther back. Mark had asked her out about once a month since she'd moved to Willow Ridge. He always seemed to take her rejections in stride, but that never stopped him from trying every time he saw her. "Talk about what? I thought the festival was all settled."

He fumbled with a cigarette, but didn't light it. "About whatever it is that's on your mind."

Rebecca decided to use the same tactic on him she had a dozen times before. "You know you're almost young enough to be my son, Mark—"

"Well, not quite."

"Close enough."

"I guess that means lunch is out?" he asked, the unlit cigarette clenched between his teeth.

She picked up her purse and headed toward the exit. "Thanks, but I don't think lunch is a good idea." He followed her down the hall.

"It's that Jordan fellow, isn't it?"

Rebecca turned back to face him. "What did you say?"

"It's him, isn't it? Steve. Steve Jordan. You've got the hots for him, don't you?" With each word, the cigarette bobbed up and down between his lips.

She could feel the heat creep up her neck and spread across her face and chest. A surge of anger seethed below the surface of her emotions. "Mark, you and I have been friends for a long time, but *that* is none of your business."

Mark's full cheeks flushed a ruddy color as he stuttered, "Do . . . Do . . . Don't . . . Don't get your d-dander up, Re . . . becca."

She felt terrible that she'd caused his stuttering, but Mark had overstepped his boundaries. Her own anger dissipated as Mark labored to finish his remark.

"I-I-I just thought . . . if th-that's what you want, then I hope you'll be ha-happy." He pulled his too-short tie back over his bulging stomach.

"Oh . . ." It was one of the few times that Rebecca was at a loss for words. She muttered a heartfelt, "Thanks, Mark," and left.

Rebecca's face brightened at the sight of her oldest, dearest friend in the world walking across the open field next to Riding the Wind. Hawk had supported her emotionally when her husband had died. He'd helped her start a new life in Willow Ridge, and had been her confidant and friend for more years than she cared to count. He stopped and waved to her.

"I'll be there shortly," she yelled to him. She pulled a cap over her head and followed him over to the festival site.

Hawk had a way of bringing out the best in everyone. His volunteer builders proved it in the way they methodically followed his lead and worked long and hard to make the festival a reality.

"You men have done a terrific job," she heard Hawk tell a group of workers hammering away on booths. "It's been a busy morning, but I think we're almost finished."

Doug gathered up the scrap wood and put it in a pile. "Yep. The end's in sight, Dad."

One of the workers yelled out, "Then it's Miller time!"

Rebecca laughed as she caught up to Hawk and his crew. "I don't have any beer, Burt, but I do have a gallon of lemonade and a mile-high stack of sandwiches waiting on the porch when you guys finish for the day."

She used the refreshments as an excuse to walk through the maze of wooden booths, but secretly she hoped to run into Steve.

"Hello down there," a voice called from the top of a ladder.

She'd recognize that voice anywhere. His husky tone broke through the deafening sounds of hammers and saws. She drew the brim of her hat down as she searched the ladder for Steve's face.

"Don't inspect things too closely, okay?" Steve climbed down a couple of rungs. "I prefer to think I'm a master craftsman."

She bent to retrieve a bar level from the tool chest on the ground beside her. "I guess I shouldn't check things out with this, huh?"

"Not if you know what's good for you," he threatened. "Where have you been all day?"

So, he had missed her.

"Didn't you know? I'm invisible." She drew her cap down tighter on her head.

"Invisible. Right." He yanked a rag out of his back pocket and threw it at her. "Afraid of a little hard work?"

She retrieved the rag and noticed Hawk nearby. "Me? Afraid of work? Not a chance. Right, Hawk? I just don't like getting in his way."

Straight and tall, Hawk padded over to Rebecca, his moccasins barely leaving a mark in the hard, red clay. She noticed a strand of jet black hair had worked its way loose from his braid.

"Tell me the truth, Hawk, she's not the construction type, is she?" Steve dropped to the ground from his perch. "I'll bet her hammering technique is lacking."

Hawk smiled easily, his voice low and even. "That is one subject I would advise you to avoid."

Steve gave Hawk a quizzical look. "Does that mean she can or can't build?"

"The middle is an uncomfortable place to be," Hawk said, his smile widening.

"Leave poor Hawk alone." Rebecca said. "Can't you see he's trying to save you from being embarrassed by a lady?"

She realized the noise from the saws and hammers had halted, and everyone had stopped to watch. "Is that a challenge?"

"You bet!" Steve handed her a ten-penny nail and a hammer. "It's all yours."

She waved the hammer. "What's the bet?"

"Your choice. Name it."

Rebecca weighed her options before answering, "Dinner."

"Dinner it is."

Rebecca nailed the booth's corner joist together with four solid blows of the hammer, then stood back and gloated. "I'm the fastest nailer in Willow Ridge."

"And the straightest." Hawk took a multi-colored headband from his pocket and slid it down his forehead to secure his loose hair. "It is good that you did not bet much, Steve, since this is a losing proposition. Rebecca does handiwork in her house for *fun*."

"I should have known!" Steve shook his head.

She worried that she had injured his pride. "Do you concede? Without even trying?" Rebecca was mature enough to know how fragile a man's ego could be, but independent enough not to back down from a challenge.

Steve moved closer, grabbed her hand, and raised it as if she'd just been declared the champion of a world-class boxing match. Hawk simply smiled, but the others cheered her on. She obliged with a winner's jig before the small crowd dispersed to find the food she'd prepared earlier.

"I admit, I secretly hoped you couldn't do it."

"Isn't that a bit sexist?"

"Guilty."

Steve moved closer to her until he left no room at all between them and whispered, "It's hard to imagine those pretty, delicate hands wrapped around a hammer."

What *do* you imagine them holding? she wondered.

* * *

Rebecca took Hawk's arm, and together they walked through the crowded field which had been cleaned and mowed until it resembled a city lawn. Riding the Wind was more than her home; it was Hawk's home, too. In a way, Hawk and his son were the only family she had left. And since she was hostess to the fall festival, Hawk saw himself as the host—a role Rebecca willingly let him assume.

"You've been at it since sunrise, my friend." Rebecca touched Hawk's elbow. "It's time to quit and enjoy the festival."

Lines of concentration deepened under Hawk's headband, along his brows and under his coal black eyes. He left her side to repair a loose board on a nearby booth with a hammer from the tool belt around his waist. She had to get that thing off him, or he wouldn't stop until the last person drove off into the night.

The high school football coach approached, carrying a tray of treats. "Peanuts, cotton candy," he boomed. "Peanuts, cotton candy." He knocked the dirt off his cleats and peered at Rebecca from under his Braves baseball cap. "How about something to eat?"

"Maybe later." As he left, the sweet, salty smells

trailed after him, reminding her of the way the sticky concoction felt on her tongue as a child.

Hawk rejoined her and they continued down the grassy aisles. "Look at all of this!" He motioned to the white-washed booths filled to the brim with stuffed animals, bowls of goldfish, and woodworking crafts.

"Yeah, isn't it great?"

"If people truly want it, I guess it is."

She could hear the doubt in his voice. But today wasn't the time or the place for a philosophical debate about materialism, particularly with Hawk. He'd win. He always did. That man could defend a point he believed in better than anyone. Rebecca let his comment drop and they walked on without talking.

"Fourteen," Hawk said, breaking their silence as they strolled past the Boy Scouts' ring-toss booth.

Rebecca handed fifty cents to one of the uniformed boys, but her orange plastic ring flipped and missed its mark. "Fourteen what?"

"Fourteen times in the past ten minutes you've looked at your watch."

"You're counting?" Without thinking, she lifted her left wrist again to check the dial. "I can't hide anything from you, can I?"

"Old friends never can. He'll be here soon."

She rolled her eyes at Hawk's last remark. They stopped to catch a magician's vanishing hat trick, then continued on to the next aisle. "Well, old friend, what do you think?"

"If you are asking what I think about your friend, Steve . . . he's a worthy man, well-respected, one the gods sent especially for you."

She swiveled slowly and stared at Hawk in surprise. "Don't be shy, now. Tell me what you *really* think."

Hawk saw things with such clarity. Rebecca envied that in him. His visions were full of reality. Reality she couldn't deny. But was what she felt about Steve real, or an illusion?

"Your happiness is very important to me, Rebecca." Hawk's voice was low and direct.

"I know. I just wish I was as sure about things as you always are."

Hawk put his arm around her. "You will be. You just don't know it yet."

"Miz Rebecca!"

She recognized this voice, too. Jeremy's voice, so Steve must be close by. Rebecca searched the crowd in earnest, finally spotting the boys and their grandfather moving her way.

What a handsome man he was. He reminded her of lightning—compelling and dangerous—lean and sinewy, full of confidence and strength. Yes, that was it, strength. It was etched in his firm mouth, the set of his jaw, his deep, observant eyes.

Jake's face split into a smile. "There's Miz Rebecca!" Dropping Steve's hand, the young boy bolted toward her with Jeremy on his heels.

"We've been looking and looking for you all over the place," Jake said.

"Yeah," his brother agreed. "Granddad didn't want to do anything 'til we found you."

Steve walked up and stopped behind the boys. "That's a little exaggeration, boys." He offered his hand to Hawk, who shook it firmly. "But not by much." He lowered his eyes to find Rebecca watching him.

"Granddad!" Jake tugged at Steve's sleeve. "Now can we go watch the dunking booth, p-l-e-a-s-e?"

"I think that's a terrific idea." Rebecca grabbed each boy by the hand, and together they strolled to the dunking booth. Mayor Oliver sat perched, waiting for a good drenching. Hawk and Steve followed, but not before the pungent smell of roasted peanuts lured them to stop and buy a couple of bags.

Hawk shelled one, popped the peanut into his mouth, and dropped the shells back into his paper bag. "Your grandsons have a great fondness for Rebecca."

Steve wondered where this conversation was going. He knew the tall, dark-skinned man meant more than his words indicated.

"Yes, I'd say they were fond of her. It's nice to see them having a good time."

"And you?" Hawk's words were as unhurried as his long, even strides.

"Me? I'm having a good time, too."

Hawk stopped and stared directly into Steve's eyes. "Are you fond of Rebecca?"

From the intensity of his gaze, Steve felt Hawk could read his innermost feelings. After a long pause, he answered, "I'm very fond of her."

Hawk broke his stare. "Good." He didn't say another word, but walked to the dunking booth and watched in silence until the mayor had plunged into the cold, murky water. Then he left.

Rebecca walked over to where Steve stood at the edge of the crowd. "What was that all about? What was going on with you and Hawk?"

Steve looked over at her, then glanced back at his grandsons pressed against the dunking booth. He wasn't sure what *had* really happened. Hawk wanted what was best for Rebecca, that much Steve knew. "Hawk was just looking after you, that's all."

"Whatever that means . . ." Rebecca gave him a questioning look, but said nothing more.

"It's about time for a break, boys," Steve said. "Run on to the concession tent and order drinks and some curly fries." He followed to help them and pay the bill. "This won't take but a minute," he called to Rebecca. But she knew better. The boys weren't going to let him get away without a fight.

Waiting for Steve to return, Rebecca watched a boy throwing balls until finally the teacher got dunked. He came up drenched, his shirt and pants matted against his body. Her mind slipped from the present dunking victim to the first time Steve had visited her hot tub. She clearly remembered the way his boxers had clung to his skin. In her mind, she could envision the outline of his thighs and the bulge between them.

She thought of the bubbly warmth of the hot tub and the emotions it had stirred in her. Lately, she had caught herself fantasizing about seducing and being seduced by Steve. Alone in the frothy bubbles, she had allowed herself the pleasure of pressing up next to the powerful jets to intensify the passion awakening within her. Watching Steve in his snug-fitting jeans today, she couldn't keep her thoughts from drifting . . . drifting back to the way he looked in those wet boxers . . .

Steve tapped her on the shoulder. "Earth to Rebecca?"

She jumped at the sound of his voice. "What? Oh, sorry." Her cheeks burned as she tried to compose herself.

"Didn't mean to take you by surprise." He took her arm and guided her toward the tent where the boys were finishing their snack. "You seemed a million miles away."

Less than a mile, she thought. Much closer than

he could imagine. Much, much closer. She could feel the burning heat in her face again, as Steve observed her with an indulgent, musing look.

When Jake and Jeremy left the tent, the foursome headed out to hit all the high spots in the festival. Rebecca was delighted when Steve won her a stuffed giraffe as a "sharp shooter." She even coerced him into laying out big bucks for his grandchildren to shoot hoops. The children were excited when they finally won fake leather wallets.

Steve pointed to two gigantic metal tubs filled with floating red apples. "Let's try our hand at bobbing, boys."

Jake squinched his nose at the suggestion. "Bobbing? What's that?"

Jeremy asked his grandfather the obvious. "Won't we get wet?"

"Yeah, that's the point. You're supposed to stick your head down into the water and fish out an apple with your teeth. The first person to grab one wins."

Rebecca watched in amusement as Steve demonstrated exaggerated chomping techniques with his mouth open and teeth bared. Steve winked when he caught her eye.

Jake joined in with his own chomping version, but Jeremy shook his head. "You guys are crazy if you think I'm gonna stick my head in a cold tub of water and look like a moron just to get a dumb apple."

The adults shared a knowing smile. Steve's face was eager and alive with affection for his grandchildren. Rebecca's attraction to him was increasing by the minute.

Flapping his arms and clucking like a chicken, Jake ran around Jeremy until his brother popped him on the arm.

"That's enough, Jake. Come on. We'll just have to go it alone." Steve and his younger grandson stepped into the long line and left Jeremy and Rebecca on the sideline to watch.

"This is definitely a Polaroid moment." Rebecca dropped the stuffed giraffe at her feet, then elbowed Jeremy and pointed. "Look." His grandfather and brother were practicing their chomping while waiting for their turn.

Jeremy tried to stifle a snicker. "What I'd give for a picture of this."

"It would make a great Christmas card," Rebecca suggested, as she ruffled his thick, tawny-gold hair.

"Naw, not a Christmas card. April Fool's maybe." His toothy grin was irresistible.

Rebecca liked this kid and his mischievous mind. "Better yet, how about Halloween?"

Jeremy leaned over and whispered, "I don't know about Granddad, but blackmail works with Jake."

"Why, you little stinker—" She pretended to be shocked, but didn't finish when she saw him stiffen as though she had hit him. "Jeremy, what is it? I meant it as a joke—"

When he spoke, his voice wavered. "My grandma used to call me that—" He swallowed hard in an effort to keep back the tears.

In one motion, Rebecca put her arms around him and squeezed tightly. "I didn't know. I'll bet she was a terrific grandmother." She loosened her hold on him, keeping one arm across his trembling shoulders. "I'm sure she knows how much you love her."

She felt him relax and knew they'd passed a milestone in their relationship. She was glad he had been comfortable enough to tell her his feelings about Dolores. Now if she could only get Steve to do the same.

Rebecca dropped her arm but remained close by. She knew better than to be too pushy. Boys Jeremy's age could tolerate only so much public affection. He could make the next move if he wanted to. If not, she knew it was only a matter of time before he reached out again. She didn't want to take the place of Steve's late wife. But she definitely wanted her own spot in his life, and his grandsons' lives as well.

"I've got an idea." Rebecca snapped her fingers.

"Don't let your grandfather out of your sight. Wait here, okay?"

She picked up the giraffe, poked it under her arm, and hurried into the crowd in search of Doug. Luckily, she found him in the refreshment tent. She returned and gave Jeremy a conspiratorial wink as she produced a 35mm camera with a built-in zoom lens. "We're in business now."

"All right!" he crowed. "What happened to your prize?"

She chuckled at Jeremy's excitement. "Doug's storing it for me."

By the time Steve's and Jake's turn came, Jeremy had worked himself into a frenzy. Rebecca had to admit that he was a handful to keep up with, but she loved his spirit and spunk. She only wished they had more times like this with the boys. But Melinda always saw to it that Jake and Jeremy were busy when she and Steve planned any sort of family outing. According to Steve, Melinda had allowed her sons to come today only after making it perfectly clear that she would be there as soon as humanly possible after her business meeting.

Thinking of Melinda brought back memories of working on Saturday—one thing Rebecca was happy to give up when she retired. All those hours. All the missed events. She hadn't regretted it then, but now, she wondered sometimes if she hadn't sacrificed too much for the sake of her career.

Jeremy shook her arm and shouted, "They're up!"

Rebecca lifted the camera to her eye and took a deep breath to steady her hands for the best shot. She didn't plan to miss this opportunity . . . for Jeremy's sake, and her own.

"No head starts. No cheating. No hands. Get it?" A bald-headed man wearing a plastic garbage bag raised his hand. "One, two, three, go!" His hand sliced through the crisp afternoon air.

Decked in the latest trash-bag attire, both Jake and Steve tentatively approached their target apples. Jake coaxed one into the tub's wall with his chin so he could gnash his teeth into it without getting soaked, but his plan failed. He came up empty, complaining, "They're slimy!"

"Slippery," the bald-headed man corrected with a chuckle. "Oiled. Makes it more fun for the spectators."

The crowd started clapping and egging them on. "Stick your chops in!"

"Don't let the pint-sized guy beat you, Steve—"

"You've got a big enough mouth there—"

"Afraid of a little water?"

Steve sucked in a deep breath and buried his face in the layer of bobbing apples.

Rebecca snapped the camera just as he went under, and again as he pulled out, slinging water everywhere like a wild, shaggy dog.

"Ah-h-h-h," he screamed to catcalls and loud applause.

"Just nippy enough to keep you awake," the bald man told him.

"N-nippy?" Steve put on an hysterical look for the onlookers.

Rebecca snapped again. "Perfect." Right at that moment she realized how much she cared for Steve. Not just because he stirred her emotions, but because he was the best grandfather she'd ever come across. These kids were so lucky. Her own grandfather had only been around at holidays and special occasions.

Jeremy held his sides. "I . . . I can't . . . believe we got this on . . . film," he haltingly told her between spasms of laughter.

"But you don't have the apple," Rebecca screamed above the noise.

The crowd chanted, "Ap-ple! Ap-ple! Ap-ple!"

The bald man swabbed Steve's dripping forehead with his large red kerchief, then pushed him toward the tub. "Haven't got all day, you two."

"Ap-ple! Ap-ple!"

Steve winked at Jake and stuck his face under a second time. Jake took the lead, closed both eyes tight, pursed his lips, and dunked his head.

Rebecca snapped just as Jake pulled up, his eyes open wide and the apple dangling from his two front teeth. Steve must have looked like that when he was young.

Before the stem broke off, the bald man grabbed it with one hand, raised Jake's arm with the other, and declared him the winner. The little boy grinned from ear to ear as he ripped off his wet trash bag. He ran over and hugged his grandfather.

The man scooped out a dozen apples, threw them in a basket, and gave them to Jake. "For the winner. You can pick them up here when you're ready to leave the festival." He herded them to a nearby table where two volunteers from the local beauty college whipped out battery-operated hair-dryers and coiffed their hair to new heights.

"Aw, man," Jake protested when Jeremy ran up and teased him about being primped at the beauty parlor.

"You gotta get a shot of this," Jeremy told Rebecca. She obliged with the last two shots in the roll.

"Evidence." She raised the camera.

Jeremy grabbed her free hand. "Yeah! We've got you both!"

"Where have you been? I've been looking all over for you boys." All eyes turned to Melinda.

Rebecca could sense her indignation.

Jeremy jerked the tail of the oversized denim shirt she was wearing. "Mom, you shoulda been here! Granddad and Jake bobbed for apples."

"And I won!" Jake said.

Melinda looked from Jake to Jeremy and smiled. "I'm glad you're having a good time with your grandfather."

"And Miz Roswell," added Jeremy.

She peered at Rebecca and nodded. "Hello, Rebecca. I'm surprised to see you here."

"She lives here, Melinda," her father told her in an agitated tone. "Where else would she be?"

His daughter cut her eyes at him. "What I meant was, I assumed she'd have responsibilities with the festival and wouldn't have time to entertain you and the boys."

Rebecca didn't miss the sarcasm in her voice or the way she refused to make eye contact. "I always have time for the boys . . . particularly Steve." She summoned up a light tone, but emphasized the last part for Melinda's benefit. She wasn't sure if Melinda got the message, but from the look on Steve's face, he certainly did.

"Now that we're all here, let's see what else we can get into." Steve grasped Rebecca's hand, and they briskly walked down the row, pausing only when they met the peanut vendor.

"Peanuts all around," he ordered, letting go of Rebecca's hand to twist his wallet from his back pocket.

"None for me." Melinda patted her stomach. "All that salt's not good for the baby."

Steve nodded and passed out the warm packets

to everyone except his daughter. He lifted the paper holder to his nose and took a sniff. "I love the smell of roasted peanuts. Reminds me of ball games when I was a boy."

"And the boardwalk at the beach," Rebecca added.

"And movie marathons." Steve popped another peanut into his mouth, licking the salt from his lips.

"Did you ever see the Frank Sinatra movie-thon?" Rebecca pretended to swoon, with the back of her hand against her forehead and her eyes rolled back.

"Yeah, yeah, I guess 'ol' Blue Eyes' was okay, but what about those sirens like Lana Turner or Rita Hayworth?"

"Sirens?" Jake looked confused. "Like the fire engine?"

Rebecca and Steve burst out laughing, but Melinda just cocked her eye at her father and waited for his explanation.

"Well, a siren was our term for a looker." When the boys didn't seem to understand, he tried again. "A knockout . . . a beauty . . . a movie star."

"Sounds like my girl, right here." A compact, muscular man walked up from behind them and fell in step with Melinda.

"Dad!" the boys said in unison, attacking him with bear hugs.

"Joey." Melinda ground the word out from between her teeth. "What do you want?" Her tone remained cool, but her gaze was glaring a hole straight through her husband. She reached into her baggy jeans pocket and pulled out some change. "Here's some money, Jeremy. Take your brother and get some drinks."

"Joey." Steve pumped his son-in-law's hand. "This is Rebecca Roswell."

Rebecca watched Steve for a reaction to Joey. He was cordial, even friendly, to his daughter's husband. In fact, he seemed genuinely glad to see him. There was no mistaking that the boys were thrilled. Melinda was a different story.

The strong, almost formidable-looking man took Rebecca's hand and firmly shook it. He wasn't what she had expected of Melinda's estranged husband. He was rugged, even handsome, with a Clint Eastwood kind of face and a not-so-subtle hint of arrogance to his gait.

When the boys started back in their direction, Joey looked squarely at Melinda. "Let's not ruin the day for them, okay?"

His wife nodded woodenly, but put on a big smile for the boys.

"What's next?" Joey asked his sons.

"Tattoos," Jeremy suggested.

But Jake had another idea. "Pony rides."

Joey scratched his chin. "We'll do both. First the tattoo, then the ride."

Melinda shot him a killer look. "Joey, not tattoos."

It sounded as if Steve's daughter was looking for anything to start a fight.

"Come on, Melinda, this is a festival, not a motorcycle brawl." He leaned closer and whispered so the boys couldn't hear, "You know they won't be real."

Steve grasped Rebecca's hand. "We'll catch up with you later." He waited to speak until Joey and Melinda trailed after the boys to the tattoo parlor. "Tattoo?" he asked.

"A creative version of the old-stand-by—face painting. It gets the kids to sit down a few minutes—"

"And that gives the parents a chance to catch their breath," he finished. "Why didn't we think of that earlier instead of bobbing for apples?"

"You had a ball and you know it." She reached up and ran her fingers through his hair. "And you got a new 'do' out of the deal."

"Some 'do.' I look like an Elvis impersonator. How could you let them do this to me?"

"I was busy taking the pictures—"

"You—" He pointed his finger at her and pretended to be angry.

But she knew better. He was loving every minute of it. And so was she.

They walked in silence for a while until they found themselves at the perimeter of the festival, away from the crowds. Steve propped his arm on the trunk of a large oak and looked down at Rebecca. He brushed a gentle kiss across her cheek, then the tip of her nose, before smothering her lips with his. "I've wanted to do that all day."

Rebecca was caught off guard by the sudden stillness of his voice. She put her arms around his neck and buried her face against his chest. "Ummm, me, too." Smiling in contentment, she relished the salty taste of his kiss and the faint aroma of his aftershave.

For a moment, it seemed as though time stood still, and they were alone in a field with only their thoughts and the late afternoon sun beating down on their shoulders. A faint breeze rustled the remaining leaves in the trees. When they heard footsteps coming their way they broke apart, but their fingers remained linked tenderly.

As a couple passed them on the way to their car, Steve spoke. "I'd better get back to the family."

"I know. I've got some things to check on, too."

"Can we meet again later?"

She hesitated. "I've got to get this place cleaned up and cleared out after everybody leaves."

"Sounds like a long night."

"It will be."

"Count me in then."

With a slow, secret smile she knew that it was only one of many more nights to come.

Six

Rebecca sat on a picnic bench in full view of the action at the pony ride area. Melinda and Jeremy sat on one side, while she and Steve watched Jake from the other.

"Ride 'em cowboy!" Steve swung his arms as if he were roping a steer with a lariat. "You look like a natural!" he yelled to his grandson.

Joey led the chestnut-colored pony around the course by the reins while his son held on to the saddle horn. Rebecca didn't know who resembled a proud peacock more, Jake or his father.

"Relax your legs, Jake, and sit up extra tall in the saddle to distribute your weight properly," Doug called from the middle of the riding ring. "Don't kick the horse with your heels. This isn't a western movie."

Rebecca knew how much Doug loved horses. He had learned to ride bareback almost before he could walk.

"That a boy," Steve encouraged, as Jake weaved

around the bright yellow marker flag on the course's third leg.

Hawk was conspicuous by his absence. Rebecca knew he disapproved of the pony rides. He had always told her that animals shouldn't be locked up and kept from doing what horses have done for thousands of years . . . running free, slaves to no man. Hawk still believed in the old ways of his people. She had once heard him ask Doug how he would like to have someone new on his back every fifteen minutes in a tiny arena.

But she knew Doug loved children, loved teaching them how to respect the ponies. So she decided to let father and son work it out on their own. Maybe I should do that more often with Melinda and Steve, she thought.

"Lean your body to the left. That's it. See how he responds?" Doug coached.

"Look Mom!" Jake squealed.

When Doug joined them, Joey turned the lead over to Jake. Near the end of the course, Doug showed the boy how to do it himself. "Grab the reins here with your hand."

Melinda gasped when Jake started riding on his own. Rebecca looked over at her and saw the color drain from her face. Steve saw it, too.

"He's in good hands, Melinda," Rebecca said, in an effort to reassure her. "Doug's a wonderful teacher."

"As far as I can see, he's not in any hands at all. The kid's riding that damn horse by himself."

"Mom!" Jeremy started to say more, but stopped when he saw the stern look on his mother's face.

Steve patted Jeremy's back, but addressed his comments to his daughter. "He's hardly moving, and Doug's right there, only feet away."

"What if that pony decides to run off with my baby?" Melinda's voice took on an excited pitch that Rebecca was beginning to recognize . . . and despise.

She wanted to deflect Melinda's attack if she possibly could. But from where she sat, Melinda was looking for a reason to condemn Joey, and he'd just handed her a doozy on the end of those reins. Rebecca didn't think Melinda was as upset over Jake's solo ride as she was that Joey didn't do what *she* thought he should do.

At the finish line, Joey helped his son scramble off the pony.

"Got yourself a little horseman there," Doug said.

Melinda gave him a shrug and a nasty look, but not nearly as deadly as the one she gave the boys' father when he got close enough to know it was meant for him.

"What's wrong?" Joey asked.

Melinda squinted her eyes and glared at him. "How could you, Joey Camden? What ever possessed you to turn our son loose on a horse? Don't you know any better?"

"For crying out loud." Joey kicked the dirt with his boot.

Rebecca could smell a fight in the air. Joey had innocently opened the door, and Melinda was about to barge through and dump all her pent-up anger on him. The signs were there. She herself had been prone to tantrums when the stresses of work and home had been too much. Rebecca wished she could tell Melinda that it didn't make things better. Twenty years of experience had taught her that much. But experience had also taught her that such unsolicited advice was rarely welcomed, particularly by someone in Melinda's state of mind.

Instead, she settled for steering Steve and the boys out of the range of fire.

"Look at my tattoo." Jeremy pushed up his sleeve to show off a hideous eagle-like bird soaring into a neon orange sunset with the letters J S C across the bottom. "Ain't it something?"

"It's something all right." Rebecca hid her smile and winked at Steve. Bending down, she inspected the letters. "S?"

"For Steve. For Granddad."

"That's sweet." She noted his expression of complete pride.

Jake vied for his fair share of attention, too. "My name is Matthew Joseph Camden."

"After Joey's father," Steve explained.

"What a great name." Rebecca wanted to make sure she didn't leave Jake out. He was obviously jealous that Jeremy had this grandfather's name and not he. Steve had once told her that the boys only had a chance to see their paternal grandparents every couple of years. It stood to reason that the name didn't mean as much to Jake as Steve's did to Jeremy.

Jake pushed up his sleeve. "Want to see *my* tattoo?"

"He's got a wimpy ol' rose on his. Yuck!" Jeremy made gagging sounds to emphasize his disapproval.

Rebecca managed a reply without laughing. "A rose, huh?" She inspected Jake's neon red masterpiece.

Steve interjected with a straight face, "When the man at the tattoo parlor told him that the rose was the most popular tattoo of the Navy Seals, that cinched it."

"He could just do that one faster," Jeremy countered. "Come on, there're Mom and Dad. Let's go show 'em."

Amusement flickered in Steve's eyes as he watched his grandsons run off. His laugh had a deep, rich, husky sound that made Rebecca want to join in. She grabbed his hand and they half-ran to the stage area in the middle of the festival where the loudspeaker was announcing something over the static.

When they stopped to catch their breath, Steve asked, "Where in the world are you going in such a hurry?"

"There." Rebecca motioned to the wide tables covered in white butcher paper, weighted down by tin after tin of pies smothered in meringue.

"For dessert?"

She pushed him toward the wooden stage. "Sort of, except this time you get to eat as much as you want, and nobody will raise an eyebrow."

"You aren't serious." He playfully dug his heels into the dirt.

"Deadly. We need volunteers for the pie-eating contest, and I know how much you like lemon pie."

"I like to eat my pie with a fork, not my face."

She dropped her arms and passed him. "Well, I can't force you." She mounted the steps to take a seat.

A local radio personality used the fog horn to generate more interest. "We need a few more participants. Come on, this is for a good cause."

Rebecca saw Steve standing near the stage. She knew he wasn't *that* shy, but she didn't plan to push it. If he didn't want to, he didn't have to.

"Anybody out there? We need two more people up here—" the emcee pleaded. "The contest starts in three minutes."

Melinda, Joey, and the boys wandered over to where Steve stood. Rebecca was almost glad when the emcee zoomed right in on them. "Wouldn't you youngsters like to see your—" he waited for the boys to fill in the blank.

Jeremy quickly responded. "Granddad!"

"Wouldn't you like to see your *Granddad* up here in the pie-eating contest?"

"I don't know . . ." Steve answered as the boys egged him on.

"Don't you worry, boys," Rebecca said in her sweetest voice. "Steve doesn't stand a chance."

Jeremy worked his grandfather for all he was worth. "O-o-h, Granddad, are you gonna let a girl take you out?"

"Them's fighting words," Joey agreed.

Steve took a step toward the stage, then turned to Joey. "I will if you will."

"Do it, Dad," Jake cheered him on.

From the crowd, Mayor Oliver yelled, "I'll donate a hundred dollars apiece to the courthouse fund if you two will participate."

"I'll donate another fifty," a voice hollered, but Rebecca couldn't tell who it was.

"I'll make it an even five hundred," blue-haired Flora from the fund-raising committee bid.

"She's just trying to buy our hearty appetites," Joey said.

"Well, I think she just hit my price." Steve gave

Flora a deep bow that sent the crowd into thunderous applause.

"Dad!"

Surprised at the turn of events herself, Rebecca caught the hateful look Melinda shot Joey when he jumped onto the stage, bypassing the steps.

"You're on, then." Joey scraped back a metal chair and held it for Steve, ignoring his wife's disapproving stare. "I didn't have lunch, so you're in serious trouble here."

"You may have youth on your side, son, but I've got more room to hold it." Steve rubbed his stomach and took his seat next to Rebecca.

Instantly, Rebecca felt a hand on her leg and knew it was Steve's. An embarrassed warmth spread up her neck, even though the butcher paper tablecloth concealed his gesture from everybody but her. "What in the world?" she blurted out softly.

"Revenge." He mouthed the word.

Rebecca could feel the print of his palm on her thigh. Discreetly, she put her hand over his, never looking in his direction, then moved his hand back to his own lap.

"Dirty pool," she whispered.

"What, me?" He gave her an innocent look.

"You're trying to sabotage my concentration."

"Did it work?"

She flashed him what she hoped was a devastating grin. "Like a charm."

"Would you two stop flirting?" Joey pushed two pies their way. "Pie-eating is serious business."

This was the first time Rebecca had actually met Joey Camden, but she'd heard lots about him from Steve and the boys. His sons adored their father. Steve had once told her that he thought Joey resembled a young boy in a man's body—full of good intentions, but lacking maturity. So far, she liked the young man.

The emcee dropped brightly colored scarves on the table in front of them. "Tie up those hands, people."

Steve raised his eyebrows. "You've got to be kidding."

Securing one of Joey's nylon ties, the emcee joked, "Don't knock it 'til you've tried it, right?"

Rebecca loved the look of disbelief on Steve's face. She tugged on his knotted scarf before she surrendered her own hands to the emcee for tying.

"I'm sitting here between a couple of heathens," Steve said, a look of implacable determination on his face. "And I'm going to beat you both."

The emcee went over the rules. "No hands. Sit up when you're ready for another pie . . ."

Steve cocked his head and asked Rebecca, "Another?"

". . . and most of all, ladies and gents, don't make yourselves sick. At the sound of the bell, dig in."

R-i-n-g. R-i-n-n-n-n-g.

Rebecca stuffed her mouth down into the billowy white meringue, covering every inch of her face with the citrus-smelling fluff. She thanked goodness she'd pushed her hair back with a headband.

She dug, her tongue tasting the tart filling as the scent of lemon filled her nostrils. She swallowed bite after bite of the lemony mixture, raising up only for air . . . and a peek at how her rivals were doing with their own frothy concoctions. Steve, using an inventive method of licking at the meringue, looked as though he was ahead of her.

She plunged her face back in and tried to take large bites using her lips, then teeth, but resorted to copying Steve's licking approach. Rebecca ran her tongue along the edge of the pie tin, then sat up for another one, thankful that the pies were crustless.

She wondered how Joey was doing, but didn't risk looking up again, for fear of falling even farther behind Steve's lead. She snuck a peek and found Steve wiping another tin clean with his tongue, while several of hers still remained.

"Uncle!" she heard Joey yell above the screaming and cheering.

The emcee untied him and announced Joey's total of four pies. After that, the other contestants started dropping like flies, all finishing with three to four pies under their belts.

Pretty soon, Rebecca realized she and Steve were the only ones left in the race. She knew her pace was slower, but she kept plugging away.

The emcee gave the audience a play-by-play of both their efforts. "Rebecca rates a ten for lip-smacking. But Steve's overall licking ability seems to give him the edge. Look at that over-and-under technique of his."

She knew she had reached her limit when the fifth pie was placed before her. Rebecca pushed the sickeningly sweet mixture around in the tin. She hated to throw in the towel, but she knew it was time. Finally, she sat up and shook her head.

Steve slurped away almost as if he was enjoying the stuff. It couldn't be good after downing five of those lemony monsters, she thought. After wiggling her hands loose from the scarf, she used it to wipe some of the meringue off her face, then sat back, astounded to see Steve chowing through his sixth pie.

The emcee thrust his hand over Steve's head. "We have ourselves a winner, ladies and gents. Steve . . . What's the last name?"

"Jordan." He licked his lips and blinked the meringue out of his eyes.

"Steve Jordan's our winner with six pies." The emcee raised his voice even more. "Six. Did you hear me?"

A messy Joey waved to Steve and Rebecca, still

on stage, as he herded the boys and a fuming Melinda off to the booths. "Catch you later," he mouthed. "Congratulations!"

By the time the contest had ended, the whole stage smelled like a truck load of ripe lemons that had been run over and left on a hot highway. Rebecca couldn't wait to get away. She offered Steve a sticky hand. "Gracious, you can sure put away the pie."

He showed her his wrists, still tied. "Do you mind?" He pushed them as far in her direction as he could.

She worked her nails into the knot's loop. "Be my pleasure." In more ways than one, she thought.

He groaned, "I never want to see another lemon meringue pie as long as I live."

"But you *looked* as if you were enjoying every bite."

"Anything for a good cause—" He rubbed his wrists when she got the knot loose. "Even a sticky mess like this."

"You don't look so bad." She wiped the meringue off his chin and put it in her mouth, sticking her whole finger in, then pulling it out with a low smack. "Um-um, good."

He returned the gesture by dipping his finger in the leftover pie and dotting her nose with meringue. "Rudolph would be jealous." He picked patches of pie off his shirt. "Gross, as Jake would say."

"Gross is right." Rebecca wiped his cheek clean. "Do you have any adventurous bones in your body?"

"Plenty. What do you have in mind?"

"My house and a hot shower."

"Sounds decadent."

"Decadent it is, then."

Seven

Steve felt like a teenager sneaking into the house after curfew, except this time the girl was going with him into her own house, and there weren't any parents to remind him of the consequences.

He escorted Rebecca down the steps to the back of the stage area. "Which way?" He gestured first to the maze of booths, then to the grove of pecan trees edging the festival.

Rebecca reached out and laced his fingers with her own. "Let's take the back way."

"I hoped you'd say that."

For once in his life, Steve was doing something spontaneous—and he hoped he didn't live to regret it. As they slipped behind the booths, through the trees, and around parked trucks and vans, his heart pounded so loud he was afraid she could hear it.

They made their way past rows of school buses and the last vestiges of the festival. Nothing but a wide, grassy field lay between them and their destination—Rebecca's house, and privacy.

What had possessed him to accept Rebecca's invitation? Lust, he thought. Pure, unadulterated lust. But it wasn't just the physical attraction, although that had become a growing hunger. It fed on Rebecca's every move, every word, every glance. He was attracted to so many things about her, but there was no mistaking that she was different from Dolores. Rebecca spoke her mind, made her own decisions, took the bull by the horns. Her independence scared him—and made him want her in a way he'd never wanted any other woman in his entire life.

"I think we're in the clear." The sound of her voice was as welcome as an oasis in the desert—cool enough to quench the thirst that welled up inside, making him want to take her in his arms every time they were alone . . . and even when they weren't.

Steve stopped and reluctantly relinquished her hand to empty a rock out of his shoe. "This reminds me of when I was a kid. I skipped Sunday School with my buddies to drink soda pops filled with peanuts at the filling station."

She ran her fingers through her lemon-splattered hair. "Oh boy. I can't believe it. Steve Jordan, a juvenile delinquent."

He stood and pointed an accusing finger at Rebecca. "Don't tell me you were one of those girls who loved the bad-boy type?"

"I wish. I dreamed about those leather jackets

the 'hoods' wore back then." She snapped her fingers. "But darn it, they never gave me a second glance . . . or a leather jacket. I was one who—"

"Let me guess. You were the cheerleader who went steady with the captain of the football team."

"Nope. But I'm flattered that you'd think so."

Steve felt exposed to watchful eyes when they left the shelter of the pecan orchard and walked into the open field. They followed the matted path through the grass made by the dozens of cars parked at the festival. He enjoyed the rhythm they fell into and checked his stride to match hers.

"I know. You were the valedictorian who dated the guy voted most likely to succeed."

Her brows drew downward, but one corner of her mouth twitched into a slight smile. "Wrong again."

"Am I warm?" Warm. Hot would be a better word. Around Rebecca, he felt as hot as a teenage boy just before his first sexual experience—excited, urgent, ready.

"Cold as a cucumber in Alaska."

In spite of himself, he chuckled. "Well, give me a hint."

"Do I have to? I'd hate to deflate your illusions of me."

He surveyed the play of emotions on her face and wondered what caused them. "I'm dying of curiosity. Tell me."

Her smile vanished. "There's not much to tell. I wasn't anything. Not athletic. Not smart. Not popular. Not noticed, actually."

"I can't believe that. You're beautiful, successful—"

"And the typical ugly duckling when I was young."

"If that's true—and I'm not absolutely sure your account is the unbiased truth—then you've turned into the most beautiful swan Willow Ridge has ever seen."

Her face brightened. "I . . . I don't know what to say . . . except thank you." Her voice was determined. "Now it's your turn. What niche did you fit into as a teenager?"

"I was the buddy, not the boyfriend." To his surprise, she showed no outward reaction to his light-hearted, yet true, confession. "The girls liked me, just not enough to date me."

"Or maybe they didn't date you because they liked you too much."

Steve raised his voice, being purposefully patronizing. "That's the kind of rationale I was up against. The girls did nothing but tell me their problems. The guys resented me because their girl-friends used me as a shining example of what they were supposed to be like."

She laughed a low, throaty laugh that set his skin

tingling. "I can just see it. You were James Dean with a pocket protector."

"Close enough. But I never got the girl."

"Shhh." She placed a finger over her mouth. "Listen. A car's coming."

"We've been caught."

"Not on your life. This swan's gonna make a run for the house. Are you with me?" Her mouth curved into a captivating smile. Without warning, she bolted off the path toward the house. "Race you."

Minutes later Rebecca stumbled onto the porch swing with Steve barely a yard behind her. Gasping for breath, he slid down beside her and stretched his long legs out in front of him.

Now that they were at Rebecca's house, Steve could feel his old insecurities washing over him. What did she expect? What was going to happen? What if it didn't happen? How could he risk their friendship for a few minutes of pleasure? What if he couldn't perform?

Rebecca shivered. "It's getting cooler."

"Ready to go inside?" He said the words tentatively, as if testing the idea. Nervously, he flicked some dried meringue from his pants.

Rebecca laughed and the tension between them began to melt. "First dibs on the shower." She moved toward the beveled front door, opened it, and flipped on the lights.

Smothering a groan, Steve trailed after her. "But I've got more of that gunk in my hair than you do."

With long strides, Rebecca crossed the living-room. Pausing at the bathroom door, she reached in, grabbed a towel off the bar, and threw it to Steve. A bright smile curved her mouth. "I'll concede to the winner." She curtsied deeply with wide-open arms.

Steve gently pulled Rebecca to her feet. His gaze riveted on her delicately formed features. He put his hand to her waist and gathered her in a tender embrace. His heart fluttered wildly as she buried her head against his chest. Her mere touch sent a thrilling shiver through him as she locked her arms around his neck and touched her lips to his cheek like a whisper.

Rebecca was sure her heart had stopped beating when Steve moved his mouth over hers. He caressed her lips with tiny kisses, then with a lush, full kiss that left her burning for more. She kissed the hollow of his neck, then let her mouth graze his earlobe. He uttered a small sound when she gingerly explored his ear with her tongue. Her senses reeled as she remembered the delicious way Steve's tongue had devoured the pies earlier at the contest.

Huskily, Steve whispered, "You feel so good."

"Ummm, the feeling is mutual."

Rebecca felt as if she was roller skating downhill on ice, backwards, unable to stop. But stopping was the last thing on her mind. Pressed against him, she had no doubt what was on his mind, too. There was no denying the evidence of his desire. When they stood together like this, she almost forgot about everything except how passionate he made her feel.

But was she ready? Steve's companionship was important to her. Could she risk what they had—friendship—for the unknown?

"You'd better take that shower," urged Rebecca, easing herself from his embrace. She straightened her clothes, resisting the impulse to join him in the hot, steamy water.

Not one to let opportunities pass her by, she couldn't explain why she held back. But she did, and she knew it was the right thing to do. For now.

Steve followed Rebecca's lead. "Might work better if you stick me in the dishwasher. With all this lemon meringue, I need the pot-scrubber cycle." He disappeared into the bathroom.

Seconds later, she heard the water start, then the pulsating shower. It had a distracting hum that she had never noticed before. Rebecca imagined Steve's nude body covered in soapy bubbles, the undulating water splashing over his hard muscles.

On the other side of the door, Steve was suffering with at least one hard thing she'd caused that afternoon. And a cold shower was the only cure that worked. When he got out, he quickly dried off with an oversized towel. Now that he was back in control of his emotions and his body, he realized how good it felt to have cleaned that gooey mess out of his hair and off his skin. He knew Rebecca would feel the same, so he hurried to turn the bathroom over to her.

Looking around for the first time, he noticed the simple white-tiled room, with rose-colored floral paper and accents. He felt clumsy in such a feminine room, but had to admit the large, double-sized shower with dual sprayers had possibilities. Under other circumstances, he would have lingered to enjoy the heavy, pulsing water. But today, it only prolonged the agony.

A loud rap on the bathroom door startled him. He yanked a towel around his lower body and cracked the door a couple of inches. "Yes?"

"Thought you could use these." She handed him a heavy red velour robe and a mesh laundry bag for his dirty clothes. "If you'll put your things in that, I'll run them through a rinse cycle and have them ready by the time we finish our drinks."

He took them and closed the door. Dropping the towel, Steve contemplated which clothes he should give her. The shirt was a disaster, so it had to go. The pants were splattered, too, so he emptied his pockets onto the counter and deposited the denims into the bag. But the rest—his shorts and socks—were fine. He'd keep those with him.

Steve stepped into his white boxers before cracking the door to push out the mesh bag to Rebecca. He knew she'd seen him in his underwear before, that night at her pool, but it was different somehow. Maybe because so much had happened between them since then. Maybe because now that he knew her, it mattered more what she thought.

He lowered the toilet lid and sat down to put on his socks. He stood up and looked into the mirror, combing his hair with his fingers. Satisfied that he'd done all he could do to make himself presentable, he pulled on the red robe, tying it closed at the waist. At once, he knew it wasn't her robe. It was a fair fit for him. Certainly not too small.

A nagging thought made him wonder why Rebecca would have a robe big enough for a man his size in her house. He knew it was none of his business, but still he was uncomfortable with the thought that he might be wearing some other man's robe.

He glanced into the full-length mirror before opening the door, but stopped when he saw his reflection. Something was wrong. The socks. He yanked one off and looked in the mirror again. With one sock on and one off, he labored over which looked best. The socks had to go. He took them off and stuffed them into the pocket of the robe.

A burst of cool air hit him when he opened the door. Rebecca openly stared at his damp hair and past the robe's open neck to his bare feet. "It's all yours," he told her, walking into the living room.

"Great. I'm ready." She sailed past him into the bathroom. "The water's ready on the stove. Just help yourself to some hot chocolate."

Steve was glad he had a minute alone. He sat down on the white wicker sofa, tugging the robe together in the front. When he couldn't get it to close, he stood and adjusted the belt, then sat down again. He was nervous. Nervous about being alone in Rebecca's house. Nervous about being alone with Rebecca. Nervous about being alone with Rebecca in her house in some man's robe with nothing on under it but a pair of old boxer shorts.

A loud knock on the front door knotted his stomach in panic. Should he answer it? Tell Rebecca? Do nothing? A wave of apprehension swept through him as the visitor knocked again with renewed force.

"Dad? I know you're in there. Open up."

His body froze in shock. Melinda. His paternal concern kicked in. His first thought was for the baby. No. If something was wrong, she wouldn't be standing there knocking away. His daughter was here for her own reasons. He might have known she'd show up here on Rebecca's doorstep.

His shock yielded swiftly to exasperation as he jerked open the door. "What do you think you're doing, Melinda?"

She glared at him with reproachful eyes. "Me? What are *you* doing, Dad? Or do I have to ask?"

He knew it looked bad . . . standing there in a robe and little else. But it was none of her business what he did with his private life, and it was high time he told her so.

"You're acting like a teenager, sneaking around like this!" Melinda said accusingly.

"Sneaking around? I'll assure you that I'm old enough to do what I want, with whom I want . . . and I don't have to sneak anywhere." He motioned for her to come into the room and shut the door behind her. No need to advertise their family squabbles to anyone within earshot.

She lowered herself into a chair and tensed her fingers across her widening stomach. "Then why didn't you tell me you were coming here?"

His voice was strained when he answered. "Melinda, I know this is hard for you to grasp, but I don't need your permission or approval to see Rebecca. You're going to have to accept that."

"*Seeing* her is one thing, but this . . ." Melinda flipped her hand at the closed bedroom door—this is something entirely different."

"This . . . as you so scathingly put it, is not what you're thinking." He glowered at her, his face burning with anger. "But if it were, it would still be my business."

"What if I'd brought the kids with me? How could I have explained their grandfather standing here half-naked with a robe on in a strange woman's house?"

"The kids are smart enough to know not to barge into someone's house without calling first, a common courtesy their mother apparently hasn't mastered."

"I'll be damned if I'll sit back and watch her make a fool out of you."

"Make a fool out of me? How?" He choked out the words, thankful that the water was still running and Rebecca couldn't hear the insults his daughter was hurling.

"She's after something. I'm sure of it."

Steve stood motionless in the middle of the room. "What in the world could she be after, Melinda? She's successful, wealthy, owns her own home, her own business . . . if anything, she should be worried about what I want out of her."

"So that's it." Her mouth took on an unbecoming curl. "You're after her money. I should have known. I knew there had to be some reason for your behavior."

"Get out, Melinda," he yelled, "before I say something we'll both regret."

Rebecca opened the bathroom door and Melinda immediately pulled her into the heated exchange. "You—"

Steve turned and saw that Rebecca met his daughter's accusing eyes and sharp tone without wincing. He was proud of the way Rebecca stood up to Melinda's belligerence with a stiff back and an even stiffer upper lip.

Rebecca joined Steve, placing a reassuring hand on his arm. "You don't know your father at all if you can say those horrible things about him." In spite of her reserved tone, he knew she was seething underneath her calm exterior.

Melinda struggled to pull herself to the edge of the wicker chair. "I know my father and he would never," she gestured broadly, "never . . . do this. So it has to be the money."

A new anger seared his heart. "I've asked you to leave."

"I'll leave, but not before I tell Ms. Roswell a thing or two." Melinda's harsh voice reverberated through the room. "You're a conniving bitch who latched onto my father as soon as he came to town. You've tried everything in the book to lure Dad into your bed, and it looks as though you've succeeded. But I'll do everything in my power to stop this."

Steve felt impaled by her stunning words. "Melinda, you apologize this instant." He was caught off guard, rendered powerless against his daughter's senseless attack.

Rebecca's voice was uncompromising. "I think we're way past apologies, Steve. Let's be adults and talk this out. Your daughter has had her say, now, I think she should listen to ours."

"Nothing you say is going to change my mind."

"Maybe not, but you've barged into *my* home, laid your accusations at *my* doorstep, and now I deserve the chance to speak. You don't know your father very well if you believe that he could be manipulated so easily. He is a caring, considerate, charming man— the kind of man lots of women would love to spend time with." She paused. "There's no arguing he's a good catch, but I'm too old to fish or to play the kind of games you're accusing me of."

"I'll bet."

Steve stared at his daughter. Melinda reminded him of a wild animal who guards her young with her life, only it was he, not her children, who was being guarded.

Rebecca took a deep breath and continued. "And as far as luring him into my bed . . . at this moment, I haven't had the pleasure, no the *honor* of being anymore intimate with this lovely man than—"

Steve interrupted. "Rebecca! You don't need to explain." He put his hand on her arm. "If we ever do have more than a friendship, and we very well may, then it will be by mutual agreement between us. And, Melinda, I hope that you'll be happy for me. If that's too much to ask, then at least be civil."

He had accepted that his daughter was an unhappy person and may have been for months. For a long time, Steve had been caught up in his own miseries—his wife's death, the inevitable loneliness, selling his home, moving—to notice his daughter's pain. By the time he had moved in to help with the kids, Melinda had become a bitter stranger.

He turned to his daughter. "I've let you make your own mistakes. I'm letting you live your own life—even when I think you're wrong. All I ask is that you do the same for me." He wanted Melinda's blessing, but he wasn't about to compromise himself for it.

Melinda lifted her gaze to Steve's, then swallowed hard. "I see your point, Dad. I know you're trying to help. I'm just not ready to accept this." She took a heavy breath. "But I'll try."

Steve knew Melinda had taken a big step, but not quite big enough, considering the things she'd said to Rebecca.

This time he expected more. "I think you have something to say to Rebecca. You owe it to her."

Melinda's voice faded to a whisper, losing part

of its steely edge. "My father means I should apologize, Ms. Roswell."

Rebecca jumped in. "You don't need to do that."

She's trying to let Melinda save face, Steve thought. He was astonished that Rebecca could feel anything but animosity toward his daughter.

"I'm sorry I said all those things to you." Melinda looked from her father to Rebecca. "I know better."

"That's okay, Melinda. You were upset," Rebecca said.

"I should go find Joey and the children." She walked to the door, but turned and addressed her father one more time before leaving. "Are you coming soon? People will talk."

She just couldn't leave well enough alone.

He gathered enough strength to counter, "I'm too old to care what people say about me."

"Well, maybe you should." With that parting barb, Melinda was gone. Steve settled into the plump floral cushions of the sofa and propped his feet on the ottoman. He yanked the gaping robe together, but was no longer embarrassed. After all that had been said, he felt closer to Rebecca than ever. She'd taken up for him, spoken in his defense. And she hadn't run screaming into the woods when his daughter had acted like a shrew. So what did he have to lose? "What about that hot chocolate and some music?"

"Don't you want to get dressed?"

Rebecca had no idea how silky her voice sounded, nor what it did to him.

"Nah. I'm getting used to this get-up."

"I don't want to cause you anymore trouble. You won't hurt my feelings if you think you should go."

"Are you trying to get rid of me?"

"Not a chance."

"Then I propose you sit here and relax, while I fix us that hot chocolate." He squeezed her knee affectionately and walked by. "Let's sit here and sip our cocoa for a very long time . . . hours, maybe." He gave her a devilish grin. "And really give Melinda something to talk about."

Rebecca brought her hand up to stifle a giggle. "You're so-o-o bad. You truly missed your calling in high school—you would have been the ultimate bad boy."

"Do you think it's too late for a bad boy to give you a second glance?" His heart hammered, waiting for her answer.

Standing, she cupped his face in her hands and planted a tantalizing kiss on his lips. "I guess it's never too late."

Eight

Rebecca's heart jolted as she looked down to land the balloon and saw a lone man sitting on the picnic table next to the barn. Could it be?

She fixed her eyes on the man until the figure came into focus. It was Steve, holding a package tied with a big red bow. After a week without a word from him, he was there. Relief flooded through her. She was angry that he hadn't called, but she was glad to see him in spite of herself. Maybe he had a good excuse, or maybe Melinda had something to do with it.

Steve waved and she waved back with a tentative flip of her hand.

Whatever the reasons, she was happy he was here now. The powerful set of his shoulders and his long, lean form sent her senses soaring back into the clouds she'd just descended from. Rebecca could hardly maneuver the controls, she was so eager to land. Her fingers trembled with anticipation. Had it only been a week since the festival and the last time they'd been together?

She busied herself with the task of tying down the balloon with Hawk's help, half in anticipation, half in dread, at finding out why Steve hadn't called in days. She'd picked up the phone herself at least a dozen times, but had placed it back into the cradle before dialing. She knew it was the nineties, knew she didn't have to wait for him to call her, but she hadn't dialed his number.

Sure, she'd called men before, had even taken a few out and paid for the date, but this was different. After the festival, she'd made her intentions abundantly clear. Now it was Steve's turn.

With apprehension gnawing at her confidence, she walked toward Steve after securing the balloon. Not sure whether she should be cool or warm, questioning or concerned, she decided to follow his lead. After all, he had come to see her. If he'd decided not to date her anymore, then he wouldn't have dressed up, come all this way, and brought a gift. Would he?

Steve jumped off the table and greeted her warmly. "Hi, stranger." He seized both of her hands and stood swinging them back and forth. His eyes brightened with pleasure when she smiled. In that instant, she knew he was as glad to see her as she was to see him. She studied his face intently, looking for answers to her unspoken questions.

Nodding toward what she now could see was a

plastic food container, she broke the silence. "What's that?" she asked.

Steve released her, straddled the bench, and sat down. "This, my dear Rebecca, is a peace offering."

She stepped on the bench, then sat on the table. "For what?" She spoke in a casual, jesting way, yet she felt anything but casual. Jittery, yes. Anxious, no doubt about it. Doubts. Those devilish qualms that had crept into her thoughts with each passing day he hadn't called.

The lines deepened above his brows as he moistened his lips. "For my bad manners at not calling this week. I apologize." He slid the plastic container in front of her and popped off the top, ribbon and all, with his thumbs. "Here's a token of my sincerity."

She offered him a forgiving smile as the sweet smell of apple cobbler wafted out. "Thank goodness it's not lemon meringue!" She leaned close to the rim and took a deep whiff, filling her lungs with the scent of cinnamon and brown sugar. "Smells like heaven." She reached in and broke off a piece of the flaky crust, browned to perfection, not burned the way most of her own culinary experiments ended up. "Ummm, it's scrumptious. Who made it, Melinda?"

He clutched his chest. "I'm wounded—"

"No. Not you?"

"And why not me?" His voice was warm, yet teasing. "Don't you think men can cook?" His expression turned smug.

"Okay, so you caught me." Rebecca frankly admired the cobbler and the chef. "I admit, I didn't think you'd be able to bake a masterpiece like this."

"Well, if I'm forgiven for my past mistakes, then you're forgiven for this tiny indiscretion." His face grew serious. "Besides, I have a favor to ask you, and I want the slate clean before I do."

"Clean as a whistle. What's the favor?"

"Rebecca . . ."

She tingled as he said her name.

"Will you go out with me?"

She exhaled a short sigh of approval before answering. "That's not much of a favor. I'd be delighted to go out with you."

He shifted on the bench. "That's not exactly the favor part."

"Oh?"

His dark, earnest eyes sought hers. "It's in Atlanta—"

"Yes?"

"It's a benefit for the Garden Society." He flushed, but continued after she nodded. "Dolores and I hosted it for twenty years, and now they want me there in an honorary capacity." The look on his face mingled eagerness and anxiety.

"And the favor?"

"That *is* the favor. I'd consider it a big one if you'd be my date to the ball." He nervously swept his fingers through his hair. "Melinda will probably be there." He paused. "I know it's asking a lot, since I can't promise she won't be an ass again. But I'll do my best to keep her in line."

"Her actions are not your responsibility. I'd be delighted to go with you." She hoped her voice didn't reveal the insecurity she felt. "Melinda doesn't scare me, although I was beginning to wonder if she'd scared you off."

"Because I haven't called?"

"That did make me wonder."

He stared past her. "I have no excuse except that I had to take care of the kids more than usual. Melinda wasn't feeling well—"

She kept her features composed. "It doesn't take but a minute to pick up the phone and call." How well she knew that, since she could have done the same thing herself, but hadn't.

"Then why didn't you call me?" he asked. "I thought after Melinda's outburst that you too might have had second thoughts about our, uh . . . friendship."

"Point well taken," she admitted.

"I just had my hands full with the boys . . . and Melinda."

"It all comes back to Melinda, doesn't it?"

"Rebecca, last week marked the anniversary of

Dolores' death." His voice cracked. "For the first time since she died, I almost forgot. *Almost* forgot." He swallowed hard and closed his eyes. "Melinda took it hard. She needed me to help with Jeremy and Jake. I had to be there for her."

Startled at his confession, Rebecca moved from the table to sit beside him on the bench. "Of course you had to be there." She cradled his head against her chest and stroked his temples. "I understand."

She wanted to comfort him, wanted to take away the pain she herself had felt after her own husband had died. But she could only wait and be there for him while he worked through his sorrow. She couldn't do it for him. No one could.

"No, you don't really understand." His voice was a broken whisper. "I took it hard, too. I felt . . . guilty . . . about us." He searched her face, his dark eyes glistening. "Last week made me think about Dolores and all our years together. She was a good woman, a good wife and mother, and . . . I miss her." After a long pause, he added in a quiet, almost dejected, tone, "But she's gone, and after a hell of a week, I finally realized that Melinda wasn't standing in my way. Dolores was."

"Dolores?" Rebecca sat up, uneasy with what Steve was telling her. A faint thread of awkwardness threatened her composure. She never dreamed that after all this time he would be in such pain, still working through his grief. She wanted him to stop, but she had to know the truth, even though it hurt.

"Dolores was the biggest part of my life. I thought I'd never live without her, but I have." He gave her an affectionate look. "Since I met you, I've even been happy. I just couldn't shake the guilt I had over finding someone else to . . . share my life with. I didn't mean to cut you off last week, but I had to think about where our relationship was going."

"Relationship?" She hated that word. What the hell did it mean? Not friend, not boyfriend, not husband, not spouse, not even the proverbial "significant other."

"Rebecca, you've become my best friend, but we both know we want it to be more. Don't we?"

She nodded. "So what do we do?"

He gazed at her a long moment before answering. "I think it's high time we had an official date. None of this 'outing' business. None of this meeting for lunch or babysitting the boys. We owe ourselves a genuine, honest-to-goodness, boy-picks-up-girl kind of date for starters." There was an invitation in his eyes. "Then we'll see what happens from there. What do you say?"

A warm glow of happiness drowned her earlier reservations and fears. "What time?"

"Saturday. Seven o'clock. Sharp." His composure in check, he gave her an exaggerated wink. "Oh, did I mention it's a masquerade ball?"

"A what?"

Excitement added a shine to his eyes that had been missing all morning. "Masquerade. You know, dress up."

"I'm not sure—" She watched him as he rose to his feet.

"Trust me. I'll take care of everything. Just leave your size with the costume store at this number, and I'll make the arrangements." He pulled a slip of paper from his shirt pocket and slid it across the table. "They've been taking care of me for ages. What do you say?"

This was a big step. He was introducing her into his former life—the life he'd shared with Dolores. Rebecca didn't know if she was ready. She'd thought she was before they started this conversation; now her emotions were twisted up tighter than a flag wrapped around a pole in a hurricane. She inspected her options quickly, then decided she really had none. It was now or never, and "never" sounded so final. She wasn't ready for never, so it had to be now. "On the condition that you don't turn me into an animal, a punk-rocker, or Shirley Temple. Can I count on that?" she asked dubiously.

"No problem. I had something a little more . . . daring in mind."

Her cheeks burned with embarrassment at the

possibilities. "No French maid outfit, either. Promise me it'll be decent."

"As beautiful as you are, that's a promise I can't keep. But it will be in good taste."

"My good name is in your hands—"

"I'll have the costume delivered in plenty of time for your approval. If you hate it, we'll get something else."

"Then you've got yourself a date."

A date. The beginning, or the end.

Rebecca lined her lips with a raspberry pencil, filled in the outline with a luscious red-amber lipstick, then dabbed a spot of powder on her nose. She smacked her lips on a tissue and surveyed the results in the vanity mirror. Definitely not her color. Not yet, at least. But when she donned the costume she'd received that morning, she knew the results would be spectacular.

She walked to the bed and uncovered the large white box from the costume company. Even though she knew what was inside, she smiled to herself at the thought of actually wearing it out in public for all the world—including Steve—to see.

She pulled the silky sheer stockings out of the box first and draped them across her mauve comforter. Rummaging through the tissue-wrapped items, she found what she was looking for, the crimson garter belt. She stepped into it, pulled it to her waist, then let the straps fall to mid-thigh. Rubbing her hands together, she coated them with lotion to avoid picks and runs in her only pair of stockings. Rebecca slid her foot into the right stocking, smoothed it up her calf and thigh, then hooked it into the garters, front and back. She repeated the procedure for her left leg. When she finished, she stood in front of the full-length mirror behind the bathroom door to observe the results.

Not bad, she thought, feeling more than a little risqué. She hadn't worn the real thing in decades, and never with such a racy garter. Never. She blushed the shade of the belt when she wondered if Steve had picked it out himself, then dismissed the idea. The outfit was probably a package deal.

The delicate, black lace bustier corset came next. She loosely laced the boned garment and slipped it over her head. She tightened the ribbons until it snugly fit her waist and breasts. The curvaceous top barely covered her ample bosom, made more voluptuous by the boning. She had never felt so sexy in her life.

At her dressing table, she put the finishing touches on her make-up by penciling a dark mole in the appropriate spot. She took the burgundy and black pin-striped, full-length dress off the hanger and held it up to her bodice. It was such a deliciously wicked costume. She never would have picked it out for herself, but she was glad Steve had. He must have thought she would look good in it. Why else would he have chosen it?

She stepped into the dress and secured it up the front over the corset. The lacy edge of the bustier peeked above the fitted bodice, and the full skirt billowed from hundreds of tiny gathers at the waist. Underneath, a black net crinoline filled out the gown. Rebecca tugged the long, fitted sleeves to her wrists, then carefully buttoned the tiny onyx buttons that stretched from wrist to elbow. The dress dragged the floor until she slipped her feet into black leather ankle boots.

Almost done. Carefully spreading her skirt over the vanity stool, Rebecca sat and opened the smaller box from the costume company. The *pièce de resistance*—her crowning glory—the wig. With both hands, she slipped the wig over her own hair and stared at the woman in the mirror. Rebecca Roswell had been transformed into Dodge City's very own Miss Kitty. Thick copper ringlets fell from the crown, and tiny tendrils framed her face. For a finishing touch, she tied a black velvet ribbon around her neck, and was spritzing perfume behind her ears when the doorbell rang. Almost as an afterthought, she lifted her heavy skirt and sprayed behind her knees. Leave an aromatic trail, her mother used to say. She placed the bottle on the table, took one last look in the mirror, and headed toward the door.

Watch out, Steve, here I come!

Steve took another look at his reflection in the window before ringing Rebecca's doorbell. He looked pretty good in a hat, even if he hadn't worn one in ages. For fun, he whipped the Colt .45 replica out of his holster and stood poised for action. It was definitely action he was looking for tonight, but not at gunpoint. He shoved the gun back into its holster and adjusted the leather belt riding low on his hips.

When his old buddy at the costume store had suggested the Dodge City duo as their outfits for this shindig, he'd balked at first. But after one look at Miss Kitty's saloon attire, he couldn't get the image out of his mind of how Rebecca would look in it.

Now Steve's pointed-toe cowboy boots tapped a rhythm on Rebecca's porch floor. He rang the bell again and waited. When he heard footsteps on the other side, he posed with one hand on his gun, the other on his well-shaped hat.

Rebecca flung the door open and light flooded the porch. Steve tipped his hat and swung down low, stopping in mid-bow as he caught sight of Rebecca's radiant image framed in the doorway.

Her fair skin was finely complemented by the deep auburn-colored wig. Her lips had never looked more lush and inviting than at that moment. "You look gorgeous!"

"Why, Matt, darling, you're a sight for sore eyes yourself." Rebecca batted her eyelashes and curtsied with a rustle.

"I'll be the envy of every man at the ball tonight." Steve lifted her slender hand to his lips. "Miss Kitty herself never looked this good."

"The original Dillon might argue that point."

"Not if he'd seen you in this dress." His gaze lowered to the satiny fullness of her breasts and her cinched waist that flared into rounded hips. When his appraisal turned back to her lovely face, she colored fiercely, but her eyes smoldered with delight.

"We'd better leave now. Your chariot awaits."

"You mean stagecoach, don't you?"

"This modern-day Matt can do a little better than that." He moved aside, motioning to the black stretch limousine and chauffeur waiting at the curb.

"Oh, Steve! A limo. It's been ages since I've ridden in one."

The surprised look on her face made it worth the extra effort he'd gone through to get the limo. "Only the best for my Miss Kitty."

They walked the short distance to the elegant car and climbed into the wide back seat. "You are the best, Matt Dillon," she whispered as they waited for the chauffeur to close their door and position himself in the driver's seat.

This wasn't Miss Kitty talking to Matt Dillon. This wasn't television, this was real life—with no script and no director telling him what to do. Steve was falling in love with this woman, and it scared him to death. After losing his wife he'd thought there would never be anyone else, but Rebecca had proved him wrong. He tapped the chauffeur on the shoulder and directed, "Dodge City, and step on it."

The privacy glass silently slid into place.

"Are we in a hurry?"

"Hurry?" He gave an impatient shrug. "The sooner we get there, the sooner we can leave."

"Leave? I've been looking forward to this evening all week, Steve Jordan." She tossed her copper ringlets in mock defiance. "I'm not leaving until the very last dance is played."

"It's just been years since I've had a beautiful woman in the back seat of my car, and I don't want to waste a single minute dancing when I can do this." He softly pressed his lips to hers, savoring the taste, drinking in the delicate aroma of her perfume. He lingered, not wanting to tear himself from her arms.

Steve saw the familiar facade of the French Quarter Inn in Atlanta as the limousine pulled into the covered valet area. He jumped out and beat the chauffeur to Rebecca's door.

Her full skirt inched to her knees as she slipped across to the edge of the seat. The sight of her shapely legs clad in black stockings sent his heart to pumping wildly. His thoughts strayed, imagining her silky white thighs against the wicked crimson garters. He wrenched himself into the present and offered his arm to escort her into the hotel.

As the doorman held the door for them to enter, Steve said a quick prayer that Melinda would behave herself tonight.

"Steve, old man, glad you made it." A chubby Robin Hood in bright green leotards enthusiastically pumped Steve's hand as they walked into the five-story atrium that served as the ballroom for the event. "Isn't this damn thing hideous?" He slapped his bulging green stomach. "My wife just had to be Maid Marian."

Steve smiled to himself. It felt funny to be here with Rebecca, talking to friends who had known him all his adult life.

"Well, howdy-do, Miss Kitty. This fellow you're with sure does leave some big shoes to fill." Robin Hood tipped his face toward Rebecca.

"Rebecca, this is Norman Bakerson. Norman has my old job as chairman of this lavish event," Steve explained. "Norman, this is Rebecca Roswell."

Steve searched his old friend's face for a reaction. Norman was jovial enough, but unreadable.

"Not *the* Rebecca Roswell from Roswell Developments?" He gave a long, low whistle. "I've always wanted to meet Atlanta's most famous real estate tycoon," Norman gushed. He vigorously shook her hand. "This is a real pleasure. You've got to meet George Heatherton. He's a big admirer. Used that merger you did as a model for—"

In deciding to bring Rebecca to this event, Steve had worried about exposing her to so many of his old friends, couples he'd seen for years with Dolores. It never occurred to him that many of these same people who were involved in business might know, or have heard of, Rebecca from her other life. Her life before him.

"It's been ages!" another old acquaintance interrupted.

Steve could only watch as Norman kidnapped Rebecca, leaving him to make polite conversation with his former business associate. As soon as possible, he hurried to retrieve his date from Norman's clutches.

"Here you two are! Norman, I turn my back for a moment and you run off with my woman."

"Sorry, old man. I couldn't pass up the chance to show off one of the best damn negotiators Atlanta's ever seen."

"Now, Norm, you're embarrassing Rebecca." It

took a lot to render Norm a blubbering idiot, but Rebecca had managed it without trying. She must have been something in the business world for old Norm to act the way he did. He usually reserved that kind of adulation for corporate presidents.

Before the party, Steve had worried about how his friends would react to Rebecca as the new woman in his life. He hadn't expected to find himself in her shadow. Yet instead of feeling jealous, Steve was proud of her accomplishments, even if he hadn't been a part of them.

"Thanks for rescuing me."

"I didn't realize you were such a celebrity."

"Me? *You're* the celebrity."

He *had* been with Dolores. He knew Dolores had been satisfied to stand back and let him be the center of attention. It felt odd realizing that Rebecca had been as successful—more so, even— as he had in his career. This was a foreign concept to him, even though his own daughter was a career woman now.

Through the years, Dolores had been content to let him do most of the talking. She'd stood quietly by in public, laughing at his jokes and being a "good wife," but that was the way Dolores had wanted it. She was most comfortable in her kitchen, baking or doing something for the family.

Rebecca wasn't Dolores and he knew it. She

wouldn't be happy taking a back seat to anyone. He just hoped his ego could adjust.

Just then, several people crowded around them. Old friends kept stopping by to say "hello" and meet the new woman in his life. A steady stream of costumed characters greeted them cordially, hindering their entrance into the main function area. They finally broke loose and pushed past the hand-lettered sign balanced on an easel that read Garden Society Masquerade Ball.

Arm-in-arm, they stepped into the lavishly decorated atrium filled with exotic flower gardens and gaudily dressed benefactors. A gazebo bar flanked one side of the room, and a multi-level buffet was set up on the other. But their gaze riveted to the elaborate bronze fountain splashing into a lighted pool across from the stage.

"It's beautiful!" Rebecca's infectious laugh was as intimate as the kiss they'd shared in the limo.

From a waiter's tray, Steve lifted two fluted champagne glasses filled with the sparkling amber liquid. He handed one to Rebecca and raised the other to his lips. "Ummm."

Right now, Steve would give almost anything for a few minutes alone with the lovely Miss Kitty. He couldn't take his eyes off her. Neither could most of the other men in the room.

"You certainly have a lot of friends."

"I seem to have more tonight than usual." He

ran his finger along the rim of his crystal glass. "They're all curious about you."

"Or maybe they're just big Gunsmoke fans."

He loved her sense of humor. In the last weeks, Rebecca had taught him to laugh again. He steered her to a linen-covered table near the stage and podium. "Gladys, Bill, meet Rebecca Roswell." He gestured to the couple on their right. "And this is Maid Marian, better known as Ellen."

"Norm's better half." The whole table laughed as Ellen flipped back the hair on one side of her long, brown wig. "Norm's working the room, but he'll be disappointed if you two don't sit here." She patted an empty chair.

Rebecca sat down next to Norm's wife, while Steve finished the introductions. "The Wellingtons, Nan and Elbert." He wished he hadn't promised Norm they would sit at his table. At the time, he hadn't counted on how much attention they would stir, but he'd wanted an excuse not to sit with Melinda, in case she asked.

When the conversations reverted away from them, Rebecca leaned toward Steve. "Where's Melinda? I thought you said she was coming."

His jaw twitched involuntarily. "She is." He dreaded his daughter's arrival. "She loves to make a late entrance, complete with fanfare. She'll show, never fear."

"Are we having a good time yet?" Norm boomed

into the microphone on stage. "I appreciate your generous participation in the thirty-first annual Masquerade Ball benefiting an organization near and dear to us all—the Garden Society of Atlanta." A smattering of applause interrupted his speech. "Tonight we welcome back someone who is also dear to us—although he's not that near anymore since he moved out to the boondocks—our old buddy and past chairman of this event, Steve Jordan. Steve, come on up and say a few words."

When he'd been in charge, Steve hadn't minded speaking. But tonight Rebecca was here listening to his every word, and he didn't want to embarrass himself by messing up. He was too old to be this insecure, yet his palms were sweaty and his mouth was dry as he started up the steps.

On stage, he paused and looked across the crowded room. "Twenty years ago when I took over this event, a lot of people showed up as gangsters and hippies—but tonight, you guys have gotten a lot more creative."

"We can afford better costumes now!" Henry VIII yelled from a table near the buffet.

Steve laughed with the others. "That we can. And from the looks of the early totals, we can raise a lot more money for this worthy cause, too. The Garden Society thanks you, and I thank you. In the eternal words of Robin Hood," he waved toward Norm, ". . . eat, drink, and be merry . . . and pay your bar tab before you leave." As he left the stage, a slap on the back and a couple of well-wishers caught him before he could retreat to his table . . . and Rebecca.

A few minutes later, he excused himself to find Rebecca engaged in an animated conversation with the Wellingtons and Norm. He needn't have worried; she could take care of herself. She wasn't a social neophyte by any means.

"Steve, old buddy, old pal of mine," Norm started. "I need a favor."

Oh, no. What now? Steve looked at his date for any hint as to what was coming, what they'd been talking about.

"This bum back of mine is giving me a fit—hauling in all these damn plants, I guess. Ellen wanted me to personally take care of those exotic ones myself. It was a pain keeping those beauties out of the wind."

"Norm, the favor?"

"Oh, yeah. I can't do the traditional first dance any justice. Would you do it for me?"

"With Ellen?"

"Are you kidding? She's got two left feet. Hates to dance. She's hiding out in the powder room now, waiting for me to find somebody who'll take her off the hook."

Steve's stomach lurched. How could he dance in front of all these people with Rebecca, whose very touch sent electric shocks to parts that didn't need waking up? "I don't know, Norm. I'd like to help you out, but Rebecca didn't count on this when I asked her out tonight." He tried to catch her attention, but she was watching Norm. He was stuck. It wasn't that he didn't want to dance with her. He did. Couldn't wait to get her into his arms and feel her body pressed against his, swaying to the music. He just didn't want to do it with three hundred pairs of eyes scrutinizing their every move.

"I guess my achy-breaky back's in your hands, Miss Kitty. What do you say?" Norm by-passed Steve and went directly to Rebecca. "If you can't, Ol' Matt here's gonna have to shoot me like a lame horse. If he doesn't, Ellen will."

"Well, we wouldn't want a shoot-out on my account. I'd be happy to." She offered Steve a sudden, irresistible smile.

How could he refuse after that?

"I'll be damned! Thanks, Steve." With a relieved sigh, Norm added. "Just give the band leader a signal and they'll start the dance music."

Steve helped Rebecca up and they started across the room.

"By the way, it's a waltz."

Steve shot Norm a venomous look. A waltz, of all things. He could do a scandalous tango—thanks to Arthur Murray—and his two-step was passable, but his waltz was another story. That monotonous one-two-three, one-two-three rhythm was unforgiving. One false step and the whole room would notice, particularly in a spotlight.

"I'm a bit rusty," he confided as they paused at the gazebo for a glass of water.

"This is probably not a good time to tell you that I have a tendency to lead. Comes from dancing by myself all those years without dates." Rebecca laughed nervously.

"Great." He wasn't sure if it was or not. "I wish we'd had time to practice." What he really wished was that he could snap his fingers and Matt Dillon could be curled up in Dodge City in front of a roaring fire with his boots kicked off and Miss Kitty in his arms. He never realized how badly these ill-fitting boots would cramp his toes. At the moment, his foot apparel was the least of his problems.

"Why can't we practice?" She surveyed the room. "Wait here." He watched her whisper something to the bartender, who nodded in the direction of the exit. "Let's go. Hurry."

Rebecca pulled him along through the crowd, past the entrance sign, and produced a key that opened a side door.

"What are we doing?" Steve froze, so she pulled him into a large room lined with row after row of coats. "Are you crazy? What if somebody saw us come in here? What will they think?"

"You *are* getting old. They'll think that Matt and Miss Kitty want to smooch in the coat closet."

"Rebecca!"

"Steve, do you want to practice or not?"

"I guess so."

"Fine. Let's do it." She opened her arms and waited for him to join her in the empty center of the dimly lit room. "Pretend it's a dance hall and I'm Miss Kitty, not Rebecca."

Steve looped his left hand around her waist, barely touching her back. Gently, he pressed his palm against her outstretched arm, avoiding the urge to look down at her breasts. He felt so awkward, but he started to dance. Pushing his right leg forward to the swish of Rebecca's skirt, they fumbled through, with Steve muttering the counts under his breath. He felt her pick up speed, smoothing out the steps until their movements resembled the dance as it was meant to be. Then he forgot about counting and pulled her closer, closer, until his chest pressed against hers.

They moved easily now, each stride fluid and graceful. His emotions reeled with each swirl of her skirt brushing against his thighs, awakening an intense urgency he could no longer ignore. The smoldering flame he saw in her eyes only stoked the fire in his own heart.

As if in slow motion, the two glided to a stop. Still holding her in his arms, Steve knew the wave of passion between them was more than sexual desire. At last, he broke their self-imposed silence when strains of the Tennessee Waltz brought them back to reality. "I believe they're playing our song."

Nine

Melinda walked through the grand atrium of the French Quarter Inn with a fixed smile on her face and a tall, handsome man on her arm—a man who wasn't her husband. Showing up at her father's big event with a strange man had seemed like a good idea in the beginning. Yet now that she was actually here in front of all these people who knew and loved her, a pang of regret hit her—but it was too late.

If her father could bring someone besides her mother, then she, too, could bring whomever she pleased. She'd dragged Joey to too many of these fancy banquets, and he'd hated every single one. In her line of business, she had formal obligations. Joey had escorted her—under duress—because she'd convinced him it was good for her career in corporate insurance.

Standing here in familiar surroundings, amidst all of her father's friends, she was having second thoughts about her decision. Even with his "shotgun" attendance, Joey had always made her feel special. Melinda knew he'd much prefer taking her to a Braves double-header or a matinee at the Fox Theater.

But tonight was different. She and Joey were separated, and she'd had no desire to ask him to escort her under the circumstances. So she'd brought a date. Besides, there was nothing she could do about it now. They were here.

"We're a little late," she told her escort, knowing full well she'd planned it that way. She looked up at William Davis, III. She'd picked him because he was good-looking, knew how to handle himself in a social setting, and most importantly, was convenient.

"We could have skipped the drink at your house." William helped her out of her coat and handed it to the man behind the registration counter. "At the risk of sounding presumptuous, have I told you how beautiful you look tonight?"

"I gave it my best shot." Melinda awkwardly covered her eyes with her mask and hoped her smile was noncommittal.

She preferred the Cinderella look, but now that she resembled the pumpkin coach, feeling attractive was an impossible proposition. So instead of coming as a Princess, she'd opted for the traditional hand-held Mardi Gras mask with a flowing black silk evening pantsuit. William, however, was a perfect double for Prince Charming in his white dinner jacket. It set off his jet-black hair combed back in a slick city style. Only someone with a mountain of confidence could carry that hair-do off, and no one had ever accused William of lacking self-confidence.

Inviting William this evening had had nothing to do with romance. Her own love-life was the last thing on her mind. Tonight was, in part, a rebellious statement to her father. She wanted to embarrass him by showing up with someone besides Joey, the way she'd been embarrassed to have someone other than her mother with her father. She wanted to make him see how ridiculous he looked dating another woman. But would he? Melinda was going for shock value, and she grimly set out to accomplish her goal.

Entering the ballroom, she instantly recognized a familiar waltz. The immobilized crowd and lull in the noise meant the traditional first dance was underway. Memories of her parents sliding across that very same floor came flooding back to her. She could close her eyes and still see them slowly dance around the circle, greeting their friends as they passed nearby, laughing at some unspoken joke only they could hear. She bit her lip to kill the sob in her throat and forced herself to settle down. This memory, etched in the recesses of her mind, was the very thing she had vowed to preserve.

Breaking away from William's grip, she pushed through the throng of onlookers to the edge of the dance floor. There she halted, shocked at what she saw—her father and Rebecca dancing cheek-to-cheek in a shaft of blue light, oblivious to everyone else. Miss Kitty and Matt Dillon were in their own private world. In all the years her parents had been together, she'd never seen her father look at her mother the way he was staring at Rebecca now. Melinda took a quick, sharp breath. A stab of panic threatened to shatter her last ounce of control. She wanted to run out and push them apart. How could he dance with her here, of all places?

"You're a hard lady to catch."

Melinda flinched at the sound of William's voice. Displacing her anger, she turned on him. "I'm a woman. A person. A mother. And . . ." She caught herself before she added "a wife." "Lady sounds condescending and insulting. Like little lady. Lady of the evening. Lady luck."

Why had her father put her in this untenable situation? At first, she blamed Rebecca for taking him away from her when she needed him most, but now she'd come far enough in her thinking to realize her father was no easy target. If he was with *that woman*, it was because he wanted to be, not because Rebecca had tricked or manipulated him.

"Careful, Ms. Camden, your green fur is show-

ing. I didn't mean anything, I just didn't think—"
William's mouth flattened into a straight line of
displeasure.

"Typical. Men usually don't . . ." She was suddenly sorry she'd ever invited this man to escort
her here. "Think, that is."

He thrust both hands in his tuxedo pockets. His
features were as cool as his tone. "And I'm no
exception. Is that what you mean?"

She'd expected him to be angry after her ridiculous outburst, but he didn't seem to care enough
about her to be very angry. Annoyed? Maybe. But
she knew he had gotten exactly what he wanted,
and that was to be here with the movers and shakers of the town. Melinda was just the vehicle that
had made it possible.

"Yes. No. William, I don't know what I'm trying
to say." Melinda impatiently ripped out the words
from a confused place within.

"Let's quit playing games, Melinda. You're here
because of them, not me." William motioned toward her father and Rebecca, who were gradually
being surrounded by other couples joining in the
dance.

An equally cold expression settled on her face.
She hated being caught red-handed, hated for
someone to read her motives. When she'd broken
the house rules as a teenager, Melinda had made
up elaborate stories to cover her tracks, even for a

minor infraction. She would have done or said most anything to keep her parents from knowing that she wasn't their perfect little girl. Nothing had changed in that respect. But William was not her father, and she didn't owe him an explanation, so she simply didn't respond.

"Isn't it?" He asked again, and nodded perfunctorily at the dance floor. "We're adults. We're at a perfectly marvelous affair with a luscious buffet, tolerable music, and enough high society to make or break a hundred careers. You . . . well, you take care of whatever personal agenda you came here for. And I'll just take care of myself until you're ready to be politely escorted to your front door."

Abruptly, Melinda wanted to escape from scrutiny. His reproachful words rang in her ears as she watched him retreat to the far side of the room to sample the food on the tiered buffet tables.

She turned her attention back to her father. Those costumes must have been Rebecca's idea. Her father would never have picked out anything so revealing for her mother. Dolores was too modest for such a low-cut bodice that only someone with little class would prance around in. Deep down, Melinda felt a tinge of jealousy at how sexy her father's date looked. Her own costume suddenly felt like old draperies.

It hadn't been this way with her other two pregnancies. Joey had been by her side, making her feel special, beautiful, as if she were the only woman in the world who'd ever been pregnant. The problem was, Joey wasn't around this time. And she had no one to blame but herself. He'd made it clear he was interested in a reconciliation. Her irrational pride had kept her from considering it so far. Maybe she was punishing him for letting things deteriorate to this sorry state.

Still, she missed him. For the first time tonight, she wished he were here. He'd know just the right thing to say to put a smile on her face, to lighten her mood, to ease the tension between her and her father. Maybe that was one of the reasons she hadn't invited him. She didn't want to feel better, didn't want to act like an adult, didn't want to be "big" about Rebecca taking her mother's place.

"Melinda, darling." One of her mother's oldest friends jolted her out of her thoughts. The plump, white-haired woman dressed as Queen Victoria offered her a fluted glass brimming with golden liquid. "Have some champagne. Maybe it will cheer you up."

"I'd love a glass or two, but I'm not allowed." Melinda lightly patted the mid-section she'd tried so hard to camouflage. "Doctor's orders. Thanks anyway."

"Of course, how silly of me!" The two of them were joined by Snow White, another member of her mother's bridge group.

Queen Victoria boldly patted the baby the way Melinda had done herself only seconds before. "You remember Melinda." Her voice dropped as if she were whispering a well-kept secret instead of stating the obvious. "Melinda's having a baby. So, I guess you can have her champagne."

Snow White greeted her warmly. "I'm so glad you could make it, Melinda. I was afraid something had happened when I didn't see you earlier."

The trio chatted for a few minutes, then turned back to observe the dancers. Odd couples—Captain Kangaroo and Mae West, Frankenstein and Katherine Hepburn from the African Queen—were two-stepping to the latest country hit as partners mixed to dance.

"Scandalous, isn't it darling?" Queen Victoria asked.

Melinda shrugged her shoulders, unwilling to acknowledge what she knew the woman was referring to. "Pardon?"

"Those two are so close, one would have to wonder how they can breathe. And that corset. Land sakes, nobody who's anybody would ever wear such a thing at home, much less out in public."

Melinda nodded, slightly embarrassed, yet encouraged that other people—people who had known her mother—reacted the same way to her father dancing with another woman. She tried to catch her father's eye, tried to make him notice her, but he was totally engrossed in his conversation with Rebecca. The red-headed hussy flipped her auburn locks back with a full-hearted laugh.

"Who can blame Steve? He's bound to be lonely. After all it's been such a *long* time since the loss of your dear mother." Queen Victoria was living up to her reputation as a queen of gossip.

Long time, indeed. Melinda knew exactly what she meant. It was okay if Melinda said bad things about her father. After all, he was her father. It was something else, entirely, to sit back and let someone else criticize him, even if she did agree.

The woman swigged down her last swallow of champagne. "Excuse me, dear, it's not a real party without a full glass in your hand." And she was off to find a waiter and another ear to bend.

Melinda had almost forgotten her mother's other friend, she'd been so quiet. "So where's your dwarf or prince or whatever? I get my fairy tales mixed up."

"I'm here alone. My real-life Prince Charming died of a heart attack three years ago." Snow White's eyes filled with tears and her voice cracked. "Your mother was a good friend to me during that time."

Melinda's cool tone warmed slightly. "That's the way she was."

"I remember she once told me that my late husband wouldn't want me to be a wallflower in the dance of life. I thought that was very poetic and very true." The woman placed her still-full glass on a passing waiter's tray, pulled out a lace handkerchief from underneath her watchband, and dabbed the corners of her eyes.

It felt good to talk about her mother to someone else who had loved her. Her father might have forgotten what a good, kind, loving person Dolores was, but Melinda never would, and neither would her boys.

"Mom was a wise person." Melinda blinked back her own tears.

"Wise . . . and lucky to have spent thirty years with your father, who is also wise. After all, he married your mother, didn't he?"

Her stomach churned in frustration. *"That* was the best decision he ever made."

"Maybe, but now that she is gone, he can't be a wallflower either."

The last thing Melinda had expected was for one of her mother's friends to come to her father's defense. She swallowed hard and managed a curt question as she searched the dance floor for Steve and Rebecca. "But *her?"*

"I never had the good fortune to find someone else, but it seems your father has."

Melinda tried to keep her heart cold and still, but images of her father and the two women in his life—her mother and Rebecca—burned clear.

"What bothers you so much about this new woman?" Snow White's tiny voice barely carried above the music.

"She's nothing like my mother."

"Maybe that's why they get along. Steve's obviously not trying to replace your mother." The woman shook her head and sighed. "Can't you see that?"

"I know I should be happy for him. I just don't feel happy right now."

"That's not his fault, so don't take it out on him . . . or his friend. Think about it. It's what your mother would have wanted."

Why did everyone pretend to know what her mother would have wanted? She was Dolores' daughter. Wouldn't she have known if her mother had felt this way? How could this woman, who professed to be her mother's friend, approve of her father's new girlfriend?

"How can you say that? How can you know?" Pain was gripping her from the inside—the kind of pain spawned from unresolved grief.

"I knew her. I know she'd want your father happy." Snow White placed a reassuring hand on her arm. "And deep down, you know it, too. You need your daddy now, honey. Don't do anything you'll regret later." The woman wrapped her arms around her in a comforting hug, then left Melinda alone to consider what she'd said.

Melinda was conscious of where the woman's thin, bony arms had held her, the embrace dredging up the countless times her own mother had gathered her close, the memory of her tenderness almost unbearable. And the image of her father coming in and enveloping them both with the long, strong arms of his love.

Melinda realized deep in her heart she was just a little girl who needed her daddy. A little girl who saw the new woman in his life as a threat.

On impulse, she took a brusque step forward and stiffly walked toward the swaying couple. She'd lost her mother, but she had no intention of losing her father, too.

Steve didn't see Melinda until she was standing right beside them. He looked up to see his daughter's disapproving eyes staring directly into his. "Melinda!" He froze in mid-dance, but not before he squarely stepped on his partner's toe. "Rebecca, I'm sorry."

One curly auburn lock fell forward as Rebecca warmly smiled first at Steve, then at his daughter. "Must be those two left feet you were talking about."

Melinda snapped, "My father's an excellent dancer."

Steve noticed his daughter's clamped jaw and fixed, angry eyes. "It's a joke, Melinda."

"Inside joke, maybe." Melinda's tone was sarcastic as she waved her black and purple sequined mask back and forth in front of her face.

The three of them stood in the center of the dance floor, with all the dancers filing by, the music droning in their ears, and the silence between them deafening.

Rebecca raised her eyebrows at Steve. "I'm a little hot."

"You look it," Melinda added.

Disconcerted, he looked to Rebecca. She answered his apologetic frown with a reassuring smile—unaware of the captivating picture she painted, or the peace she brought to his soul.

With renewed strength, Steve turned to his daughter. His high spirits were dampened, but not doused, by Melinda's barbs. He put a hand on each woman's arm and started to lead them both off the dance floor. "Let's go get some drinks and—"

"That's not necessary. I need to freshen up a bit and take a break." Rebecca sent him another reassuring look. "Why don't you two dance?" She gently laid his hand on Melinda's arm and walked away.

"I believe she wants us to dance. Shall we?" For Rebecca's sake, he wouldn't cause anymore of a scene. He would dance with his daughter. She wanted things to work out for him . . . and for his relationship with his daughter. Steve stuck Melinda's mask in his pocket, then took her in his arms.

His resolve to stay angry crumbled a little when he felt her bulging stomach between them. A new life. His grandchild.

"Why did you come out here?" He carefully maneuvered her away from listening ears to an empty section near the edge of the parquet floor. "What did you want?"

"I didn't come out here to force you to dance with me, if that's what you mean." Her lips quivered.

"Did I say you did?" He closed his eyes a moment, reliving the agony of their last fight. "You looked as if you had something on your mind."

He felt her body grow rigid, her grip on his hand tighten. The color drained from her face and he thought she was going to pass out. "Are you okay? Do you need to sit down?"

"No! Please, not yet."

Her voice was shakier than he would have liked, but she continued to sway to the music. Steve warily observed her face for signs of fatigue. "What's going on, honey?"

"I wish I knew." Her exasperation was evident in the lines creasing her eyes and brow. "I was thinking of Mom."

"I've thought of her a lot myself tonight."

"You have?"

Steve felt the tension ease from her body as the strain lessened between them. Yet the disbelief in her tone and the surprise on her face had hurt him. Over his daughter's shoulder, Steve caught sight of Rebecca at the buffet table, engrossed in conversation with some of the other guests. She was good for him.

He stroked Melinda's hair, tilted her head back and looked into his daughter's face. "You have your mother's smile."

Her tight expression relaxed into an easy grin, the first one he'd seen in weeks.

"Yeah, that's the one—a little crooked, with your nose wrinkled." He touched the tip of her nose with his finger. They rocked together, hardly dancing at all.

"Oh, Daddy! I've missed you so much." She leaned her head against his chest.

"I'm right here, honey. I'll always be here for you." Father and daughter moved slowly around the dance floor for a few minutes without speaking. Steve chuckled aloud to himself. "Remember when you were a little girl and you'd stand on my feet and I'd dance you around the room?"

Her face softened. "Yeah! I loved it. I've always regretted not having a photo to remember that by."

"You have the memory right up here." He pressed her forehead with his index finger. "That's what really matters. Nobody can ever take that away from you." He felt a warmness that he hadn't felt for his daughter in months.

"Sometimes I still feel like that little girl."

Her fingers trembled. Steve wanted to protect her the way he'd done when she'd been that little girl staring up at him with adoration in her eyes.

They danced to a less crowded spot before Steve hastily stopped, dropped her arms and cried, "Did you feel that?" He pushed his daughter back a few inches and riveted his gaze on her stomach. "Was that what I think it was?"

She looked surprised, but happy at his reaction. "Absolutely." Melinda took his hand and placed it on her belly. "Daddy, meet your newest grandbaby."

"He feels like a field-goal kicker."

"He?" Melinda's face split into a wide grin. "Why not she?"

Steve was filled with awe at the miracle of feeling his newest grandchild—boy or girl—for the first time. "I'd be proud to have another girl in the family."

"Really, Daddy?"

"Of course, honey." He wrapped his arms around Melinda, feeling a renewed closeness. "Don't you know I love you?"

By the time Rebecca reached the buffet, her pounding heart had quieted and her rapid pulse was nearly normal. Nothing would have made Melinda happier than for Rebecca to have balked when she'd cut in on the dance floor. Those two had unresolved business to take care of and didn't need an audience or any added pressure. It would do Melinda good to dance with her father, talk to him one-on-one. Rebecca was sure Melinda would come around, because she loved her father and wanted him happy. How long it would take for Melinda to do more than tolerate her was anybody's guess.

Rebecca turned to discreetly observe father and daughter. Then Steve looked her way, sending Rebecca's heart thudding again. The long deep look she and Steve exchanged said it all: they would somehow work things out.

She turned to the buffet and filled her plate with lobster Thermidor, Swedish meatballs, and boiled shrimp covered with spicy cocktail sauce. Jabbing a piece of Swiss cheese with a toothpick, she popped it into her mouth. No one looked familiar until she spotted Snow White—the woman Melinda had been talking to earlier—at the other end of the table. She made her way to the corner, ostensibly to pick up a linen napkin, and introduced herself. "I'm Rebecca Roswell. Didn't I see you talking to Melinda Camden earlier?"

Snow White patted her mouth with a cocktail

napkin. "Yes. I'm Florence Barnett." She extended a small, pliable hand.

Within minutes, the two of them were chatting like old friends, but nothing else was said about Melinda. Rebecca found herself liking this genteel, soft-spoken woman. She even felt comfortable enough to offer, "Maybe you'd like to come up to my place in Willow Ridge for lunch in the country sometime."

Florence Barnett didn't hesitate. "I'd love it. Since my husband passed on, I haven't gotten out much, except for the occasional fund-raiser like this."

Rebecca understood what she meant. Couples are invited, not single women who throw the male/female ratio off. It was one of life's little cruelties that no one told you about.

When the two women moved on to the dessert table, Rebecca noticed that Florence had turned quiet. Since they'd only just met, she decided it was the quelling silence that sometimes falls over people who don't know each other well enough to keep a conversation going for long periods of time. After a while, though, she concluded that this wasn't it at all. Florence obviously had something on her mind, and Rebecca was curious to know what it was.

"Is anything the matter? All off a sudden you seem preoccupied."

"Melinda's mother and I were close friends."

So that was it. Dolores and Florence had been friends. This was probably an awkward situation for the woman. Perhaps Florence didn't approve of her friendship with Steve. After all, she and Melinda had looked pretty chummy when they had stood together earlier. "Steve speaks so warmly of Dolores. She's very much missed by her friends and family."

"She was a wonderful woman. But that's not why I bring it up," Florence explained.

Rebecca paused, wondering what Florence was trying to say to her.

Florence wiped her lips again before continuing. "I knew Dolores, and she would want Steve to go on with his life."

Rebecca's mouth flew open in surprise. "Did you tell his daughter that?"

The wiry woman smoothed her billowy white skirt and answered with an amused glint in her eyes. "Of course."

"And?" She couldn't believe Florence had lived to tell about it.

"There are twenty single, widowed, or divorced women for every eligible male in Atlanta, so you'd better get out there and get that charming man before the vultures start circling."

"Twenty?" The odds were as bad in the big city as they were in Willow Ridge. At least her small-town situation had spared Rebecca the embarrassment of blind dates, since she was acquainted with everybody in town. Except for an occasional date with a summer vacationer, Rebecca had found the pickings slim.

"At least twenty, maybe more." Florence wiggled her fingers. "It would be a shame to let him slip through."

With wide-eyed innocence, Rebecca probed, "If he's so perfect, then why didn't you go after him yourself, Florence?"

The woman laughed out loud. "Oh, you!" Her fingers fluttered to her neck. "I waited too long. All the good ones get away."

They shared a long, frank look. The determination Rebecca felt from Florence permeated the air between them. This tiny Snow White had shocked her into action. "Well, I don't intend to let *this* good one get away," she promised, as much to bolster her own courage as anything. With a sidelong glance of thanks, she put her plate down and made that first step out to the dance floor and Steve.

"That-a-girl!" Florence gave her a discreet thumbs-up before turning her attention back to the buffet.

Past the point of no return, Rebecca's legs turned to jelly as she made her way across the dance floor. She lightly tapped Melinda on the shoulder. "May I?"

Melinda gave an enigmatic look at her father and surprised Rebecca by answering in a pleasant tone. "Okay," she said, releasing his hand. "See you later, Dad." She retreated without so much as a nasty glance.

The music slowed to a lilting ballad. Steve wrapped his arms around Rebecca's waist. She automatically linked her hands around his neck. They danced the way young teenagers do, barely swaying.

"What did you do to Melinda? You're a miracle worker," she complimented him.

He shook his head, his hands exploring the hollow of her back as they moved. "A miracle watcher, maybe."

She dropped her head on his chest, conscious of his pounding heart. "Miracle watcher?" She sighed, content with holding him close, forgetting that they were still in the middle of a crowd.

"I felt my grandchild kick while we were dancing."

She lifted her head and gazed into his eyes, feeling a rush of emotion wash over her. "You must be so excited." The dull ache from the pain of childlessness hit her, along with the realization that she'd never have grandchildren of her own, either.

When the song finished, Steve asked, "Would you mind if we sit this one out? I've been at it for nearly an hour—"

Rebecca had no desire to back out of his embrace, but she did, leading him to their seats. Thankfully, the table was empty when they reached it. She'd had enough small talk for one evening. She wanted to ask about Melinda, wanted to know what they'd talked about.

"Finally." She relaxed, sinking into her chair. "A moment alone."

He cradled her hands in his, the warmth immediately spreading up her arms and throughout her body. "I have a proposition for you." He leaned close. "Let's go back to your house for a nightcap. I know you wanted to stay to the bitter end, but if you'll agree, I promise you a last dance you'll never forget."

"That's an offer I can't refuse." Rebecca felt a lurch of excitement within her as his powerful arms pulled her up.

They searched out their table partners, thanked their host, waved goodbye to Melinda, and left the ballroom.

He grinned. "These boots are killing my feet!"

As if by magic, their limousine drove up. The driver jumped out, opened the door, and waited for them to get in.

Once inside, Rebecca leaned down and pulled off his boot, then peeled back his sock. "If you're good, Miss Kitty will give you a massage." She did the same to his other foot before moving out to the edge of the leather seat. "Slide back."

A disbelieving smile found its way to his mouth as she lifted one of his legs into her lap and worked her fingers between his toes, kneading them with moderate pressure. One toe after another, she squeezed and released until Steve laid his head back and groaned in pure pleasure. In time, she shifted his other foot to her lap and started the process again.

"This is Heaven!" Steve muttered in a husky whisper, contentment evident in his voice.

"Heaven," she repeated, but her thoughts of Steve were anything but heavenly.

Ten

Two weeks and a half-dozen tether rides later, Steve found himself suspended thirty feet up in a brightly colored balloon, alone with Rebecca. He positioned himself against the side of the woven basket, finally able to move about without hanging on for dear life. He couldn't honestly say he felt comfortable, but his feet weren't frozen in fear any more.

"Just when I thought it was safe to come out to play," he chided, "you throw another kink into things."

Rebecca's brows arched a fraction. "Bite your tongue." She secured a loose line with a slip-knot. "We'll have no talk of kinks on this ship."

"Ship?" He swung his arms upward to the envelope in one sweeping motion. "I thought this was a balloon."

She chuckled, shifting the blower on for a moment, then checked the tethered lines again. "A sailing ship is a sailing ship, whether you're in the air or on the water," she shouted over the roar of the burner. "Both use the same principles of wind." Apparently satisfied that the balloon was filled to capacity, Rebecca fiddled with the instrument panel, then moved toward Steve, stepping over the picnic basket he'd prepared for the trip.

"Wind." He stretched his arm out and grabbed her hand. "That's what it all comes down to." When she closed the short distance between them, he kissed her hand lightly.

"Actually, wind is what makes it go up, not down." Rebecca peered over the side of the basket to check something below.

When the basket tipped slightly, Steve held his breath. It had gotten easier each time they'd gone up, but panic still registered at the least little unexpected movement. "Speaking of up and down, I've been perfectly happy doing just that. Why do we have to venture into unknown territory?" He knew she was waving to Hawk and Doug, but he couldn't bring himself to look down. Not yet.

Where was that darned beeper of hers when he needed it? The last two times they'd planned this outing, she'd been called away on an emergency— and he hadn't minded a bit. Most of the time he hated that beeper, resented her being called away to a fire. But today a little interruption would have been welcomed.

Rebecca wrapped her fingers tighter around his. "Where's your adventurous spirit?"

"On the ground about now."

Her gaze was filled with understanding. "As your teacher, I feel we've covered up and down to death." She squeezed his hands before letting go. "It's about time we move on to stage two: left and right."

His uncertainty was growing. "I've got nothing personal against left or right. It's just that moving vertically has such a nice motion to it. Why tamper with perfection?"

Rebecca stepped back to the controls. He hadn't noticed how lovely she looked, her loose silver curls softening her features.

He had to face this fear of heights head-on and come to grips with it; he had something to prove to Rebecca. And something to prove to himself.

"I've become very attached to that tether line." He gestured toward the heavy nylon ropes that still kept the balloon from flying off into the clouds. Steve knew that today was the day they would sail off without it, but he still liked the security it gave him for the moment.

"Face it, Steve, we can't stay tied to the ground forever." A soft, loving smile curved Rebecca's lips as she patted his back. "You're ready to spread your wings."

"If you're about to make the analogy about the mama bird and her babies, then I'm in serious trouble. I recall she threw them out of the nest, and they were forced to learn to fly."

Rebecca worked the knots loose on the tether lines and wrapped them around a steel cleat. "That's not exactly what I was going to say, but now that you mention it, that's a pretty good idea."

"Good idea?" He worked at keeping his voice even as she got ready to untie the other tether line. "What have I gotten myself into?"

"Nothing as drastic as getting thrown out of the basket." Rebecca shook her head and laughed. "We're just going to take a little ride. Are you ready?"

"Ready as I'll ever be." Steve grabbed the edge of the console with both hands.

"That's what I like to hear. Confidence."

"Absolutely . . . if that's a synonym for scared. You'd better do it fast, before I change my mind."

Rebecca signaled Hawk on one side and Doug on the other, then unwound the lines from the cleat. "Cast off," she yelled, before throwing the ropes clear of the basket. She gave Steve a sidelong glance and said, "It's going to be terrific. I promise."

He took a deep breath and wiggled his fingers, keeping one hand firmly attached to the instrument panel. He watched Rebecca juggle the controls. The colorful, striped material billowed in the wind until the burner cycled on, sending a puff of hot air into the burgeoning balloon. Steve didn't bother to conceal his anxiety. "Why's it doing that? Is something wrong?"

Rebecca snapped the blower off, bringing blessed silence. "I'm sorry, Steve, I should have warned you that when we lift off, the shape of the balloon is deformed until we pick up our traveling speed to match the wind's speed."

"Oh," was all he could muster in response. He wanted to enjoy this, but right now he couldn't get past the fact that they were floating up into the sky with nothing holding them down and no brakes to stop them from running into things . . . things like trees, houses, power lines.

Oh Lord! Help me get through this without passing out or getting myself killed.

"Hawk and Doug will follow us in the truck, ready to retrieve the balloon after we land."

They continued to move upward, away from the landing strip and solid ground.

"That's good." Did she realize they were about to be swallowed up in a bank of low-lying clouds? She didn't seem concerned. Maybe it was all right. Maybe it wasn't.

Rebecca linked her arm in his and whispered into his ear, "I'm proud of you for doing this."

"You should be," he joked, "because I may kiss the ground when I see it again." He looked around at the swell of white clouds surrounding them. He wanted to reach out and touch them, but resisted the urge, not wanting to rock the basket.

"Kiss the ground?" She brushed his mouth with her index finger, sending shock waves of desire to his core. In a playful tone, she added, "Lips that touch dirt may never touch mine."

"Is that so?" He snaked his free arm around her waist. For a moment, the feel of her lithe torso distracted him from the fact that they were sailing through the clouds. "You might like it." He bent forward to kiss her just as the basket lunged and threw them both against the control panel. "What the hell?"

"Just a little turbulence," she told him in her soothing voice.

He could feel his knees buckle, even though the basket quickly leveled out. "When that happens in an airplane, the pilot comes on and tells the passengers to put on their seat belts. I don't see any seat belts handy in this breadbasket."

Smiling, Rebecca pointed to the sunlight bursting through the cloud cover. "Look! The early morning fog is burning off. It's going to be a gorgeous flight."

"Just as long as it's quick." Steve kept his gaze glued to the horizon. She'd said that would reduce the chance of motion sickness. He desperately hoped she was right about that, but his stomach was a little unsteady.

She placed an encouraging hand on his arm again. "Quit worrying. You're going to love it. You can see the whole town as we pass over."

His fingers raked a lock of hair off his furrowed forehead. "And the power lines?" He hoped his voice didn't sound as shaky as he felt.

"They're well below us." Rebecca pointed in the distance to the thin black lines cutting the blue sky. "See?"

"Where are we going, exactly?"

She broke into a wide, open grin. "Exactly?"

"Okay, if not exactly, then how about the general vicinity?"

"I can't say." A devilish look shone in her eyes. "It's a surprise."

"Didn't I mention I hate surprises?" he asked in a resigned voice, "especially five hundred feet above the ground."

"You're safe, then. The surprise part doesn't come until we land."

"Land?" His tension increased. "How do we land this thing?"

"Pretty much the way we do at Riding the Wind. We deflate the balloon and descend to the ground gradually, then roll out of the basket and wait for Hawk and Doug to do the hard work of putting the whole thing into a nice, neat package that will fit into the pick-up truck."

This wasn't the first time Rebecca had explained

the process to him. She'd prepared him fully for this outing, but he needed to hear it all again. She'd made it a personal goal to help him get past his fear of flying. He just couldn't forget that his whole life depended on little more than hot air and a wicker cup dangling from some nylon.

"But at the barn we're tied to the ground and Hawk and Doug simply pull us down," Steve reminded her. "Who's going to pull us down in the middle of nowhere? And how do we steer this gigantic balloon to a certain spot without a tether?"

Rebecca reached around him to tug a line that had tangled around one of the pulleys. "I've landed at this particular spot a hundred times. It's wide open, clear of trees, and gives us plenty of room to spare. We'll drop our altitude until we touch the ground, then I'll pull the rip cord and deflate the balloon completely."

"Okay, so the landing strip is big enough, but what about getting out of the basket?"

"No problem." She squatted down to coil a spare rope that had sprawled out across the floor when the basket had jolted earlier. "I've never had a passenger hurt himself getting in or out. We'll touch down, then the basket will roll over on its side and we'll scramble out."

"I'm a little old to scramble—"

"You can keep up with me." She met his uncertainty with a reassuring gaze. "Trust me."

At that second, he knew he did trust her. She was the first and only woman he'd ever confided his fears to . . . his fear of heights, his fears for his daughter's predicament, his fears about starting his life over again in a new place. He'd always been the strong one in his first marriage, never giving in to his emotions, never opening up with his insecurities. But with Rebecca he could.

"Would you like the nickel tour?" she offered.

"Sure. I'm not going anywhere."

Her smile widened. "To your right is Miller's pond. Coming up on your left is Main Street and downtown." She pointed out several recognizable markers as they passed overhead, high enough for safety, but low enough to make out what they were seeing.

Steve put his arm across her shoulder, pointing. "What's that dot over there?"

Rebecca squinted, then a look of recognition crossed her features. "That's one of the guys washing the fire truck in front of the station."

Before he thought, Steve said, "I'm surprised you aren't there pitching in." When he saw her look of reproach he added, "You do spend an awful lot of time there."

She moved to the controls, slipping out from under his arm. "I'm there when they need me. The fall leaf-burning season is our busiest time of the year for runaway fires."

He hadn't wanted to get into this now. Steve had already made it clear that he resented it when her duties took her away from him. Her job was such a high priority in her life and it was dangerous. Now that the door to this subject was open, he was afraid his frustrations would pour out as fast as the blower spewed hot air into the envelope.

When she didn't comment, he didn't have the good sense to stop. "If it wasn't leaf-burning, then it would be something else."

"Is that a complaint?"

He noted her set face, her clamped jaw, her curt tone. This wasn't the way he wanted things to go. He thought a minute before trying to explain. "I guess so. Half the time I try to reach you, you're out on a fire call, or down at the station pulling duty, or saving somebody's cat—"

"Steve Jordan, you sound jealous."

"Me?" He was. He'd never had to compete for attention before. He'd had his job, his schedule, his activities. He hadn't had to give his family and house a second thought, because Dolores was the perfect wife and mother. She had taken care of all the details, so he'd just had to show up at home. Everything had revolved around him. With Rebecca it was different. She had her own life, her own schedule, even her own career. He hadn't learned how to handle the changes yet.

She persisted. "Yes, you. Are you jealous?"

"I guess I am, a little," he admitted. That was another thing. She always seemed to see right through him. Dolores had let sleeping dogs lie. "No, a lot. You're always helping somebody, always busy doing something."

Her brows lifted. "As opposed to sitting around waiting for you to call?"

"I hardly think you're sitting around," he lowered his voice, "but you *could* be available a little more often."

"I'm not a homebody, Steve." There was a dangerous sparkle in her eyes. "For Heaven's sake, you met me when your daughter's house was on fire. You knew then that I was a volunteer firefighter. What did you think? That I only go out on a call when it's convenient?"

"Of course not. I don't mean to be . . . what's the word?"

She glared at him. "Domineering? Controlling? Pig-headed?"

"Yeah, take your pick." He had never seen Rebecca angry about anything, especially not at him.

"I did," she corrected. "It takes all three to describe how unreasonable you're being."

"I know I have no right to ask that you give up your interests to spend time with me, but I—"

"I'm my own person now, Steve, and have been for about five years. I won't give that independence up for anyone. You wouldn't have liked me the way I was, believe me."

He couldn't imagine not liking this feisty woman. Rebecca was strong, secure, and independent. Maybe he was being too harsh. Maybe seeing the way Melinda and her husband were falling apart was wearing away at his own confidence.

Steve scratched his chin. "I just like to be with you, and sometimes I feel it's hard when you're so busy—" His last words came just as she yanked on the blower and released another blast into the crown.

"I don't complain about the time you spend with Melinda or the boys, or even your landscape business."

It was true. Rebecca had been understanding, even under the worst of circumstances where Melinda was concerned. She'd bent over backward to help him adjust to life with his two grandsons and their mother. Even though he hadn't done much business since he'd moved to Willow Ridge, she'd been supportive of the jobs he'd had to finish in Atlanta.

"You've been terrific about including the boys in our plans, as much as Melinda will allow. You'll never know how much I appreciate that."

"I love doing things with Jeremy and Jake. They're like the grandchildren I never had."

The silence between them spread into minutes. He'd said enough.

"We're here," she told him in a hushed voice. "We'll land over there." She motioned to a large green swath of flat land stretched between a mountain ridge on one side and a thick forest on the other. "Prepare to land."

He studied her while she readied the lines and set the controls. She puffed just enough hot air into the envelope to keep the balloon from descending too quickly. Her long, beautiful fingers moved deftly as she adjusted the pulleys, and it suddenly dawned on him that he hadn't given his fear of heights a second's thought since they'd started the argument several miles back. He'd made the journey, looked at the passing landscape, and carried on a heated conversation without cringing at every wind spurt.

Was it possible she'd staged this whole thing on purpose? No, she wouldn't do that. Or would she?

"Hawk and Doug are here already," she announced, apparently putting their argument on hold.

"Where?" He scanned the meadow, then finally focused on a pick-up truck parked at the edge near the forest. Rebecca's Jeep was right behind it. As they drifted lower, he could make out Hawk's tall frame walking toward them. "It's amazing that they can find us way out here in the middle of nowhere."

"I told you, they've been here before. Many times. We used to bring clients out here all the time." Her words were halted by the roar of the blower and the flapping fabric of the balloon as it deflated.

"Used to?" He didn't understand.

She turned and faced him, cutting the blower completely. "Now I save it for only my closest friends."

"Do I still fall into that category?"

Before she could answer, they descended the last few yards to the ground. Rebecca reached high and pulled the rip line, spilling the hot air into the sky through the wide gash in the envelope's side. The basket touched down with a jolt, dragging the grass until it tipped over on its side. She grabbed Steve's arm and together they crawled out, forgetting about everything except the excitement of what was happening around them.

The once-perfect symmetry of the colored giant was destroyed as the massive folds of fabric collapsed against the green grass. The sound was deafening after the quiet solitude of the flight, which had been broken only by the blower and their exchange of harsh words.

Hawk and Doug jumped into action. Within fifteen minutes, they'd stashed the folded balloon in the truck bed and tied the basket onto the trailer behind it. While Rebecca inspected the tie-downs on the trailer with Doug, Hawk walked over to Steve with the picnic basket.

"How was the ride?" Hawk put the basket at Steve's feet and extended his hand in greeting. "It was a beautiful day for a sail in the clouds."

"Was . . ." Steve mumbled. "I blew it. We got into a stupid argument." Doubts about Rebecca's motives nagged at Steve again. He had to know if she'd set up their argument to help him make it through the flight . . . or if they'd just had their first bona fide fight.

"Many arguments seem stupid, after they are over." Hawk stooped to tie the leather laces of his moccasins. "What happened?"

Steve shook his head. "We landed before I could straighten things out."

"When did this disagreement start?" Hawk stood and began coiling a length of tangled line.

Steve thought for a second. "Right after we passed over Willow Ridge."

"Did anything happen before that?"

Hawk was heading somewhere with this line of questioning. Even though Steve had only known him a short time, he'd come to respect the wise man's opinion. His new friend was a man of few words, but those words were usually full of truth. "We did have a bit of turbulence."

"That's when the argument began?" Hawk's voice

was deep and resonant, almost hypnotic. "Am I right?"

Realization hit Steve again, and his earlier suspicions were confirmed. "Are you saying that Rebecca engineered this whole thing to keep my mind off flying?"

"No. I cannot say that, because I was not there. But she has been known to go way beyond the call of duty to distract—"

Rebecca walked up, dropped a pile of rope into the basket, and interrupted their conversation. "What are you two talking about?"

"I have been asking Steve about the flight. I see that Doug is ready, so I will head back to town." Hawk started to leave with a wave.

"Hawk?"

"Yes, Rebecca?" The erect man stopped, facing the two of them with his head held high, his chin jutting, and the wind blowing the ebony hair not captured in his braid. He gazed at them both with solemn eyes.

"The car keys?" Rebecca held out her hand.

The tall man reached into his faded jeans with long, dark fingers and pulled out a key ring with two keys attached. He flipped them to her, turned, and trudged toward the truck and Doug.

"I know that man, and there's definitely something on his mind," Rebecca commented as she dropped the keys into her shirt pocket. "I'm starving. Ready for our picnic?"

He walked to her and pulled her to him in a warm embrace. She relaxed, sinking into his arms, her head buried against his chest. "Thank you," he whispered into her soft, silver locks.

With a startled expression, she tipped her head and kissed him tenderly on the cheek. They stood, suspended in time for what seemed like an eternity, until the growl of Rebecca's stomach brought them both back to the present.

"Hungry?" Now that he was back on solid ground, he could set his mind to more important things. He let go of her reluctantly.

"Famished."

Steve grabbed the picnic basket. "Lead the way." He followed her across the field into the pine thicket, stopping only while she grabbed a quilt from her Jeep. A hundred yards or so into the forest, the green canopy opened up and the sun glimmered on the surface of a winding creek.

"Beautiful!" Dropping the basket, he helped Rebecca spread the quilt out in a sunny spot. He inhaled the mossy smell of the low-lying shrubs growing wild under the shade of the towering pines, and dipped his hand into the frothy water of the shallow creek as it splashed against the rocks. He was surprised that the water wasn't freezing, especially at this time of the year.

"It is a beautiful place for a picnic," she agreed.

Rebecca squatted to unpack the basket of food, her jeans molding the curve of her hips and slender legs. Steve savored the feeling of joy he felt when he looked at her. But the feeling was more than sexual desire.

"It wasn't the place that I was referring to," he told her. "Although it is perfect."

He looked into her eyes. When he spoke, his voice was filled with emotion. "I'm sorry we argued." He guided her down onto the faded patchwork blanket. "But I have to know . . . did you encourage it to take my mind off flying?"

Rebecca sat up ramrod straight, her eyes wide. "Why in the world would you think such a crazy thing?" Her lids came down over her eyes and she turned away.

He touched her chin, turning her face back toward his. "Did you?"

Her clear, tender gaze met his, and she nodded. "I thought it would make things easier."

"But I started it. Remember?" He straightened to relieve his tense shoulders, his mind racing back to the night she'd massaged his feet in the limousine. He bet she could also work magic on his shoulders.

Rebecca started to unpack the picnic basket. "Yeah. But I got more than I bargained for. I just wanted to stir you up a little."

Steve leaned over, then pushed stray tendrils of silver curls away from her cheek. "You did that, all right."

"I stirred myself up pretty good, too," she admitted.

Steve laughed. "I noticed."

Her eyes narrowed and her voice caught. "I *did* mean everything I said."

"And you're right to feel the way you do," he firmly agreed. "I have no intention of being an overbearing male—"

She stopped him with a finger against his lips. "I know. You don't need to say anything else."

They unpacked a stack of turkey sandwiches, a bag of chips, and some sodas in companionable silence.

"What a lovely lunch," she complimented as they hungrily munched away to the creek's soothing music. She gathered their trash after they'd eaten, but knocked over her empty soda bottle as she stood.

Steve watched it spin against the worn fabric of the quilt. As it came to rest with the top pointing toward him, he grinned, remembering a childhood game that had initiated him into adolescence. "Spin the bottle." He picked up the bottle. "You've got to kiss me or tell a secret."

"That's not the way I remember it." She put her hands staunchly on her hips and stared down at him. "Because I'm such a good sport, I'll play along anyway."

"Which is it then, secret . . . or kiss?"

"Kiss, of course."

Steve stood, and without touching Rebecca, kissed her. His tongue traced the velvety smoothness of her lips. "Good choice," he told her, his voice thick with desire.

"Maybe. You'll never know what a delicious secret you might have learned," she teased.

He reached down and spun the bottle between them. This time it pointed toward Rebecca. With a wicked grin, he demanded, "Secret."

"Follow me."

He didn't move. "Not before you tell me your secret."

"Wouldn't you rather I show you?" she asked, enticing him past the creek's curve, deeper into the forest.

Steve jammed the rest of the trash into the basket, snapped it closed, snatched up the quilt and followed her. "Wait up!"

"Catch up," she challenged. But she paused, picked up a stone, and skimmed it across the water as he closed the distance between them. She took the quilt from him, and side by side they continued into the woods, leaving the creek's edge when it sharply swung to the right at a large boulder.

"Where in the world are we going?"

"It's a secret."

Eleven

Rebecca had mixed feelings about bringing Steve up here. She didn't want him to associate this place with her past, although it did represent a piece of her history. Her former life was now so foreign to her that it seemed to have belonged to someone else. But her desire to share this special place with Steve won out over her misgivings.

Rebecca led him through a slash in the pine thicket as they hiked away from the winding path by the creek bed. The strong scent of flowering wintersweet bushes mixed with the musky smells of damp earth and pungent pine. "We're almost there."

Steve set the picnic basket down to get a better grip on its handle. "Are you sure we're not lost?"

"Not a chance. I could find this place in the dark—blindfolded." Rebecca walked a step ahead of him on an unmarked path only she could follow.

Steve grasped her wrist firmly as she approached a fallen loblolly pine. "Watch out."

In her surprise, she dropped the quilt. The intensity of his grasp halted her steps. "What? What is it?"

"Never step over a dead tree," he warned. He eased his hold on her. "It's a perfect spot for snakes."

"Snakes?" Her mouth dropped open. "This time of year?" A soft gasp escaped her lips as she shuddered, but she was determined not to let the thought of a snake destroy their outing.

Steve picked up the quilt, handed it to her, then led her around the tree. She glanced down at the tree's decaying trunk, thankful that nothing moved.

"Snakes don't follow a calendar. It's unusually warm this year and the slithering fellows don't hibernate until after the first good frost." He grinned. "I'm not *afraid* of snakes. I just hate them."

"Didn't you run across them in the landscape business?" she asked.

"Yeah, a few . . . occasionally. I learned to respect them and avoid them whenever possible."

After a few tentative steps, Rebecca picked up the pace, dodging the dark green foliage of wild azalea clusters scattered under the pines.

"You used to come here a lot?" Steve broke the silence as they padded across an area covered in pine needles, the meandering creek barely in sight.

"Back when I worked in Atlanta, my husband and I made it a habit to bring our big clients up here once a year." Her voice seemed distant, faraway.

"Was . . . was it a special place for you two?"

Rebecca could feel the importance of his question. He wanted to know about her life before Willow Ridge, about her life with her husband. How could she tell him how full it had been, yet how empty at the same time? How could she admit she hadn't even known she'd missed anything until she'd met Steve?

She was keenly aware of his scrutiny. "Are you kidding? Harold, well, Harry had two agendas in life—getting business and keeping business. This was his lure for the big fish. I doubt if he paid much attention to the scenery—only the clients. He probably never realized how beautiful it was up here." Her gaze clung to Steve's, analyzing his reaction. She almost held her breath waiting for him to speak.

"His loss." Steve's face displayed an uncanny understanding as he hoisted the basket to his other hand and moved forward.

"Half the time Harry would skip the balloon ride and just meet us here with a lavish buffet spread out on the creek bank."

"Now there's something he and I might have had in common." Steve lightened the moment with his devilish grin. "Did he hate ballooning?"

"Harry? No, it was just too slow for his taste. He didn't like anything that slowed him down for one minute. Sometimes I think that's what killed him. He used up a whole lifetime in fifty-five years. Rush, rush, rush, then bang—he was gone."

He studied her face, feature by feature, his dark eyes seemed to reach her most intimate thoughts. Rebecca was quickly learning that nothing got past those eyes. She changed the subject, not wanting her past to intrude on her present.

"Come on, let's get a move on, or we'll never get there."

Steve hurried to catch up. "There, where?"

"You'll see."

The look in his eyes made her want to be there already. Rebecca's stomach fluttered every time he looked her way, and her pulse raced just thinking about his earlier kiss. Together they steadily moved through the forest, their footsteps disturbing the quiet of the still, autumn day.

When they reached a small clearing, Steve paused to catch his breath. "How do you remember how to get here?"

"That's easy. You follow the creek until it veers sharply to the right, go through the brush, then follow the line of pines until they end, make a right and—" she threw her free arm out in a grand gesture, "—here we are." She watched as his smile widened in approval.

Steve put the basket down and stared. "Where are we exactly?"

Rebecca lingered a moment. She tried to view

it the way Steve was, for the first time. She wanted it to be as beautiful to Steve as it was to her. In the clearing was a cave nearly hidden under a screen of twisted honeysuckle vines dotted with berries. Moss-covered rocks partially blocked the dark, shadowy entrance. Bluish-green clumps of lacy ferns surrounded by a carpet of thrift flanked both sides.

"Come see your surprise—one of my favorite places in the whole world—the cave." Rebecca dropped the quilt onto a rock, then took his hand and led him to the misty opening.

Steve stepped behind her and looked over her shoulder into the inky darkness. "I've never seen anything like it."

"Wait until you see the rest. You won't be disappointed."

Hawk had once told Rebecca that his ancestors had visited this cave to purge their souls of problems. She believed the cave did the same for her. Rebecca felt centered here—at peace with herself. She'd wanted to share the cave with Steve weeks ago, but she'd waited, reserving it as a special reward for his virgin flight.

He cupped his ear. "Do I hear water?"

"Yes. I'll show you as soon as I get the light on. Stay here, okay?" With a giddy sense of excitement, Rebecca slipped between the rocks and the earthen wall. It took a moment for her eyes to adjust to the dimness. She slid her hand against the damp wall, then inched her way to the citronella candle in a bucket she'd left in the cave. Fumbling in her pocket, she found the disposable lighter she'd brought just to light the candle with, and flicked it rapidly until it sparked. She jabbed the wick with the flame until it sizzled and burned on its own. The smell of citronella burned her nostrils as a whirl of smoke rose from the large metal bucket. She stood up and motioned for Steve.

Steve squeezed through the rocks and walked toward Rebecca, loaded down with their supplies. "Gosh. It feels like it's seventy degrees in here." He blinked, adjusting to the contrast between the shady daylight and the eerie darkness broken only by the glimmering candle glow and the faint shaft of light near the entrance.

Rebecca picked up the bucket, and together they descended a dozen or more steps to a landing at the edge of a glassy pool. Shimmering light reflected in the clear, green water and from the stalactite-covered ceiling.

"This is what the Indians called a 'water cave,' " she explained. "It's filled by the same creek we had lunch by earlier."

"But how?" Steve deposited the quilt and basket on the damp earthen floor. "We left the creek a long time ago and followed the trees to the clearing."

Her mouth curved into an unconscious smile.

"The creek divided, and this part went underground."

Rebecca squatted, running her fingers through the crystal-clear water. "Feel this." She cupped both hands and stood up, holding out the water toward him as if it were an offering.

Steve placed his hands under hers, letting the streams of water flow through his fingers and over his palms. "It's warm."

"That's my other secret." She brushed her hands along her back pockets, drying them on her jeans. "On cold days, the cave is filled with a thin layer of fog rolling off the warm water."

"Why isn't this place packed with tourists?"

"It's private property." She retrieved the quilt and spread it out near the pool. "An old friend of mine owns it—from here all the way to the nearby state park."

"I'm surprised people don't wander over here."

"It's not that easy to find, thank goodness, so we'll have it all to ourselves." They both sat down. "My friend threatens to deed it all to the state once he's gone, so I suspect it eventually will be full of tourists."

Rebecca inhaled deeply, taking in the natural, moist scent of the cave mixed with the burning citronella. "But for now, we're alone. No one can get in touch with us." She leaned back on her elbows and stretched her legs out on the quilt.

"No one? What about the fire department?" He gave her a dubious look.

The question irritated her, but she maintained control of her temper. "Not even the fire department can get us way out here."

"Can't they beep you?"

Rebecca didn't want to condemn Steve for wanting privacy. She wanted it, as well, so she kept her anger in check. "Nope. We're safely out of range. Besides, I told them I was off duty and left my beeper at the house."

"I'm glad, Rebecca, because I want you all to myself."

A slender, intricate thread of understanding began to form between them. Maybe it had been there since the moment they'd met. Steve wanted to be here with her—wanted her. And she felt the same way about him.

"I thought it would be a great ending to a beautiful day."

"It is. The balloon ride, the picnic, the cave, and now . . ."

"Now . . . how about a swim?"

She could feel the heat of his skin only inches away, could imagine the two of them in the warm, bubbly water.

Steve tugged her chin gently and smiled. "I didn't bring my suit. Did you?" He let his finger slide down her neck to the open collar of her blouse.

She smiled. "No. My mind was on the balloon flight."

"And on helping me through it?" He laughed softly, adding, "It's okay to admit it."

"Maybe a little." Rebecca was trembling—not from the cool winter breeze making its way through the cave's mouth, but from Steve's closeness, his touch.

"Do you trust me?" His gaze was riveted on her face.

She felt an almost uncontrollable urge to rip off his clothes and run her fingers across his chest. She wanted to scream "yes" to whatever he suggested, but years of experience cautioned her to wait. "What do you mean?"

"Rebecca, I trusted you with my life on the flight over here." There were questions in his deep, dark eyes as he asked again, "Do you trust me?"

"Absolutely," she whispered. At this moment, she was more certain than she'd ever been about anything in her life. She knew she trusted him, but did she trust herself? "Why do you ask?"

"I was thinking that we shouldn't miss this golden opportunity."

When he didn't continue, she prodded, "And . . . ?" almost afraid to know what he wanted.

"And take a swim."

She smiled up at him, completely charmed by

his proposition. Before she lost her nerve and did the "right thing," she answered. "Let's."

She could feel her lips tremble as she heard him reply, "Good." Steve moved toward the edge of the quilt and hesitated for only a moment before kicking off his shoes.

The longing to touch him was almost unbearable as she watched him unbutton his shirt. Sitting with his bare feet dangling in the warm bubbling water, he quickly slid his belt buckle open and unzipped his pants. With a slight glance her way, he stood and shed those, along with his underwear. Her only clear view was his nude posterior slipping into the clear, green water—broad shoulders, a smooth back, and well-shaped buttocks.

Rebecca tried to relax as she prepared to join him, willing herself to think that this was a perfectly acceptable situation for two consenting adults to be in. But it had been a long time since a man— any man—had seen her completely nude. Even though he'd seen her in a swimsuit several times in the past few weeks, the nagging thought that he'd be disappointed crossed her mind. While Steve paddled across the ten feet to the far ledge, Rebecca quickly undressed, then dropped over the rim into the hot basin.

Steve's totally nude body, only a few feet away, restrained by nothing more than tantalizing bubbles, excited Rebecca. She wondered if the warmth of the water intoxicated him as much as it did her.

Steve turned his head when she splashed water in his direction. For a while, they laughed and splashed and raced. They swam around each other, sizing one another up, but neither wanting to make the first move.

After a time, they braced themselves, side by side, on the smooth lip of the pool, sharing a left-over soda Steve had retrieved from the picnic basket.

"When was the last time you went skinny-dipping, Steve?"

"I can't remember the last time . . . no, wait, it was back when I was a teenager spending the summer with my uncle on his farm. My cousins and I went swimming in the pond after working in the fields one day. Buck naked, as we called it."

"Sounds like a fond memory."

"Having lived in the city all my life, I couldn't believe how liberating it was to take off my clothes in broad daylight and jump into a pond with a bunch of other guys. I learned to let go and have a good time that summer."

Rebecca shifted to face him, managing to keep everything from chin down under water. "Oh, really? What else did you learn that summer?" She knew what he meant by liberated. The warm bubbles were caressing her body in a sensuous rhythm.

"Got my first taste of 'hooch,' smoked a store-bought cigar—both made me sick as a skunk, I might add." He grinned, then dove under the water, his bare buttocks skimming the surface on his way down.

When he came up for air, Rebecca asked, "Anything else happen that summer?"

"Well, there was that older woman of sixteen . . ." he teased, pushing back his wet hair with his fingers.

She splashed him when he didn't finish. "Yes?"

"We spent most of our time together behind the barn practicing the fine art of French kissing."

"Such sophisticated habits for a young boy." Caught up in the conversation, Rebecca rose out of the water until the soft mounds of her breasts were exposed, but didn't realize it until Steve's gaze dropped to the pool's glimmering surface. Hesitating a second before sliding back into the water, she sensed her nipples harden as waves of desire swept over her.

Steve picked up the conversation as if nothing had happened. "Well, she needed the practice and I just couldn't say no."

"I'll bet you couldn't." Rebecca managed to keep her voice on an even keel, but found she was having trouble doing the same with her emotions. "I'd like to meet that girl someday."

"Why in the world would you want to do that?"

His playful tone took on a low, husky sound—the first tangible sign that he was being affected by her, too.

"To thank her for getting you off to such a good start."

"After my uncle caught us one day, he gave me this big speech about sex and handed me a condom . . . a 'rubber' as we called them back then."

"Maybe it's the uncle I should thank, then—"

"Maybe . . . he told me something that's stuck with me all these years."

She could feel his piercing gaze on her face. "What's that?"

"My uncle always told me that it's not what you do, but who you do it with, that counts. He said that if I couldn't be happy just holding a girl's hand, then I had no business doing anything else with her."

"Your uncle sounds like a wise man."

"I believe he was."

With a twinkle in his eye, Steve switched the subject to Rebecca. "Now that we know my sordid past, when was the last time you went skinny-dipping?"

Her eyes darted around the cave in embarrassment. "Me?"

"Yes, you."

She wanted to lie, to make up some wonderful story about her youth, but couldn't. She never did anything she wasn't supposed to in all her years of growing up, not even as a teenager. But she was making up for it now. Here she was, naked with a man in the middle of the woods in a watery cave, sharing secrets. Except that she didn't have a secret to share. "I've never—"

"Never?" He splashed water her way, his brows drawn together. "Not even once?"

Rebecca wondered if he thought she was being coy. "Not once. Honest. I was too shy when I was a teenager, then as I got older, I was too busy."

"And as an adult?"

"Then, I was just too . . . adult." Fleetingly she thought back over all the missed chances to have fun in her life, and immediately vowed to make better use of the next fifty years.

"So-o-o-o, this is your first time?"

She detected a gleam in his eyes. "Yes. Does that surprise you?"

"A little. I thought the independent Rebecca Roswell had done everything at least once in her life."

"I have to admit I've always wanted to . . . just never had the nerve."

"Why now?" The question caught in his throat as he moved closer to her, propping an arm on each side of her head, their faces inches apart, yet their bodies not touching.

"Don't you think it's about time?" Every nerve in her body tingled.

"I'm glad you decided to do it with me."

"Me, too." Her heart fluttered wildly in her breast. Yes, youth was good, but Rebecca was terribly thankful to be a full grown woman right now.

Steve wasn't sure what he should do next. He didn't want to assume too much, but he couldn't wait another minute to take Rebecca in his arms and feel her smooth, silky skin next to his. He'd tried to be a gentleman when she'd undressed earlier, but he couldn't keep from looking. The image of her slender waist and full breasts had almost driven him crazy. He'd swum around in circles to keep from pinning her against the rocks and taking her right then and there.

Hungrily he took her face in his hands, kissing her deeply until they were both breathless. He gathered her close when she uttered a sigh of contentment and moved against him for the first time. Steve could hardly think straight anymore, a moan of satisfaction escaping his lips. First he admired, then massaged, her breasts with his hands, kneading her nipples until they hardened with desire.

With added urgency, Rebecca pressed her lower body against the growing evidence of his arousal. The fizzing water churned anew between them as she ran her fingers along his chest, returning the pleasure he'd given her by teasing his nipples with her thumbs.

"Oh, Rebecca . . ." The water's warmth, her beautiful face, the curves of her body—all combined to send his senses reeling. He buried his face in her neck, nibbling her earlobe as he glided his hand down the roundness of her hip, pausing on her thigh. Before he could continue, she reached for his hand, moving it to where she wanted it the most. There was no doubt in his mind that Rebecca wanted him as much as he wanted her.

He lightly touched her and she groaned with pleasure. She welcomed him eagerly, so he stroked a finger along her opening, barely touching her skin, then stopped. Without moving his hand, Steve pressed his lips to hers.

She returned his kiss with wild abandon, forcing his lips open with her tongue, lifting her body against his fingers, demanding his attention. Every time she was roused close to the crest of her desire, he pulled back, teasing her over and over again to greater heights.

Steve encircled her waist with his hands and lifted her higher so his face crushed against the soft flesh of her breasts. His teeth closed gently on one nipple, then the other as she surrendered completely to his masterful seduction. The turbulence of their passion swirled around them, churning the water at the same time.

It had been a long time since he'd been with a woman, even longer since his whole being had flooded with the desire of new and exciting love.

"Oh-h-h, ye-s-s-s," she moaned as Steve tenderly kissed the base of her throat.

Suddenly, Rebecca yanked out of his arms. Her soft murmur turned into a bloodcurdling scream in his ear. "Oh, no! Look!" She flailed her arms, pointing at something behind him. "Look! There!" She scrambled backward to the ledge.

Steve turned to see what was causing the commotion. "What is it?" His rude return to reality ended any sexual thought he'd anticipated for the afternoon. He stared in the direction of the offending interruption, aware that Rebecca was standing open-mouthed, her chest heaving in panic.

"Sn-snake . . . a snake," she uttered hysterically.

"Where?" he asked, frozen in place, afraid to move. It was one thing to find a snake when he installed bushes or cut someone's grass, it was another thing entirely to have a snake swimming undetected in the water with him. "Where is it now?"

"Back there," she shrieked, pointing behind him.

Steve scanned the area, but didn't see anything. "Are you sure you saw a snake? Couldn't it have been something else?"

"Like what? I'm sure it was a snake. It looked like a snake, wiggled like a snake, and it's still in there. Get out, please. Get out."

Steve drew a deep breath and started swimming to the ledge and safety. With every kick, he prayed he wouldn't snag the snake with his foot—or worse. After a couple of strokes, he saw it. Near the wall, a brown form slithered in the water.

"Damn!" The sound of his voice echoed in his ears as the blood pounded in his temple. Fear took control and he swam rapidly to get to the rim. The span of water suddenly seemed as wide as the Gulf of Mexico.

"Hurry, Steve! It's swimming this way!" Rebecca grabbed a rock and threw it over Steve's head at the snake.

"Oh Lord, Rebecca, don't make it mad!"

Sheer fright knotted his muscles. He propelled his body the last few yards. Breathless, he reached the pool's lip, pulled himself out of the water, and yanked his feet up.

Stark fear shone in her eyes as she roughly hugged his dripping body. "Thank goodness you're safe."

He could feel her uneven breathing as he held her close, his own heart beating rapidly.

When they'd both calmed down, he asked, "That snake sure did break the mood, didn't it?" He offered her a small, shy smile. The water no longer a shield to cover his manhood, Steve realized he was openly naked in front of Rebecca for the first time.

"Sure did." Apparently Rebecca noticed her lack of clothes, too, because she strode over to the quilt and wrapped it around her shoulders.

"Hard to be romantic with a snake slithering by," he added with a shake of his head.

"Romantic?" She threw back her head and laughed. "Not with a snake."

Keeping an eye out for the snake, they dried the best they could with the quilt, then donned their clothes.

"The quilt's soaking wet—and heavy. Let's lay it over the rock to dry," she suggested. "We'll get it another time, okay?" She spread it out before gathering their things, then blew out the candle. Together they started up the path to the creek and home.

About halfway to the Jeep, Rebecca interrupted their awkward silence. "Steve?"

"Hmm?" He was conscious of the note of tension in her voice.

"We *were* good together, weren't we?"

"Did you doubt it?" He cut his gaze toward her, but her attention was fixed on the path.

"Actually, I doubted myself."

"If I'm to be completely honest, then I'd have to admit I was worried about my . . . ability, too."

Her look was one of faint amusement. "You? I can't believe it."

"What? You think women have a monopoly on insecurity?"

"Steve Jordan, you are the most secure man I know." She returned his smile and grabbed the hand he offered her.

"I'd rather be the sexiest."

"That goes without saying."

"That's what I like to hear." He squeezed her hand. "But I can always stand to hear it again . . . and again."

"I think I can manage that."

The intense pleasure Rebecca gave him was so perfect, he had to do everything in his power to make her feel the same way—safe, secure, loved.

Twelve

Rebecca scribbled a name into the appointment calendar on her office desk, and braced the telephone with a raised shoulder. "Ten o'clock will be perfect, Mr. Sanders. We'll be expecting you and your wife for our champagne brunch flight on Thanksgiving morning." She jotted down the rest of the information, then replaced the handset in its cradle without looking up.

Doug swung his long legs from their perch on her desk to the floor, and leaned forward. "Another one, huh? With the two reservations Father took yesterday, we're booked solid for turkey day. It's a good thing we're not doing dinner flights, or none of us would get to eat before dark."

Rebecca shuffled through the stack of reservations. "If the wind is good and our clients are punctual, we'll call it a day by late afternoon."

"Those are a couple of big ifs, but I love your optimism."

"Where's your faith? After all, Thanksgiving is supposed to be about faith, right?" She observed her young assistant for a long moment. In the many years she'd known him, he'd grown into a sensitive, thoughtful man, much like his father.

"Right, but remember last year?" Doug sat back with his hands behind his head.

Rebecca grabbed a piece of paper, wadded it up, and tossed it at him. "Thanks for reminding me! What a disaster! It rained buckets and cancelled out our whole day."

"Maybe we should pray for rain." Doug let out a peal of laughter.

She couldn't keep herself from laughing, too. "Bite your tongue."

"But that would free up your day—" Doug broke into a wide grin as he added, "You'd be able to spend it with your beau and his grandsons."

Rebecca's brows drew together into a frown. "It's Thanksgiving, not the Fourth of July. If I showed up for dinner, Melinda would have fireworks instead of turkey and dressing. It's just as well that I'm up to my ears in work."

Doug picked at the stack of reservations. "That sounds to me like a good excuse to avoid confrontation."

Rebecca was surprised. Doug rarely—if ever—interfered in her personal life. Sure, he'd made jokes in the past, even kidded her about Steve, but never offered any serious advice. This time, though, he sounded like his father—quiet, assured, and insightful.

"I thought Indian culture advocated peace, not fighting." She spoke in a casual, jesting way.

His smiled faded and his tone turned defensive. "This isn't a history lesson, Rebecca, but Indians have always stood up for their beliefs . . . and if that meant fighting to protect themselves and their rights, then they fought."

"I didn't mean anything . . . I was trying to avoid the subject."

Doug's concern was obvious in his somber, yet sympathetic expression. "I know. That's what I'm trying to explain. Avoidance is no good. Whether it's my question or Melinda or Thanksgiving—you can't hide from it."

"I'm not hiding." Her mouth was tight with displeasure. How dare Doug suggest that she—Ms. Independent—would hide from anything . . . or anyone?

"Maybe hiding is the wrong word. But you *are* dodging the issue . . ."

"Oh, really?" Her tone was clipped. She was overreacting, embarrassed that he'd put into words what she'd been afraid to admit: She wanted to be with Steve on Thanksgiving.

"And the Indians? What do *they* think I should do?"

Doug stared at her pointedly. "I don't know what

you should do. All my life, I've been taught never to back away from anything important. You're backing away."

"I'm not doing any such thing." Rebecca instantly regretted her strong tone. It wasn't Doug's fault he was right.

It had been a long time since she'd worked on a relationship with a man, and even longer since she'd had a family to contend with. She'd forgotten how to "give-and-take." Most of her life she'd been the one doing all the giving. Taking was something she'd never learned. She didn't know how to make her place in Steve's life.

She struggled to regain her composure. "I am going to be busy tomorrow."

"Too busy for the people you care most about on a day designated to give thanks for just such things?" Doug's voice faded into a hushed silence.

Rebecca carefully thought about her answer before speaking, but she couldn't come up with a good response. Finally, she threw up her hands and chuckled. "I hate it when you get philosophical."

The old familiar humor sparkled in his intense eyes. "You hate it when I hit the nail on the head."

"That doesn't sound much like an old Indian saying."

"Well, my old Indian father said it to me a thousand times. Does that count?"

Rebecca let out a long, audible breath. "Hawk would skin you alive if he heard you call him old."

"He would, at that." Doug slapped his thighs and chuckled. "Still . . . aren't you avoiding Steve's daughter?"

"Melinda? I guess I am avoiding her. Thanksgiving is going to be tough enough for everybody with Melinda and Joey separated. I don't want to make things any tougher by causing a confrontation with Melinda. I can't spoil the holiday for the boys."

Doug leveled his gaze to hers and flatly asked, "Or Steve?"

"Or Steve."

"But won't it ruin it for him if you aren't there?" He picked up a pencil, then tapped it on the desk.

Would it? she wondered, secretly hoping Steve would want her there. "He thinks I'm busy with the balloon flights, Doug."

"Steve's a wise man, Rebecca. You don't honestly think you're putting something over on him, do you?"

Her fingers fluttered to her neck. "But he hasn't said anything . . ."

"Neither have you."

"True." How could she expect Steve to read her mind? He knew she cared about him, knew she was attracted to him, knew what she wanted to do, practically before she did herself. Why didn't he know she wanted to be with him on Thanksgiving? Wasn't that something he should know?

Doug sighed. "Don't you think you should?"

"Should what?" Hawk's booming voice reverberated from the open door, slicing into their conversation.

"Your son gave me some friendly—though unsolicited—advice."

Hawk looked from his son to Rebecca and back to Doug again. "About Steve?"

"About Thanksgiving," she corrected, trying to divert the subject. Did *everybody* know about her personal problems?

"Son, I hope you told her to find time to spend with Steve and his family on such a special holiday." Hawk leaned his powerful shoulders against the door frame.

"I did, Father. Maybe you'll have better luck with the stubborn lady than I did," he muttered under his breath as he left.

"Is this a conspiracy?" Rebecca placed her hands on her hips and smiled at her old friend to cover her uncertainty.

"You should be with Steve on Thanksgiving."

"It's not that easy." Feeling Hawk's gaze bore into hers, Rebecca blushed.

"Nothing worthwhile is ever easy," Hawk said.

"If it's just the same to you, I think I'll stick to flying balloons next weekend."

"If you won't take our advice, then at least come with us to our tribal feast. Giving thanks is universal. You should be with friends."

"I'm honored that you'd include me in such a revered event of your people. But I can't. Not this time. Thank you for asking, Hawk."

"You'd rather be alone?"

Alone was a state of mind. She could feel lonely at home, in a crowd, or with someone else's family. She didn't feel comfortable in Melinda's home, because Steve's daughter didn't welcome her there. Wasn't it obvious? "I can't. I hope you'll understand."

"Understanding is not mine to give, but I'll accept your decision and won't press you any more."

"You're a dear friend, Hawk." She forgave him for meddling. His intentions were good. Hawk wanted what was best for her. How could he be so sure what was best, when she wasn't sure herself?

Rebecca wound up her paperwork and headed home for a few laps in the pool, a warm bath, and a quiet night in front of the fire.

Later, wrapped in a thick, navy velour robe and fuzzy slippers, Rebecca sat down on a couple of floor pillows, propped her elbows on the oversized hearth, and warmed her hands by the flames. Her shoulders ached from the vigorous swim she'd had earlier, and she felt strangely empty. It had become routine for her and Steve to do their exercises together, whether they decided to swim, run, or dance to golden oldies in her living room. It wasn't nearly as much fun to exercise alone.

But with Thanksgiving only a few days away, Steve was too tied up with his own family to spend much time with her. She knew the boys were home and Melinda was busier than usual. Steve's days— and nights—were spent taking care of his grandsons, shopping for the holiday, and preparing for the biggest meal of the year. Rebecca understood, but she missed him. Missed having his company. Missed his arms around her. Missed the man who had become such an important part of her life. She realized that without Steve, her life wouldn't be fully satisfying anymore.

Sitting there alone, she wondered if she was making a mistake by staying away, and letting Melinda and the boys have Steve's full attention on Thanksgiving. In the past few weeks his daughter had blossomed into a very pregnant woman, complete with all the aches and pains associated with her condition.

Facing the first major holiday without Joey must be hard for Melinda. The situation certainly hadn't helped her already frayed disposition. Rebecca wished she and Melinda could talk about it; Rebecca understood what it was like to lose a husband. She remembered the long, lonely nights, the painful memories surrounding her husband's death. And though Joey wasn't dead, the death of a relationship must be just as painful, maybe more so. The memories couldn't be tucked neatly away, because Joey would be forever popping into Melinda's life to see his sons.

In many ways, death was a clean break, a way to allow the surviving spouse the option to move on, to live again. There was nothing clean about divorce; it was like murder in slow motion with a blunt object. Maybe that was why she had overlooked the shortcomings of her own marriage. Considering divorce as her alternative, she'd decided to stay and make the best of her situation. And it hadn't been all bad.

But life was so much better with Steve. Their friendship was what a companionship should be. Their brief time together had shown her what she'd missed all those years with Harry. But things had been different for Steve and Dolores. *His* had been a happy marriage, and Dolores was a hard act to follow. They'd loved each other. They'd raised a daughter together. Did Steve feel the same need to grab happiness that she did? Maybe not. After all, he was happy before. What did Steve expect from her? What did he want from their relationship?

The noxious buzz of her beeper interrupted her musings. Having the beeper was the only way she was certain she could be reached in case of a fire. Flying into action, Rebecca threw off her robe and quickly dressed. She stepped into her boots by the door and pulled the uniform and suspenders up simultaneously, before grabbing her keys off the hall table. Flinging the door open, she raced across the yard and jumped into her Jeep.

Rebecca was glad Steve wasn't here. Their last three evenings together had been cut short by alarms calling her back to the station. Fires were fairly common this time of year. She was used to it, but Steve wasn't. He didn't like the interruptions, didn't like her to run off to the station and leave him there alone. But she had to go where she was needed—and if Steve was to be a part of her life, he'd have to accept that.

Minutes later, Rebecca pulled into the station driveway and slammed her car into park. She grabbed her helmet from the driver's seat and slipped it on, then ran in to answer the fire call.

"What's up, Mitch?" she panted, fastening the helmet strap. Mitch was her partner and the volunteer firefighter on duty.

"False alarm, Rebecca. I tried to reach you, but you're too fast. I guess you were on your way before I could dial your number. All I got was a ring."

Rebecca smiled at the short, stocky man with unruly hair who had obviously been awakened by the call. His clothes were disheveled and a dark, thick stubble was evident on his chin. Mitch had been the first one to volunteer for duty when she'd organized the fire department over ten years ago. He'd been with her ever since. They'd long since passed the point of being embarrassed about seeing each other at less than their best.

His mouth and eyes revealed touches of humor. "Do you practice jumping into your suit in your free time?"

"Of course." Rebecca slipped her helmet off and placed it on the table. "I can't have anybody ruin my record as the fastest dresser in Willow Ridge, now can I?" She grabbed the chair opposite Mitch, flipped it around, and sat down with her arms propped across the back. "So what was it this time—cat up a tree? Some kid playing a bad prank?"

"Nope. You'd never believe it in a million years." He scratched his stomach and stretched his arms out, yawning loudly.

"For Pete's sake, Mitch, what?"

Rebecca had thought she was about to fight a fire, so the adrenalin had kicked in with a bang. Now that the emergency was past, she was weary and a little depressed at the idea of going home alone. She didn't want to fool around with small talk. If everything was okay, then all she wanted to do was go home and warm herself by the fire.

Suddenly she felt chilled right down to the bone. She missed Steve and his warm arms around her.

"Some kid locked himself in the bathroom . . ."

"Why didn't they just unlock the door?"

"The parents weren't home. It was a baby-sitter who called, scared as hell that the little boy would get into the medicine cabinet and take drugs or drain cleaner, or drown in the toilet or something."

"Tell me what happened." She took a deep breath to settle her nerves. "Did you go over there to help her?"

"Didn't need to. Before we got a crew together, she called back and told us her boyfriend had climbed out the bedroom window, across the roof, and into the bathroom."

"Lord have mercy! Lucky for them he didn't fall off the roof." She shook her head. "I guess they were also lucky the bathroom window was unlocked."

"Those kids were lucky in a lot of ways," he said.

Mitch stood up and slid his suspenders down. He stepped out of his boots, leaving his uniform pooled around them, ready for the next call. Underneath, he wore a tattered pair of jeans and a flannel shirt.

"Yeah," she agreed. "Many times the worst happens, and we can't do a thing about it." Rebecca watched him yawn again. This time Mitch attempted to cover it with his hand, but she could tell he was tired. "I'm glad it all worked out. I'll get out of here and let you get some rest."

In a serious voice, he asked, "Are you okay, Rebecca? You seem a little down."

She threw a quick retort, turning her face away from him. "I'm not up to my usual jovial self, huh?"

"Don't try to kid a kidder. I can see behind that smile that something's bothering you. I just thought you might want to bend an old pal's ear, that's all."

Rebecca stood, turned the chair around, and pushed it under the table. "I'm sorry, Mitch, but I don't really have anything to talk about." She tilted her head to one side as she leaned on the back of the chair. Mitch was a good friend, but a nosy one. "I think I'm just tired."

"I'm here if you change your mind," he said.

"Thanks, but I'll be fine. I'll see you in the morning. Good night."

On the return trip home, Rebecca drove much slower, resisting the urge to drive past Melinda's house. The need to do something like that hadn't reared its ugly head since high school when she'd had a crush on a guy and wanted to know if he was at home on a Saturday night when he hadn't asked her out. Of course, this was different. At least that's what she told herself.

Back at home, she heard the phone ringing and

fumbled with her front door key. She thought of those days back in high school again, when she'd sat at home waiting for boys to call. More often than not they never did. Now old enough to know better, she had vowed not to sit alone waiting around for anybody, not even Steve. Yet secretly, she hoped it was Steve on the telephone.

The stubborn lock finally surrendered. Rebecca shoved through the door, tossed her helmet on the carpet, and reached for the phone. "Hello?"

"Rebecca?" The voice was female.

Rebecca couldn't place it immediately, especially since she'd been expecting Steve. "Yes?"

"It's Fran." The woman paused. "From Atlanta. Your best friend. Remember?"

"Oh, Fran. I'm sorry. I didn't recognize your voice." She tried to hide the disappointment she felt.

"I know it's been a few weeks since we last talked, but surely it hasn't been long enough for you to forget me."

Rebecca kicked off her sneakers. There was no such thing as a short conversation with her old buddy, Fran. "How was Europe?"

"Wonderful. Awful. You know the routine. Can't wait to go. Can't wait to get home."

"When did you get back?"

"A couple of days ago. When I didn't notice a message on my machine from you, I knew something was up. I bet it's that handsome man I heard you're seeing. Am I right?"

Rebecca took in a sharp breath. "Where in the world did you hear about Steve?"

"Steve, huh? Nice name. Tell me all about him."

"But Fran, you're the one who's been touring Europe. I'd rather you told me about your trip. What did you see this time?" She wanted to divert the conversation from her relationship with Steve.

"Okay, but I can't imagine why you'd want to hear about it again for the fifth year in a row."

Fran was so dramatic . . . but Rebecca loved her anyway. When she had needed her over the years, Fran had been there for her. After Rebecca's husband died, some of her friends had treated her as if she was the carrier of the seven-year itch. They saw her as a threat. Not so with Fran. She'd been a friend from the beginning . . . and still was.

"Three weeks. Ten cities. Bad weather. The Eiffel Tower. Rome. The Leaning Tower. Paris." Fran gave a long, loud sigh. This habit annoyed Rebecca, but it was as much a part of Fran as her long-winded talks.

"Sounds great." Rebecca stifled a yawn. Though she usually enjoyed catching up with her friend, tonight she was tired.

"It all means nothing, my dear Rebecca, if you don't have somebody special to share it with.

Maybe next year I'll meet *my* Prince Charming, but for now I want to hear about yours."

"I'm sorry." Rebecca knew how it felt to need someone. She, too, had been lonely before Steve.

"Don't be. I ate a lot of scrumptious food. I got away from my hum-drum routine. But it's nothing compared to finding a man. So tell me about him."

Rebecca shrugged even though Fran couldn't see her. "You didn't tell me how you heard."

"Word travels fast, my dear, in the ranks of the widowed and single. When one of our own snags a live one, we're all proud."

Rebecca chuckled. "You're terrible. You're talking about Steve like he's a piece of meat."

"A prize, maybe," Fran corrected.

Prize? Rebecca remembered the fair and the pie-eating contest and how Steve had brazenly tempted her with his pie-eating skill.

"Are you still there? Rebecca?"

If she were younger, maybe she'd have enjoyed a good girl-to-girl, no-holds-barred gabfest about the new man in her life. But she was a grown woman, and she wanted to keep her friendship with Steve to herself. Fran's persistence was beginning to irritate her. Rebecca was beginning to wish she hadn't answered the phone. "I'm still here."

"You're such a doll, I'm sure Steve must be handsome."

Fran hadn't had a decent relationship in over a

decade, but it didn't stop her from looking. Rebecca smiled to herself, remembering that Fran had once told her she would never give up hope that the "love of her life" would sweep her off her feet, even if he had to do it while holding on to a walker.

Fran tried again. "Tall, dark, and handsome?"

"Hmmm? Yes. He's very handsome, with salt-and-pepper hair."

"Is he the strong, silent type or the witty, gregarious type?"

Rebecca thought about the choices before answering. "He's . . . he's a little of both, I guess."

"Old, older, or ancient?"

"You're impossible!"

"Well, which is it?"

"Steve's only a couple of years older than I am, so you decide."

"So what's he like?"

"Steve?"

"No, Santa." Fran giggled. "Of course, Steve."

Rebecca didn't say anything for a moment, then gave her friend what she wanted. "He's fun to be with. We laugh together. He makes me feel young again."

Now it was Fran who hesitated. When she spoke, Rebecca heard a wistfulness in her voice. "You're in love with him, aren't you?"

"Don't be crazy, Fran. I didn't say that. I have

no idea what you're talking about." Rebecca felt a hot flush spread across her face and trickle down her neck and chest.

"Having trouble with the 'L' word, huh?"

"We're just friends."

"Ah, the old friend ploy, is it?"

"It's not a ploy, Fran."

"Whatever you say—"

"Let's talk about something else. Have you got plans for Thanksgiving?"

"Have I got plans! I'll spend the morning having brunch with my daughter and her brood, then I'll slip over to my second husband's in-laws for their big get-together. Then I'll have a late dinner with my third husband's daughter and her husband. They have a catered affair in Atlanta, complete with movers and shakers of both the married and the unmarried variety. It's a blast."

"Whew! That's a lot of Thanksgiving dinner! How in the world can you eat that much?"

"No problem. Since I'm not doing the cooking, I just eat what I please and leave the rest."

"Fran!"

"I'm not a kid any more, and I don't have to eat my veggies. Nobody cares if I eat a balanced diet or not, so I can pig out on all my favorites and have a ball."

"I forgot your late husband had children." Rebecca immediately sat up. Fran had had stepchildren. Maybe she could shed some light on Rebecca's relationship with Melinda.

"Yes, Peter had a daughter, an only child. Buffy hated me."

"You must get along if you're spending part of the holiday at her house. How did you get from hate to whatever it is now?"

Fran's tone was matter-of-fact. "Buffy's a piece of work, all right. She hated the fact that her father was getting married again, but she managed to remain civil once she realized there was nothing she could do—and found out my bank account matched her dad's dollar for dollar."

"She sounds awful."

"Not really. But once Buffy and I worked out the financial situation, the sex part was worse."

Rebecca was taken aback. "Sex?"

"Yeah, you know that thing people do between the sheets. I'm sure you'll remember if you think back . . . I believe Buffy had convinced herself that Daddy had no desire to do such things. She couldn't stand the fact that we were sleeping in the same room, much less in the same bed."

"She knew?"

"Knew?" Fran gave a wicked little laugh. "She probably heard us when she visited on the weekends. My late husband knew how to have a good time in the sack."

"Fran!"

"But about that getting along part—Buffy and I came to an understanding. She didn't bother me, and I didn't bother her. We both loved her father, and eventually we both accepted the situation."

"But how?"

"It was pretty bad until she got out on her own. After that, we took it one step at a time. First we spent holidays together, then we worked up to birthdays. Before long, we were catching dinner together every Sunday at the club."

"And you still spend Thanksgiving with her?"

"Yep. And Christmas, as well."

"Christmas. Ahhh. I hate the thought of picking out a gift for Melinda. That's Steve's daughter."

"Grown?"

"Yes. And married—about to be divorced—with two kids."

"Ouch. Bad situation to jump into, but not impossible."

"Any suggestions for a gift? She's a business-woman."

"Go for the unusual. The different." Fran snorted. "Even the tasteless will work"

"I couldn't possibly give her something tasteless."

"Why not? She's probably going to find fault with anything you give her, so you might as well make it something really obnoxious so she'll have something good to talk about. Oh, listen, there's someone at the door—I have to run. It's been fun catching up with you, Rebecca. Talk to you soon. Invite me to the wedding, okay?"

Startled, Rebecca almost dropped the phone. "Wedding?!"

Before she could say more, Fran was gone, but her parting words echoed in Rebecca's head. Marry Steve? Rebecca tried to imagine what life would be like with Steve . . . sharing his bed, being his wife.

But doubts and insecurities filtered into her thoughts, as well. What if he didn't want a commitment to her, to their relationship? Would he want to live in her house? What about Melinda?

But she felt so right in his arms. Steve was so right for her.

Was she afraid to fall in love?

The Publishers of Zebra Books
Make This Special Offer
to Zebra Romance Readers...

AFTER YOU HAVE READ THIS
BOOK WE'D LIKE TO SEND YOU
4 MORE FOR *FREE*
AN $18.00 VALUE

No Obligation!

ONLY ZEBRA HISTORICAL ROMANCES
"BURN WITH THE FIRE OF HISTORY"
(SEE INSIDE FOR MONEY SAVING DETAILS.)

MORE PASSION AND ADVENTURE AWAIT... YOUR TRIP TO A BIG ADVENTUROUS WORLD BEGINS WHEN YOU ACCEPT YOUR FIRST 4 NOVELS ABSOLUTELY *FREE* (AN $18.00 VALUE)

Accept your Free gift and start to experience more of the passion and adventure you like in a historical romance novel. Each Zebra novel is filled with proud men, spirited women and tempestuous love that you'll remember long after you turn the last page.

Zebra Historical Romances are the finest novels of their kind. They are written by authors who really know how to weave tales of romance and adventure in the historical settings you love. You'll feel like you've actually gone back in time with the thrilling stories that each Zebra novel offers.

GET YOUR FREE GIFT WITH THE START OF YOUR HOME SUBSCRIPTION

Our readers tell us that these books sell out very fast in book stores and often they miss the newest titles. So Zebra has made arrangements for you to receive the four newest novels published each month.

You'll be guaranteed that you'll never miss a title, and home delivery is so convenient. And to show you just how easy it is to get Zebra Historical Romances, we'll send you your first 4 books absolutely FREE! Our gift to you just for trying our home subscription service.

BIG SAVINGS AND FREE HOME DELIVERY

Each month, you'll receive the four newest titles as soon as they are published. You'll probably receive them even before the bookstores do. What's more, you may preview these exciting novels free for 10 days. If you like them as much as we think you will, just pay the low preferred subscriber's price of just $3.75 each. *You'll save $3.00 each month off the publisher's price.* AND, your savings are even greater because there are never any shipping, handling or other hidden charges—FREE Home Delivery. Of course you can return any shipment within 10 days for full credit, no questions asked. There is no minimum number of books you must buy.

4 FREE BOOKS

TO GET YOUR 4 FREE BOOKS WORTH $18.00 — MAIL IN THE FREE BOOK CERTIFICATE T O D A Y

Fill in the Free Book Certificate below, and we'll send your FREE BOOKS to you as soon as we receive it.

If the certificate is missing below, write to: Zebra Home Subscription Service, Inc., P.O. Box 5214, 120 Brighton Road, Clifton, New Jersey 07015-5214.

FREE BOOK CERTIFICATE

4 FREE BOOKS

ZEBRA HOME SUBSCRIPTION SERVICE, INC.

YES! Please start my subscription to Zebra Historical Romances and send me my first 4 books absolutely FREE. I understand that each month I may preview four new Zebra Historical Romances free for 10 days. If I'm not satisfied with them, I may return the four books within 10 days and owe nothing. Otherwise, I will pay the low preferred subscriber's price of just $3.75 each; a total of $15.00, *a savings off of the publisher's price of $3.00.* I may return any shipment and I may cancel this subscription at any time. There is no obligation to buy any shipment and there are no shipping, handling or other hidden charges. Regardless of what I decide, the four free books are mine to keep.

NAME _____

ADDRESS _____ APT _____

CITY _____ STATE _____ ZIP _____

TELEPHONE ( ) _____

SIGNATURE _____
(if under 18, parent or guardian must sign)

Terms, offer and prices subject to change without notice. Subscription subject to acceptance by Zebra Books. Zebra Books reserves the right to reject any order or cancel any subscription.

ZB0694

GET
FOUR
FREE
BOOKS
(AN $18.00 VALUE)

ZEBRA HOME SUBSCRIPTION
SERVICE, INC.
120 BRIGHTON ROAD
P.O. BOX 5214
CLIFTON, NEW JERSEY 07015-5214

AFFIX
STAMP
HERE

Thirteen

Steve stared into the bedroom mirror, knotting the tie Jeremy had selected for him to wear for Thanksgiving dinner. He loved his daughter, but he wished she could be more understanding where Rebecca was concerned. He felt pulled apart inside, wanting to share the holiday with his daughter and with Rebecca.

At times like this he wished he could turn back the clock. More than once he'd wanted to send Melinda to her room when she had started acting like a spoiled child. But she was an adult now. He wished she'd simply act like one more often. Melinda didn't understand his feelings, nor did she want to understand. The closer he and Rebecca grew, the more irrational his daughter became.

"Dad, can you spare a minute?" Melinda called from the kitchen. "I need you to peel the rutabaga for me."

"Coming."

Steve walked from his bedroom to the back of the house, consciously putting on a smile at the kitchen door. "At your service for kitchen duty." The room smelled of fresh-baked goods and roasting turkey.

He sat down at the table where a laminated cutting board and paring knife waited for him. Melinda handed him a large, round rutabaga. Steve attacked the vegetable and worked on the tough skin while his daughter mixed the cornbread dressing in a large metal pan. The sight of his daughter feverishly whisking the mixture reminded him of her mother.

Thanksgiving had been one of Dolores' favorite holidays. She had loved to cook, particularly when she had a houseful of family to feed. She would spend days getting everything ready for the huge feast.

Jeremy ran through the room with Jake close on his heels. They grabbed cookies from the platter on the counter and surrounded their mother.

"Smells good, Mom. When do we eat?" Jake bit into one of the large chocolate chip cookies.

"Heavens, Jake, we aren't eating for hours yet. Why don't you and Jeremy make yourselves a snack?" Melinda leaned down and kissed his forehead. "You can sit with Granddad while he tackles that rutabaga. How about it?"

"Oh, Ma, do we have to?" Jeremy snatched another cookie and stuffed it into his mouth. Chewing, he continued, "I want to wait for the turkey bird."

"Don't talk with your mouth full, young man." Melinda picked up the cookie platter and placed it on top of the microwave, out of the boys' reach. "If you don't eat something now, you'll be ravenous before the meal is ready. How about a sandwich?"

Steve could see his daughter's frustration growing. "Boys, how about fixing me one, too?"

Getting his grandsons' attention was easy. They loved to do things for others, especially their grandfather. They had inherited that trait from their grandmother, he thought. Now that they were older, Steve regretted that Dolores wasn't here to see how loving and considerate their grandchildren were.

He glanced at Melinda. "Your mother used to do that."

"What?"

"Just now, the way you poured each of those spices into your hand before putting it into the dressing—that reminded me of your mom."

Melinda turned and stared at her father with tears in her eyes. "Really? I remind you of her?"

"Honey, you're a lot like your mother. Don't ever doubt that."

Melinda took a tissue out of her apron and dabbed her eyes. She whisked with renewed vigor, but this time she had a smile on her face.

Dolores had always made holidays special, and celebrating without her was hard. Steve missed her most during this time of the year. The noises, smells, conversations, family buzzing around the kitchen—all reminded him of past holidays. He wondered if Melinda felt the same way—if she had the same memories about her mother. Maybe that was why his daughter was so adamant about not inviting Rebecca to their family dinner. She would be an outsider, not part of the memories.

Maybe that was why Steve wanted her there, to help exorcise the sad feelings he couldn't seem to shake.

Jake and Jeremy set out to find the sandwich fixings and quickly filled up every spare inch of space Steve wasn't using on the table.

On his knees in a chair, Jeremy slathered a glob of peanut butter on a piece of bread. "I'm making a double-decker. You want one, Granddad?"

"I think a regular old sandwich will be plenty."

Steve wasn't fond of peanut butter, but it was the only thing the boys could make without adult supervision. Jake was taking great pains with spreading his peanut butter and grape jelly on the bread. Steve smiled, seeing signs of his father in Jake—Joey's meticulous attention to detail, his artistic talent, his total immersion in whatever he undertook. Did Melinda notice the similarities, too?

"Mom, have we got any strawberry jam or that

orange stuff?" Jake slid off his chair and started toward the refrigerator.

"Marmalade?" Her brittle smile softened slightly.

"I guess. Do we, huh?"

"Don't you like the grape jelly?" She threw him a sideways glance as she chopped more celery for the dressing.

Jeremy scowled. "He's making a natural-born mess, Mom, trying to make a stupid picture."

"Leave your brother alone and eat your own lunch." Melinda shot him a warning glare. "Dad, my hands are full. Can you handle this?"

"Sure, hon, let's see what you have here." Steve stood up and moved to where Jake had been sitting. The little boy ran over and jumped back onto his chair.

"It's a balloon, Granddad, just like the one Miz Rebecca has. I just wanted to paint the stripes on."

In an instant, Steve saw his daughter's face turn to granite. The melancholy in her eyes evaporated and a dark remoteness replaced it. He wanted to communicate with her, to sympathize with her emotions—those holiday blues, made worse this year by her separation from Joey.

His grandson waited for a response about what he obviously considered to be his masterpiece. Steve cast a frustrated glance at Melinda, then turned his attention to Jake. "It's a great balloon, but how do you think it will taste with all those different jams on it?"

"Gross." Jeremy held his nose and made a gagging sound.

Steve shook his head at Jeremy, still standing behind Jake's chair. When the boy caught his grandfather's look, he rolled his eyes at his brother, but didn't say anything else.

Jake shrugged. "Didn't think about that. I guess it would be yucky."

"Why don't you eat your sandwich first, then go and make a picture with your markers? That way you can use all the colors you want in your balloon. Don't you think that's a good idea?"

Jake enthusiastically agreed and took a big bite out of his sandwich. "Can we give it to Miz Rebecca?"

Jeremy tipped his head back and rolled his eyes again. "She wouldn't want your old picture."

"Would, too. Wouldn't she, Granddad?"

Steve answered with a hearty nod of reassurance. "Of course she'd love it."

"I sure wish she could be here today." In those few words, Jeremy said what Steve had felt in his heart all day, but had been afraid to verbalize for fear of upsetting his daughter. "Maybe Christmas, huh?"

Jeremy and Rebecca had gotten close over the past few weeks. The boy would have gone to Riding the Wind every day if it was up to him. He loved the puppies and the balloons, but most of all, he seemed to need Rebecca.

"I'll bet she'd eat a double-decker with me easy. She loves peanuts."

Steve immediately looked at his daughter to see her reaction. Melinda's eyes clouded and her shoulders tensed. She put down her pan and wiped her hands on the large apron that stretched across her growing abdomen. "How in the world could you know she likes peanuts?"

"Sometimes at the barn she'd give us sodas, and we'd put a whole bag of peanuts in them. Boy, do they fizz!" Jeremy slapped his knee and chuckled. "Specially if you shake 'em up."

"Of all things to give young, growing boys." Melinda's voice was fragile and shaky.

"Now, Melinda, it's an old southern tradition and it won't stunt their growth a bit." Steve patted his stomach. "I've had my share, and I've never had a problem."

In a grudging voice, Melinda added, "You would say that."

"What is that supposed to mean?" he barked, before he could stop himself.

"Nothing." She rubbed her lower back with both hands. "I don't want to talk about *her* today, okay?"

Steve took the rutabaga to the sink to wash it before dicing it. He kept his back to Melinda, and she couldn't read what he was feeling from the massive shoulders that remained strong and straight, but unresponsive. She reached out and touched his arm in a gesture of apology. "Daddy, I'm sorry."

He nodded and continued to chop without looking at her. "I know, Melinda"

She could see the hurt on his face, hear it in his voice. For a minute, she regretted her decision to exclude Rebecca from their festivities. But she needed her father today and didn't want to share him with anyone. Couldn't he understand that? Couldn't he see how much *she* was hurting?

Thanksgiving played out like most holidays did. For every minute spent enjoying the meal at the table, an hour had been spent preparing for the event. By the time they sat down to eat, the boys were starving, Steve was exhausted, and Melinda wished they'd gone to the all-you-can-eat buffet at the diner downtown.

"Dad, would you do the honors?"

Steve walked over to the perfectly roasted turkey, picked up the carving knife and long-handled fork, and started to slice the breast, then stopped. "Shouldn't we give thanks first?"

"Oh, sure, of course." Melinda blushed. Her mother would never have forgotten something as important as that. She should have remembered. She'd been so caught up in getting the meal right, the table right, the timing right, that she'd forgotten the most important part. But then, Joey always said grace, and he wasn't here anymore.

"Jake, why don't you say the blessing," she said to her younger son.

"Do I have to?" He set his chin in a stubborn line.

"Let me do it," Jeremy offered.

"No," Jake's eyes narrowed, "she asked me to."

"But you didn't want to, bonehead." Jeremy jumped up, leaned across his mother, and swatted his brother's ear.

Melinda placed a restraining hand on Jeremy's arm. "Boys!" She could feel her eyes fill with tears. "Dad, would you say grace?"

"I'd be happy to." Steve put the carving utensils down and held his hands out to the boys. They each stood, clutched a hand, and reached for their mother's hand. She joined them without getting up. "Lord, let this be the beginning of another happy time in all of our lives. We have our health. We have each other. We have a new baby on the way. We have so much . . . don't let us ever forget how much You've given us. Amen."

After the prayer, Melinda didn't want to look at her father because she knew that if she did, she'd burst into tears.

"It's turkey time," shouted Jake.

"Finally," Jeremy agreed.

Melinda nodded to them both, busying herself with her napkin while Steve made a grand show of carving the bird for the boys' sake. Joey had always done that, too. Funny, her husband and her father were a lot alike. She wondered why she'd never noticed that before.

"White or dark?" Steve interrupted her thoughts.

"Huh?" she muttered, not aware that he'd already served everyone else. "Oh, white, thanks."

The rest of the meal was served without incident. Melinda allowed the boys to engulf the conversation with chatter. Steve obliged their requests for talk about the "old days" with story after story about his childhood holidays. And she was grateful to have the time to her own thoughts.

Stuffed to extreme, they all agreed to wait until later for dessert.

"Why don't you take a little snooze, and we men will clean up?" her father suggested.

"We will?" Jake asked in a high-pitched voice.

Jeremy poked his brother. "Yeah, we'll have this mess cleaned up like *that*." He ended with a hard snap of his fingers and a frozen stare at his brother. "Right, Jake?"

"Oh, yeah, right."

"Aren't you boys sweet." Melinda took one last look at her family and the dishes scattered on the table, then waddled down the hall and collapsed on her bed.

When the last dish was washed, Steve tiptoed down to her bedroom to check on his daughter. He heard her snoring slightly. She looked so contented lying there on her side with a pillow tucked under her stomach. She groaned and shifted when he pulled up the cover—a tattered afghan. Dolores had made it when Melinda was pregnant with their first grandchild. The faded old rag had lasted through two pregnancies and several winters before being retired to the cedar chest. Steve was touched that Melinda had unpacked it. He felt a twinge of guilt that he hadn't thought of it himself. This baby deserved the same joy of expectancy that Jeremy's and Jake's arrivals had merited. He was glad Melinda had remembered.

Steve eased the door shut and continued down the hall to the boys' room. They were busy making the last of a dozen pictures, each one less detailed than the one before. He could sense that their attention was wandering and knew he'd better get them out of earshot before they woke Melinda from her well deserved nap.

He gathered up the supplies and helped the boys put them away. "What do you say we sneak out for a few minutes and take a walk?" he suggested. "We want to give your mom a chance to catch a little catnap."

"Why do they call it that?" Jake stacked his paintings into a haphazard pile, putting the balloon one on top.

"What do you want them to call it, *dog*nap?" Jeremy flipped his brother's papers with his thumb, sending the whole pile tumbling to the floor.

Steve caught himself before he raised his voice, remembering Melinda wasn't the soundest sleeper in the world. "Jeremy, help your brother pick those up right this minute." With each word, his tone got lower and lower until it was barely a whisper. "Then follow me without making a sound. Not a peep, okay?"

With exaggerated steps, he tiptoed across the room with the boys on his heels. "If you make it all the way to the sidewalk without waking your mom up, I'll give you each a quarter." A little bribery never hurt, he thought. Besides, he was the grandparent, and grandparents were by nature supposed to do all those things that drive parents crazy. Lately, he'd been acting too much like a father for his taste. It was time he spoiled them a little. What better time than Thanksgiving?

Outside, Steve paid off his debt after a couple of rounds of heads or tails. Then the trio strolled down the sidewalk. They waved at the neighborhood children as they spotted them playing on their lawns. Steve could place some of the kids' faces, but he hadn't lived there long enough to know who belonged and who was just spending the day. He was amazed at how many of the children the boys knew.

"When's dessert, Granddad?" Jeremy asked.

"Yeah, I'm ready," Jake agreed.

"You're hungry already?" Steve was amazed that they could even think about food after all they'd devoured at dinner, on top of their substantial snack that afternoon. He rubbed his waistline. "I'm still about to pop."

"Not hungry," Jeremy corrected, "just starved for that pumpkin pie you made last night after we went to bed."

"Why, you little sneak!"

Steve had waited until everyone in the house had retired for the night before he started his baking frenzy. He'd wanted to surprise them with his top-secret pumpkin pies as a treat for today. Back home he was known for his unusual concoction. It had been the hit of all the Sunday suppers and dinner parties and the most requested item in his less-than-extensive culinary repertoire.

He should have known he couldn't put anything over on his grandsons, particularly Jeremy. That kid had a nose for finding whatever he wasn't supposed to find . . . Santa's projects, the Easter bunny's stash of candy, and even an occasional birthday present or two. "How did you find out?"

"The whole house smelled go-o-o-d." Jeremy drawled out the last word with obvious delight.

"That, and we found them in the laundry room this morning," Jake added.

"The laundry room? I thought that was a safe place to hide them, for sure. You guys treat laundry like the plague."

"Just lucky, I guess." Jeremy imitated Steve's Groucho Marx routine, wiggling his eyebrows and holding an imaginary cigar. Steve chuckled. The kid probably had no idea who Groucho Marx was. Steve had to remember to rent an old Marx Brothers video. For now, they simply thought he was doing something hilarious and wanted to do it, too.

"That," Jake said and laughed, "and no clean socks."

Steve made a mental checklist in his head over the past week's chores. Sure enough, he hadn't done the laundry. Apparently, neither had anyone else.

The threesome walked the last few yards up the sidewalk and plopped down on the bottom step of the front porch. Steve pressed his finger over his lips. "Shhh," he told the boys. "I'm trying to hear if your mom is up yet." He strained to hear any sounds from inside. But the house was quiet, so he took advantage of their cooperative silence to contemplate Plan B, the next step to keeping them busy. Satisfied that all was well, he asked, "What do you want to do next? Your wish is my command."

"Anything?" Jeremy asked.

Steve immediately knew he'd made a tactical error. If there was a loophole to be found, Jeremy would find it.

"Within reason," Steve quickly added. From the look in Jeremy's eyes, he could tell the little tiger was coming up with something that would test his grandfather to the limits. That was one of the reasons Steve loved him so much.

"I say we go visit Miz Rebecca, then. I'm sure she's lonesome without us."

"What about dessert?" Jake asked, a tinge of disappointment on his face. "What about the pie?"

"Stupid, we can take a pie with us," Jeremy beamed. "Granddad made three."

Steve wondered if the little rascal had been hatching this plan all along. "Don't call your brother stupid," he told him, buying some time to think about the luscious prospect of seeing Rebecca, even if he'd have two overbearing chaperons to deal with. He might even be able to sneak a kiss or two while the boys were busy with their pie. The memory of Rebecca's arms around him and her warm lips touching his made up his mind. He wanted to see her, had wanted to talk to her a thousand times today. "I'll get the pie," he told them before he could change his mind. "You guys meet me at the car."

Steve slipped into the house and quietly selected a pie from the laundry room. Every nerve in his body tensed when he crackled the tin foil, afraid that he'd awakened Melinda. Each step out of the house brought new creaks and squeaks. The noise was amplified in his mind, matching the pounding of his heartbeat as he escaped through the front door to freedom from Melinda's accusing stares and the biting words he knew he'd get if she caught him.

Caught him! He felt like a teenager sneaking out to date a girl his parents had forbidden him to see.

"Ta-da!" he announced, proudly presenting the pie to the boys. He hustled them into the back seat and fastened their seat belts after wedging the pie safely on the floor between them.

"Hurry and get there, Granddad," Jake begged. "The smell of that pie is driving me crazy."

"I can already taste it," Jeremy said.

"Me, too," Steve agreed. But his thoughts had nothing to do with pie. Instead, they were on the sweet taste of Rebecca's kisses.

Fourteen

By the time Steve turned onto the gravel road that led to Rebecca's house, his stomach was doing somersaults. He felt as if he were in the front seat of the Scream Machine at the local amusement park.

He checked the clock on the dash, surprised to see it was nearly five o'clock. A fleeting trace of apprehension cooled his excitement over seeing Rebecca. He should have called before barreling over for an unannounced visit. After all, he wasn't invited. He'd acted on impulse—something he rarely did. His need to see her, spend some of the holiday with her, had outweighed his good sense.

He told himself his lack of common courtesy was what bothered him, but his real concern was that Melinda was going to be angry when she found out where they'd gone.

What if Rebecca had company? What if she wasn't at home, but had made other plans for the holiday? What if she didn't want to see him, much less the boys? Questions kept jabbing away at his confidence as the tires crunched that last mile, spitting gravel under the car with steady pings. He usually slowed to a crawl at this point. Today, he ignored the possible damage the jagged rock missiles might cause to the underside of his car. He was looking forward to seeing Rebecca, secretly hoping to capture a few moments alone with her and take her in his arms.

"Granddad?" Jake interrupted Steve's thoughts. "Can we play with the puppies?"

"What?" Steve took a moment to reorient himself. He had heard the boys talking, but hadn't paid attention. "I'm sorry, what were you saying?"

Jake grinned at his brother, then asked a second time, "The puppies. You know. Do you think we can play with them?"

Steve answered before he thought things through. "I don't see why not." Once again he mentally ticked off the reasons he should have called before showing up on Rebecca's doorstep with two exuberant boys filled with enough sugar to pay for a dentist's second home. "We aren't expected, so we'll just have to wait and see what she's doing before we make any definite plans."

"She'll be glad to see us, I just know it." Jeremy's features became animated when he talked about seeing Rebecca and the pups. "We haven't been to visit her in over a week."

It appeared that Steve wasn't the only one with a huge crush on "the balloon lady." Jeremy missed her as much as he did. Well, maybe not quite *that* much, but almost.

He just prayed that Melinda didn't wake up before they returned. Steve knew he'd have to explain skipping out with the boys and the dessert, but he decided a few minutes spent arguing with his daughter was a small price to pay for a few minutes with the beautiful, charming woman he couldn't get out of his mind.

"We're here," he announced as he parked the car near Rebecca's Jeep.

Her Jeep is here! She's home! The only sight that would make him happier than that Jeep, would be Rebecca's smiling face. He was glad he'd come, even if apprehension did slightly nick his excitement.

"Hang on, I'll let you out." After months of taking care of the boys, he'd learned to childproof the door locks so they couldn't jump out before he was ready for them.

Snatching his buckle with one swift move, Jeremy let his seat belt slap into its holder and pushed Jake's hand aside to undo his, as well.

"I can do it myself," Jake snapped.

"You're too slow." Jeremy whipped his brother's buckle back.

"Am not," Jake responded as the strap slid off, releasing him from its grasp.

"Are, too," Jeremy shot back as he moved to his door, ready to pounce out when the lock clicked open.

"Boys! Stop bickering this instant or we'll go home without visiting Rebecca or the puppies." All three of them knew the threat was meaningless. In his heart, Steve had absolutely no intention of leaving this yard without the satisfaction of hearing Rebecca's voice or seeing those deep, green eyes that drew him in with a magnetism as strong as the force of gravity.

Steve jabbed the button and the hard click indicated the doors were ready to be opened. He swung his door wide, stepped out, then turned to check his reflection in the car's window. "Jeremy, bring the pie," he directed, combing his fingers through his windblown hair.

Jeremy's smile widened. "Yes, sir." He picked up the pumpkin pie, slid back across the seat, and closed the door with his backside. When he joined his grandfather, he was grinning like a Cheshire cat and elbowing his little brother in the side.

"What are you grinning about?" Steve could feel a warm flush rising from his neck as he took the pie from his older grandson. He offered a forgiving smile to the boys as he took the lead, sorry he'd snapped at them in the car. Together, the trio walked the short distance to Rebecca's door in happy silence.

"Can I ring it?" Jake looked up at his grandfather before pushing the doorbell. Steve nodded.

As the old-fashioned chimes sounded, a surge of anticipation racked Steve. He'd never dropped in on Rebecca before and now wondered if he had the right to be so forward. He knew times had changed, but good manners weren't a thing of the past, and he was breaking one of the "cardinal rules of etiquette," as his mother used to say.

His apprehension turned into joy when he heard footsteps somewhere in the back of the house after Jake rang the bell a second time. Steve let out a slight sigh of relief and stretched his head to peer into the beveled glass of the heavy wooden door.

"I hear her. I hear her. I told you she'd be here." Excitement was evident in Jake's voice.

Steve chuckled to himself as he realized he and Jeremy weren't the only two taken with the talented and beautiful Rebecca Roswell. It seemed she appealed to "men" of all ages, especially a fifty-six-year-old widower with a penchant for gardening and a fear of flying.

* * *

Rebecca thought she heard something—the telephone, maybe—but when she stopped blow-drying her hair, the chimes had stopped. She turned on the blow dryer again. The second time, she was sure she wasn't imagining a noise, but when she picked up the telephone receiver, the steady buzz of the dial tone was all she heard.

When she'd first moved to the mountains, she'd been nervous about living alone. Every little sound had set her nerves jangling, but after all these years, she'd forgotten what it was like to be afraid of the noises.

She had gotten used to the sounds of the country and had grown accustomed to living alone. But lately, she found herself wondering what it would be like to live with someone again. Steve, to be exact. How would life with Steve be? To sit down and eat their meals together. To plan their daily activities and outings as a couple. To watch television or listen to a little music on the porch swing in the cool of the evening. To wake up with his handsome face lying beside her. To be a wife and partner again.

The droning sound of the dryer left a sudden quiet when she switched it off. Even though she had the feeling she'd heard something, the third ring of the doorbell startled her. Who could be visiting this late on Thanksgiving? Her first reaction was that there must be an emergency, a fire, or someone who needed help. The adrenaline started pumping before she could remind herself that her beeper hadn't sounded, and people with emergencies didn't generally come calling at the front door.

Her next thought was that she'd forgotten someone's reservation for a hot-air balloon ride. Her last appointment had been at two. She mentally went through her list for the day's rides as she slipped her green satin robe over her bra and panties. But everyone was accounted for on her reservation list. And she didn't get much walk-in business. Not at several hundred dollars an outing.

Halfway down the hall, Rebecca decided that it must be Hawk. He hadn't been happy when she'd turned down his invitation to join the tribe's big celebration tonight. Maybe he was back to give her one more sales pitch to convince her to join him. That was just like Hawk, a true friend, even on a holiday usually reserved for family.

But when she looked through the glass and saw Steve, Jeremy, and Jake grinning back at her, a subtle gasp escaped her lips. Rebecca pulled her robe together with an unconscious tug.

Although her body remained absolutely motionless, her thoughts surged ahead at the speed of sound. He hadn't let the day go by without seeing her!

"Are you going to open the door?" Jeremy cried out to her, pressing his face up to the beveled glass.

"Jeremy!" Steve chided. But he wondered at her hesitation, as well.

He was relieved when Rebecca yanked open the door and grabbed both boys into her arms with a hug that engulfed them both in silky satin. Steve knew he'd never forget her expression: disbelief laced with pure happiness, all wrapped in an irresistible smile that lit up her face and warmed his heart.

She unwound herself from the boys, stood gracefully, and glanced at him as if she were a child on Christmas morning catching Santa under her tree with a bag brimming with gifts.

"It's Casey," Jake yelled.

"Huh?" Steve tore his gaze from Rebecca's face long enough to notice a sleepy-eyed dog waddle into the hall.

"Can we see her, Granddad?" Jake turned to search Steve's face for an answer as Jeremy inched closer to Rebecca and the entrance.

"Go on in," Rebecca told the boys. They immediately dashed past with arms flying to see who could get to the beloved dog first. "The puppies are in the den," she shot after them.

Steve watched the boys disappear into the den with the tail-wagging dog bounding right along at their heels. This was more than he could have hoped for. The boys were happily occupied. Casey and her brood were getting all the attention they could ever want. And Rebecca was standing only inches away.

"Am I invited in, too?" he asked.

"Is that delicious-smelling gift for me?" To Steve's surprise, Rebecca leaned toward the dessert he held in front of him and took a deep whiff. "Smells heavenly," she told him with a look that would have made an angel blush.

"My secret recipe." He lifted the tinfoil, exposing a quarter of the spicy dish.

"I see you put plenty of whipped cream on top." She stuck her finger into the creamy topping, brought it up to her lips, and hesitated before slowly licking it clean.

Steve swallowed hard. Rebecca was flirting with him like a breathless girl of sixteen, yet she played the part of a tempting vixen. Girls could do that when he was a teenager, since their parents were always close by to provide the safety net when things heated up too much. Back then, he'd hated the teasing. Now that he was older and more experienced, teasing was fun, even exciting. Especially since he knew her parents weren't an obstacle to his romantic advances . . . and he could always take the boys home to their mother.

He checked his breathing and boldly raked her

body with his gaze, pausing at the swell of her breasts before continuing down the silky folds of her wrap. Every time he met her eyes with a direct look, his heart leaped in an urgent response.

Two could play this game.

He turned his attention back to the pie and took a dab of the topping from the foil cover. Gently, he smudged her cheek with the cream, letting his finger glide down to her chin. Moving so close he could feel her warm breath on his face, Steve cupped her chin in his hand, and caressed away the sticky white cream with whisper kisses until nothing remained but his lips.

Rebecca closed her eyes and Steve felt her body shiver. Only then did he carefully pull back. He didn't know which he liked better, to tease, or be teased. From the look on her face, neither did she.

Rebecca was conscious of where his warm lips had touched her cheek, searing a path down her face with each velvety kiss. What she'd started as a simple flirtation had turned into a sensual encounter.

She opened her eyes and returned his steady gaze. "I don't know about the pie, but the topping is magnificent." Her voice was warm and throaty.

"Whipped cream is my specialty," he told her with a wink.

"Is that a promise?" She felt her face grow flushed. "Or just a tease?"

"A promise," he said in a husky voice, "that I can deliver with pleasure."

"Granddad," Jake called from the den. "I think Casey wants to go out. Granddad, are you there?"

Steve's hand brushed Rebecca's shoulder as he broke away. "Duty calls." He bowed, then handed her the half-covered pie.

"Whose duty, mine or yours?" she laughed, folding down the foil again. She'd forgotten all about dessert. At least, she'd forgotten about the pie.

"Both," he said. "I'll take care of the animals—"

"Two- or four-legged?"

"Both," he told her as he walked to the den. "Why don't you set up for dessert? We'll join you shortly."

"I'll do that just as soon as I get dressed." She grabbed the knotted sash, aware of how the thin, silky material clung to her body.

"Don't go to any trouble on my account." Steve gave her a wicked grin and winked.

"But the boys . . ." She was flattered by his open praise. "It will only take a minute."

Steve brushed against her again, causing her skin to tingle at his closeness. "You look gorgeous, but suit yourself." He kissed the tip of her nose, then went into the den to find his grandsons.

* * *

Rebecca began cleaning away the dessert dishes, astounded at how big a mess two little boys could make in a matter of minutes. They'd devoured Steve's excellent pumpkin pie with vast quantities of milk in record time. She had almost died of embarrassment when Jeremy had asked, "Don't you like it?" after she'd eaten only a couple of bites.

It wasn't that she hadn't enjoyed every morsel, she just couldn't look at the creamy topping without remembering the velvety smoothness of Steve's kisses on her face.

And Steve had sat there with his commanding air of self-confidence, grinning from ear to ear as she stammered out an excuse to cover the real reason she was having trouble.

"Can we go out and see the puppies again?" Jeremy asked as he helped Rebecca stack the last of the dishes in the sink.

"Absolutely, if it's okay with your grandfather."

Steve came up behind her and put his arms around her waist. "Let's all go out. What do you say?"

"Great!" Jake answered, tugging at his grandfather's arm. "Can we, Miz Rebecca?"

"What are we waiting for?" Laughing, Rebecca untied her apron while Steve hung the dishcloth out to dry.

The group made its way through the house to

the front door. "Oh, wait," Rebecca directed them. Stopping at the hall closet, she opened it and rifled through the pile of items on the top shelf until she found what she was looking for. She handed a red Frisbee to Jake. "Casey loved to play catch with this thing before she got so big when she was pregnant with the puppies. I guess I forgot about it after they were born. Would you like to use it?"

"Cool," he answered, his face breaking into a toothy grin.

"It's a bit chewed around the edges, but it still works."

"Good idea." Steve nodded, approval evident in his voice. "You boys go ahead and play."

"All right." Jake sprinted down the steps and offered the toy to Casey. The proud new mama sniffed it, but ignored the boy's attempt to get her to fetch.

"Let me show you how, goofball." Jeremy yanked the toy from his younger brother's hand, but neither of the boys had much luck in getting Casey to retrieve the disc for their benefit. The dog watched with a matronly air as the children took turns demonstrating what they wanted her to do. Her own offspring, tiny brown fluffs of fur, preferred to chase after the boys instead of the Frisbee.

"What's your pleasure, the steps or the porch swing?" Rebecca asked Steve.

"Either would be pleasurable with you," he replied, taking her hand lightly into his as he sat down on the top step and pulled her down beside him. "But the steps will do for now."

"You know, you didn't tell me how you ended up coming out here today."

"No, I didn't, did I?"

After a pause, she playfully ruffled his hair. "Well?"

He dipped his head and gave her a wicked look. "We snuck out."

"Be serious."

He placed his palm over his chest as if he were pledging allegiance to the flag. "Cross my heart. How in the world did you sneak away from Melinda?" His daughter's absence had been noticeable, but he hadn't mentioned it, so neither had she.

"We cooked for ten hours, ate for ten minutes, then Melinda fell asleep, so we took a walk. We ran out of places to walk, and Jeremy came up with the brilliant idea of coming to see the "balloon lady" so here we are."

"It wasn't your idea?" She pressed the back of her hand to her head, pretending to be offended.

All day, she'd fought the overwhelming urge to call him at Melinda's. Deep down, she knew that if she asked him to come and see her, he would drop everything and do it. The fact that he had come on his own was so delicious, she could taste the sweetness.

He moistened his lips before speaking. "No, the credit's all Jeremy's."

"It's obvious who my fans are." She waved in the boys' direction, then changed her tune. "Or maybe it's obvious who Casey's fans are."

"Does it count that I thought of you every hour of the day? I wished over and over that you were with me." He bowed his head and murmured, "I started to call a hundred times."

"And?" It had hurt her feelings when he hadn't called at least to say hello. She'd been feeling a little sorry for herself when they'd shown up earlier. To celebrate the holiday, she'd fixed herself a Cornish hen after her last balloon ride had ended. Thanksgiving just wasn't the same without someone to share it with. But that had been her choice. More than once, she'd regretted not taking Hawk up on his gracious offer to include her in his plans.

Steve cleared his throat. "I don't have a good excuse. Melinda needed me. She misses her mother more than I realized." He lowered his voice. "She opened up to me . . . probably because Joey wasn't there for her to confide in."

"I'm glad you had some time to talk." Rebecca managed a tremulous smile. She really was glad

Steve had made some progress with his daughter. She took a deep breath, reassuring him with a touch on his shoulder.

"I missed you." He reached out and took her hand in a possessive gesture. "We're going to be together on the next holiday, no matter what."

"Don't make promises you can't keep."

He squeezed her hand. "I never do. This is one promise you can take to the bank."

His firm mouth had a stubborn set to it she'd never seen before. His features had a way of appearing sensitive, yet strong, but today his resolve seemed carved in granite. Somehow she believed him when he said nothing was going to keep them apart.

Rebecca stretched her back, while Steve shifted his long legs to a different position. The boys had moved farther from the house, but were still close enough to keep an eye on where they were sitting.

Steve yelled when he noticed what they were doing. "Get that Frisbee out of your mouth." Using the demonstration method, the boys were teaching Casey how to fetch. "You have no idea where that thing has been."

"Or what kind of germs it has on it," Rebecca agreed.

Steve shook his head and laughed. "I sound just like a parent, don't I?"

"Yes, we've turned into those responsible adults we used to hate," she said.

"You could at least have disagreed with me."

"Why? When you're right, you're right."

"You . . ." He pulled her up with his powerful arms and stood towering over her, handsome as ever with his hair ruffled by the wind. "You, Rebecca Roswell, are challenged to a game of Frisbee. Are you up for it?"

"Up for it?" She raised her voice. "I can beat you with one hand tied behind my back."

"You're on!"

Jeremy flipped Rebecca the Frisbee and she caught it, much to her surprise. Her first attempt to throw it whizzed two feet over Steve's head.

"You're in for it now," he threatened, letting the disc fly with a snap of his wrist.

"Whoa, Granddad, what a shot." Jake's eyes widened.

"Getting fancy on me?" Rebecca asked, after she jumped for the high-flying saucer, but missed.

"If you can't take it, we can call it a draw."

"Not on your life." She bent forward and sent the Frisbee sailing straight up.

"Now you're talking, Miz Rebecca." Jeremy clapped his hands. "That's a beauty."

Rebecca had a soft spot for Steve's grandchildren. They were a joy to be around, even though they kept her on her toes. Who would have imagined she'd be out in the yard playing a game of Frisbee at her age? She felt younger than she had in years! And she felt aching muscles she hadn't felt in decades. Rebecca shuddered to think how sore she'd be in the morning, but she didn't care. Right now, the most important thing in the world was to stomp the daylights out of Steve at Frisbee.

She let another deadly throw spin upward, almost out of sight. Steve stepped back, back, back, to retrieve it, but misstepped and stumbled backward, going down hard onto the leaf-covered ground. Rebecca bolted over to where he lay with his eyes closed.

Her stomach knotted in fear when he didn't sit up right away. She squatted down, calling, "Steve! Steve! Can you hear me?" When he didn't answer, she placed her hand on his neck, checking for a pulse. Assured that his heart was beating, she leaned down to listen to his breathing. She refused to panic, because she didn't want to upset the boys.

Steve captured her in his arms, then rolled her over on her back.

She'd been had! Her relief that he was fine melted into anger, but Rebecca covered her feelings, not wanting a scene in front of the boys.

The boys ran over and joined Steve, who was doubled up in laughter, tears streaming down his face. She wriggled free from Steve's grasp. He was sneaky, all right. Rebecca had to admit she loved a good joke as well as the next person, and this had been a whopper.

"You two were in on this, weren't you?" she asked Jeremy as he wiped his eyes on his sleeve.

"We had nothing to do with it," Jeremy said between laughs. "Honest."

"Granddad played possum real good," Jake told her.

"Possum, nothing." She rolled over next to the little boy and started to tickle his ribs. "I smell a skunk. No, I smell three skunks." She turned her tickling skills on Jeremy.

"It was all in good fun," Steve told her with an innocent look on his face. "Am I forgiven?"

She winked at the boys and moved to Steve's side. "I'll forgive you on one condition . . ."

"Anything," Steve promised, propping himself up on his elbows in the grass.

"You have to cry uncle." She attacked his funny bone.

"Never," he vowed, twisting from side to side to avoid her roaming fingers vacillating from his ribs to his armpits.

"You two had better pitch in if you want to have another piece of that pumpkin pie." She didn't have to ask them twice. Jake helped tickle Steve's underarms with Rebecca, while Jeremy tugged off his grandfather's shoes and one sock and concentrated on tormenting his feet.

"Give me back my shoe!" Steve yelled. "It's cold! My feet will freeze."

"It's not that cold." She paused. "Have you had enough?"

"Never," he gasped.

Rebecca pinned down his arms for the boys to get a good shot at his ticklish spots.

"Cry uncle," she demanded.

"No." Steve drew a deep breath. "Never."

In tandem, the three went after his bare feet with renewed vengeance. Steve squirmed harder than ever on the cold ground. They'd found his Achilles heel, his weak spot—his feet.

"Give up," Rebecca urged as he gasped in mock torment.

"Okay. Okay," he finally yelled as the phone rang inside the foyer.

Rebecca released him and stood up, brushing the leaves and grass from her jeans. She was starting to get stiff already. Boy, was she going to pay for all this merriment tomorrow. "I'd better get that."

"Ignore it." Steve's gaze met hers without flinching.

But Rebecca raced toward the house. "Can't. It might be an emergency." The holidays were the worst. People did things they didn't normally do.

They drank too much, ate too much, tried to accomplish too much, and expected too much. It wasn't surprising that they often ended up sick, hurt, in an accident, or worse. She let the door slam as she reached the phone and answered, "Roswell residence."

"This is Melinda Camden. Is my father there?"

No "hello." No "Happy Thanksgiving." No "howdy-do."

"As a matter of fact, he is. He and the boys are out in the yard. May I take a message?" Rebecca imposed an iron control on herself. She had no intention of upsetting this woman, or of being upset herself. "Or would you like me to call him to the phone?"

"I'd like to talk to my father, if you don't mind."

"Not at all. Let me get him, okay?" Rebecca didn't wait for an answer. She stiffly walked outside with her remote phone and motioned for Steve to come to the porch. "It's Melinda," she mouthed when he got close enough. She wanted to add, "and she's not happy," but decided to let him find that out for himself.

"Melinda?" He sat down on the steps and patted the spot next to him for Rebecca. "Did you have a nice nap?"

Rebecca couldn't hear what his daughter's reply was, but from the grimace on his face, she guessed it wasn't pleasant.

"I'm sorry to hear that, honey. No . . . No . . . we just . . . Don't get upset." He kept his tone pleasant, but Rebecca could see the frustration in his eyes. "We did take a walk, then decided to bring Rebecca a pumpkin pie—"

Rebecca tried to focus on the boys, tried to tune out Steve's telephone conversation. But her curiosity was too great and Steve was too close. She listened in spite of her good intentions. She started to get up, but Steve caught her wrist before she could make her getaway.

He patted the step again, and she sat back down. This was his business, and she wanted to keep it that way. The less she knew, the less she had to hold against Melinda.

"I'm not asking you to spend time . . . here." He listened for a moment. "When the boys asked to see Rebecca, I didn't see anything wrong with coming here." He grew quiet again.

Rebecca tried again to concentrate on something else, but it was impossible not to hear every word.

"I don't think a little pie hurt them a bit. Actually, they're ready for a second helping." While his daughter was talking, he lightly ran his fingers up and down Rebecca's arm.

"Sweetie, I know you're tired. And I know the holidays are hard for you." His voice lowered. "As if they're not hard for me."

Rebecca started to get up, but Steve shook his

head and pulled her back. The more he and his daughter talked, the more uncomfortable she grew.

"You calm down!" His grip on her hand tightened and his voice grew tense. "That didn't occur to me, but, Melinda, you knew I was with them." He scowled while Melinda's agitated voice filtered from the receiver. "If that's what you want, okay." Steve shrugged his shoulders and gave Rebecca a smile. "We'll be home shortly." He poked the antenna back down and handed the phone to Rebecca.

The two boys ran over to the porch.

Jeremy plopped down beside Rebecca. "We've been busted, huh, Granddad?"

Steve's expression grew serious. "Seems like it."

Jake pushed into the spot between Rebecca and Steve. "Don't worry. By the time we get home, Mom will be over being mad."

"Yeah, she gets mad all the time these days," Jeremy said without emotion.

"Well, don't you two worry about it," Steve reassured them.

"Why don't you both go in," Rebecca suggested, "and clean up before you leave."

The boys scurried up the steps and into the house before either Rebecca or Steve spoke again.

"Is Melinda upset?" Rebecca finally asked. She knew the answer, but wanted Steve to confirm it.

"You might say that. She told me she thought the boys had been kidnapped."

"Kidnapped? You *are* kidding." Surely, Steve couldn't actually mean what he was saying. Kidnapping! That was more than she could imagine, even from Melinda.

"Nope. She thought Joey had snatched them." His expression was a mask of stone. "At least that's what she said."

Rebecca had never been in Melinda's position. She'd never had children, never been in the middle of a divorce, never been pregnant without a husband. It was hard to imagine what Melinda must have felt, with things so crazy in the world today. She obviously reacted before she thought.

Rebecca straightened to relieve the tense ache in her shoulders. "Joey would never do such a thing."

"I know that, and so does Melinda. She just had to have some wild story to tell me when she called over here to complain."

"You did leave a note, didn't you?"

"No." A frown flitted across his features. "I honestly thought we'd be back before she woke up."

"Steve! No wonder she was worried." Rebecca knew Melinda was manipulative, but this time the fear might have been real. If she actually thought something had happened to the boys, no wonder she was so tense on the phone. What parent wouldn't be? Rebecca actually felt sorry for her.

"I'll tell her you agree with her." The frown reappeared, creasing his brow. "That should thrill her."

"I don't think that will get you back into her good graces."

He sighed deeply. "Maybe I don't care if I'm in her good graces or not anymore."

"You don't mean that. You're just angry and tired."

"You're right. She's had these unexplained fits of fear since she got pregnant. Like when I'm driving her somewhere, she thinks we're always going to run over the car in front of us, no matter how far behind we are."

"You're not serious?"

His faint smile held a touch of sadness. "Yeah, it's weird."

"What do you do?"

"I just pat the brake every so often, to make her comfortable." He gave a resigned shrug. "It's aggravating, but I know she's really scared. All I can do is put the brakes on and make her feel better."

Rebecca touched his cheek. His skin was cold beneath her fingertips. "You're such a good father."

"I'm more than a father . . . I just wanted to spend the day with all the people I care about." He glanced up and added in earnest, "And that includes you."

"I'm glad." She felt a wave of happiness. "I've had a wonderful time."

"Me, too. I just regret—"

She gripped his arm tightly. "Don't."

The boys barged through the door and she loosened her hold on Steve.

"We're ready to go," Jake told his grandfather. "I sure had a swell time, Miz Rebecca. I wish you could go home with me." He reached around her neck from behind and hugged her.

Rebecca pulled him around in front of her and into her lap. "You can come back very soon." After a good hug, she helped him to his feet, straightening his collar and hair. Jeremy then moved in close, kissed her cheek, and ran off in the direction of the car before she could say anything.

"You boys get in the back seat and buckle up. I'll be right there." Steve stood and reached for Rebecca's hand to pull her up to her feet.

"I'll miss you when you go," she told him. "It will be terribly quiet here with the boys gone."

"A little quiet sounds good to me."

"You know where you can find it. Any time."

"I'm sorry I didn't call you before we came over. I should have. I saw an opportunity to visit the most beautiful woman in Willow Ridge and jumped at it."

"It wasn't a problem. I'm flattered that you went to such great lengths to see me today."

He glanced at the boys, who were still making

their good-byes to Casey. "I'm very thankful to have you, Rebecca Roswell."

His voice sounded so sexy—that low, throaty rasp that made his words soar right to her very core.

"I feel the same about you, Steve Jordan."

He put his arm around her waist and squeezed affectionately. "Does this mean we're going steady?"

"Yes," she agreed with a grin. "On one condition . . ."

"Uh-oh. The last condition I agreed to got me into a world of trouble. What is it this time?"

She leaned her head against his chest. "Promise you'll never pretend to be hurt or dead again." She didn't want him to see the look of real fear she knew was in her eyes. "You scared the life out of me earlier."

He tilted her face toward his. "I didn't mean to frighten you. I thought you'd see that I was just fooling."

"My husband died right before my eyes." Her voice caught. "And I couldn't do a thing to help him."

"Oh, Rebecca. I'm so sorry." He pressed her close once more. "Please forgive me for being so thoughtless."

"You didn't know. You had no idea how frightened I was when I saw you lying there. Just don't do it again, please."

"I promise," he said as he stroked her hair. "I'll never, ever, do such a thoughtless thing."

She withdrew from his comforting embrace. "While we're apologizing, I should say I'm sorry for tickling you the way I did. It wasn't fair to gang up on you that way."

"Yeah," he grinned, "you turned my only grandchildren against me. You should feel ashamed." He motioned toward the boys, who were now in the car.

"I do. A little." She smiled thinking about it.

His brows arched mischievously. "I see very little remorse in those eyes."

"I'm trying," she said with a lopsided grin.

"That's what counts."

"I'll call you tomorrow," he promised.

"Tomorrow."

He took a couple of steps, then turned and stopped. "Rebecca, I can't leave without confessing something."

"What?" She couldn't imagine what was coming next.

His voice became deep and thoughtful. "You remember the tickling?"

"I told you I won't ever do it again." Her stomach lurched at the thought that she'd really upset him by her silly trick.

"I'm sorry to hear that—"

She was confused. Was he kidding her again or did he mean it? "What *are* you talking about?"

"I liked it." A flash of humor crossed his face. "A lot."

"You're incorrigible," she said.

"You love it," he accused.

"Yes, I do."

And I love you, too, Steve Jordan. There. She'd admitted it, even if only to herself.

Rebecca shivered in delight, remembering the warmth of his touch, as she watched him leave in the dim light of dusk.

Fifteen

"Hey, Mitch!" Rebecca straddled the thick, black hose that snaked from the yellow hydrant to the fire truck, showering the fire truck's hood with a torrent of water. "Adjust the pressure down, okay?"

"Will do," Mitch yelled over the roar of the water. He stopped sluicing the hoses and headed for the hydrant. Halfway there, he yelled back, "Rebecca! Visitor."

When she turned, Mitch motioned to the other side of the fire truck. Her gaze followed his waving arm and came to rest on Steve's smiling face. Steve's jeans were streaked with dirt and his knees were caked in red Georgia clay, but to Rebecca he looked just about perfect.

Her heart gave a leap as their eyes met. She'd missed him over the past few days. He had become such an important part of her life that when he wasn't there, she felt an ache, a longing that she could no longer deny.

She tightened her grip and fought to maintain control of the bucking hose still gushing water onto the truck. She was usually careful to wash the vehicle quickly to conserve water, but today Steve's presence distracted her. With a conviction that was part of her character, she grappled with doing her job well, instead of dropping everything and rushing over to him.

When Steve started toward her, she shook her head and yelled, "Wait!" She was afraid the powerful hose might get away from her. Dousing him with a strong stream of cold water would certainly spoil his visit. "Wait there for me."

He cupped his ear with his hand and gave her a quizzical look. She couldn't hear, but rather read, "What?" on his lips.

Rebecca shifted the hose and held up her palm to stop Steve. He nodded and moved back a couple of steps.

To Mitch, Rebecca made a slashing sign across her neck with her left hand, and managed to keep the mammoth hose from flailing loose with her right. She watched him adjust the hydrant's knobs until the pressure subsided. The water drained out of the hose and dwindled down to a trickle before she dropped it on the jumbled pile Mitch had been scrubbing earlier.

"Hello." She waved Steve over. "The coast is clear now."

"I didn't mean to take you away from your

work," he said, but the expression on his face contradicted his words.

Rebecca pulled a red bandanna out of the back pocket of her jeans and swabbed away the droplets of water on her arms and face, residue from her bout with the cold hose. "I'm glad you did." She was elated to see him, but was puzzled that he would come to the fire station just for a friendly visit.

Rebecca suspected that Steve had begun to avoid the station and anything to do with her volunteer fire fighting. He knew how she felt and she knew how he felt. He'd told her he was worried about her safety. He'd also reminded her that she shouldn't try to do everything her younger counterparts on the team undertook. And she'd made it clear she wasn't going to quit, nor was she planning to cut back on her level of participation in the department.

Stalemate.

When Rebecca was called away on a fire alarm, Steve always asked her about it later. After the fact, he seemed genuinely interested, never failing to ask how things had gone. But he stayed away from the station, and never showed up at the scene of a fire like most of the rest of the town gawkers did. In a small rural town, the alarm blast was something of an event.

She shivered involuntarily, yet felt anything but

cold as his gaze roamed over her damp chambray shirt and jeans.

"Aren't you cold with those wet clothes on?" Steve asked.

"No. Well, maybe a little."

"It's December, for heaven's sake! You shouldn't be playing in water outside at this time of the year." He gave her a small, tentative smile, but his eyes were twinkling with humor.

"Playing?" She swatted his backside with her damp bandanna. "I'll have you know I was giving this baby an official bath." Rebecca patted the truck's red fender.

"And getting a bath yourself." Steve turned to her stocky partner and threw up his hands. "Mitch, what am I going to do with her?"

"Leave me out of this!" Her partner laughed richly as he started to coil up the scrubbed hoses. "But if I was a betting man, I'd bet on Rebecca."

Steve quirked his eyebrows. "Bet on her doing what?"

Squatting on the sidewalk, Mitch slapped his thigh and snorted. "Any damn thing she sets her mind to." He straightened, sighing loudly. "If she gets something in her head, it's like a Pit Bull gnawing and gnawing, but never letting go."

"Thanks, Mitch, for such a lovely analogy." Rebecca stood with her feet apart, hands on her hips, and exchanged a relaxed smile with her fellow firefighter. "Don't believe a thing he says." She walked past Mitch, playfully clenching her right hand. "He's just pouting because he's got clean-up duty."

"Yeah, yeah, yeah." With a grunt, Mitch hoisted the heavy hose into the truck's first bay area. "Why don't you quit rubbing it in and get out of here before you catch your death of cold?"

"You know I never catch anything," she boasted. "I'm never sick."

"A woman after my own heart," Steve said. "Let's go before Mitch changes his mind."

"Or puts us both to work." Rebecca stuffed the bandanna in her pocket and took Steve's offered hand. "I know when I'm outnumbered. See you later." Together the two strode to the fire station.

Steve stopped to wipe his feet on a hand-painted doormat decorated with a likeness of Rudolph, complete with a cherry-red nose. "Great decorations. Did you put them up yourself?" He pointed at the pine garlands and gigantic, red velvet bows that framed the doors and window.

"No. The other volunteers pitched in, too." She walked into the day-room. "So what brings you here in the first place, Mr. Jordan?" Without bending down, she slipped off her wet sneakers and padded across the cold concrete floor in her socks. "Not that your being here isn't a pleasant surprise."

"What makes you think that I have a reason to

drop in on my best g—?" he stopped in mid-word. "To drop in."

She observed him before asking, "Best what?"

"Oh, nothing." He shuffled his feet. He always did that when he got nervous.

"Steve," she drawled out his name with an accusing tone. "Your best what?"

He shuffled again, then met her gaze with his own. "Girl. My best girl, okay? I think of you as my girl."

"And?" She waited.

"Melinda hates it when I refer to a woman as a girl. I just figured you wouldn't like it either."

Rebecca took both his hands in hers. "I'm not your daughter. I can understand her point, but . . ." She hesitated and felt her face grow warm.

"But?" he pressed her to continue.

"But, I kind of like your thinking of me as your girl." She squeezed his hands and let go. The cool December air made it harder to stand still in her wet clothes.

"Cold?" He started to take off his blue and yellow windbreaker and hand it to her. "Here, put this on."

"No, thanks." She shook her head. "I'll just get it wet."

"That's no problem," he assured her.

"Give me a minute to change, and we'll finish this conversation over a cup of coffee. What do you say?" She gave him a conspiratorial wink.

"I'll start the coffee perking if you'll point me in the right direction."

She waved him toward the makeshift kitchen. "A gentleman and a gourmet. What a lucky girl I am."

"We're both pretty lucky, by my estimation."

She stopped on her way to the changing room and turned to look at Steve. She felt his gaze caress her face. Even though it had only been a few days, she longed for his touch, his kisses, the closeness they had come to share. "Yes, we are two very lucky people."

In the changing room, Rebecca tugged her wet jeans down and stepped out of them, leaving them puddled on the floor while she unbuttoned her damp shirt. Flicking open her locker, she searched for a clean shirt and clean underwear. "Damn!" she cursed softly to herself when she found only a pair of jeans and sneakers to put on. "I can't believe I forgot to bring replacements."

She removed her panties and socks, toweled dry, and slid into the jeans. The heavy seams felt foreign as they pressed against her soft inner flesh. She opened a few of the other lockers and searched for a presentable shirt to wear as the heavenly smell of freshly brewed coffee wafted into the room. "Bingo!" she said, yanking a worn, but clean, light blue flannel shirt off a hanger. Slipping out of her wet blouse, Rebecca hesitated, then removed her bra, as well. The wet lace and nylon would only stain the clean shirt in a matter of minutes. She had no choice. But the idea of joining Steve sans lingerie was exciting. He'd never know. It would be her delicious secret.

When she returned to the day-room, Steve greeted her with a mug of dark, steaming coffee. "There. Isn't that much better, now that you're all cleaned up?" With a nod, he motioned her to the unpainted Adirondack chair beside him.

"Much better," she agreed, and sat down. "Ummm. Coffee's wonderful. Speaking of clean . . . What happened to you?"

Steve glanced down at his dirty attire and frowned. "I completely forgot I looked like this." With a self-conscious gesture, he tried to dust the grimy spots away with his fingers. "I've been working," he explained.

"Working where?" He looked as though he'd been up to his knees in newly-turned earth, but she knew he hadn't taken any new landscaping jobs since he'd moved here. Steve had supervised the projects that he'd committed himself to before his life in Willow Ridge, but had turned everything else down. He'd devoted all his free time to getting involved with his grandsons and to helping his daughter with her problems—and to spending time with Rebecca whenever she wasn't busy with hot-air balloon rides or the fire station.

"You know perfectly well where." He arched an eyebrow.

"I don't. I promise." She searched his face, trying to figure out what he was talking about. "I had no idea you had a landscaping job."

Steve flushed. "You really don't know, do you?"

She gave him a bemused grin. "Don't know what?"

"Didn't you volunteer me to do the landscaping for the town square?"

"Me?" Rebecca gasped.

Steve swallowed wrong, causing a fit of coughing. After a moment, he asked in a choked voice, "You didn't do it?" He cleared his throat, his eyes still misty from coughing. "All this week, I thought you were the person who gave the mayor my name."

"No, I can't take credit for it." She hastened to add, "but they picked the perfect man for the job."

"I don't know about that, but I do know I wouldn't have taken the job if I hadn't thought you were the one who got me into it."

"And now?"

"Now, I'm glad I did it." His face creased into a sudden smile. "It's been terrific getting my hands back into the soil again. I've missed it."

Rebecca curled her legs under her and set her mug on the chair arm. "I'm really happy you're gardening again. I know you love it."

"That I do." Steve absently brushed his jean-clad thighs, then reached over and covered her hand with his long, strong fingers.

Rebecca studied his hands, now stained the terra-cotta tint of the common clay ever-present in the area. Steve had the rough palms of a worker, someone not afraid to get dirty. Since they'd started seeing each other, she'd answered her door numerous times to find his hands dipped into her planter boxes, picking off dead leaves or checking for moisture. And her plants had never looked better, she had to admit. He did seem to have the magic touch, both with her and her flowers.

"But I'm still dying to know who turned my name in for the project," he said in his low, husky voice, his eyes narrowing.

"To thank them . . . ?"

"Of course."

"I'm glad you came by to tell me this," she said suspiciously. "Or did you come by to complain?" She released his fingers and adjusted herself in her seat, cautiously slipping the jeans down her thighs a bit to keep them from cutting in anymore than they already did. She was afraid to look up for fear he could read her mind, afraid he'd figure out she didn't have anything on underneath her clothes. Did she really care if Steve knew her secret, or was it the fact that Mitch might walk in at any second?

Steve thrust his fingers through his thick hair. "That's not why I'm here."

She'd never seen him so nervous. He wasn't the type of man to hedge, but today he couldn't seem to find the words. "What is it, then?"

"I'm a little embarrassed to admit this, but I haven't taken the boys to see Santa yet."

She was careful to wait and see where he was going with the conversation. A simple "Yes?" was all the encouragement he needed to continue.

"It's been a tradition in our family to take the kids to see Santa on the first Saturday in December," he explained without looking at her. "I missed it this year. Dolores always took care of details like that."

Rebecca sensed a hint of pain in his voice and could only guess that it had to do with his late wife—or maybe his disappointment at missing a family tradition. She wanted to say the right thing, she just didn't know what that was.

"I'm sure the boys will be happy, whenever they go," she reassured him. "We've barely rolled into December, so you have plenty of time to fight the crowds and visit the jolly old man."

"Maybe . . ." he said, but his voice didn't sound convinced.

"No maybe. I'm sure of it." As badly as she hated to step into Dolores' shoes about anything, Rebecca knew Steve needed her now. He was reaching out for her, even in this small way, and she wasn't going to let him down. She just hoped she wouldn't have to fight his daughter to do it. "I've got some free time. I think this Saturday might be the perfect time to remedy this oversight. What do you think?"

"Sounds good to me," he agreed, relief evident in his eyes.

Steve was strong ninety-nine percent of the time. Strong for his daughter. Strong for his grandsons. Strong enough to pull his life together and carry on, even start over. But in that one percent of the time when he faltered and needed a helping hand, a shoulder to cry on, a friend to hold his hand, Rebecca was determined to be there for him.

Together, they made plans to meet early on Saturday to trek to Atlanta with his grandsons to visit Santa and do some Christmas shopping. They'd make a day of it. Rebecca had the good sense not to mention Melinda or Joey. She was just thrilled to be visiting Santa for the first time since she'd sat on the old guy's lap forty years ago and asked for a "real" bicycle with training wheels. Maybe she was overdue for a little visit to Santa herself. She had a few things on her Christmas list she'd like him to deliver. Things that wouldn't fit into his bag.

* * *

Steve chewed his lower lip and stole a final look at his freshly scrubbed grandsons on Rebecca's porch. They'd been so excited they'd hardly slept the night before, waking him up at the crack of dawn. His own sleep had been interrupted by periodic waves of anticipation. Steve knew his personal eagerness was about seeing the woman he'd grown to care about a great deal. He couldn't decide from their enthusiasm where the boys' allegiances lay—in going off with "Miz Rebecca," or in seeing Santa.

They were early, but not as early as they could have been if Steve hadn't created a few distractions along the way. He'd taken the long way through town, stopped at the cafe for breakfast, dropped off some letters at the post office, filled the car with gas, and even washed all of its windows before driving the last few miles to Rebecca's house.

As he listened to Rebecca's footsteps tapping toward the door, Steve glanced at the blue-black clouds sagging with moisture overhead. He could smell the rain, anticipating the sting of droplets hitting his face. Lightning danced across the sky. The awkward, dangerous, slashes were bathed in light one moment, then hidden in the storm's semidarkness the next. Thunder reverberated in the distance, sending an echo against the barn's tin roof nearby.

The day's gloomy appearance brightened as Rebecca pulled the door open with a warm smile and welcoming eyes. Steve hoped she would still be smiling after the hour-long trip to Atlanta in the car with his exuberant grandchildren.

"Isn't this a glorious day?" she greeted them, looking over their heads to Steve.

The impending storm was forgotten as Steve and Rebecca generated their own brand of electricity. Every fiber in his body made him want to take her in his arms. He openly gazed over every inch of her—her creamy complexion framed with loose silver curls, tiny gold hoops in her ears, a jeweled balloon brooch pinned high above her right breast, and slender black pants with a simple green sweater. His fingers fairly ached as he imagined how soft the sweater must be against her fair skin.

He approved, but then he always did. Rebecca was beautiful, no matter what she wore . . . or didn't wear.

"It's fixin' to rain buckets." Jeremy's comment broke into Steve's thoughts. "Don't you think we oughta get going?"

"Yeah, let's go, Granddad," Jake said, tugging on Steve's arm. "I want to be the first to see Santa."

"Santa—" Jeremy started, then snorted a laugh.

"Is sure to be waiting on us," Rebecca added, taking the older boy by one hand and his brother by the other.

Steve knew that his oldest grandson wasn't sure he believed in Santa anymore. The biggest fear for

Steve was that Jeremy would ruin the day for his little brother by telling him the "truth" about Santa. Maybe Rebecca could keep him from blurting anything out. It was evident from the way he allowed her to take his hand that Jeremy would do almost anything for her.

"Sorry the weather's not so great," Steve told her as they climbed into the car.

"The weather is perfect," she told the boys with a wink, "for us to play the cloud game."

"Game?" Steve asked.

"Sure. We look out the window and find all kinds of objects in the clouds. Right, boys?"

He should have known she'd find a silver lining in the bleak, gloomy sky looming overhead. Before long, the three were rounding up dinosaurs and dragons in the fast-moving storm clouds while Steve steered the car down the highway to Atlanta.

Steve was relieved that the boys played and chatted during the entire ride into Phipps Plaza, one of the fanciest malls in the city. It was fancy in the way that most in-town, newly renovated malls were—spacious, lots of glass, plants and woodwork, and plenty of specialty shops to make the most sophisticated shopper happy. He didn't come into town often, but he had it on good authority that Phipps Plaza had the best, most realistic Santa in the state.

He whipped into a parking spot, herded the boys

out of the car, and led them into the mall as claps of thunder and bolts of lightning ripped open the clouds. The four of them had barely made it through the heavy glass doors before the pelting drops hit the sidewalk.

"Whew! Just in time." Jeremy turned from the door and started toward the center of the mall, squeaking his sneakers on the slick marble tiles. He followed the signs to Santa's display, with Jake right behind him, mimicking every move his brother made.

Rebecca touched Steve's arm before he could reprimand the boys. "They'll settle down in about two seconds. They're just excited."

"You're probably right. How did you get so wise about children?" Steve draped his arm around her shoulder. The sweater material was as soft and downy as he'd imagined. He rubbed her shoulder with his fingers, content with her closeness and the warmth that radiated between them.

"I've been hanging around this man who's a wonderful grandparent."

She leaned her head against his chest, and he couldn't resist running his fingers through her satiny curls. "And he taught you a lot?"

"More than he realized."

Steve detected the gentle sensuousness in Rebecca's voice and instantly regretted that they were in such a public place with a couple of underage chaperons. "We'd better catch up before the boys upstage the elves."

"Or before Jeremy tells the whole shebang there's no such thing as Santa Claus." Rebecca led him through the long, store-lined corridor to the center atrium and Santa. "I detected his skepticism earlier, but I think when he sees Old St. Nick right there in front of him, he'll buckle under, just in case there's a chance he might be the real thing."

Rebecca and Steve caught up with the boys at the end of the line that had formed between thirty-foot-tall Christmas tree shapes made of thousands of scarlet poinsettias. Myriads of twinkling white lights were intertwined among the plants, giving the whole display a festive glow. Swirling sounds of carols and Santa's laughter echoed off the high ceiling and marble floors.

"We'd better get in line," Steve urged.

"You don't need to stand with us," Jeremy assured his grandfather. "I'll stay with Jake."

"I can stand by myself," Jake stuck out his lips and poked his brother's arm. "I'm not a baby."

"Of course you're not a baby." Rebecca placed her arms around Jake. "But we'd love to wait with you both. It would be fun."

"But Granddad, only babies need their parents with them." Jeremy's face flushed to a bright crimson that nearly matched the poinsettia blooms. "Do you have to?" His voice reached a squeaky pitch.

Steve quickly assessed the situation and relented. "I see your point." As much as he wanted to stand with them, he knew it was time to give them their independence. He could move to the end of the line and catch the best part without infringing on their newly-found need to prove themselves. "We'll meet you over there." Steve pointed to the over-sized sleigh filled with brightly wrapped presents.

"Thanks, Granddad." Jeremy gave Steve a half-hug, then clasped Rebecca around the neck, too. He pulled away, drew his brother into the growing line of children waiting to rattle off their Christmas lists, and looked very pleased with himself.

"You did the right thing," Rebecca told him. "But . . . there's nothing that says we can't immortalize the moment—" She turned to the lady at the nearby photography booth and put in her order. "I'd like a videotape of each of the boys and Polaroids, too, please." She signed the order, paid, and took her receipt before Steve knew what she had done.

He wished he'd thought of it. The last time Steve had brought the boys to visit Santa, he'd remembered to bring his own camera. Today, he'd been too busy getting them ready to plan ahead to the memories afterward.

"Come on," Rebecca told him, moving toward the appointed spot. "We can see as much from there as we could if we were right behind them."

"The eternal optimist." He took her elbow and led her through the maze of familial onlookers waiting for their darlings' turns with Santa. "The video's a good idea. Thanks for thinking of it."

"Oh." She laughed. "You thought I got those for you?" She hesitated, a gleam in her eyes. "Those are for my own selfish pleasure. You see, I've never brought anyone to see Santa before, and I wanted the moment captured for time immemorial. And to prove to all my friends that I really did visit Santa."

"Well, okay." He stumbled over the words, not sure if she was kidding him or not.

"Don't be so serious," she chided in a good-natured tone. "Of course I ordered copies for you and Melinda, too. Lighten up and enjoy being here with your grandsons."

"I'm sorry. I don't know what I was thinking."

"I do. You weren't thinking. Or you were thinking what a ditz I was. But I forgive you. Now why did you say Melinda and Joey couldn't bring the boys themselves?" They pushed through the crowd at the sleigh until they found an unobstructed view of the boys and their destination.

"I didn't. But since you asked, I'll tell you. Melinda's too pregnant to do anything but drag herself to work and back. She couldn't stand the thought of driving to Atlanta, fighting the crowds, and keeping up with two very rambunctious boys." He waved at Jake, who was trying to get their attention. Jeremy pretended he was studying something on the other side of the courtyard.

"That's understandable. Were her other pregnancies this tough?"

"Not that I remember, but you have to realize that Dolores and I weren't in the same town for the other two. We saw Melinda a few times for family gatherings and showers, then we came up to Willow Ridge after the big event. By the time we arrived, Melinda was resting comfortably and the baby was all cute and cuddly in the nursery."

"Why didn't Joey come today?"

"I'm not exactly certain that Joey even knows it's Christmas yet. He's too pre-occupied with the situation with Melinda. He loves the boys, don't get me wrong, but right now all his attention is directed toward getting back with his wife."

Steve realized Rebecca was concerned about his family, interested in what happened to them, yet he felt a little resentful at her questions. He wanted her to care, but he shivered at the thought of sharing so much of his personal life with anyone besides Melinda's mother. The holidays were having an adverse effect on him, dredging up painful memories that needed to be buried in the past. Memories that had to be exorcised so he could get on with his life and open up to Rebecca without this needling urge to hold back.

"That's good, isn't it?"

Rebecca's question jolted him back into the conversation. Her piercing, beautiful green eyes struck deep into his thoughts as he hoped—no, prayed—she wouldn't detect his waffling reservations. "Yeah, but if Joey has one fault, it's that he works too hard." He fought to maintain an easy, level tone, to regain his lighter mood.

"Maybe he's just trying to provide for his family," she suggested.

"I'm sure in his mind he thinks so."

"Melinda doesn't see it that way?"

He didn't want to talk about Melinda. Not today. Or was it that he didn't want to talk about his daughter to Rebecca?

Steve shifted from one foot to the other. "Melinda believes that it's because he doesn't want to have another baby."

Her eyes widened in surprise. "What little time I've spent with Joey, I can say with all certainty that that man wants this baby in the worst possible way."

"I know that, and you know that, but convincing Melinda of it is harder than walking on the moon." Steve forced a laugh. "Look, the boys are up next. I hope they'll be on their best behavior." He rolled his eyes upward. "Please don't let Jeremy pull Santa's beard." Together they pressed forward to the barrier rope in full view of Santa in his large, green velvet chair.

Rebecca felt a flutter of excitement herself as she watched the boys tackle the last few steps. For an instant she forgot she wasn't their grandmother, and she felt part of a family, part of a holiday tradition. For a moment, she belonged. Her eyes misted and an eagerness gnawed at her composure.

Jake went first. A pretty young elf helped him climb up into Santa's lap. Curled up under Santa's arm, Jake rattled off a long list of wishes as he touched the old man's beard with a tentative finger. When he crawled off Santa's knee, he ran straight to Rebecca to show off the photo the elf had given him. When Jake turned his attention to his grandfather, Rebecca straightened to catch Jeremy's visit with Santa. She watched as he furtively glanced both ways before edging onto Santa's knee, keeping one leg firmly planted on the floor.

Jake was bubbling over, reciting his wish list again so loudly that Rebecca couldn't hear his brother's wishes. The only thing she could tell was that Jeremy's list was short. So short, in fact, that he must have requested only one or two items before he dropped off Santa's lap to join them with his picture in hand.

Rebecca slipped away and picked up their video cassettes. She tucked them into her bag and rejoined the boys, who had moved away from the Christmas display.

"What did you wish for?" Jake asked his brother.

Before he could answer, Jake started on his own litany of hopeful requests again.

"Whoa, boy," Steve told his younger grandson, "you've got such a long list you're going to have to prioritize them to help Santa's elves out with the shopping."

"Pri- or- what?" Jake asked with a puzzled look on his beaming face.

"Tell them what you want the most, bonehead," Jeremy told his brother with a shake of his head and a conspiratorial wink at Rebecca. "Or you might get socks and underwear."

"No way," Jake yelled, "Santa wouldn't do such a lousy thing."

Everyone laughed at the horrified look on Jake's face. It was one second in time that Rebecca wanted to freeze. She realized how many of these special moments she'd missed in her life. This just might end up being the happiest holiday season of her life. Every day spent with Steve was a new beginning, a new experience. She couldn't remember a time in her fifty-odd years when she'd been as excited to get up each morning and face the day.

For her, the weeks between Thanksgiving and Christmas were usually purgatory. She hated the crowds, the materialism, the stress. She had mistakenly blamed her Scrooge imitation on living in Atlanta, but when she'd moved to Willow Ridge, she'd found the problem to be common to small town and large city alike. Knowing Steve and his two adorable grandsons had made this year's mad dash to the Christmas countdown one she'd never forget.

Steve herded them to the next event on their holiday outing—lunch at the Pheasant Restaurant. They watched the flickering lightning overhead as they munched on gourmet burgers and homemade chips in the glass sunroom.

Their astute waiter earned his tip when he suggested, "Would you two young gentlemen like to rock in our super-duper rockers on the veranda in the waiting area while your grandparents finish their coffee?"

"We couldn't impose," Steve told him half-heartedly.

"Sure you can," the waiter assured him. "Consider it an early Christmas gift." With a flourish, he whisked the boys off to the large, white rockers in the lattice-lined foyer. Seeing the boys clearly from their vantage point, Steve relaxed. The waiter checked on the children every time he whizzed by with an order, so they were in good hands.

"Having a good time?" Rebecca asked.

"A day shopping with my grandsons, lunch with a beautiful lady, and a successful visit with Santa . . . what more could a man ask for?" He lifted her hand to his lips and kissed it tenderly. "Now, little one, what's on *your* Christmas list?"

"That's a secret between Santa and me," she said.

He groaned and moved in closer, rubbing his strong leg against hers. "My dear Rebecca, does this mean you believe in Santa?"

"Absolutely, without a doubt. Don't you?"

Rebecca felt like a schoolgirl. She was aware of his closeness, his breath on her neck. Her senses stirred in a way that was becoming second-nature because she felt it every time Steve touched her.

They hastily separated when the waiter brought the bill. Steve busied himself with the details of paying the check. After he finished, he sighed. "We should probably leave. The boys are waiting for us."

She heard the note of reluctance in his tone.

"I'm ready." Ready for anything, she decided. Arm in arm, they started toward the boys still rocking away on the veranda.

Sixteen

Rebecca watched Steve as he worked in the courthouse gardens. Letting her gaze follow his movements, her thoughts rambled to the last time they were alone. If she closed her eyes, she could almost feel his arms around her, his warm lips on hers. Opening her eyes wide, she blinked the image away, replacing it with the equally appealing one in front of her.

Steve's long, strong arms spread pine straw around the base of huge mounds of camellias. He reached into the dark green leaves and plucked off a flower's dead head, then dropped it into the bush's center. His nimble fingers stroked the thumb-sized petals of one of the variegated pink and white blooms.

Rebecca could have stood and watched him all afternoon, but she decided to make her presence known. "This place is gorgeous!"

"Rebecca! What a surprise!" Steve stood, brushed dirt off his hands, then stepped out of the flower bed. "What are you doing here . . . dressed like that?"

Rebecca fingered the lacy cuff of her starched white cotton blouse. "I had to drive into Atlanta this morning to take care of some end-of-the-year company business. I'm on my way home and I saw you toiling away out here, so I couldn't resist stopping to say hello."

She moved from the sidewalk to the grassy area of the courthouse gardens, which Steve had been renovating with the proceeds from the fall festival. Her fitted green skirt, and her heels sinking into the ground, caused her to take slow, cautious steps. Reaching the flower bed, she touched one of the colorful blossoms. "You do have the magic touch."

"Thanks." He picked a stray pine needle off his rolled shirtsleeve. "I'd give you a proper hello if I weren't covered in dirt."

Rebecca swiveled slowly to face him, closing the distance between them with a few deliberate steps, never taking her eyes off his. "What's a little dirt between friends? I'll take my chances."

His brow rose a fraction and one corner of his mouth creased into a smile. "With that pretty white shirt?" He pointed his finger at the sheer lace bodice, almost touching, but not quite. "You'll get filthy! Look at me!" Dusting his thighs with short swipes of his palm, Steve succeeded in knocking off several loose clumps of rich dark soil.

"How about a compromise?" Stretching upward, Rebecca leaned forward and gently kissed the tip of his nose. "See . . . clean as a whistle." Running her hand across her blouse, she felt a tingle of excitement at her boldness. Or was it his nearness that caused her reaction? With her gaze piercing into his dark eyes, she leaned near his face and kissed one cheek, then the other, careful not to touch him with her hands or her body.

"If you don't stop that, you little tease, I won't be responsible for my actions."

She *was* teasing him . . . and enjoying every second of it. But was he? The smoldering look on his face told her everything she needed to know. He loved it. Rebecca wanted to be close to him— right here—right now, in broad daylight. She was too old to worry about what people thought or about how things looked.

She lightly ran her finger down the side of his face, wiping away the lipstick smudge she'd left imprinted on his cheek. "What did you have in mind?"

A red flush stained his cheeks as he groaned. "What I have in mind would get us arrested. We're already attracting a great deal of attention." He nodded upward to the courthouse. "If you don't believe me, look."

She squinted her eyes into the midday sun, trying to focus. "Oh, that's just the mayor—"

"The mayor!" he cried out.

". . . Yes . . . it's Mark and his secretary." She threw up her arm, waving and grinning as if she were a beauty queen in a parade. "Smile. They're watching," she directed through clenched teeth.

He looked at her with disbelief. "Are you crazy?"

"A little." She laughed without breaking the wide grin. "Wave back at the good mayor, or he'll be disappointed."

Steve stared up at the second-story window, nodded his head, then waved along with her, a lopsided grin plastered on his face. "How long do we keep this up?"

She switched her waving hand. "Until they move away from the window."

He chuckled. "Is this what they called a standoff in the old westerns?"

"Why, yes, Matt Dillon, that's exactly what this is . . . a standoff . . . and I'm not backing down. I'll wave 'til the sun goes down."

The memory of the ball and of Steve dressed as Matt Dillon swung her emotions into the recent past. A flurry of excitement rushed over her as she remembered her provocative costume . . . dancing cheek-to-cheek in the coat room . . . the limousine ride and her impromptu massage. Who needed Prince Charming with the good sheriff around?

"Miss Kitty, your standoff may end sooner than you think." The velvety sound of his voice and the glint in his eyes convinced her that he, too, fondly remembered the ball. "It's almost lunchtime, and since I've been working here, I've never known the mayor to miss a meal."

Her lips trembled with the need to laugh. "They'll surrender, just you wait and see," she mumbled through her smile. As if they heard her words, the secretary moved away first. "One down." The mayor lifted a pudgy hand in greeting as though he'd just noticed them, then closed the blinds. "And the other one bites the dust." She dropped her hand.

Steve pinched his mouth into various shapes and shook his arm. "Whew! I'm worn out. My cheeks are sore from all that smiling."

In spite of herself, she chuckled. "Mine, too. I can't believe this is the same place! A week ago it was full of dead shrubs and red clay. I couldn't go anywhere near the courthouse without getting that stuff caked all over the heels of my shoes."

Steve motioned to her feet. "Now you have potting soil all over them."

"At least it matches the black leather." She noticed as his gaze lingered on her black-stockinged legs and the slim skirt that hugged her hips and made her feel sexy. Rebecca didn't dress up much anymore, so when she did, she wanted to look feminine and sophisticated. From Steve's reaction, she must have accomplished her goal. "Now that I've probably ruined your reputation for good, why don't you give me the grand tour of the garden?"

His face lit up at the mention of the garden. Renovating it had been good for Steve, whether he admitted it to himself—or his daughter. Until lately, he'd gotten too wrapped up in Melinda's life to make room for his own interests. He needed time away from the boys and Melinda . . . needed goals that had nothing to do with anyone but himself. The courthouse garden project had accomplished that, if only for a week or two.

The whole garden centered around two slender weeping willows planted on raised mounds covered in evergreen candytuft, surrounded by a strip of newly laid sod. Anchored to the sidewalk were wrought-iron benches facing the courthouse.

She caught his enthusiasm as he showed her all of the changes he'd made. "I can't wait to see what it will look like when everything starts to bloom."

"Close your eyes." He swung her around to face him. "No peeking."

She did as he directed, feeling silly, yet doing it anyway. "Now imagine those azaleas overflowing with shocking pink flowers and the ground cover under the weeping willows thick with dense puffs of white."

"Sounds lovely." In her mind's eye, she could visualize every bloom, every branch . . . and she could see herself sitting on one of the green benches with Steve, feeding the birds sunflower seeds or sharing a sandwich. She opened her eyes to find him smiling at her. Steve wasn't usually this descriptive, this talkative, this excited over anything except maybe his grandchildren. Flowers and plants were special to him . . . they brought out a part of him she really found attractive.

Without touching her, he raised his hand as if to shield her eyes. "Not yet. Close your eyes. Now think fall."

She shut them again, not tightly, but enough to keep out the light. What next? A hint of excitement ran up and down her spine as she let herself be pulled back into his vision.

"Do you see it again?"

Rebecca nodded, not wanting to speak, not wanting to break the spell he had wrapped her in. She wanted, instead, to have the sound of his voice wash over her, wanted to feel his words, see the images in her head, let her senses flow away to another season and a future with Steve.

"Along the back of the courthouse, picture the pink and white camellias under the reddish-orange leaves of the sourwood trees. Take a deep breath." Steve waited.

She inhaled and exhaled, the aroma of freshly turned earth and grass filling her nostrils. She also detected a hint of aftershave and a masculine smell she instinctively knew was Steve.

"English lavender borders that bed." He breathed in and out himself. "It's a fragrant plant with fuzzy heads and spiked grayish leaves. This whole area will be full of color and wonderful perfume."

Sensing his pride, his joy, she could understand how much he loved his work . . . and why it would be a shame for him to give it up. Rebecca opened her eyes to find Steve gazing at her face with a shy, quiet smile. "That was lovely!"

He shuffled a pebble with his foot, studying it intently. Seeming embarrassed, he responded in a low voice, "I'm glad."

Rebecca reached for his hand.

"It's dirty," he protested.

She took hold of it anyway. "I told you, I don't care." She guided him to one of the benches and they sat down.

"I have a big favor to ask you." She could feel her heart pounding, feel her hands grow clammy. She removed her hand from his under the pretense of straightening her skirt, keeping it in her lap when she finished. She didn't want him to know how nervous she was.

"Shoot. Just name it. Anything . . . for you." He shifted sideways to face her. When she didn't answer, he added, "What is it? Is something wrong?" His mouth dipped into a frown and his brow furrowed with worry.

"Anything?" she stalled, clearing her throat.

"Anything," he assured her.

But she was anything but reassured. She wasn't convinced this was the right thing, didn't know if she should do what she was about to do. Her insecurities rivaled her earlier excitement. She fidgeted with the lace around her neck, forgetting her hands were smudged with dirt from Steve's.

"I have this *thing* to go to . . . in Atlanta . . . next week." Her words came out in gulps. What was the big deal? She'd asked men out before, why was this time so hard? Because this time it was important . . . this time it was Steve . . . this time "no" would really matter, would hurt.

"Yes . . . ?"

Her invitation burst out in a rush. "And I wondered, well, I wondered if you'd go with me." Avoiding his gaze, she stared down at her dirt encrusted heels, waiting for an answer.

Steve tipped her chin. "I'd be happy to go with you."

"You would?" She wasn't sure if it was his touch or his answer that lifted the tension from her shoulders, but both things made her deliriously happy.

"Of course, I would."

Beep. Beep. Beep. The beeper attached to her alligator belt started its incessant call. Someone had an emergency. Someone needed her.

Steve's jaw tightened and he roughly sat back on the bench. "Perfect timing."

She unclipped the offending gadget, checked the number, and stuck it back on her belt. "It's the station. I'm sorry, but I have to go." Reluctantly, Rebecca stood up, looking down at Steve.

What lousy timing! she thought. But it still made her angry that Steve didn't understand that she couldn't ignore it any more than a doctor could. No matter how many times he told her he was worried about her safety, no matter how annoyed he was at having her called away . . . no matter that he couldn't understand why she didn't just quit.

"Take care of yourself." His tone was dejected and his frown had deepened.

She gave him a crooked smile. "I always do." Hastily, she took off her shoes and walked across the grass, leaving Steve sitting on the bench.

Every week she faced danger—in flying, in fighting fires, in answering emergency calls. She'd learned to protect herself in those life-threatening situations. Yet reaching out to Steve was much more dangerous. Her heart was in jeopardy. Why couldn't she protect herself from falling in love?

Just before she reached the sidewalk, Steve called out, "Rebecca?"

Turning, not sure what he would say, she only asked, "Yes?"

"By the way, what is that *thing* you invited me to?"

"The company Christmas party." She gave him a tentative smile and climbed into her Jeep. As she turned the key, she hoped she'd done the right thing.

Rebecca turned up the car's heater, adjusting the vents away from her face to keep it from blowing her hair. Switching on the radio, she rolled the dial until she found the local "oldies" station. She hummed along to "Blue Moon" until the car rolled to a stop in Steve's driveway. In the rearview mirror, she checked her make-up and pulled a curl into place. Running her hand along the chrome door handle, she tugged it open and got out, careful not to snag her beaded gown.

As she started up the steps, she lifted her slim-fitting designer gown above her ankles. On the porch, she dropped the heavy beaded material, then pressed the bell. Surprised that she'd gotten this far without Jeremy or Jake greeting her, she glanced at her diamond-studded dress watch. Eight o'clock on the dot. She was right on time. Maybe they were already in bed. Or maybe they were spending the night with Joey.

More than once lately, Rebecca had seen Joey at Melinda's house, and more often than not, the four of them had been doing things together. Steve was cautiously optimistic when she questioned him about the chance of those two working things out and reconciling by Christmas. His answer was always the same, "Be prepared for the worst, but hope for the best."

Rebecca shivered as she jabbed the bell a second time. She should have brought a wrap, but she hated furs and she had nothing else that looked good with this evening gown. Once she got inside, she'd be comfortable. Years of dressing for these fancy events had taught her to wear short or sleeveless gowns, regardless of the season. It was better to be a little cool than to be a hot. She found she could always move around, dance, or drink some coffee to warm up. But cooling off was a lot harder, and a lot more noticeable.

Hearing footsteps in the hall, Rebecca straightened her dress and waited.

Steve opened the door and gaped at the sight of her. "You are breathtaking!"

She stared back at the tall, handsome man dressed to the nines in a formal black tuxedo. This is not a rented tuxedo, she thought, it fits too well. He didn't have the usual too tight or too loose jacket, the too long or too short pants. He even sported a lovely set of onyx studs and probably cufflinks, too, although she couldn't see them from where she stood. Her gaze lingered on his neatly trimmed hair, and his perfectly tied bow tie.

"Where are my manners? Please come in." With a sweeping gesture, he offered his hand. Rebecca took it and entered the foyer, aware of his clean, sophisticated scent. She hadn't smelled this cologne on Steve before. Maybe it was new, or one he saved for going out.

Going out. Alone. Without the boys—a rarity these days. And she'd done the asking. But he'd said yes, she reminded herself for the hundredth time. "You look very handsome." He would have made Fred Astaire envious. She'd never seen Steve in formal attire before. He was a good-looking man, but she'd never thought of him as cosmopolitan or debonair. Tonight he'd surprised her by being both. But she had a few surprises of her own. "Are you ready to go?"

"Just let me lock up." He took a key from the hall table, then opened the door again. "Oh, wait!" He went down the hall and into the kitchen. She heard the refrigerator door open, then close. When he returned, he carried a white florist's box with a gold ribbon around it. "For you."

She took the box he offered and untied the elaborate ribbon. Inside she found one long-stemmed white rosebud wrapped in tissue. "How beautiful . . . so thoughtful of you . . ." She could feel a blush rise up her face. He'd bought her a flower, and she hadn't even *thought* of getting him a boutonniere. His business *is* flowers. How could she have forgotten! "I'm sorry. I didn't remember to get you a boutonniere."

Steve was gracious to a fault. "That's quite all right." He put his arms around her and held her close. "Besides, if I wore a flower, I'd never be able to do this. I'd be too afraid I'd mash it." He hugged her closer. "Now we won't have to worry about a thing."

As Steve fiddled with the lock, Rebecca wondered where his daughter and grandsons were tonight. Maybe they were with Joey. Anxious for Steve to see his surprise, she walked on ahead. Stepping onto the porch, Rebecca consciously decided to avoid the subject of Melinda altogether . . . unless Steve brought her up. Hurrying down the steps, she hiked up her dress again to protect the fragile beads, and positioned herself by the car so she could see his face when he turned around.

Her gold beaded gown glimmered in the moonlight, casting a warm glow on her creamy face and arms. A high collar and fitted bodice slid across her body, molding itself to her every curve.

"There! I've got to get this lock fixed. Half the time we leave the darn thing open—" Turning from the door, Steve couldn't believe his eyes. In front of him was Rebecca propped against a '57 Ford Thunderbird porthole convertible—a solid white hardtop model with shiny chrome fenders. "I haven't seen one of these in years! What a beauty!" Steve bounded down the steps and circled the car, running his hand over the spotless hood.

"It's ours for the night." She smiled and opened the passenger door. "Want to drive?"

"Does a baby cry? I'd love to get behind the wheel . . ." He caught the key she flipped to him and held her door as she struggled to maneuver into the low-slung body.

Steve momentarily forgot the car as Rebecca lifted her skirt enough to climb in, exposing a pair of lovely legs and strappy gold heels. He leaned down and pushed a portion of her gown inside so he could shut the door, accidentally brushing his arm against her thigh. A pang of regret hit him that they had to attend a crowded party full of strangers. He wished he could have Rebecca all to himself on this glorious moonlit night with the top down and a beautiful angel by his side.

But he was wise enough to know that suggesting they remove the convertible's top was inappropriate. Maybe later, when their time would be their own . . . but for now, they had a party to go to and no time to spare.

Steve strode around the car, touching the fender,

then swung his door open. He took a deep breath. "Smells new inside." He rubbed his hand along the black-and-white two-toned interior and climbed in, bending his long legs to fit under the steering wheel.

"It's just been redone." She cut her eyes at Steve.

"It looks it." He touched the dials and knobs on the dash, adjusted the mirror, then cranked the car. His right hand groped for the gear shift, but it wasn't there.

"It's an automatic." Her voice had an apologetic tone. "I know it's not a real sports car without a stick shift, but—"

"But nothing. I'm glad it doesn't have gears to shift. I haven't driven a stick shift since I got old enough to realize they made cars that shifted by themselves. Oh, at sixteen I might have been disappointed, but now I don't mind a bit not having to bother with all that trouble." He put the car in "drive" and pulled out into the street, then clasped her hand on the seat between them. "Besides, I couldn't do this if I had to shift every five minutes, now could I?"

"That's a good point." He felt her relax and lean back.

The throaty hum of the car's motor lulled them into a certain rhythm. They drove in comfortable silence, both absorbed in their thoughts. It was as if on some unconscious level their emotions were communicating through the sense of touch. And everything was right between them.

Traffic picked up when they pulled onto the interstate near Atlanta. He released her hand and concentrated on changing lanes and getting the right exit. When he glanced her way, she was smelling the rose, looking out the front window. But her gaze was far away, not on the cars and trucks and the congestion of city driving, but on something peaceful and calm—something that made her smile, a distant smile that told him she was happy. He hoped he had something to do with that smile!

Steve followed her directions and pulled up to the covered valet parking area in front of a towering glass office building. In all the years he'd lived in Atlanta, he was always near the suburbs, so he didn't often deal with valets and parking decks. In those days, he had worried about turning his car keys over to a complete stranger who would park his car somewhere he couldn't see, drive it who knows how, and expect a tip to do it. It was even worse this evening because it was Rebecca's car— at least for tonight—and he would be mortified if it came back with a ding in the perfect body of the '57 Thunderbird.

As they waited in line for the valet, Steve had to ask, "Are you sure the car will be safe?"

"Of course. I parked here for years, remember? The guys take extra care with my cars. I even have my own special parking spot." She patted his hand as he guided the car to a stop next to the waiting uniformed valet. "Don't worry."

Shoving the gear into "park," Steve was greeted by a boy who looked barely old enough to drive, while another young man helped Rebecca out on her side. He reached into his jacket pocket for his wallet and some insurance money for the driver. Stuffing a couple of bills into the boy's hand, he mumbled in a stern voice, "Don't let anything happen to this car."

The freckle-faced boy nodded. "Yes, sir. I'll handle it personally, sir."

That was what Steve was worried about.

"Hello, Freddy. How's your father?" Rebecca called across the car to the boy standing with Steve.

"Hello, ma'am. He's doing great. I'll tell him you asked about him." The grinning boy got into the car, a ruddy blush covering his face. He carefully steered into the parking deck, disappearing into the darkness.

"You know your valet's name? And his father?" Steve stepped back to let Rebecca walk through the door first. He was impressed at how much the boy obviously liked Rebecca. "Freddy, wasn't that his name? seemed to be quite taken with his boss."

"Former boss," she corrected. "My job here is mostly in name only, now that I'm up in Willow Ridge." She smiled at everyone in the atrium—the doorman, the waitress taking drink orders, and even the hat-check girl.

He couldn't believe how friendly all of these people were to Rebecca. "Do you know everybody?"

"Just about. I made it my job to know my employees. If they were willing to spend forty hours a week working to make my company a success, then I felt I owed them at least the courtesy of knowing their names."

Her straightforward, no-nonsense approach to life apparently didn't start when she moved to Willow Ridge. She had been the same kind, compassionate, thoughtful person in the business world—and had made it work, because if this building was any indication, she had done well. Very well.

Steve warily looked at the glass-enclosed elevator carrying people up the center of the atrium. His chest tightened at the thought of having to ride in it to the party, knowing he couldn't ask Rebecca to take the stairs, even if she were willing. He had to get a hold of himself. He'd thought he had this fear of heights licked. After all, he'd been flying in the hot-air balloon with Rebecca for months now and could do it without an anxiety or panic attack. Sweaty palms and a semblance of apprehension when they lifted off were the worst he experienced now. But he still didn't appreciate it the way she did. He wished he could, but he'd learned to tolerate it because he was doing it with her. He might not enjoy the activity, but he certainly enjoyed the company. Even the agony of flying was worth it . . . to be with Rebecca.

Rebecca led him out of the atrium, through a maze of corridors, into a well-appointed conference room. She punched a couple of buttons on the wall and a floor-to-ceiling bookcase opened up, revealing an elevator.

"Harry hated waiting for an elevator, so he put in his own. Even the executives weren't allowed to use it. Only Harry and I knew the combination. It led into his old office . . . which is still unused by anyone else. He used to drive the other execs crazy. They'd walk by and see him working in his office, then wait for the elevator, thinking they were punctual and even early. Then they'd get down here to Harry's private boardroom and Harry would be sitting there, as if he'd been there all day. They knew it was impossible, but they couldn't find the elevator to prove how he did it."

"Harry sounds like quite a fellow." A pang of jealously reared up in the pit of Steve's stomach. He wanted to dislike Harry, although he had no good reason to, except that he'd had all those precious years with Rebecca . . . and Steve hadn't. He knew that his dislike was irrational. After all, he'd had a wonderful life with Dolores. But now that she was gone, he saw things differently where

Rebecca was concerned. And he was jealous of Harry, even if he wasn't here.

"He was one of a kind." Her voice sounded wistful, almost sad.

Steve's heart twisted as he stepped into the elevator. "Shall we join the party?" He needed a crowd, people around to dispel the ghost of Rebecca's dead husband, to bring the life back into the evening. Nothing a little music, champagne, and a slow dance with Rebecca in his arms wouldn't cure.

She gave him a questioning stare, stepped into the elevator, and punched the button. The old machine groaned, then moved slowly upward like a giraffe reaching for a leaf high in a treetop.

"Freddy's father, by the way, was a valet here for nearly thirty years," she explained, "before they took away his license because of eye surgery."

He leaned against the wood-paneled wall, feeling the vibrations as they scaled the building to the top floor. He tried to make conversation, but Steve hated elevators even more than he'd once disliked ballooning. "So his son took over?"

"Well, not exactly." Her voice was soothing to his nerves. "His son only works here during the summers and when he's on vacation, like now when he's out for Christmas."

Steve's fingers touched the brass, curling around the bottom railing for support. "Out of what?" His chest was pounding. Pounding louder and louder. Rebecca must be able to hear it!

"College. It's his holiday break. He's studying engineering at Georgia Tech—wants to design cars when he graduates."

For a second, she caught his attention. "That boy I met in the parking lot?"

"That young man is very talented."

Her voice sounded impatient. Or did he imagine it?

She went on, "He's going to college on our scholarship program. He works here when he can, and most importantly, he has to keep a B average or better to stay in the program." The elevator ground to a halt. They had reached the top of the building—thirty floors up. The doors slid open and they entered a large, elegant office.

Steve let out an audible sigh of relief as he stepped from the elevator. Even in the dark, he could make out the shapes of heavy wooden furniture and leather chairs. Her husband's office. *Late* husband's office.

Rebecca gingerly walked across the room toward the desk, sidestepping a table and a pedestal with what appeared to be a sculpture on it. She'd obviously been in this room often enough to know it by heart. The thought made Steve even more uncomfortable than being here in the first place. The room suddenly filled with a low light coming from a green banker's lamp on the desk. Her husband's. Her rich, powerful, successful husband.

"There, that's better. Now you can see two feet in front of you. I don't want to use the overhead fluorescent lights, because I don't want anyone to come snooping in here from the party." She picked up a silver letter opener and ran her fingers along its length, staring out the picture window that filled the entire wall behind the desk. Through the glass, Steve could see the lights of Atlanta, the skyscrapers lit up for Christmas, the moving cars weaving in and out of the ribbons of highways linking the rest of Georgia to its largest city. From here, he was mesmerized by the way she looked in the moonlight—dressed in her glamorous gown with all of Atlanta at her feet.

He wondered if she missed it on nights like this. Her former life had been so different from her present life. So different from what he could give her.

Like a man with a mission, Steve walked across the shadowy room. When he reached Rebecca, he gathered her in his arms and drew her near. His lips slowly descended to meet hers in a warm, inviting kiss. "I've wanted to do that all evening," he confided.

Rebecca shivered. "What took you so long?"

He put his hand to her waist and drew her closer, the curves of her body molding to his. His lips recaptured hers, this time more demanding, more intimate. Close to her mouth, Steve whispered, "I think we'd better go now."

After a long sigh, she nodded, then eased out of his embrace.

Seventeen

Rebecca and Steve slipped into the party through an obscure side entrance. The top floor of the building had been converted into an elaborately decorated ballroom for the special evening. It normally housed the executive dining room and several smaller specialty suites created just for wining and dining clients. But tonight the area had been opened up to make one large room with panoramic views of the city on all sides.

As soon as they entered, they were spotted. A woman wearing a shimmering red dress and too much make-up pounced on Rebecca. "Darling, I didn't know you were bringing a date," she cooed. She lifted her hand to Steve's face as though it were a present and batted her fake black eyelashes. "I'm Isadora Feldmire, darling, and who, pray tell, are you?"

Not knowing what else to do, Steve took her hand and tipped his head, not actually kissing the woman, but making a showy bow to satisfy her obvious need for attention. He couldn't get a read from Rebecca on whether this woman was friend or foe, so he hid his repulsion, for Rebecca's sake, until she gave him a clue.

As soon as he could, he dropped her limp hand with the dagger-sized, blood-red nails.

"Isadora, I'd like to introduce you to Mr. Steve Jordan. Mr. Jordan, this is Mrs. Malcolm Feldmire, the wife of one of our board members. Darling, where is Malcolm? I'd like Steve to meet him." Darling, indeed! The consummate professional, Rebecca's voice was forceful enough to put things in perspective, yet as cool as lemonade on a scorcher in July. He was getting used to that in her and was beginning to like it. People never had to guess where they stood with Rebecca.

The woman in red fluttered her eyelashes at Steve, ignoring Rebecca. Didn't she know when to give up? "Mr. Jordan . . . Steve . . . it's all right if I call you Steve, isn't it?"

He quickly looked to Rebecca, whose attention was focused across the room. When she didn't say anything, he nodded "yes" to the woman.

"Steve . . ." she clutched her claw-like hand to her skinny throat, "where did you say you two met? Do you do business with the company? I can't imagine overlooking you at any of the company's banquets." Her raspy voice was drowned out as the orchestra in the middle of the room started playing Big Band music.

Speechless, Steve stared at the woman's eyes. He watched in awe as she batted those inky black eyelashes again. Each time the lashes closed, the top ones clamped down on the bottom ones. He half expected the lashes to stay enmeshed in the bottom lair of fringe when her eyes opened. How could anyone think those stiff, uneven spidery spikes around her eyes were attractive?

Rebecca grasped Steve's arm. "You must excuse us, Isadora. We have to go and greet the other guests." With the grace of a queen, she led him away from the spider woman and her litany of questions.

When they were in the clear, Rebecca smiled. "Don't mind Isadora. She's harmless."

"Harmless as a tiger in heat. Did you get a look at those nails?" Steve raised his hand and pointed at his own neatly clipped nails. "They should be registered as lethal weapons."

With an amused laugh, Rebecca grabbed his hand and yanked it down. "Stop that. Isadora might be looking. So you'll know you're safe, her nails are glued on and plastic. They wouldn't do anything but dent your skin and pop off if she tried to attack you."

"That sounds awful!"

Rebecca batted her eyelashes, "Oh, what we women go through to be beautiful."

Steve cleared his throat, acutely aware of the desirable woman flirting with him, causing a reaction not accepted in polite society. This evening was important, he couldn't lose control. Not yet, anyway. But Rebecca—dressed in that glittering second skin—was driving him wild. "Beautiful! There's nothing beautiful about that woman."

Rebecca walked along the wall, passing several empty tables, to one in the middle of the room. Checking the place cards for their names, she pointed to his seat, then placed her purse on her own chair. Surprised Rebecca wasn't sitting at a head table or dais, Steve surveyed the room and found there was none. He hoped she hadn't picked this table because of its location away from the many floor-to-ceiling windows that lined the room. His fear of heights was embarrassing enough; it would be worse if she'd chosen their seats just to accommodate his phobia. Unwilling to draw even more attention to his problem, he said nothing, but felt helpless and uncomfortable.

"Don't get too cocky. Isadora flirts with all the men that way," she said, grinning. "She was an unusual choice for Malcolm to pick as his second wife, but he seems happy enough, and he's the one who has to live with her."

"He doesn't mind her flirting? That would drive me crazy if she were my wife."

"Heaven forbid! But I'll keep that in mind. Malcolm seems proud of it in a convoluted sort of way." A waiter appeared out of nowhere. "I'll start with a glass of champagne, Roger, then ginger ale for the rest of the evening." Steve nodded in agreement, aware that she also knew the waiter's name. She wasn't kidding when she said she knew them all.

With his back to the rest of the room Steve murmured, "Plan to keep your wits about you?"

"At all times. Nothing is fun if you can't remember it in the morning."

The waiter appeared with the champagne. Steve took one and handed it to Rebecca, then as if he were making a toast, he lifted his glass to hers and added, "*I'll* keep *that* in mind."

Steve noticed a hint of blush creep into her flawless features, making her face appear warm and inviting.

Her eyes filled with an eagerness that took them both to a private place and time, but her voice maintained control as she continued the conversation. "Malcolm is a crackerjack businessman and he has the good sense not to bring Isadora to events where she might be a . . . problem. I've worked with him for twenty years and trust him implicitly. He's a good man with strange tastes in wives. It would be unfair of me to hold that against him as long as it doesn't affect his work."

The room was gradually filling up with festive employees dressed in everything from sport coats to tuxedos—Sunday dresses to designer gowns. Steve's eyes swept across the tables, surprised at the diversity of the group—all ages, all races, and from appearances, all economic groups. When Rebecca had said all her employees would be here, she had meant it literally. Somehow Steve had thought she'd meant the middle and top management, not the office employees and mail clerks, alike. But that's who appeared to be here—every employee in the company from the bottom up. And it appeared that they were all mixed in together, not seated according to placement on the rungs of success.

"Speak of the devil." Rebecca smiled at a tall, stocky, balding man who approached them. "I've been looking all over for you." Malcolm's tanned, leathery skin looked as if he'd spent too much time in the sun when he was young.

"I want you to meet my escort, Steve Jordan. Steve, this is one of the best business executives this side of the Mississippi."

Malcolm shook his head. "I think the Mississippi is pushing it a bit . . . Maybe the Chattahoochee; it's only a few miles away." Tough, leathery folds crinkled around his nose and mouth, and his jaw jutted forward when he smiled. His hands were rough on the top, but noticeably smooth underneath as he vigorously shook Steve's hand. "Nice to meet you. I want you to know we think the world of Rebecca, so you'd better take good care of her or you'll have the whole company to answer to." The man didn't stop pumping until he stopped talking.

Rebecca laughed. "You'd better watch out, Steve. Malcolm's infamous in the boardroom for administering thirty lashes."

"Metaphorically speaking, of course." The man's shiny head bobbed as he laughed. "Do you know what table you put me at this year? Give me a hint, or I haven't a chance in hell of finding my seat or my wife."

"That's the fun of it, Malcolm I want people to mill around and talk, as they look for their place cards."

"I'm sixty-six years old. I can't even see the darn place cards, much less read the names on them."

She patted his arm. "Next year I'll have them printed in one-inch letters just for you."

"My eyes thank you and so do I. Well, I'm off to find the elusive seat. Can you at least point me in the right direction?"

"Maybe Isadora's found it," Rebecca suggested. "Where is she?"

"She can't see any better than I can. The woman's too vain to wear her glasses in public."

Rebecca turned him toward his wife and gave him a gentle push in the right direction.

"You did the seating assignments?" Steve tried to hide the surprise in his voice. He figured she would have some underling do that for her. He didn't realize how much input she still had with the company.

"Absolutely. I have great fun putting unusual tables together." She looked at the people milling around the tables and smiled. "I believe if all the employees know one other, there will be less disagreement between management and non-management. If you know someone, you're less likely to dislike them for no apparent reason."

"Who did you put old Malcolm and Isadora with?"

She suppressed a snicker. "Actually, I have them matched up with the company's chaplain and a pair of newlyweds from the art department."

"You let employees marry each other? I thought there was some kind of rule against that in most companies." He was fast learning that Rebecca didn't follow any rules she didn't want to follow.

"Not in this company." She waved at a passing group of people. "If two people fall in love in the workplace, I think it's stupid to make one quit just because they get married."

"What if they get divorced?"

"What if anybody gets divorced?" Rebecca threw her hands in the air, palms up, sending the beads of her gown shaking. "It generally works itself out. If not, one or both can transfer to a different office or job or, as a last resort, we help them relocate to another company. I don't like to lose my employees, but I want them happy. Ah, here come some of our dinner partners." Rebecca stepped out to greet a lovely young black woman with an African turban wrapped elegantly around her head. She introduced Steve to Yolanda and her companion, as well as to another, older couple standing behind them. The four of them took their seats on the other side of the table.

"Yolanda has brain cancer," Rebecca whispered in Steve's ear. "She hasn't been able to work much this year because of the surgeries. I was so thrilled she and her husband could make it tonight that I arranged for them to sit with us.

"There's Cappy! Excuse me a minute." Rebecca left Steve and went over and hugged a striking white-haired woman wearing a pale blue dress and sitting in a motorized wheelchair next to the wall. After a moment, Rebecca and the woman wheeled her chair to their table. One of the waiters made room next to Rebecca's spot for the woman to guide her machine into place. Apparently everyone else at the table knew her. Steve waited to be introduced.

"Don't get up, gentlemen." The woman's voice was smooth as molasses, thick and sweet. "Yolanda! How wonderful you look! You've got to show me how to wrap one of those turbans. It's the only way I'll ever look taller."

"Cappy, if I had your pretty hair, I'd never cover it up." The young African woman laughed, touching the brightly colored bands of cloth wrapped around her head.

"You are stunning, Yolanda, and don't you ever forget it. Hair will grow back, but what you have— your beauty, your intelligence, your style—that, you're born with." Cappy picked up her water glass. "To Yolanda. Welcome back."

Steve joined in the toast as did the rest of the table. He wondered who Cappy was and what significance she played in Rebecca's life. As the waiters started serving the first course, he and Rebecca sat down.

"I know everyone except the gentleman on your right." The feisty woman peered at Steve and extended a well-manicured hand.

Rebecca quickly introduced them, but Steve still had no idea who the woman was. Was she an employee? Probably not. She looked old enough to be retired. Maybe he'd pick up a hint during the meal.

The dinner was delicious—Caesar salad, grilled trout Almondine, and a raspberry torte for dessert. The conversation was light, catching up on one another's doings and families. And intense—debating politics and the state of world affairs. Rebecca's face was animated as she admired photos of children, listened to stories about vacations, and defended her stand on civil rights.

After dinner, the orchestra picked up the pace and people began to dance. Rebecca excused herself to check on a few details and shake a few hands. Steve was left to play host, but not for long.

"Yolanda," Cappy addressed her dinner companion. "May I borrow your young man for a few minutes? I feel like a song."

"He's all yours, Cappy."

Yolanda's husband followed the older woman to the aisle, making room for her wheelchair along the way. He bent down to talk to her, then escorted her around the perimeter of the room, down the center, and across the dance floor to the stage where the band was playing. Then he strode across the stage and talked to one of the orchestra members. After a minute or two, and a couple of consultations with other band members, the young man returned to Cappy. With her arms around his neck, he whisked her up and onto the stage into a chair positioned in front of the glossy black grand piano.

What was this woman up to? And what was Rebecca going to say when she saw Cappy on stage about to take over the orchestra? Steve searched the room for Rebecca's face, but found it too late as the band stopped playing, the lights dimmed, and the microphone was turned over to Cappy. He'd have to wait and see what happened, along with

five hundred other people now concentrating on the
tiny woman in the spotlight.

"Good evening!" Her soft, syrupy voice flowed
out over the room. "Most of you know me as
Cappy . . ."

A murmur shuffled through the crowd. Steve noticed nods and smiles as all eyes turned to the
woman in blue. He caught a glimpse of Rebecca
at the back of the room. Was that a smile on her
face?

"I've been with this company a thousand years . . ."

Another ripple of laughter flowed around the
room.

"I started as a telephone switchboard operator,
back before they had machines to do my job. Then
Harry, God rest his soul, took me aside and told
me it was time to learn something new. He sent
me to accounting school and the rest, as we say,
is history." She paused, moving the microphone
away for a second. "I've signed a million checks
as comptroller, but now it's again time to learn
something new. I'm taking my cue from the big
boss, Rebecca." She pointed the microphone toward
Rebecca, then brought it back to her mouth, speaking into it with a softer tone. "Taking a break from
the everyday nine-to-five seems to be working for
you. I hope retirement is as good for me, too."
Cappy looked from Rebecca on one side of the
room, to Steve on the other.

With a smile, she ended. "Now that my speech is over, I'm officially retired. Let's have a little music." She stuffed the microphone into its holder on the piano and played an arpeggio that ran up and down the keyboard. "Harry, wherever you are, this one's for you, for giving a girl a chance . . . and for you, Rebecca, for all the good times."

In a clear, sweet soprano, the spry old woman began, "Farewell every old familiar face . . ." Steve didn't recognize the lyrics, but the tune sounded vaguely familiar. When Cappy belted out the refrain, "I'm looking over a four leaf clover, that I overlooked before . . ." it all came back to him. Her silky soprano had turned into a torchy ballad in a matter of a few bars, sending the crowd into spontaneous applause for the petite woman in the middle of the stage, confined to her seat, yet swaying and swinging to the beat. When she finished the first tune, she revved it up by swinging into Irving Berlin's "Alexander's Ragtime Band," then slowed it back down with the grand finale, ending with "Shine on Harvest Moon."

After a couple of verses, the crowd joined in at the chorus. Steve left to find Rebecca. He wanted to hold his "gal," wrap his arms around her and do a little "spooning" of his own. He wanted to hear her voice, listen to her sing. He'd never heard her sing before, but he knew her voice would be lovely and haunting—tempting him beyond reason.

When he found her, it was as though she was the only one in the room. They walked toward each other in the cover of darkness, with all the crowd's attention on Cappy. They met and joined hands, swinging them to the beat of Cappy and five hundred other voices serenading them. As if on cue, they both turned to the stage. Steve wrapped his arms around Rebecca from behind, gripping his wrists in front to secure her in his embrace. Together they sang and danced to a rhythm of their own.

Steve sang along with renewed vigor, the words holding more meaning than even he himself could comprehend. ". . . All he has to say is, Won't you be my bride, for I love you . . ." Steve knew in his heart he loved Rebecca. Somehow he had to find the words to tell her.

". . . So shine on, shine on harvest moon, for me and my gal . . ." Rebecca. His gal.

Eighteen

Usually Rebecca stayed until the lights came on and had a cup of coffee as the band packed their instruments, reveling in the party's success. But tonight, she'd never been so eager to leave a party in her entire life. For the first time ever, she—Rebecca Roswell—sneaked out of her own party without so much as a by-your-leave to anyone, not even the caterers.

While Cappy happily played an encore, Rebecca slipped over to the now-empty table, grabbed her purse, and spirited Steve through the office, down the secret elevator, and out into the fresh air before he had a chance to be nervous. The whole ride down, she kept him pleasantly occupied, so much so that neither of them noticed when the elevator's door slid open. From the conference room phone, Rebecca called for their car to be brought around, so that when they pushed through the exit, Freddy and the unscathed Thunderbird were waiting for them—with the convertible's hardtop removed.

Surprised, Steve looked at Rebecca. "How? Where?"

That made twice in one night she'd been able to pleasantly surprise Steve. From his expression, he was eager and ready to try it out.

"Safe and sound as promised, sir." Holding the door for Rebecca, Freddy handed Steve the key. Walking around to the driver's side, Steve reached for his wallet. "It's been taken care of, sir." Freddy touched his finger to his cap. "Good night, ma'am. Drive safely."

Climbing into the seat, Steve shifted so his legs were comfortable, flipped up the visors, turned the key, and waited until the engine's initial roar settled to a throaty hum. Before turning into the street, he turned to Rebecca. "You should have let me take care of Freddy. I would have been happy—"

Rebecca interrupted before he could say more. "Of course you would have . . . but that would have spoiled my surprise. I needed Freddy to take the top off for me, so the car would be ready when we decided to leave. You and I weren't exactly dressed for the occasion."

She hadn't meant to embarrass him by tipping. It hadn't crossed her mind that he would think anything of it. Steve needed to be less sensitive about her spending money when they were out together, and she needed to be more so about how she handled things. She made a mental note to talk to him about finances some other time.

"Where is the top? Won't we need it later?" He steered the car through the near-empty streets of Atlanta to the interstate and home.

To knock the chill off her feet, Rebecca adjusted the heater to full blast. "All taken care of. Doug had some errands to run near here, so he whipped by in the truck and picked it up from Freddy. It's probably at home as we speak."

"You think ahead, don't you?"

"Have to, to surprise you."

They drove through a lighted tunnel and under a MARTA public transportation track. A few miles later, Steve switched on the blinker, then exited up a side ramp. "Here's something I'll bet you didn't count on." He made a couple of quick turns and eased the Thunderbird into a spot at one of Atlanta's oldest fast-food eateries, The Varsity. The other diners already parked honked their horns in a ritual "hello" and Steve honked back. The '57 Ford gave a loud, demanding peal, instead of the high shrill sound of most modern horns.

The sprawling flat-roofed diner was wrapped in blinking white lights. Christmas wreaths decked the numerous doors to the restaurant and the poles holding up the covered picnic area. Even the curb-side waiters and waitresses had gaudily wrapped silver garlands around their bodies, letting some of

the tinsel swing across their backs as they skated
from car to car taking and delivering orders.

With "This Magic Moment" blaring on the loudspeaker, they ordered two large milk shakes and
some french fries from a teenager wearing what
appeared to be a cheerleader's uniform and roller
skates. When the order came, Steve cranked his
window down almost all the way and snapped the
tray securely in place. He paid the bill, then handed
Rebecca her vanilla shake and some napkins.

"With or without catsup?" he asked her, holding
up the plastic packets.

"Don't you mean ketchup?" she joked. "After
all, this is The Varsity, not The Coach and Six."

He raised a brow. "I doubt the Coach serves
either one."

"You're probably right." She laughed. "I'll take
mine plain."

Steve picked out one of the long, skinny fries
The Varsity was famous for, holding it near Rebecca's lips. "I wouldn't want you to get that gorgeous dress messed up, so I'll have to feed you
one fry at a time."

Rebecca opened wide in anticipation and took
the french fry from his fingers with her mouth,
licking his fingertips as she took in the last bite.
She chewed slowly, enjoying every morsel, then
tried to sip her shake. The thick, creamy mixture
was so dense she couldn't get it up her straw no

matter how hard she sucked. In desperation, she finally took out the straw and licked the shake off the end, then sucked the plastic end clean.

"That's a novel approach." Steve's eyes blazed with what Rebecca had come to recognize as desire. He wanted her as badly as she wanted him. "I'll buy you a shake every week, just to watch you drink it." His voice was as thick as the shake in her hand and every bit as delicious.

As they devoured their fries, Rebecca sat back and enjoyed the colorful crowd packing the local establishment—everything from rowdy teenagers to families—all there to capture a piece of the past. "What do you say we take this party on the road?" she suggested, wrapping a napkin around the bottom of her cup.

Steve agreed and motioned for the tray to be removed, along with their trash. Minutes later, they were heading north to Willow Ridge, the wind blowing through their hair, the city lights growing dimmer as they put some distance between them and Atlanta.

Rebecca stretched her neck, leaned back against the seat, and stared out into the blue-black sky dotted with twinkling stars which seemed so close she wanted to reach up and touch them. She thought of the trees on Atlanta's many Peachtree streets, their branches bare of leaves, but filled with tiny white bulbs draped haphazardly over the limbs forming odd shapes and designs. No pattern, no schematic theme, only lights bursting out hither and yon drawing the eye to the simplicity of the scattered illumination in the darkness.

The closer they came to Willow Ridge, the less Rebecca wanted to get there. It was almost two in the morning—far past her normal bedtime—but she wasn't sleepy. Perhaps she could talk Steve into a nightcap at her place or maybe a swim. The thought of their last swim together in the cave brought back the feeling of desire that now crept cautiously near the surface whenever Steve was near.

When he parked the car in front of his daughter's house, Rebecca noticed the house was dark, except for one, lone bulb shining by the door. "Looks as though everyone's asleep." Of course they were. It was the middle of the night. She chastised herself for the inane remark, but couldn't think of anything to say that wouldn't be too serious or heavy for the moment. The ride home had been a joy, fun, even romantic. She didn't want to spoil it by expecting too much, by pushing Steve too far. The next move was up to him. She'd control her emotions—physical desires and all—if it killed her.

Steve leaned toward her, putting his arms around her, pressing one hand against the small of her back, bringing together as much of their bodies as was humanly possible within the confines of the convertible and her snug-fitting gown. His mouth grazed her earlobe with a soft nibble as his fingertip gently traced the outline of her breast before cupping it in his palm.

Rebecca quivered in delight at his tentative touch, her nipples hardening against the heavy silk lining of her dress. She squirmed to get closer, then wound her arms inside his jacket and around his sides, aching for the touch of his skin.

Then she remembered where they were and gently twisted away. Trying to calm her growing desire, she pulled back. After all, they were sitting in full view of anyone who happened to drive by or look out the window. "We'd better behave." Her words hung in the early morning air between them. "What if Melinda caught us? What would she think?"

He buried his fingers in her thick, silver curls and drew her face to his. "The boys are at Joey's and Melinda is sound asleep."

She responded by raising her mouth to his, parting her lips for a warm, tender kiss. There was a sweet intimacy to their lingering kiss—a newness, born not only of desire, but of love, as she realized how powerful her feelings had become for this man.

When the kissing stopped, they both were breathing heavily, their bodies responding with the kind of lust usually reserved for two teenagers who can't tear themselves away from each other at the end of the evening. Rebecca burst out laughing when she noticed the window. "We've fogged up the windshield. That's hard to do in a convertible! I can't believe it."

"You can't believe it? I'm crushed." Steve stretched back in his seat, smiling. "And here I thought I was sweeping you off your feet."

What a great idea! Sweeping her off her feet reminded her of a balloon ride. The mood was perfect, the moon was full, no one was keeping tabs on their whereabouts . . . why not? Rebecca knew she'd have to do some powerful persuading to get Steve to do it, but the results would be worth the effort.

She leaned over to Steve's side of the car, resting her head on his shoulder, and curled her arm around his waist. "It's been such a lovely evening . . . I hate it to end."

She felt Steve's body stiffen. "I don't want it to end, either. Why don't we go inside?"

"I don't think that's a good idea." She wasn't lying. The idea of anything intimate with Steve in his daughter's home turned Rebecca's stomach inside out. And with Melinda home, it was out of the question.

"Why not? I live here, too."

"I know. I'm just uncomfortable about . . . doing anything in her house."

"Melinda's asleep, so she won't hear us." His voice was insistent.

How can he be so certain?

"I don't think I could enjoy it."

He sighed. "Then let's go to your house. Nobody will bother us there."

Her heart was thundering with anxiety. What if he said no? She'd never know until she asked. "I've got a better idea."

"What's that?"

"Let's take a balloon ride. Look how beautiful it is. The sky's clear, the stars are out, and the moon is full. What could be more perfect?"

Steve inhaled sharply. "A balloon ride? I don't know, Rebecca. We don't have Hawk or Doug to trail us—"

He reacted strongly, his resistance to the suggestion evident. How could she convince him to go up with her? "We don't need them. We'll just go out and back to Riding the Wind. In and out. I've done it a hundred times before. By myself. Trust me."

"Trust you." He moaned and laughed in the same breath. "The last time I trusted you I almost got bitten by a snake."

She detected a note of humor in his voice, her heart thudding wildly against her ribcage at the prospect of Steve agreeing to fly. "But you didn't, did you?"

"No, but it was touch and go there for a while."

She snuggled up close, giving him a pleading look. "Where's that lovable guy who was tearing my clothes off a minute ago?"

"That's different," he groaned.

"Imagine how romantic it will be up in the balloon with the moonlight beaming down on the basket. What do you say?"

"Oh-h-h-h," he drawled, making her wait for his answer. "Okay. I can never say no to you, even when my better judgment says "run." Let's do it before I change my mind. And this had *better* be romantic."

"The most romantic ride of your life."

Later, at Riding the Wind, Steve laid out the nylon envelope while Rebecca changed into comfortable clothes, then set about making the pre-flight checks on the ballooning equipment. Steve had changed at Melinda's, so he was ready to go. As ready as he'd ever be. If someone had told him a year ago he'd be flying off into the moonlight in a hot-air balloon with a beautiful lady, he'd have told them they were hallucinating. But this was no dream, and he really was going to sail into the morning sky with Rebecca.

Within fifteen minutes, the balloon was inflated and they were in the basket, gradually gaining altitude with each burst of hot air Rebecca shot into the billowing cavity. The outside wind was cool against his skin, yet Steve wasn't cold because of the heat emanating from the burner—and Rebecca's closeness.

He'd learned to stare up and out without concentrating on how high they were flying, now that he'd done this many times before. Without looking, he knew Rebecca was closely watching their ascent on the variometer—to tell how fast they were rising—and the pyrometer—to monitor how hot it was inside the top of the balloon. For a long time, he'd referred to the instruments as gadgets or thingamajigs, until he finally felt comfortable enough to look at them and learn their proper names. Once they reached a safe height for the direction they were going, he knew Rebecca would relax and join him.

The earlier darkness had been eclipsed with a glowing brightness as the full moon had risen above the tree line. Illuminating the night with moon shadows, the golden globe hung over the balloon, riding with them over the fields, past the town to the northern end of Lake Lanier.

Rebecca stepped to the center of the basket and slipped her arms around Steve after the balloon was high above the sparkling, tranquil lake. They floated peacefully without the roar of the burner, using the wind currents over the lake to push them quietly over the open water. Crickets echoed from the distant shores of tiny islands dotting the flat shimmering expanse. An occasional rock jutting out from the surface stirred the murky water, generating tiny waves that lapped and seemed to dance in the moon's rays.

"How high *are* we going?" His voice sliced into the silence.

She broke into a wide, eager smile. "Darling, we're going so high, it's as if we're going over the moon!"

Steve could see Rebecca's face clearly in the moonglow, her eyes casting a scintillating shine of their own. He could no longer deny himself her soft, velvety lips. The memory of her burning kisses earlier in the car left an imprint on his heart, rekindling a fire she'd been stoking for months.

Wrapping his arms around her, he felt her heart pounding in tandem with his own. He traced the fullness of her upper lip with his tongue, then urgently covered her mouth with his own tantalizing persuasion. Moving his hands down her back, he rested on the swell of her hips, his passion exploding into a million sparkling stars, filling his senses with the need to share what he'd wanted to share with her all night.

"I love you, Rebecca." Steve couldn't control the emotion in his voice. He loved this woman with all his being and was finally able to tell her under the resplendent beauty of a starry night. "I love you."

Steve's heart-stopping words rang in Rebecca's ears, stirring her soul to rise up and take flight on its own. Her senses flooded with the uncontrollable joy of knowing Steve loved her. Rebecca savored the feeling of completeness she felt, then showered him with kisses—around his lips, his chin, his nose, his jaw, his neck—ultimately capturing his mouth with a passionate hunger stronger than she cared to admit.

"I love you too." Her breathless response was met with another kiss, a more urgent and demanding one.

A lapping sound sent currents of fear through her body. "Oh Lord, no!" she screamed, jumping for the blower as the basket touched the water's surface, breaking the ominous water into a million ripples. As they ascended a foot or two, she could still see the widening rings of waves from where they'd almost splashed down in a watery landing. "We're going to be fine, Steve. Are you okay?" Her sharp voice was filled with fear and concern for his state of mind. "Speak to me."

How could she have been so careless? She should have kept one eye on the instrument panel. Would Steve ever forgive her?

When the balloon's basket was ten feet or more off the lake, Rebecca exhaled in relief. She shifted her position so she could continue to yank the blower valve on, to increase their altitude and also see Steve. With his back to her, he hadn't said a word since they'd hit the water.

Steve turned away from the rim of the basket, sure now that he was safely airborne again. He hadn't been much help, but then nothing could be done except to yank on that damn blower. And Rebecca had done a good job of that. They had barely scratched the lake's surface before she'd bounded into action. She was good at emergencies, even when the emergency was her own.

Steve pulled himself together enough to speak. "That was a close call," he yelled over the insistent howl of the blower. He stepped forward and clasped his hand over hers clutching the valve. "I'd like to talk to the captain about the entertainment aboard this ship. It's a little intense for me."

She broke into a ragged laugh, hollering back, "You had me worried . . . why didn't you speak?"

"Speak? I couldn't move. Even my vocal cords were frozen."

"But you're okay now?"

He heard the concern in her voice. "When I realized I could swim better than I could fly, I thought how ridiculous it was for me to be afraid." Resting his hands on her shoulders, Steve massaged the tense muscles.

"What are you talking about?"

The balloon had risen high enough so that now they were talking between blasts, instead of over them. They were moving straight up, but oddly enough they weren't making much progress across the lake.

He waited for a pause in the roar. "We were fixing to hit the water, right?"

"Technically, we did skim it a little."

"Well, I can swim like a duck and so can you, so we weren't in any real danger."

"Well . . ."

Rebecca tugged the blower to raise the settling balloon a few feet. When she stopped, he continued. "And I can certainly swim better than I can fly . . . it's heights I'm afraid of, not water."

"So you're not mad?"

"Mad? I'm mad about you. Mad we were interrupted." He dropped his eyes before her steady gaze. "But mad at you because you were kissing me so passionately that you forgot everything else? Never."

"Even to forgetting a little thing like piloting the balloon?" Her tone was apologetic.

"You're forgiven." He gave her an exaggerated wink. "I'm sure it won't happen again. Besides, how dangerous could a little evening swim be?"

"Well . . ."

"You said that before. Were we in *real* trouble?" Rebecca exhaled a long breath. "Yes. The water's so cold, probably no more than fifty degrees. Even good swimmers couldn't make it to shore in that temperature without suffering from exposure."

His stomach lurched, but he kept his voice even. "The worst is over. We're safe . . . and dry." He laughed. "Now sail this thing back home. I'm ready for solid ground."

Rebecca checked the instrument panel, then took a tiny nylon strip from the floor and tied it high on one of the lines extending upward to the envelope. When it didn't move, she wet her index finger in her mouth and held it out over the basket's rolled lip. "There seems to be another problem."

"I don't like the sound of that."

"It's almost daybreak and it seems we've lost our air."

"How big a problem is that?"

She set her chin in a stubborn line, then tugged to release another puff of air. "I can keep us high enough for several hours with the amount of fuel we have left, but I can't move us forward without the damn wind."

"So we're stuck here." He would give anything to be out of this balloon. Now she was telling him he was suspended above the lake indefinitely.

The lines of worry deepened along her brows. "It looks that way."

"Any alternatives?"

"Not unless you can blow real hard."

* * *

The twilight gave way to the blush of morning as the starshine mingled with the breaking dawn. For what seemed an eternity, the brightly colored giant yo-yoed. Rebecca and Steve took turns working the blast valve and resting on the woven floor, exhaustion overtaking them both.

Steve broke the silent pause between them. "Why don't you try to sleep a few minutes? We've been up all night, and we might be here a while."

Instead of leaning back, Rebecca scrambled to her feet. "Do you hear that?"

"What? I don't hear anything."

She stood motionless in the middle of the basket. "Shh. Listen. I'm sure I heard something."

Steve shook his head in disbelief. "It's your imagination."

"No! Look! It's a boat!" Pointing into the distance, she saw a rumbling speck rounding an island, moving in their direction.

"Great. Maybe they'll motor around us in circles and cause a breeze." The sarcasm was evident in his voice. "What good does a boat do us?" He was tired, hungry, and ready to be home and out of this damnable balloon.

Her face lit up. "It can tow us."

"Tow us? Is that safe?"

"Sure. But we can't do anything if we don't get

their attention. Yell. Scream. Do something to get that boat!" Her excited movements rocked the basket.

Steve grabbed the edge of the basket and bellowed, "Hey! Hey! Over here! Help!"

Together they yelled and waved and yelled some more.

The fast-flying bass fishing boat motored close, churning the water into a frenzy. A fisherman wearing overalls and high-top yellow rubber boots cut off the powerful motor and yelled back, "I'll be damned. You folks calling me?"

Rebecca leaned out. "Yes. We need help. The wind died and we can't get to shore. This is Steve and my name's Rebecca. What's yours?"

Does she have to introduce herself to everybody? Steve wondered.

The old fisherman stood on his low-lying bow and spit a stream of tobacco juice into a can. "Friends call me Skeeter. Ain't you folks heard 'bout motors? Makes life a damn sight easier." He spit again.

"Will you help us?" Steve asked, not actually sure he wanted anything to do with the strange man. What other choice did he have? "We need a tow. Will you tow us?"

The fisherman poked the spitting can under his seat, then pulled a worn canvas Wallaby hat out of his pocket. "Sure. Fish ain't biting. Where to?"

"We need to get to the resort—Stouffer's Pine-Isle—to the golf course. We can land there," she explained.

Steve's mind was digesting Rebecca's plan. The golf course! Wasn't there a less conspicuous landing site?

"No can do. Brown's Bridge is between here and there." The fisherman wrung the hat between his hands. "Damn fine balloon to run into that bridge."

Rebecca picked up the coiled rope beneath the instrument panel. "I'll think of something. Will you do it?"

"I'll give 'er a try." Skeeter shoved the hat on his head. "Fish ain't biting nohow."

Steve was ready to tell the crotchety old man, who wasn't really old at all, that he'd *buy* him all the fish he wanted, if he'd just get him out of this balloon, but he decided against it. The guy probably didn't eat store-bought fish anyway.

Rebecca secured the spare down line to the tether shackle and let it drop over the edge of the basket. "Damn!" she muttered. The rope wasn't long enough.

Steve realized that things were getting to her, too. She had to be as tired as he was.

"Need a little mo' rope, don't 'cha?" In the bow, the fisherman opened his live well compartment and pulled out a bundle of rope. He untied the steel anchor from the end, dropped it back in the hold, then took the rope to the stern. He peered up at Rebecca's rope dangling about four feet from the water. "Kin ya'll come down so's I kin tie this piece on?"

The balloon drifted lower after Rebecca stopped pumping air into the envelope. When Skeeter succeeded in lashing the ropes together, he cranked his massive, 150-horse-powered motor and they set off down the lake. The boat's front end raised up, spitting water in every direction as the motor revved to life.

For the first time in better than an hour, things were looking up. Rebecca wanted to recapture the mood prior to the accident, but knew that the morning was lost. She and Steve held hands as they worked together to keep the balloon up. The wind whipped her face as they briskly sailed down the lake, bouncing up and down over invisible waves as the boat did the same on the real thing.

They quickly reached Brown's Bridge. Made of steel girders and concrete, the elaborate green structure rose nearly sixty feet over the main channel of the lake connecting two counties.

Skeeter killed the motor a hundred yards away from the structure. "What 'cha wanna do 'bout this here bridge?" he yelled to Rebecca.

"What do you suggest?" she asked Steve.

Steve thought for a moment. "Why don't we raise the balloon as high as we can and still stay connected to the boat, then have him pull us until he reaches the bridge? He releases the line, we soar over and he picks us up when we're safely on the other side. What do you think?"

"It's worth a try."

Steve steadied his voice. "We can't afford to try such a thing unless we're sure we can do it. After all, we're dealing with steel—"

"We can do it. I know we can." After going over the plan with the fisherman, Rebecca turned to Steve. "We're going to have to go pretty high to clear those girders. Will you be okay?"

"Don't worry about me," he assured her, yanking the blower himself, sending the balloon higher than they'd been all morning. His chest pounded and his arm ached.

When the boat slid out of sight behind the mammoth concrete supports, Steve held his breath, squeezed his eyes shut, and puffed air into the envelope. When he opened them again, the bridge was directly under them. He consciously forced himself to exhale. "We're going to make it, Rebecca." He prayed they would, anyway.

Rebecca was hanging over the edge, ready to help guide the rope back to the fisherman, which she did as soon as the balloon passed over the bridge and descended thirty feet or more. They cut it close—too close for Steve's well-being. He'd been on an emotional roller-coaster all night; one more spine-tingling loop-de-loop was the last thing he needed.

Twenty minutes later they were directly in front of the golf course and ready to land, although Steve had been ready for a long time.

"What 'cha want me to do this time?" the fisherman asked after spitting in his can.

"Let's try the same plan as before," Steve suggested. "Only this time we don't need to go up, since we have nothing to clear."

"Can you do that?" Rebecca hollered to the man on the boat.

Skeeter locked his thumbs into his overalls. "Damn right. This boat's got shallow draft, so's I kin drive 'er right up on shore almost."

"Hallelujah!" Steve cried out. "Let 'er rip!" He'd listened to the fisherman so much, he now sounded like him.

Rebecca gave the man the signal then told Steve, "Landing will be simple. We'll get just past the water, then drop the balloon, touch down, and roll out, the way we usually do."

"There hasn't been anything normal about this trip."

"You can say that again. Get ready."

The colorfully striped balloon drifted onto the ninth green, its billowy envelope wavering, then collapsing in slow-motion onto the manicured grass. The basket tipped and Steve rolled out, reaching his hand out to help Rebecca do the same.

"Ya-hoo!" Skeeter screamed from the shore. "Hot damn, we did it!"

"We sure did!" Steve yelled back, stomping the ground.

The man lowered his smaller trolling motor into the lake and started to leave.

"Wait up!" Steve ran to the water's edge. "Let me give you something for your trouble."

"Aw, pshaw! 'Twern't nothing but a neighborly thing to do." With that he was off, grinning widely. "Hot damn. What a morning!"

That's the understatement of the decade, Steve thought. This had been the most wonderful—horrible—morning of his entire life.

Nineteen

Steve felt funny asking Hawk for advice, but he didn't have anyone else to consult. Who better to ask about a gift for Rebecca than her oldest friend in town? Occasionally, Steve had run into Hawk at the grocery store or diner, but other than that he'd only seen him at Rebecca's. As long as Steve had been in Willow Ridge, he hadn't been to the man's home, but then he hadn't invited Hawk to his house either. His excuse was that he was living with Melinda, and with her being pregnant and the boys on an early schedule, he didn't feel free to have guests over.

The truth was, Dolores had always been the one to ask people over—even Steve's friends.

It was time he took control of his own social life and made his own friends. This visit to Hawk's was his first attempt—even if he did have an ulterior motive. Without being too obvious, he had to work the conversation around to asking for gift suggestions. He figured that Hawk was so perceptive, he'd know right away that his help was needed.

When Steve called and asked if they could have a private conversation away from Rebecca, Hawk had told him to "come on over." He jotted down the complicated directions, grabbed his jacket, then drove straight to the reservation. He followed the directions carefully, but still wondered if he had the right house when he pulled into a driveway lined with pecan trees, and spotted a two-story log cabin in the distance. He looked back at the mailbox, whose red block numbers confirmed that he was in the right place.

The house reminded him of Hawk—strong, sturdy, natural. The large logs were real, each one different, with the rough, grainy surfaces weathered and stained a rich brown. The house looked as if it had always been there, almost like it had grown out of the earth. Hawk was like that, too. That was one of the reasons Steve wanted to call the man his friend.

"Hi! I thought that was you." Doug greeted him from the wide planked porch where he sat in a rocking chair wearing a faded denim jacket and jeans, with his boot-clad feet propped on the wide railing. "Come on in! Dad's expecting you."

Seeing Doug's two-toned chocolate brown and bone-colored cowhide boots made Steve's toes hurt. The ones he'd worn to the masquerade ball were a poor substitute for the real McCoy Doug had on—

fancy leather overlays, flame-stitched wingtips and shafts, and two-inch heels.

"Like them?" Doug asked, looking from the goofy smile on Steve's face to his own pointed toes. "Cowboys aren't the only ones who like boots." The young man threw back his head and chuckled.

"Nice place." Although the yard didn't seem landscaped, the native flowers had obviously been hand selected to give it a "natural" look. The impressive collection of shrubs and plants appeared "wild," but being in the business, Steve knew better. A great deal of work had gone into it. "Do you live here with your Dad?"

"I grew up here, but now I have a place of my own. I'm just staying a day or two while it's being painted. This is Dad's pride and joy." The young man dropped his boots to the floor with a thud, stood, and shook Steve's hand. Leaning against a post, he slapped the smooth porch railing. "He built it piece by piece, even split the logs himself. Mom said it took him years to finish."

"It was worth the effort!" Steve stepped onto the porch. He could see the craftsmanship Hawk had put into his home—could feel the son's pride. "He did a great job. I've never seen one built this well, and I've been around a lot of houses, in the landscaping business." Steve recollected that most of them were carbon copies of the rest of the neighborhood. Hawk's place had character . . . personality. It was evident a lot of love had gone into building it.

The door pushed open and Hawk walked out. "Steve! I did not realize you were here. I did not hear you drive up." The dark-haired man grasped Steve's hand. Like father, like son—that same firm, sincere grip. "I trust you had no trouble finding us. Welcome to my home."

"I was telling Doug what a tremendous job you've done in building this place. It's a beauty."

Hawk smiled, his teeth a brilliant white against his dark skin. "Thank you. I like to tell the tourists, we Indians do not all live in tepees anymore." He padded across the porch in his moccasins. His straight black hair flowed from his face to well below his shoulders. Steve had never seen it unbraided before.

Hawk smoothed his hair back, hooking it behind his ears. "I am sorry my wife is not here tonight. She is teaching a reading course at the adult literacy center and will not be home until late. She will be sorry she missed you."

A buzzer sounded inside the house. Doug sprinted to the front door, his boots clomping loudly across the planks. "That's my laundry," he muttered. "A washer and dryer are two conveniences I wish Santa would put on my Christmas list . . . Dad." When he pulled back the screen, Steve saw that the front door was a towering slab of hand-carved oak. The deeply etched images staring back at him resembled the kind Steve had seen on totem poles. He wondered if Hawk was the artist.

Hawk shook his head in a gesture universal to long-suffering fathers. "Doug was out here because he insists on smoking a cigarette after dinner—a habit his mother and I strongly discourage. If he insists on smoking while he is here, we make him do it outside, even when it is cold." Hawk motioned toward the cozy living room Steve had glimpsed through the door. "Why don't we go in and sit by the fire?"

He graciously held the door and let Steve enter first. The room was warm and homey, with braided rugs on the rustic floor and colorful sand paintings on the walls. The furnishings were worn, but comfortable.

Steve took a seat in a honey-colored club chair next to the massive stone fireplace that covered one whole wall of the room from ceiling to floor. Sitting in a soft, plump chair opposite him, Hawk was straight and tall. "Now, friend, what did you want to talk to me about?"

Steve felt a rush of warmth he couldn't blame on the fire. "Well . . . I, uh . . . now that I'm here . . ." Steve stammered. "I feel absurd asking what I came to ask you."

He was Hawk's age, but whenever they were

alone, he felt as though he was a student, and Hawk was a teacher. The man had an uncanny astuteness Steve respected. He could sense it in his eyes, hear it in his voice, even notice it in the way he carried himself, so proud and noble.

Hawk waited with a patient smile, almost imperceptibly nodding his head. "Why not let me decide that? My people do not believe that any question is unworthy of being asked."

Steve sighed. "Okay. I need help finding a Christmas gift for Rebecca. Since you've known her forever, I thought maybe you could help me think of something."

It was a relief to verbalize it, but the relief was short-lived. Hawk's response wasn't very helpful—no questions, no suggestions, only a simple comment: "A gift." Steve couldn't tell whether Hawk was pondering the problem or waiting for him to say something else.

Steve waited while Hawk stabbed the fire with a wrought-iron poker, sending sparks flying into the air. When the flames shot up, so did Steve's frustration over Hawk's silence. After a long, awkward pause, he mumbled, "I shouldn't have bothered you with this."

Hawk sat on the edge of his chair. "It is no bother, though my wife will tell you I am not the best source for gifts."

"Rebecca already has everything I've thought of,

and if she doesn't, it's because she doesn't want it." Steve leaned forward, warming his hands by the flickering fire.

"How can I help?"

"You two talk. You're around each other all the time." Steve rubbed his hands together. "Can't you give me any hints about what she might like? Maybe something has come up in a conversation." The gleaming firelight cast dancing shadows across Hawk's already darkened face.

"No." Although the man's voice was composed, his eyes grew wider, openly amused at Steve's dilemma. "She does not talk about these things with me. Perhaps you should approach this differently."

"How? I'm open to suggestions."

"Think, my friend. What does she like? That is always a good place to start. Think about the person for whom you are choosing this gift. Think about Rebecca."

"That's simple." Shooting off the list *was* easy. "She likes hot-air balloons, swimming, fighting fires, reading, and . . . plenty of Welsh Corgis to play with."

"Umm." Hawk's expression was thoughtful. "I see your point. She either owns it, does it, or has access to it."

"Access to what, Dad?" Doug walked in from the laundry room and sat down on the large, gray flagstone hearth. When Hawk didn't answer, the young man asked, "Mind if I join you? If this is private, I'll leave."

Steve was uncomfortable about including Doug in the conversation, but he couldn't hurt Hawk's feelings by excluding his son. He swallowed his embarrassment and nodded okay. "We're talking about Christmas presents."

"My favorite topic." The young man shucked his denim jacket. "Buying or receiving?"

Steve laughed. Doug was a lot like his father—direct and to the point. "Buying. For Rebecca. Got any suggestions?" Might as well enlist all the help he could.

Doug stretched his long legs out in front of him. "What have you come up with so far?"

"The usual. You know, perfume—"

Doug shook his head. "Too common."

Steve tried again. "A leather briefcase or one of those fancy pens . . ."

"But she's not in the corporate world anymore," Hawk pointed out.

"Books . . . ?" Steve asked.

Doug made a face. "Too brotherly."

"What do you suggest?" Steve threw up his hands. "What else is there?"

He knew better than to buy a household appliance. He'd made that mistake with Dolores . . . and paid the price by eating leftovers for a month. When he was younger, jewelry had been the gift of choice. At this stage of her life, Rebecca probably had all the jewelry she could possibly wear. Besides, she never wore anything but a watch unless it was a special occasion. She'd never shown much interest in fancy adornments.

Besides, the only jewelry he wanted to buy for Rebecca would fit on the third finger of her left hand. And that would come later . . . he hoped.

The young man leaned forward with his elbows on his knees. "Lingerie?"

"Doug!" Hawk's voice reverberated in Steve's ears. "You are talking about Rebecca."

The sexy image of Rebecca in the silky blue pajamas she'd had on when he dropped in unexpectedly popped into Steve's mind.

"Dad, not every woman sleeps in flannel like Mom. Some women like frilly, sexy nighties . . ." He grinned and winked at his father. "Not that I'd know."

"Of course not." Hawk gave his son a stoic look. "I do not think that is what Steve had in mind."

Actually it *was* something Steve had in mind, but not what he wanted to give her for Christmas. He was afraid that lingerie would convey the wrong impression, would make her think there was only one thing he wanted . . . and that couldn't be farther from the truth. Oh, he *wanted* her, all right— perhaps more than he'd ever wanted a women in his life. But somehow his first gift to her had to be more than about sex. "No . . . I need something extra special . . ."

Doug's smile turned to a chuckle. "More special than lingerie?"

With a wave of his hand, his father surmised, "It's obvious what *your* girlfriend is getting for Christmas!"

Steve tried again. "I'm looking for something . . ." he searched for the right word.

"Romantic?" suggested Doug.

"Yeah," Steve readily agreed. "Romantic."

"Why didn't you say so? I've got just the thing for you." Doug disappeared into his old room and returned with an advertisement torn out of a magazine. He handed it to Steve who read it once, then a second time, to be sure he was reading it correctly.

The idea was intriguing, but Steve had a few doubts. "Is this for real? Legal? Legitimate?" He shot off his questions without giving Doug a chance to answer.

Doug seemed very pleased with himself. "All of the above. The Better Business Bureau gave them a glowing recommendation."

"What do you think?" Steve gave Hawk the advertisement and waited for him to read it. "Will this do the trick?"

Before Hawk could answer, Doug lunged in on his own. "Of course it will! It's so sappy, it will appeal to her romantic side . . . it's high-brow, so it'll appeal to her intellectual side . . . and it's so off the wall, she'd never expect it. What more could you ask for?"

Hawk handed the ad back to Steve. "I agree with you, son. Steve, this is it."

With Hawk's endorsement, Steve knew he had found the perfect gift for the love of his life. When he got through with it, even Doug would be impressed. Steve's mother had always told him the wrapping was as important as the gift . . . the presentation as important as the meal. His mind raced ahead to all he had to do before he could make it happen. It might not be the most expensive gift Rebecca had ever received, but he was sure it would be the most unique.

Swimming laps in her heated pool, Rebecca realized she had put off her Christmas shopping until it was almost too late. She'd racked her brain for the ultimate gifts for Steve and his family since Thanksgiving, only to come up empty-handed. This was the first year she'd had anyone to buy for besides token business acquaintances—and Hawk, of course.

After years of struggling with finding presents for Hawk and his family, she'd realized that what really made her old friend happy was to do something for the Indian Reservation. Last Christmas, she'd donated handicapped ramps for the cultural center on the reservation. This year, she planned to buy a computer for the adult literacy program—a pet project of Hawk's wife, Rose.

Jake and Jeremy were easy to please. Being around them when they were playing, she'd learned their gifts had to meet two criteria: they had to be indestructible, and make a lot of noise. She could always add a couple of sweaters to please Melinda and sneak in a book or two to please herself.

Rebecca took a deep breath and ducked under the warm water. She opened her eyes as she propelled herself across the pool, blinking at the brightness of the globe lighting the bottom. At the far wall, she burst through the water, gasping for air.

"Well, well, well . . ." a loud, masculine voice floated across the garden. It was a voice she'd grown to love as much as the man to whom it belonged.

She whirled around to find Steve standing by the patio table, his face washed in the light streaming through the French doors from her bedroom. He was holding one of Casey's puppies, scratching him behind the ears. With long strokes, she met him at the edge of the pool. The coldness of the night kept her under the warm water, wrapped in the mist rising from the surface.

"Some watchdog, huh? What brings you here this time of the night?"

"He's my buddy," Steve said, proving it by letting the puppy lick his hand. "I had a very good reason to be out this late . . . I wanted to see you. But I had to wait until Melinda got home . . . then until the boys were asleep. When Joey finally came over, I saw my chance to escape and took it." Steve looked good in a charcoal cable-knit sweater that brought out the silvery highlights in his hair.

Rebecca shivered from the brisk breeze that made its way over the hedge. "Is Melinda still working?"

"She's cutting back on her hours at the insurance office, but she felt she had to do all she could before the baby came. You know Melinda."

Did she know Melinda? She had *been* Melinda in another lifetime. What kind of mother would she have been if she'd had three children to care for?

Rebecca dipped under the water to wet her head for warmth. When she came back up, she kicked her legs to keep her circulation going. The air was too cold to get out of the pool. She didn't want to push Steve to go inside, so she made do where she was. "You mentioned Joey. He's spending a lot of time with Melinda these days. Is that going well?"

Steve put the puppy down and squatted next to

the pool's edge, his long, lean legs and strong thighs within easy reach. "It's anybody's guess. Melinda wants him back, but she's too stubborn to admit it yet. The poor man's around so much . . . he's there for Melinda, he's there for the boys, he's even eating breakfast and dinner with us. About the only thing he isn't doing is sleeping at home."

"Hopefully that will remedy itself soon." Rebecca moved back to keep from splashing Steve.

"Hopefully!" The enthusiasm fairly oozed from his voice. "I can't wait!"

"Won't that make it awfully crowded for you?"

"Crowded! I'm crowded already." His dark eyes gleamed when he glanced her way. If Joey moves back in, I'll finally have a chance to get a place of my own."

Rebecca stopped kicking. "That's an interesting prospect . . ." She wondered how he would feel about moving in with her. As quickly as the thought entered her head, she dismissed it. It would never work, not with Melinda and the boys so close. Even if he wanted to . . . it wouldn't be proper in Willow Ridge.

Too bad.

Not paying attention to what she was doing, she caught a mouthful of water as she slipped under the surface.

Steve waited until she stopped coughing before he answered, "Interesting indeed."

She swam to the steps a few feet from Steve and sat down chest-deep in water. The thought of having him here without chaperons or listening ears was almost more excitement than she could bear. "It's never crowded here, so when you need to get away, come on over," she offered. "The invitation is always open."

Steve's smile was a warm invitation in itself. "Thanks. I know you mean that."

She kicked off the wall and swam about halfway to the end. "How about joining me for a swim?"

He shook his head. "Not tonight. I've got to get back." The puppy rolled over and Steve obliged his eager look by rubbing his stomach. "Santa needs my help later."

It seemed that someone was always needing him. Rebecca couldn't wait until he had some time to call his own. "Is Joey putting toys together for the kids?"

Steve splashed a handful of water her way and grinned, scaring the puppy off in the process. "The kids aren't the only ones Santa will be visiting next week. What makes you think I'm not playing elf for your surprise?"

She laughed to hide her embarrassment. "Because you know I don't like surprises."

Steve stood and folded his arms across his broad chest. "How do you know you don't like surprises? Have you ever had one?"

"I've never had a good one, but the bad ones were abundant."

"So . . . let's change your 'surprise' streak. It wouldn't be Christmas if you knew what your present was, now would it?"

Presents. There was that word again, the one that had been dogging her for weeks. From the smug look on his face, he'd come up with a gift for her. Why hadn't she been able to do the same for him? She knew him so well—knew his likes and dislikes. Men were so hard to buy for, not like women. She loved everything. No wonder he'd had no trouble.

"Mind if I get out?" She stifled a yawn. "Sorry. I had two emergencies tonight, plus a full schedule of hot-air balloon rides. I'm exhausted."

Steve had looked forward to her getting out ever since he'd arrived. The thought of seeing Rebecca in next to nothing made him long for the day they'd gone skinny-dipping in the cave. The image of her luscious breasts and curvaceous figure had haunted him ever since.

Steve nodded before picking up a burgundy towel draped on the patio table. "I always welcome the chance to see a beautiful lady in a swimsuit." He unfolded the oversized towel and held it out for her.

He'd wanted to make love then and there in the cave, but the snake had made that impossible—for both of them. Later, he'd decided to wait until the timing was right, until he was sure it was what Rebecca wanted. After they'd professed their love for each other above the lake, the near-accident had managed to thwart the mood again. Since then, he'd been busy, she'd been busy, and the right mix of mood and magic hadn't materialized. He wanted their first time to be exceptional . . . and if that meant waiting a few days, then so be it. He'd wait. But it wasn't because he didn't want her.

Rebecca climbed the steps and rushed to Steve. He wrapped the towel and his arms around her, hugging her close.

"Watch it or you'll get wet," she warned, her body dripping with water.

It felt so good being close to her again, Steve didn't care if he got soaked. "It's worth it." He pulled her into his embrace and felt a brief shiver ripple through her. "You must be cold."

"A little." She pulled a few inches away and dabbed her face. "I'd better dry off."

He reluctantly let her go. Unwrapping her as though she were a precious gift, Steve began to blot the water from her arms, shoulders, and back. "Allow me." When he finished with her upper torso, he bent down and dried one leg at a time, from her silky thigh to her delicate foot . . . in a slow, luxurious massage. Satisfied she was dry, he threw the towel aside, lifted her thick velour robe, and held it for her to slip into.

"Thank you," she murmured, pulling the sash together in a bow.

He gathered her snugly into his arms and whispered, "My pleasure." He kissed the curve of her neck, afraid to give in to the mounting urge he had to devour her lips for fear he wouldn't be able to stop.

Not tonight, he told himself. It was late and Rebecca was obviously tired. There would be other nights . . . many other nights . . . he could be patient a little longer.

He draped his arm around her shoulders. "Walk me to my car?"

A look of disappointment crossed her face. "Sure."

Steve saw the look. "Sweetheart . . . we have a lifetime ahead of us . . . you need your rest tonight." He cupped her chin and tenderly kissed her lips, holding back the hunger he felt.

Rebecca snuggled into the curve of his arm. "We'd better get you home."

Together they walked through the hedge. "I'll call you tomorrow," he told her. "I've got to get up early because I've got some last-minute Christmas errands that won't wait any longer."

"Me, too." Rebecca opened his car door, then closed it after he got in. She bent down to the window as he rolled it down. "I'm having trouble finding a gift for Melinda. Any suggestions? Does she need something for the baby? . . . the house? . . . herself?"

Steve thought for a moment. "Why don't you ride to Atlanta with me in the morning? We can put our heads together and come up with something." He lightly kissed her cheek. "I'm at a loss, too, and I see her every day."

"That's a deal!" Rebecca leaned over and smothered his lips with hers. Her demanding mouth caressed his with a lingering kiss. "Tomorrow," she promised, disappearing into the house.

"Tomorrow." As he drove away, he was already counting the hours.

Rebecca was dressed early, eager to see Steve. Last night, she'd wanted him to stay over with all her heart. She'd been disappointed when he decided to leave. His reasoning was sweet, but he couldn't imagine how wrong he was—sleep, she could do without. Steve, she no longer could.

She looked in the hall mirror, smoothed her lace jabot, and tightened the leather belt around her slim-skirted plaid jumper. It had finally cooled off enough to take out her fall wardrobe.

Steve picked her up and they ate breakfast on the way to Atlanta. Even though the city was packed and traffic was terrible, they managed to run through their list of things to do faster than they'd expected.

Back in the car, Steve asked, "Could we make one more stop? I need a few things out of storage. Do you mind?"

"Of course not. We've got a few inches left in the trunk, and the backseat is completely empty."

Fifteen minutes later, they parked and went into a self-serve storage facility. Rebecca eagerly waited for Steve to open the lock and flip on the light. "I love to rummage through old attics, and this is sort of like that. It will be fun!"

After he shoved wide the door, he gave a disclaimer. "Dolores never threw anything out, so there's early college to early retirement in here."

"That's great. I'll get to see what your taste is really like." The room was filled with a mishmash of dusty boxes and old furniture.

"You're forewarned." Steve walked over to a towering stack of boxes. "Feel free to rummage around while I find those records I need and my winter coat." He dropped one of the boxes on the floor. "I'm sure I packed it away in here somewhere." Squatting down, he poked through the files.

"You know," Rebecca confessed, "most of my prize possessions are recycled from the flea market."

"The flea market?" His dark brows narrowed suspiciously. "You don't look the type."

"The type for what?" She picked up a Tiffany-style lamp and blew a layer of dust off the jewel-colored shade. "Pretty."

"Um, yes." He dismissed it with a glance. "You don't look the type to buy old junk and restore it."

She wedged herself between two chintz chairs. "I'm an old pro at refinishing. That's why my house is packed with furniture. I've enjoyed doing it so much, I've run out of space to put any more."

"Ah, here are the records." Steve set them down on a table, then moved to several plastic clothing bags hanging on a makeshift rail. He unzipped the first one, then rifled through the clothes. "Now where did I leave that coat?"

Rebecca made herself comfortable amid the tables and sofas and boxes all crammed into the tiny storage room. Inspecting nothing that wasn't sitting out, she was careful not to pry into anything that looked personal. Steve was right—it was certainly an eclectic collection. She couldn't get a feel for the "real" Steve, since nothing fit a pattern. Nothing looked like *him,* except maybe the handsome walnut-finished mantel clock with a solid brass bezel and Roman numerals, or the elegant set of framed floral botanical prints.

"Come here," Steve called from a corner. "Look what I've found."

Rebecca dodged an ottoman and a glass curio cabinet and made her way to where he was standing. "What a lovely old piece!" she cried, looking at Steve's find. Wedged into the corner was a handcrafted, slat-backed, hardwood rocker, with what once had been a cane seat.

"This old rocker belonged to my great-grandmother, who gave it to my grandmother, who passed it down to my mother and on to me. I rocked Melinda in this old chair." Fingering the natural-colored rush in the deteriorated seat, his face beamed.

"What a precious heirloom."

"Yeah. Too bad it's gotten in such lousy shape. I don't know what ever possessed me to paint it green." He ran his finger along the carved rose design on one of the dark green slats.

"You should strip it down to the natural wood for Melinda. With the baby coming, she's going to need a rocking chair handy. It wouldn't take more than a few hours to refinish it. Now, *that* would make a perfect Christmas gift." Rebecca put her hand on his shoulder. "See, your gift problem is solved."

"Not really." He blushed. "I'm not very good at that sort of thing. I'd start and wish I hadn't, then never finish."

"What an attitude!" It was such a sweet idea, Rebecca couldn't let him say no without at least trying. She knew Melinda would love having a family heirloom. "I'll tell you what . . . I'll help you . . . We could do it in the barn this afternoon. How about it?"

"I can't ask you to do that."

"You're not. I volunteered." She threatened him with a smile.

Steve sat down on the edge of the broken seat, balancing his elbows on his knees, testing the rocker's strength. "You really think Melinda would like it?"

"She's going to love it. Guaranteed."

"Rebecca, you're a genius." Ignoring the precarious seat, Steve pulled her into his lap and kissed her with an urgency she returned. Parting her lips, she moved toward him, feeling the familiar breath of passion. In an instant, the last woven shred of the seat ripped away, and they both fell downward.

Surprised, Rebecca clasped her arms around his neck as they landed, then burst out laughing with Steve at the ridiculous sight they made. "Are you hurt?" she asked, between laughs.

"My feelings, maybe." He struggled to gain his composure.

"Feelings heal fast." With great effort, Rebecca used the rocker's arms to lift herself out, with Steve pushing from below. On her feet, she straightened her jabot and offered Steve a hand.

He grabbed on and heaved himself up. "Do chairs heal fast, too?"

"Those take a little longer and a lot more elbow grease."

"Too bad." He swept her in his arms and kissed her one more time. "I had something else in mind for the evening."

Twenty

Rebecca felt as impatient as a six-year-old on Christmas Eve waiting for Santa to come down the chimney. Only it was Christmas Eve morning, and Santa Steve was coming to a lumberjack breakfast of flapjacks and blueberry syrup, plus bacon and a freshly brewed pot of coffee.

Glancing at her watch, she saw it was a little past six. Good. She was right on time. She wanted to meet early so they could enjoy their breakfast. Steve readily agreed, because he wanted to sneak the rocker into his room before Melinda woke up.

In honor of the holiday, she'd treated herself to a new outfit—casual, yet classic . . . stylish, yet comfortable. Looking in the mirror for the third time to check her make-up and hair, she was pleased with her overall appearance. She didn't generally make this big a deal out of her looks, but today was different. She wanted to look especially good for Steve.

The doorbell rang and she flew to open the door before the chime finished sounding. "Steve!" Rebecca's knees weakened at the very sight of him, and she smiled to cover her sudden flush. "Come in."

With a lopsided grin, he tugged a sprig of mistletoe out of his pocket and held it over his head. Lips puckered and eyes closed, he stood in her doorway demanding a kiss. When she hesitated, he peeked with one eye and asked, "What are you waiting for? Don't you know this is a tradition?"

Her pulse skittered as she stepped up, tiptoed to reach him, and briefly kissed his waiting mouth.

His eyes popped open before he shoved the mistletoe back into his jacket. "I'll keep this for emergencies."

She smiled. "I think you're supposed to hang that over the doorway."

"I prefer to keep it with me." He chuckled. "This way I can request a kiss any time, any place."

"I approve as long as you don't use it on just *anybody*."

Steve's hands glided down her arms to her hands. "The only body I'm interested in is yours." He cocked his head and grinned. "You look terrific! Is that new?"

With one hand, he twirled her around as she modeled her crimson red cardigan with shawl collar and roll sleeves. She flipped the end of the long collar around her neck, letting it fall across her back with the fringe dangling. "I'm glad you approve, dah-ling."

When they got to the kitchen, the radio was blaring the news. "Mind if I turn that off?" he asked, reaching for the dial.

"If it's okay with you, let's leave it on for a few more minutes." She placed a container of warm syrup by his place mat. "I heard earlier that there's a forest fire in a state park not too far from here and I want to hear an update on it."

Steve frowned. "Won't the State Forestry Service handle it?"

He held out her chair and waited for her to sit down. "Yes, if they can." She didn't want to spoil the day debating her firefighting responsibilities. "They won't start calling other stations for help unless the fire spreads."

His frown deepened. "Has that ever happened? Have they ever called?"

Not wanting to alarm him, she hedged her answer. "Not recently." Unfortunately, with fires of this magnitude, she knew the possibility of arson was better than good.

Just as they started to devour their breakfast, an update came on. When the regular programming resumed, Rebecca switched off the radio. "Nothing new."

Steve prodded his stack of thin, fluffy flapjacks. "What's got you so worried? Do you think you'll be called to help?" He cut into the syrup-covered layers and took a bite.

"It's hard to tell . . . can't hazard a guess." She chewed and swallowed before confessing. "What I'm most worried about is the Indian Reservation— that's where Hawk and Doug live."

"Is the Reservation in danger?"

"I don't know. In this situation anything within a fifty-mile radius could be in danger. One good blast of wind, one impulsive idiot, and the whole fire could escalate to massive proportions."

After a second cup of coffee, Rebecca regretfully suggested, "We'd better go if we want to get the rocker into your room before Melinda wakes up."

It took Steve a minute to load the finished rocker into the back of her Jeep. Rebecca covered their prized project with a blanket to protect the smooth, shiny finish. Running her finger across the new, sturdy cane seat, she smiled, remembering the in-cident with Steve in the storage room. "Ready." She slammed the Jeep's back door shut, then climbed in the driver's seat.

On the ride to Melinda's, Steve held her hand. Even in the dazzling morning light, the mere touch of his hand made her ache for more. She switched on the Jeep's compact disc player and they sang Christmas carols until she pulled up and parked behind the house.

"You wait here while I go in and see if the coast

is clear." Steve bounded up the steps two at a time and entered the kitchen door.

When he came back out, he propped the screen open. "No sign of Melinda, and her bedroom door is shut."

The Jeep's door squeaked when she lifted it up. Rebecca clenched her teeth and closed her eyes shut, making a face at the noise. Neither of them moved as she listened for evidence that Melinda might have heard them. Convinced she was still asleep, they gingerly lowered the rocker, walked up the steps, then sat it on the linoleum floor.

"The hall's too narrow for both of us and the rocker." Steve spoke in a low voice. "I'll manage it by myself. You follow, okay?"

She nodded and crossed her fingers in response. Although she'd walked by Steve's bedroom a few times on the way to the bathroom, Rebecca had never been inside it. The image of him stretched out on crisp white sheets sent a delicious shudder of heat through her body.

As they tiptoed past Melinda's door, she blushed at her less-than-innocent thoughts about the woman's father.

In his bedroom, Steve placed the meticulously finished rocker in the corner.

"What if someone comes in and sees it?" Rebecca whispered. "How are you going to hide it?"

"Easy. I'll cover it and leave the closet door open

to block the rocker from view." He stretched to the top closet shelf for a blanket.

Rebecca's feet froze in place as she heard a noise in the room next door—Melinda was awake.

His daughter's frantic voice echoed down the hall. "Dad! You there?" The voice got louder. "Dad, I just heard the worst news."

Both of them pivoted to see Melinda standing in front of them wearing a long, cotton nightgown and a flabbergasted stare. Rebecca's face grew warm. She knew what Melinda must be thinking. If it had been anyone else in this situation, it might have been funny.

Wide-eyed and speechless, Steve shoved the closet door ajar to impede his daughter's view of the rocker.

Melinda couldn't have looked more shocked if she'd caught her father sneaking out of an all-girl dormitory with a handful of panties. "What's going on here?" She glared at them both.

Steve's face matched the color of Rebecca's holiday sweater. "Uh, Rebecca was helping me with a . . . uh . . . Christmas present."

"I'll bet!" Melinda snapped.

"Melinda," Steve warned. "Don't say anything you'll later regret."

Rebecca felt embarrassed and more than a little amused. Watching Steve wiggle out of this mess was going to be fun. He held a blanket in one arm, and leaned the other on the door, doing his level best to divert Melinda's attention and conceal her gift.

Surprising Rebecca, Melinda dropped the issue. "I don't have time for this now. We've got bigger concerns. Joey took the boys camping . . ." her voice cracked with emotion.

"Oh, Melinda," Steve scolded. "I know that. He'll be back in time for Christmas Eve dinner."

"You don't understand . . . he might not be able to . . ." On the brink of tears, she walked to the foot of the bed and lowered herself onto it.

Steve flashed Rebecca a playful, pleading look. "What are you saying?"

Melinda sniffled. "They're camping in the park that's on . . . fire."

He recognized the seriousness of what she was saying. "The forest fire?" When she nodded, Steve strode across the room and gathered his daughter in his arms.

Rebecca's beeper blasted through the room. Reaching for her belt, she clicked off the noise and unclipped it to read the numbers. The station house. A wave of uneasiness told her it was a call about the forest fire. "May I borrow your phone?"

Steve pointed to an extension next to his bed. "Sure. Go ahead."

Punching in the numbers, Rebecca waited for someone to answer. "Mitch, I got your message.

What's the emergency?" She turned so that her back was to the others. If the news involved the fire, she didn't want to upset Melinda. The tension knotted in her neck as she listened to Mitch.

Melinda stood, stretched her back, and glanced around the room. Before Steve could stop her, she walked straight toward the corner. "Isn't that Mom's old rocker?" Tears brimmed in her eyes as she rubbed the satiny finish Steve and Rebecca had worked so hard to achieve. "No. It couldn't be. That old thing was painted a hideous color and falling apart. I thought you'd thrown it away."

So much for the surprise. Momentarily, Melinda's attention was off the fire. Rebecca was relieved to have a chance to ask Mitch a few questions without an audience.

With long, even steps, Steve walked to his daughter's side. "It *is* your mom's old rocker . . . fixed up as good as new." His face broke into a grin. "It was supposed to be a surprise."

"I'm surprised, all right." Melinda traced the intricate roses on the back slats with her finger.

"Merry Christmas, honey."

Her eyes brightened with pleasure. "Oh, Dad! It's beautiful!"

Steve hugged his daughter. "I'm glad you like it."

Rebecca swiveled toward the bed so she could see what they were doing and still manage to keep her conversation confidential. In Melinda's condition, the less she knew about the fire, the better. Rebecca tried to listen to both conversations, but instead had to focus on what Mitch was telling her over the phone. "I understand. Check it out and call me back here at Melinda's as soon as you know."

When Rebecca placed the receiver in its cradle, she didn't know whether to leave the room or stay put. Being here in Steve's bedroom was awkward enough; being here with Melinda was worse.

"Why don't you try it out?" Steve was saying to Melinda.

"I'd love to." She sat down on the now-sturdy seat and rested her arms on the chair's smoothly oiled arms. She pushed with one foot, and the rocker gently moved back and forth. "Dad! This is so sweet of you." Melinda flashed her father a trembling smile of thanks.

"I can't take credit. It was all Rebecca's idea." With a broad gesture, he motioned for Rebecca to join them. When she did, he offered her his hand. Steve's fingers were warm and strong as he grasped hers. "I was only the helper. She did most of the work."

"Rebecca?" Melinda asked, astonishment written on her face. "Why?" she blurted out.

"Is that so hard to figure out?" The frown on Steve's face was becoming permanently etched there. "You're going to need a rocker . . . and she thought it would be nice to have this old one of your mother's to share with the new baby. I think it was very thoughtful. I wish I'd thought of it myself."

Rebecca wasn't sure what to say, so she didn't say anything. She smiled and nodded and squeezed Steve's hand, but avoided eye contact with Melinda until she knew better what her reaction was. The woman seemed genuinely affected by their gesture, yet Rebecca knew not to take anything for granted where Melinda was concerned. She could be happy about the gift, yet still be *un*happy about Rebecca's involvement.

Steve was more persistent. "Don't you have anything to say to Rebecca?"

Melinda stopped the chair from rocking, and spoke very quietly. "I don't know what to say. This is one of the most thoughtful things anyone has ever done for me." She struggled to her feet and looked intently at Rebecca. "Thank you. It means the world to me to have my mom's rocker for the new baby . . . I'll cherish it always."

Rebecca fought hard against the tears threatening to spill out. She wanted to take Melinda in her arms and hug her the way Steve had done earlier, but she didn't. Instead, she simply said, "I'm glad you like it."

Rebecca hadn't planned to take credit for the idea

or the work. Her only hope was that Melinda would like it and let it go at that. For her to truly appreciate it was more than she'd dared to hope.

Although Melinda had started to accept Rebecca in her father's life, she'd still made it known that Rebecca was an outsider, not part of the family. And Rebecca got that message loud and clear, particularly when they were physically in Melinda's home.

The jingle of the phone caused Rebecca to jump. Her breath caught in her throat as she waited for Steve to answer it and hand the receiver to her.

"It's Mitch."

Aware that both Steve and Melinda were listening, she was careful not to give away too much. "Yes?" She tried to put on a smile as she listened in silence to Mitch saying what she'd suspected all along. Joey had signed in at the National Park campground where the forest fire was located. He hadn't signed out. Melinda's instincts were right. Her family was in danger.

Rebecca hesitated, unsure how much she should tell Melinda. How would such news affect her unborn child? Yet, she didn't have the right to keep the information from her.

"I'll leave right away. Be there as soon as possible."

"It's Joey and the boys, isn't it?" Melinda grabbed her father's arm. The concern in her voice escalated into fear. "Are they okay?"

"Why don't you sit down?" Steve tried to usher her to the bed.

She shook loose from her father's grip, her eyes locked to Rebecca's. "No! Not until you tell me what you've found out."

"As far as we know, they're fine." Rebecca walked over, took Melinda's arm, and led her to the bed. This time she didn't protest.

"What exactly does that mean?" Steve asked.

Rebecca faced Melinda. "You were right. Joey did camp in the park that has the forest fire in it."

Melinda bolted upright. "Oh, Lord! What's happened?"

"Nothing, so far. We know for a fact that Joey and the boys signed in a couple of days ago. According to their reservation, they were supposed to leave today, but there's no record of their departure. Since you haven't heard from them, we have to assume that they are still there."

Steve rubbed Melinda's shoulders. "Joey's smart enough to get out with a forest fire in the area."

Rebecca hated being the bearer of unwanted news. "Joey might not know about the fire."

Steve crooked his head, his eyes full of concern. "How can that be?"

"The park is huge," Rebecca explained. "Depending on where he camped, he might not have heard or seen anything."

Melinda seemed hopeful. "So he may be on his way home?"

Rebecca hesitated, but knew she had to go on. "No. They've sealed the roads, so if Joey had tried to get through, the park officials would know it."

"What do we do now? We can't just sit back and wait." Melinda was nearly hysterical. "I've got to go find them."

Steve put his arm around Melinda. "Calm down, honey. You're in no condition to go charging into a situation like this. Leave it to Rebecca and me."

"Why doesn't somebody do something?" Melinda cried. "Can't they send a helicopter out to search for them?"

Rebecca lowered her eyes. "All the available helicopters are busy."

"Too busy to rescue two little boys and their father?" Melinda yelled angrily.

"Several churches were having a joint Christmas Eve service on one side of the park . . . a second fire was started near there and now those folks are having to be airlifted out." How could she explain to a mother how her own children weren't high priority on the rescue list? Rebecca shook her head. "With such a big crowd and a limited number of helicopters, they can't spare one to search the entire park for only three people."

"Started?" Steve asked. "You mean an arsonist did this?"

Rebecca was shocked by the hostility in his voice. "I'm afraid so."

"Those *three people* are my *family.* Do something!" Melinda demanded. "Can't you pull some strings? You're a firefighter, after all."

"We just got the alarm. Willow Ridge is the fourth alarm, so three other stations are already out there. Mitch is getting the volunteers and supplies together now." Rebecca squeezed Melinda's hand. "I'm sorry. I've got to go."

"No!" Her face desperate, Melinda hung on to Rebecca's hand. "You've got to do something to get them out. You're a pilot, fly in there and find them. If not for me, do it for Dad."

"Melinda, she can't take a hot-air balloon into the middle of a fire."

"What about a plane? You can fly those, too, can't you?" Melinda clasped Rebecca's hand in an iron grip. "Please. I'm begging you . . . rescue my family." Her voice cracked. "If you don't, nobody else will."

Rebecca turned away from Melinda's pain-filled eyes. What should she do? "I'd need access to an airplane."

Relief flooded Melinda's face, but Steve's took on a look of incredulity.

"Are you serious?" He stormed around the bed to face her. "You're a volunteer, damn it, not trained to fight forest fires."

"We're the best they've got right now." Rebecca was tired, and she hadn't even started. "I've got to go."

"It's bad enough my grandsons are in danger . . . but not you, too . . . please don't go."

There had to be a solution. Steve was *her* family now and that made his daughter part of that family, too. Melinda had asked for her help. Rebecca racked her brain for a way to give it to her. "Let me check something out." She made a call, then another. "I've found a plane . . . and Mitch is working on getting the go-ahead from the Forestry Service. If they clear it, I'll help you."

The fear and pain wasn't erased from her eyes, but a glimmer of hope was added as Melinda fell back against the pillows.

Steve strode across the room and grasped Rebecca's shoulders. "If you're determined to do this, then I'm going with you."

"No, you're not." Rebecca shook her head. "That's final." As much as she wanted him with her, she had no way of knowing how his fear of heights would affect the rescue. Flying in a small aircraft was noisy and jolting and different from anything Steve had ever done. But she didn't have time to argue now. "If I'm going to fly, I've got to get into the air before the fire spreads and the visibility worsens."

Steve dropped his hold on Rebecca. He walked

over to his daughter, bent down, and kissed her forehead. "I promise I'll do my best to find them."

"I'm counting on you, Dad. I'm counting on you both."

Rebecca and Steve made a brief stop at the fire station, then headed straight for the airplane located on a farm a few miles out of town. "Whose plane is it, anyway?" Steve asked.

"It belongs to Lyle Lovett—a crop duster and pilot extraordinaire."

"A crop duster?" he cried. "What kind of plane does a crop duster fly?"

She knew he was worried about his fear of flying. The last time they'd flown in the hot-air balloon, they'd almost ended up in the freezing lake. "It's an old Cessna Skylark—a single-engine four-seater with plenty of horsepower."

"Old? How old is old?"

She thought about it a minute. "I think it's a '59 or '60 . . . that isn't terribly old in airplane years."

"That's over thirty years old!"

"Don't worry," she assured him. "Lyle's a great mechanic."

"Maybe *Lyle* ought to fly it for us."

"Lyle's out of town."

"Are we stealing his plane?" Steve gave a short,

little laugh. At least he hadn't lost his sense of humor.

"I'm *borrowing* it. His wife gave me permission and told me where everything was. Lyle's pretty generous when it comes to his plane." She turned into the lane leading to the barn and the plane. "Here we are."

"I don't see the landing strip. Is it out back of the barn?"

This was another one of those questions she hated to answer. "Sort of."

"Sort of, how?"

"It's out back all right. Lyle takes off in the pasture."

Steve's reaction was priceless. "You are kidding, aren't you?"

She flashed him a smile. "Would I kid at a time like this?"

Twenty-one

Steve was glad he had tagged along instead of waiting for Rebecca back at the station house. He couldn't just sit on his hands and be patient. Patience was not one of his virtues, particularly where his grandchildren's safety was concerned. He *had* to do something. If Rebecca was going to go through with this impulsive rescue, then he was going to be right there with her. After all, *his* grandsons were in danger.

People had depended on him all his life, but this time he was going to have to depend on Rebecca. He couldn't shake the nagging thought that they didn't know exactly where Joey's camp was located.

He followed Rebecca quickly across the grassy runway toward the plane. "What can I do?" His thoughts were plagued by a dozen things that could go wrong.

Her tone was sharp. "Nothing."

Obviously Rebecca didn't want him there. She was trying to do it by herself—the way she did most everything else in her life. One of the hardest things for her to do was to take help—even from him. This time she didn't have a choice. Though the idea of flying over a forest fire petrified Steve, he wasn't taking no for an answer.

"I appreciate your offer, but I can check faster than I can tell you how." Rebecca opened the cabin door of Lyle's Cessna Skylark, talking herself through the walk-around inspection. From the way her hands slightly trembled, she was nervous, too. "Battery switch. Off. Ignition switch. Off. Control-wheel lock. Off."

At first, Steve believed she was doing that for his benefit—just as she had in the hot-air balloon. Old fears and uncertainties about flying resurfaced as he thought about going up in this grungy-looking airplane that didn't appear capable of getting two feet off the ground. Studying her at work, he realized Rebecca was so engrossed in her tasks that she'd forgotten he was there.

Maybe she didn't want his assistance—but he wanted to make damn sure she understood that he was in this with her one-hundred percent. The very lives of his family were at stake. No matter how unhappy he was about flying in this godforsaken plane, he would do it. Loudly, he cleared his throat.

Rebecca looked up and gave him a diluted smile. "My flight trainer's motto was 'safety first.' This will only take about ten minutes." Her mouth was tightened in grim concentration as she returned to her inspection.

Ten minutes felt like ten years. He had to be productive. He opened the cabin door on the pilot's side, and stuck his head in. "What a mess!" He picked up a discarded fast-food box from under the seat and gritted his disapproval. "You can't be serious about taking this disaster up!"

"I certainly am! It's the only airplane for fifty miles. Those campers need me."

Campers! Those campers were his family. In a futile attempt to push the worry back, he drew a deep breath and busied himself with the trash. Surprised to find a bundle of T-shirts, he twisted the first one to read the slogan emblazoned on the front: "Lyle's Crop-Dusting Service. My Plane, Your Crops." Steve shook his head and tossed the bundle back onto the floorboard.

Stretching between the side by side seats, Rebecca reached a red switch and flipped it long enough to read the fuel gauges. "Fuel valve. On." She slipped out the door and strode to the rear of the plane. Even though her face was creased with worry, she tried to reassure Steve. "Relax. Knowing Lyle, it's safer than it looks."

Steve met her at the tail wing, his uneasiness across his features. "It has to be, because it looks as though it's about to fall apart."

Rebecca ran her hand underneath the metal surface and examined the hinges. "Disconnect the tail tie-down rope, will you? Just unhook it and throw it inside." She nervously chewed her lip, something Steve had never seen her do.

The possibility of Joey and his grandsons being caught in the forest fire was too real and frightening for Steve to admit out loud. He could see the worry clouding Rebecca's face as he turned to promptly follow her directions.

Rebecca had moved on to the wings. "Ailerons free. Flaps free." He watched her methodically race through the checks. How could she stay so calm? She was going to fly into a forest fire! Steve's own stomach was painfully knotted with apprehension.

"Next?" he asked, trying to speed things along.

On tiptoe, she stood on the wheel cover, muttering something inaudible, then turned toward him. "This is a high-wing plane so I can't quite reach the fuel tanks. How about finding me a stepladder? Try the barn, okay? I'm sure Lyle has one."

By the time he came back with a rickety stepladder, she looked almost finished with her walkaround. Generally, he loved to watch her work, but not under these circumstances. This situation was too serious—too dangerous. He knew they were playing with more than fire—their lives literally depended on her proficiency as a pilot and the reliability of this airplane. Steve was comfortable with risking his own life for his family's sake, but he wasn't thrilled about risking hers. Yet deep inside he knew Rebecca was the kind of person who would be doing this for anyone—even a complete stranger—in the same emergency.

Rebecca reached for the ladder. "Looks as though Lyle had it serviced recently. I need a quick look at the fuel tanks, then we're ready for take-off."

He clasped the ladder as if it were a bargaining chip in a big deal. "At least let me do that for you. This ladder isn't stable."

She shook her head and pried the ladder from him. Steve grudgingly stabilized it while she climbed up and inspected the top of the wing. "You're a dear, but it's a cardinal sin for a pilot to let anyone else check her tanks." She tittered nervously, then unscrewed the cap from the fuel tank and took a big whiff. "Good. No kerosene smell and the tank appears full. While I'm here, I'll check the vents for dirt dauber's nests."

"Dirt daubers?" Steve scowled up at her. "Are you *sure* this thing is safe?"

"Lyle uses it all the time to spray crops. Didn't you see all those attachments he had in the barn? Lyle is a jack-of-all-trades in the piloting business." She finished one tank, climbed down, then waited until Steve moved the ladder to the other wing before swiftly examining the second one.

Why the hell couldn't they just get this plane in

the air? Rebecca's thoroughness was beginning to annoy him. His grandchildren were uppermost in his mind. He didn't give a damn about dirt daubers.

As Rebecca started to climb down again, a dark-blue pick-up spun into Lyle's driveway, screeching to a halt behind Rebecca's Jeep. "Mitch!" she shouted at the approaching man. "What's up? Why aren't you with the rescue effort?"

Mitch waved a large folded paper in the air. "I got my hands on the aerial maps of the park and knew you could use them, so I brought them right out."

Before he could deliver them to Rebecca, another car came speeding up. A distraught Melinda jumped out of her station wagon. Pushing Mitch aside, she waddled over to Rebecca and Steve.

"Melinda! What the hell are you doing here?" Steve's tone was tinged with anger. She had no business being here in her condition. Didn't she think he could handle things? Didn't she have confidence in him?

"I know you both wanted me to stay at home, but I can't do that. I'm going with you." With a pleading glare, Melinda looked from her father to Rebecca to her father again. "That's my family out there . . . I *have* to go to my babies."

Steve didn't try to disguise his annoyance in front of the others. "What about the baby you are carrying? Haven't you got a lick of sense? Go back

to the station and let these people do their jobs."
He struggled to soften his tone. "I promise, I'll
call you as soon as we've located Joey and the
boys."

Determination glared in Melinda's eyes. "I know
you mean well, Dad, but I've got to do this. I may
be having a baby, but those are my *other* children
out there."

"You're pregnant!" he cried. "Aren't you afraid
for this baby?"

She swallowed hard and squared her shoulders.
"I am afraid, but my boys need me. They may be
afraid, too. I've got no choice, I'm their mother."

With a frown, Rebecca inched closer. "It's better
if you stay here."

"Please!" Melinda grabbed Rebecca by the arm.
"You've got to let me go. Don't you understand?"

Steve removed his daughter's hand and stepped
between the women. Melinda had never acted so
rashly in her life. What had gotten into her? He
knew she was worried, but insisting on going herself wasn't accomplishing anything. "Haven't you
heard a word we've said? You don't need to put
yourself at risk . . . or the baby." He loosened his
grip. "I can take care of this, okay? Why don't you
have Mitch take you home?"

"I'm not going anywhere but into that airplane,"
Melinda announced in a strong voice, challenging

her father with a cold, harsh stare. "I've got to help find them."

He felt sorry for her, especially since he felt the same fear she did over the boys' safety.

"I know how you can help." Rebecca pointed toward the aerial maps. "Show us where Joey usually camps."

Mitch took the cue and unfolded the map, spreading it out on the hood of Rebecca's Jeep. "This is the park."

Steve was expecting him to point out an area, but Mitch motioned to the entire thing. How were they ever going to find the campsite?

"This whole map is the park?" Surprise registered in Melinda's voice as she focused her attention on the shades of gray. Leaning on the Jeep, she surveyed the map intently. After a while, she shook her head. "It's so complicated. I don't recognize a thing."

Steve had never seen such frustration on his daughter's face. She was trying so hard to make sense of the map, but wasn't making any headway.

Rebecca realized how helpful it would be if Melinda did locate the campsite. It would save her hours of endless searching, precious hours that might mean the difference between life and death for Joey and the boys. She could see the anguish on Melinda's face as the woman frantically searched the map for anything vaguely familiar.

Rebecca's heart twisted as she moved beside Melinda. "Let me see if I can help." She ran her hand across the map's creases and squinted her eyes to read the tiny markings. None of the squiggly lines made much sense. "I'm afraid I can't make head or tails of this, either. I can't even find a creek or river to get a point of reference." It was going to be almost impossible to find the camp in the map's unreadable blotches.

Melinda put her hand over the section of map Rebecca was studying. "I can find them if you'll take me up. I've been there before. I know how to get there. Will you do this for me?"

She understood Melinda's determination, even admired her courage and strength . . . not letting anything stand in her way, pregnant or not. She reminded Rebecca of herself twenty years ago—relentless, self-centered, defiant. In Melinda's shoes, she'd have done the same thing, if not more. But Rebecca had learned from experience that what appeared to be the right thing, was sometimes a bad choice. Who knew what was right in this case?

"No way, Melinda." Steve shook his head. "Absolutely not." He waited for Rebecca to say something.

Rebecca didn't want to be in the middle, didn't want the deciding vote. She wasn't keen on the idea of flying with a woman who was nearly eight months pregnant over a raging fire in someone else's plane. But what choice did she have? If Melinda knew the way, then maybe she should go.

Steve took Rebecca's hand and pulled her aside. "We need to talk."

From his tone, she knew he was upset. "What is it?"

"I can't let her go up in that plane. Who knows how it will affect the baby? I can't take that risk."

"You can't take the risk?" She lowered her voice to conceal her annoyance. "You care about your daughter very much, but you can't *let* her do anything. The choice is hers, not yours."

He scowled. "But *you* can stop her."

Hating this position, Rebecca still had to be frank, even if it made Steve angry. "I can, but I won't. It is her family."

"It's mine, too." He grabbed her hand and stared into her eyes. "I can't stand the thought of *all* of my family being in danger."

She took a deep breath. "Your daughter has done her best, but she can't find the camping spot on the map. The only logical answer is for her to lead me to it."

Melinda joined them. "She's right, Dad. I've got to go."

Steve hesitated, his dark eyes showing conflicting emotions. He didn't want her to go, but knew she had to. "If I can't talk you out of this nonsense, then let's go."

Rebecca shook her head. "You don't understand, I can't take you both. With Melinda, it would be pushing the weight limit when we pick up Joey and the boys. With another person, it would be too much." The plane *would* be dangerously over-loaded, and Rebecca wasn't about to risk it—no matter what.

The reality of the situation hit and Steve stiffened. "That changes everything."

"It changes nothing," Rebecca told him.

"Daddy, you're terrified of flying! Don't you realize you can't go? We need as little weight as possible."

Steve turned to her for support. "Does it really matter that much, Rebecca?"

Rebecca knew he wanted to protect her . . . protect everybody. But she was in control, and for his own good, he couldn't go. "Well . . . actually it matters a lot. It'll be much safer without you." She continued, even after he shot her a glaring look. "Face it! I don't need to be worrying about you. Besides, Melinda can show me where the camp is. You can't."

"That's beside the point," he said through gritted teeth.

Rebecca clenched her hand until her nails bit into her palms. "That *is* the point."

"We can't stand here arguing all day, we've got to get into the air," Melinda interrupted.

"She's right. Let's do it." Rebecca swiveled

around and walked to the plane, with Steve, Melinda, and Mitch close on her heels.

"This discussion isn't over," Steve cried.

"Yes, it is. It's settled." Rebecca walked to the far side, then opened the pilot's door. She steadied herself with her hand on the back of the seat, before grabbing a strap on the inside door post. Kicking the trash from under her feet, she fastened her shoulder harness.

Steve grabbed his daughter's arm. "You are not going."

"Dad! I am!" Melinda pushed Steve back and tried to board the plane. When she couldn't hoist herself up, she demanded his assistance. "Help me up."

"You can't even get into the airplane by yourself. What makes you think you can do Rebecca any good? What would your doctor say if he knew you were flying?"

"You know he said okay when I flew to Florida on business last week." Melinda shot her father a weary, triumphant look. "This isn't that different."

"What about the stress of dealing with an emergency?" he asked. "You don't know what you'll find when you get there."

Melinda placed her hands on her hips. "I'm under stress whether I stay or go. Knowing has got to be better than not knowing. This waiting is killing me."

Rebecca could tell by the look on Melinda's face that her mind was made up. They had to get off the ground. She turned back to Steve. "Put yourself in your daughter's place . . . wouldn't you feel the same way she does?"

"I'm the only one who can find them, Dad."

Steve's brows drew together in a frown. "Isn't there another way?"

Rebecca searched her mind for an alternative. She needed Melinda to find the boys, but landing with a woman in her condition *was* risky. "If there is, I can't think of it. Melinda, I'll take you up only if you agree to my conditions."

"Anything." Relief was written on Melinda's face. "You name it."

"We go up and locate the boys and you do whatever I ask, whether you want to or not. No arguing. No outbursts. No nothing. Do you agree?"

"I guess." Melinda didn't sound confident anymore.

Rebecca reiterated her feelings. "I want it understood that once we're in the air, I'm in charge."

"Okay," Melinda agreed. "Let's not waste any more time. Let's do it."

Rebecca turned her gaze on Steve. "There's no other way for me to find them. The helicopters are too busy airlifting people from the Christmas Eve ceremony to locate them. Are you okay with this?"

"Do I have a choice?" Steve's shoulders sagged

as he conceded. He boosted Melinda up, then adjusted her safety harness before clicking it into the holder the way he had done when she was a little girl. After kissing Melinda on the cheek, he added, "Be careful."

Rebecca nodded and smiled across Melinda to Steve. "Don't worry! We'll see you soon." She set the carburetor knob to "cold," the mixture-control knob to "rich," pushed the throttle in a fraction of an inch and jabbed the master switch. She slid the window open and called, "Clear!" When she was sure Steve and Mitch were not in the way, she turned the ignition. The engine sputtered and coughed, then stopped. She tried it again. Nothing. The third time the engine caught, so she released the key.

"Thanks for taking me with you," Melinda hollered over the noise.

"Just help me find the boys, okay?" Rebecca hoped she wouldn't regret her decision. The engine idled a bit fast, so she eased back the throttle, keeping one eye on the oil gauge and the other on Steve. She hated to go against his wishes, but there was no other way. The boys' safety had to come first. She'd straighten out things with their grandfather later.

Her heart pounded as she watched him move back beside Mitch. Anxiety and frustration mingled in his glance as he mouthed "I love you." She cut her gaze to Melinda, but the woman was opening her side window—not watching her father at all.

It was clear. His message was meant for her.

It was too late now to change her mind. Melinda was going. Steve was staying.

Centering her attention on the oil gauge, she waited until the needle moved out of the red, then retracted the flaps, released the toe brakes, and taxied across the field. In position to take off, she pushed the throttle forward to the full-open position. The engine roared to life as they lunged forward, quickly picking up speed as they bumped through the pasture. In seconds they were airborne, on their way to the fire.

Rebecca wished she'd told Steve she loved him, too.

Twenty-two

Watching the tiny four-seater leave the ground, Steve felt a pang of regret ascend from the pit of his stomach to his heart. The two most important people in his life were flying into a forest fire in an unreliable airplane, with no one to depend on but each other.

"Ready to go?" Mitch started walking to his truck. "Rebecca's a damn fine pilot. If anyone can locate your family, she can. I'd put my money on that any day . . . and your daughter's pretty feisty, herself."

"Tell me I did the right thing . . . letting them go . . . without me." Steve's voice revealed the dejection he felt.

Mitch laughed, the low, growling grumble one would expect to hear from a man his size. *"You* didn't do anything. Those two are so much alike. Nothing, and nobody—least of all you—could have stopped them from flying off. Don't you know that by now? They're both as stubborn as mules."

Steve climbed into the truck's cab, then slammed

the door. Mitch started the engine, jammed into gear, and sped off. A few minutes later they pulled into the station. The firefighters were hectic as they monitored the rescue effort. They tracked the forest fire, sent out relief teams, and rounded up volunteers.

Steve stayed busy serving orange juice to volunteers who had just returned from the blaze. The smoky smell and soot-stained uniforms brought the reality of the fire home to him. These men and women had been there—digging trenches, spraying the flames, and constructing fire breaks. The snatches of conversation he overheard increased his fears tenfold.

". . . the smoke was so bad I thought I'd suffocate . . ."

". . . those dead pines were falling like matchsticks . . ."

". . . the flames were so close all I needed was basting . . ."

". . . might as well have been spitting, for all the good our hoses were . . ."

From across the room, Steve heard Rebecca's voice. "This is Cessna One-Seven-Five-Two-Bravo. North of Caldwell Farms. Due west of Smithville." Running toward the sound of her voice, Steve found Mitch frantically scribbling. When he finished, he tuned the knobs on the high-frequency radio, its cables running haphazardly across the table and floor.

"Have they landed?" Steve asked. "Are the boys safe? What did she say?"

The heavy man put his finger over his mouth, then picked up the radio microphone. "Cessna One-Seven-Five-Two-Bravo, we read you."

"Tell me what's going on," Steve demanded.

Mitch took his finger off the radio switch and set the microphone on the table. "They've located the boys."

"Thank God!"

"She'll radio back when they've landed." Mitch turned his attention back to the volunteers, while Steve paced the floor, pitching in wherever he could. But the minutes ticked into a half hour. Shouldn't she have landed by now? She'd radio back right away, wouldn't she?

"Cessna One-Seven-Five-Two-Bravo. Do you read?"

Rebecca. Finally. But something in her tone alerted him. Instinctively, he knew there was a problem.

Mitch picked up the radio again. "We read you, Rebecca. Have you landed?"

From the pained look on his face, her partner had heard it too. Something was definitely wrong.

After the longest pause of Steve's life, Rebecca spoke. "Engine trouble. With a capital Tango. Can't land. Send helicopter to rescue campers. Do you read?"

No! Steve wanted to yell. This can't be happening. It couldn't be Rebecca on the other end of that invisible radio wave telling him the worst.

Mitch sat up straight. "Ground acknowledges. Will request helicopter." He gnawed his lip. "Any sign of engine fire?"

There was a moment of hesitation. Steve nearly went mad waiting for Rebecca to answer. He visualized her peering through the windshield to look at the engine. It felt as if a hand was closing around his throat.

Rebecca's voice interrupted his panic. "Not yet. Oil pressure dropped."

By now everyone in the room had grown quiet, waiting for Rebecca's next words. From the way so many of them were staring at him, Steve knew it was bad. Alarms were ringing in his head.

The muscles in Mitch's cheek were twitching and his ruddy complexion had paled. "Can you land? Do you read?"

The ominous silence filled the air with dread. Why the hell didn't she say something?

"Rebecca!" Mitch tried again to elicit a response. "Can you land? Do you read?"

"Affirmative. Will land. Scouting for site."

"Good!" Relief flooded Mitch's face. "Give location. Repeat. Give location."

A heaviness centered in Steve's chest as he waited for Rebecca's response. Silence once again paralyzed the room.

"We're going down west of Rawlings Creek. Near the cave."

Mitch grabbed the microphone and walked several feet to the area map tacked to the wall. Running his free hand across the path of the forest fire, he located the creek. "There's no damn cave on the map," he muttered, then shouted over his shoulder, "Anybody know where it is?"

Rebecca's voice sliced into the rumbling crowd. "Mitch. Is landing location confirmed?"

"Negative! November. Oscar. No! Located Rawlings Creek. Need location of cave. Repeat. Need location of cave." Moving the radio microphone away from his mouth, he yelled to no one in particular, kicking his chair in frustration. "She used to fly clients in the balloon to some cave, but that was years ago. If Hawk and Doug were here, they could lead us to it, but they're out fighting the fire."

The creek The cave. Of course. Why hadn't he recognized it earlier? "I think I know," Steve cried. "I've been there."

Mitch walked over, grabbed him by the shoulder, and dragged him to the map. "Show me the damn cave!"

"I'm not sure I can find it again. I've only been there once."

"Once is better than never. You're our only chance." Mitch poked him in the chest. "Otherwise, I don't have a chance in hell of finding that cave. The roads are blocked. That fire is switching paths faster than you can blink."

"We were on foot," Steve moaned.

Mitch grimaced. "There's no road?"

"None. It was in the middle of nowhere."

"You've got to talk to Rebecca. Check your facts, then we'll get somebody to go after them. Okay?" Mitch shoved the microphone into his hand. "We can hear her better than she can hear us, so speak in short sentences. Slowly."

With his thumb, Steve clicked on the microphone, painfully aware that every living soul in the room was listening. "Rebecca. This is Steve. We can't find the cave on the map. Is it the one we flew to?" He stopped, waiting.

"Affirmative. Yes. It's *our* cave."

Our cave. Even in the midst of this disaster, Rebecca's reference warmed his heart.

"Okay. Help me remember how to get there . . . from the creek."

"Follow creek. It veers right, go left through brush. Follow pines to end. Turn right. Cave is across clearing."

Steve repeated her instructions.

She added, "You'll recognize it from before."

Before. When they had been there only a few weeks ago, the worst thing they had had to worry about was a snake slithering by, throwing cold water on their passion. Now Rebecca had to make an emergency landing with a pregnant woman—his daughter and unborn grandchild—then get them both to safety, assuming the fire didn't engulf them first. And all *he* had to do was locate a helicopter and a pilot, fly there, find his way to the cave, and carry them both to safety.

"Rebecca. We're coming."

"I see the clearing. Going to la—"

The radio went dead.

What had happened? What went wrong? Would he ever see Rebecca and Melinda again? Guilt swept over Steve. *He* should have been there instead of his daughter. He'd never forgive himself, if something had happened to those two.

Mitch took the radio microphone from Steve's trembling hands, then immediately began making the arrangements. After a few minutes, he came over and reported to Steve that Joey and the boys had been airlifted out.

Thank God! At least one thing had gone right. Steve paced the floor . . . waiting . . . worrying . . . and wondering. What next?

* * *

The only thing on Melinda's mind once they got into the air was whether her family was safe or not. Her father wouldn't be angry forever. He'd forgive her, he always did. Why should this time be any different? She thought about her little boys and wondered how close the fire was to their camp. Joey would do his best to take good care of them, but did he know that Jeremy had to be carefully watched or he'd be playing fireman? Would he remember that Jake was afraid of the dark—if the worst happened and they didn't get out before sundown?

When the airplane leveled off, Rebecca asked over the drone of the engine, "Is everything all right?"

It had taken a while for Melinda to get used to talking over the loud, rumbling engine and whirling swish of the propeller. Flying in a small aircraft was much different than flying commercially. She had to yell forcefully above the noise. "I'm fine."

Melinda shifted in her seat, uncomfortable and cramped. Her feet were swollen, along with the rest of her body, but they had been for weeks. Nothing had seemed to help, so she'd bought herself a pair of white elasticized slip-on sneakers to wear everywhere. She wanted to slip them off now, but was afraid she wouldn't be able to get them back on again when they landed.

"We'll be there before you know it," Rebecca

assured her in a voice too cheerful, too confident, for Melinda to believe. "A fire five miles wide should be easy to spot, right?"

Melinda gave her an uneasy smile. "Right." *Please let me recognize the way after all this time. And please, God, let Joey have camped where he said he would, and not closer to the fire.* She knew Joey was prone to change his plans at the last minute. *Don't let this be one of those times.*

A thousand times this afternoon, she'd wished she hadn't let him talk her into taking the boys camping for a couple of days.

"It will give you a chance to get some last minute Christmas shopping done," he'd said. Joey knew it was something she'd always put off to the last minute, and this year was no exception. Just to swing her over the top, he'd added a little gravy to the bribe. "And you'll have time to rest, put your feet up, even soak in the tub with no interruptions." Who could refuse an offer like that?

Melinda heard a loud bang erupt from the engine. "What was that?" she asked, gripping her seat, digging her fingers into the dirty fabric.

Rebecca gave her a reassuring smile. "Just a little morning sickness . . . you know about that, right?"

Melinda was in no mood for jokes. Being pregnant was no longer a laughing matter. "Morning sickness?" The baby flip-flopped on her spine. Her back hurt, but then it had off and on since breakfast. She'd blamed it on too much shopping yesterday, but now she was beginning to wonder if something might be wrong.

"Yeah. When an engine starts up cold and sputters and spits, it's called morning sickness—it's terrible for a short period of time, then clears up once it gets running and warm. Get it?"

"Sure." Melinda leaned closer to the window for a cool burst of air on her face. An open field, a clump of trees, and tiny unrecognizable plants dotted the ground below. Under different circumstances, she might have enjoyed the view. "Haven't we been up in the air long enough for it to be warmed up, though?"

Rebecca shrugged. "Some women have morning sickness all day long. I guess planes can have it at odd times, too."

Melinda wasn't buying that theory for one minute. This was the third time since take-off that the plane had "sputtered" and "spit" as Rebecca had so delicately put it. If this were a car, Melinda would be on her way to a mechanic. "Is there anything else it could be?" As if they could do anything about it from this altitude.

"Lyle may have just gotten it serviced." Rebecca was talking in that cheerful tone again—the one that begged to be believed but didn't fool Melinda. "Planes tend to need a little more fine-tuning after repairs. His engine might just be working the kinks out after some routine maintenance. Don't worry."

Joey had told Melinda not to worry before he left, then Mitch had told her not to worry when he'd found out her family might be camping in the middle of a forest fire. To top it off, her father had told her not to worry . . . now Rebecca was saying the same thing. From where Melinda sat, it seemed as though they'd all miscalculated. She had every reason to be worried . . . and she was.

Rebecca fiddled with some of the controls, adjusted knobs, then surveyed the gauges once more. Her face crinkled with worry, contradicting what she'd told Melinda.

Melinda's stomach cramped. She took a deep breath and exhaled slowly, wishing she'd never eaten that greasy hamburger and fries for lunch. She'd been so good for months, eating wholesomely, doing all the things her doctor had instructed her to do. For once, she'd decided to cheat a little—satisfy that fast-food craving while the boys were gone—and she had paid for it ever since.

Rebecca couldn't keep up a good face for Melinda much longer. Her smiling jaws were sore from pretending to be nonchalant, and her stomach was knotted from pretending to herself that nothing was wrong. Everything she'd told Melinda had been true, but none of it had explained what was causing the roughness in the engine.

Melinda peered out the window. "How far now?"

"Not far. Once we locate the fire break, you'll probably start recognizing some landmarks and we'll find the location of the campers—"

In a curt voice, Melinda interrupted. "Not 'the campers.' We both know it's Joey, Jake, and Jeremy. They're not just campers, they're my family."

Rebecca sympathized with Melinda, she really did, but she had enough on her mind. The engine's roughness distressed her, but she didn't want to disclose that to Melinda just yet. In addition to that, with the possibility of turbulence and smoke from the fire she could have real trouble ahead.

She resisted the urge to cover Melinda's hand, to reassure her, to comfort her—for fear they'd both give in to their emotions. They had to be strong. They had a job to do. "Once we find them," she continued in a matter-of-fact tone, "we'll land, pick them up, then fly home."

Melinda leaned forward and arched her back, releasing the tension she could feel crawling up her spinal cord. "What if we don't find them? What if the smoke is so thick we can't see anything?"

"We'll find them. You've been there before." Rebecca hoped she sounded more optimistic than she felt. "It will all come back to you. When we were looking at the map, didn't you say it was near a mountain?"

Melinda sat back, obviously uncomfortable. Tiny

airplane seats weren't designed for a woman in her last stage of pregnancy. "Yeah. Buck Mountain."

"That's not far off. We'll start there. You'll recognize something. Just keep your eye out for any kind of landmark. When we spot them, we'll call Mitch, and let Steve know they're safe. Before you know it, we'll pick them up and be back home in time for Santa."

"Sounds easy."

"If we're lucky," Rebecca agreed. Luck would be helpful right about now. She didn't want to frighten Melinda, but they were going to need more than their share of luck before this was over.

The fire had shifted. More accurately, the fires—plural—had shifted. From the strange pattern, Rebecca could see that there were several fires, not just one. Someone had started another blaze on the same side of the park they were flying over. The side on which Joey's camp was located.

Another loud noise shook the airplane, this time resembling a boom more than the earlier bang.

Melinda looked frightened. "What's that?"

"I'm not sure." The engine's noisy rumble was making Rebecca very uneasy. She adjusted the power knobs and pulled the throttle back, reducing the power long enough to check out the ignition system. She came up with nothing. Where the hell was she going to land this thing? "There's the fire break at eleven o'clock."

"I thought we'd never get here!"

"I know. I'm banking left to let the volunteers see that we're here, then I'll circle around and head north to Buck Mountain."

"Please hurry." Fear etched Melinda's features. "I keep thinking about the boys, and Joey, and I look down and see the fire—" Her voice cracked. "They just have to be okay."

"Mitch would have contacted us by radio, if there had been any . . . updates." Rebecca tightly gripped the throttle, struggling with the prospect of the unknown.

"You mean if anything had happened to them." Melinda splayed her fingers across her belly.

"But nothing has, because Mitch hasn't called."

"Maybe he's been too busy fighting the fire. Maybe he forgot."

"He'd never forget," Rebecca assured her. "He's my partner, and he wouldn't want us up here one minute longer than we have to be."

"Sometimes partners let you down."

Rebecca knew Melinda meant Joey. She felt sorry for the woman. With her own marriage to Harry, the road had been rocky on more than one occasion. Looking back, she wasn't sure it had ever been smooth. Marriage to Harry had been an eight-lane highway paved with sand. After every good-sized downpour, she'd had to go out and rake it level again or it would dry into ruts that could never be repaired.

"There's someone over there!" Melinda pointed to her right. "I'm not sure if it's them or not. It's too far away to tell."

Rebecca banked right and lowered the nose, dropping their altitude enough to get a good glimpse of the campers and the lay of the land. "Just keep looking," she told Melinda, her mind focused on flying the plane. The campers were well away from the fire raging to the south, probably unaware they were even in danger. Buck Mountain shielded them from seeing the smoke. Unless the wind made a drastic turn, she knew they would be safe.

"It's them!" Melinda frantically waved her arms. "Thank God they're safe!"

Melinda had to be told. Rebecca owed her that courtesy, although she couldn't find the words to start.

"Where are we landing? There are trees everywhere."

"That's one of the problems. We can't land under these conditions."

Melinda's breathing turned to quick, shallow gasps. "What do you mean? We have to . . . those are my babies down there. I have to get to them." Her tone verged on hysterical.

The unwelcome tension stretched tightly between

them. "I'm sorry. It's impossible." Rebecca avoided Melinda's penetrating gaze. "A helicopter can make it in and out better than we can."

Melinda resembled a volcano on the verge of erupting into anger, or tears, or both. "I don't care. We've got to get to them."

"Look! The fire's nowhere near them. Mitch will get help to Joey and the boys. They'll be fine, I promise. If we go down, we won't do them or anybody else any good. They'd have to divide their efforts between rescuing us *and* them. Right now, they can concentrate on getting to them fast."

Melinda took one last tissue out of her chambray shirt pocket and dabbed her eyes. "Do what you have to."

Rebecca talked into the radio as she circled back around the camp. "This is Cessna One-Seven-Five-Two-Bravo. Do you read?" She quickly reported Joey's location to Mitch, then flipped the radio off.

Right now, Rebecca's main concern was the plane. It was sounding worse by the minute. There was no way they'd be able to land in this hilly terrain. Even if she managed to get down safely— and that was a big if—she'd never be able to take off again. Once the engine died, it would really be dead and they'd all be stuck.

Where else could they land? She searched the landscape for a clearing, a field, anything that resembled a make-shift landing strip. But nothing acceptable came into view. The only place she knew would work was near the cave. She'd landed a hot-air balloon there before, hundreds of times, but never an airplane. Could she do it?

The engine sputtered.

Rebecca's mind was congested with doubts and fears. Not only was the engine running "rough," but the oil pressure continued to drop. To make matters worse, the oil temperature was high—a bad combination. They had to make an emergency landing and they had to do it fast, before the engine quit altogether and their landing became an exercise in her gliding ability. "I hate to tell you this, but there's an engine problem and we've got to land. I'm calling the station. Just sit tight and we'll have her down in a jiffy."

She radioed Mitch again. He had to know . . . just in case something happened. It made Rebecca uneasy when Melinda didn't say a word the whole time she was talking. She didn't respond to anything, not even her father's voice.

Rebecca turned her attention back to the radio . . . and Steve. "I see the clearing. Going to land."

But the radio was dead. Her last word cut off. This damn plane was falling apart faster than she could fly to safety.

A glazed look of despair spread over Melinda's

face. With hands folded across her stomach, she stared straight ahead. "Are we going to die?"

A warning voice whispered in Rebecca's head, telling her to handle Melinda with care. She was scared and pregnant and emotional. "Of course not!" She searched for a plausible, yet honest, answer. "We're going to have to make an unscheduled landing, that's all. I won't lie to you, it may be bumpy."

She could tell Melinda wasn't sure she believed her, but right now, Rebecca didn't care. Emergency landings didn't leave time for hand-holding or reassurance. If the landing was successful, then all they had to do was get to the cave. If they made it to the cave, they'd be safe no matter which direction the wind blew the fire.

"What will happen once we land?" Melinda asked.

"I know a place where we'll be safe. A cave." Rebecca circled around again and prepared to land.

With a note of skepticism, Melinda asked, "How did Dad know about it? The cave."

"I used to take clients there after balloon rides."

"You told Dad about it?"

In her hand, Rebecca could feel the vibrations of the throttle. It wasn't responding as it should. For the moment, Melinda's question was forgotten. As casually as she could, she answered, then prepared for the emergency landing. "Yeah, sure. Are you buckled in?" After Melinda responded affirmatively, Rebecca dropped the altitude. "The ground's rough, so don't be surprised when the plane bounces around."

"I'll be fine." Melinda braced her feet in the cockpit.

Rebecca's senses sharpened as the whir of the propeller and the roar of the engine got louder and louder in her ears. Her palms were sweating even though the wind blowing through the window was cool. Landing a hot-air balloon was easier than landing an airplane, but she knew she could do it. She'd done it plenty of times before, just not lately.

It was like riding a bicycle . . . one never forgot. But would the wind . . . the terrain . . . and the airplane all cooperate?

Twenty-three

The airplane's wheels skidded erratically across the ground. In the cockpit, Rebecca's body jolted against the throttle. She bit her tongue and didn't even feel it until she tasted the blood in her mouth. Stamping the pedals with hard punches of her foot, Rebecca managed to halt the plane in the underbrush just outside a line of pine trees, a few hundred yards from the creek.

What a bone-bruising landing!

Her first impulse was to let Steve know they were safely down. She switched on the radio, but was met with dead silence. Rebecca unstrapped her harness and wriggled out of her cramped seat, then slid into the small space between her seat and Melinda. "We've landed! Are you okay?" She grasped the quivering woman's shoulders, shaking her gently to get her attention. "Melinda? Everything's fine. Say something."

In a hushed voice, Melinda spoke. "My water broke."

Rebecca stared down at the stained seat and a

growing puddle of water on the airplane's littered floor. Her insides quaked at the obvious implication. Melinda's baby was coming . . . in the middle of a forest fire . . . with no way to get to a hospital . . . and nothing to do but let nature take its course.

Her first priority was to compose herself, for Melinda's sake as well as her own. As a trained firefighter, instinct and self-control were second nature. When she answered emergencies in Willow Ridge, she almost always knew the victims involved. But this time the emergency was with Steve's daughter—a woman who had disliked her from the beginning. Melinda had warmed to Rebecca over recent weeks, but the temperature was still only lukewarm.

And now she was about to deliver Melinda's baby.

Her second priority was taking account of what they had in the way of supplies, and getting them both to safety. She wasn't sure if she remembered all the specifics about her firefighter's birthing class, but one thing was certain—this was Melinda's third delivery, so they had no time to waste.

Rebecca wiggled Melinda's harness loose and rubbed her hands together for warmth and comfort. She had to have Melinda's cooperation on the way to the cave or they were sunk before they started. "You just sit there while I see what my ol' buddy,

Lyle, kept hidden in the cabin. He's a pack rat, so there's no telling what I'll find."

Rummaging through the trash in the floorboard and behind the seats, she collected a few packets of crackers, a couple of sodas, a bundle of T-shirts, and a much-needed first-aid kit. Under the pilot's seat, she hit pay-dirt. "Hah! I knew Lyle would have some liquor stowed in here somewhere." Pulling out a nearly full bottle of whisky, she tightened the top and added it to the supplies. "We might need this later." If Melinda didn't need it, then Rebecca very well might, herself.

Melinda eyed the bottle warily. "I can't drink . . . it's bad for the baby."

She might feel differently later on. Rebecca had no idea what they might face in the next few hours. She had to be as prepared as she could be under the dire circumstances.

Prepared.

Nothing could prepare her for delivering a baby— and that was exactly what she was going to have to do if Steve and the others didn't rescue them in time. She prayed he'd heard her message before the radio went dead.

Taking off her lightweight jacket, Rebecca dumped the supplies in the center and tied it up into a bundle. They had to get to the cave, not only because the baby could come at any time, but also because the wind could shift, cutting off their path to safety.

They would be safe in the cave—from the fire, anyway.

"That's everything." Rebecca pushed on her door. "Damn. It's stuck. It must have jammed in the landing. We'll get out on your side."

"Landing. Is that what you call it?" Melinda's laugh had a hard edge to it. "Crash is more like it."

"Crash landing then, okay?" Rebecca watched the very pregnant woman try to push herself out of the padded seat without success. "Need a hand?"

When Melinda nodded "yes," Rebecca leaned across her and accidentally brushed against her stomach. She turned the handle on the passenger side, but it didn't budge. "Damn. Give me a minute." She tried the handle again. Finally, the door creaked open. Rebecca squeezed past Melinda, then jumped to the ground.

Melinda handed her the supplies before attempting to exit. She swung her legs out with great difficulty and extended her hands for help. Rebecca grasped her under the arms and heaved her out, praying her strength and Melinda's legs would hold. Getting her out of the plane wasn't easy, but working together, they accomplished the task without incident. "Are you steady?"

With a scared, beaten look, Melinda responded, "Yes. Thanks. I think we'd better go, though. I'm beginning to have labor pains."

Rebecca nodded, afraid to say anything, afraid the very sound of the word "contractions" would send Melinda right into delivery. "It could take a while." Her tone of voice was openly optimistic. Maybe the rescue team would reach them in time.

"I doubt it."

"Are the contractions that close together?"

Melinda gave her a sardonic look. "I've been through this twice before, remember. Trust me, I can tell it won't be long."

They trudged through the pine thicket to the creek's bank and followed its winding path. Melinda walked with halting steps, pausing frequently when a spasm of pain hit. The faint, acrid smell of smoke periodically wafted over them, sending up a red flag that they had no time to waste. A smoky-smelling whiff of air hit Rebecca's face, bringing with it a cold whisper of fear and a heavy dose of reality. The fire was nearby.

As she led Melinda toward the cave, it seemed as though an eternity had passed since she and Steve had last been there.

Melinda faltered on some loose pebbles. "I've got to stop and rest."

A stab of panic hit Rebecca as Melinda stumbled. She dropped the bundle and ran to her side, hugging her before she realized what she was doing. "Thank God you didn't fall!" The blood was pounding in Rebecca's temple so hard her whole face throbbed. She avoided looking directly at Melinda, not able to disguise the fear in her eyes.

Then it hit her. Melinda hadn't winced when she'd touched her—hadn't reacted as though she'd just been branded by a hot poker. In the plane, Rebecca had been too preoccupied to notice much about how the woman had responded to her. Was it possible they were making progress?

Rebecca retrieved the supplies. "Lean on me." She locked her arm around Melinda's waist for support, then they both started across the clearing. When the young woman wrapped her own arm around Rebecca's waist, she smiled. "We'll make it, Melinda. You're a strong woman."

Emergencies brought families together in a crisis. She'd heard this and even seen evidence of it through her work in the fire department. Now she and Melinda were being drawn together . . . for the baby's sake.

"How much farther?"

She barely heard Melinda's question. The grimace on her face revealed her obvious discomfort. "There's the cave's opening. Can you make it?"

"Do I have a choice?" When Melinda met Rebecca's gaze with her own, the pain still flickered there. "Sorry. It's not your fault."

"How are the pains?"

"Painful." The bitterness was evident in her voice.

"I mean, are they getting closer together?"

Melinda's grip tightened. "Yeah." A ragged laugh escaped her lips. "Close enough."

At the cave, Rebecca released Melinda's hold, then entered first to light the candle. "When was your due date?" Rebecca made a quick mental calculation. "Five weeks from now, right?"

"Yeah. It's coming early." Melinda lumbered slowly through the cave's opening.

Rebecca's mind refused to register the significance of her words. A few tiny beads of perspiration formed on her upper lip. She was more shaken than she cared to admit. Silently, she mouthed a prayer—for guidance, for Melinda's safety, for the baby's healthy arrival—and for the rescue team to arrive in time.

Feeling along the damp floor of the cave, Rebecca found the lighter she'd left the last time she and Steve had been there. Thank goodness she'd forgotten it before, or they'd have no way to light the citronella candle now. The quilt they'd left to dry would come in handy, too. Rebecca touched the flame to the wick and held it until it sparked and flickered to life. "There, now you can see how to move around in here . . . or would you rather sit down?"

Melinda held her hand over her mouth as if she were about to be sick. "Oh Lord! That candle smells awful."

"I'm sorry." Rebecca moved the bucket farther away, but the cloying citrus scent still permeated the cave. "What can I do? It's the only source of light we have."

"I'll get used to it." She gave Rebecca a brave, little smile. "At least, I hope I will."

"The safest place for us to be—in case the fire comes this way—is on the opposite side of the pool. That far ledge is smooth and sturdy and far enough away from the cave's opening."

Melinda looked warily at the water-filled crevice as though it were the Grand Canyon. "I don't know if I can make it to the other side."

With a confidence Rebecca didn't really feel, she encouraged, "Sure you can. We can. It's shallow on the ends, so you can walk or swim, either one. I'll help you. Wait here until I get organized."

Rebecca searched the cave's interior with an eye to the task ahead. The supplies, the candle, and the quilt all needed to be moved to the ledge. She knew she could get them there. She just wasn't confident she was steady enough to do it without getting something wet.

Leaning on a rock, she took off her tennis shoes, then stripped down to her bra and panties. With deliberate motions, Rebecca scrambled into the warm bubbling pool, holding the burning candle high over her head. Other than Melinda, this would be the most important "cargo" across.

Rebecca trembled, remembering the snake and how it had disappeared under the water's surface. There wasn't time now to worry about unseen dangers. The eminent ones were scary enough. Even so, she cut her eyes over to where she'd first viewed the snake. Convinced that none was there now, she shook the image to the back of her mind and attended to more pressing matters: preparing for the birth. With the candle successfully in place, she paddled back, then made two more trips, carrying the provisions and clothes in her waterproof jacket.

Finally, Rebecca took Melinda's hand and led her to a large rock with a flat surface. "Let's get you over to the other side, okay? Why don't you hand me your shoes?"

"I guess it would be better if I took my clothes off. I'm going to have to undress eventually." Awkwardness overwhelmed her as she unbuttoned the chambray maternity blouse. Underneath, she had on a T-shirt, which she left on. She tugged the wet elasticized pants over her hips. When she got them to her thighs she surrendered and asked for assistance. "Could you help me get these off?"

Rebecca nodded, then helped Melinda remove her shoes, pants, and shirt. "I'll just put them over here to dry." Averting her eyes away from Melinda's bulging stomach, she took the clothes to a rock and spread them out.

Sitting in nothing but her T-shirt and panties, Melinda gingerly sat and dangled her swollen feet into the water. "It's warm! Maybe it will make my aching back feel better."

Rebecca offered her outstretched arms. "Ease in and get your balance. The bottom is covered in flat rocks, not mud."

Melinda inhaled sharply. The back labor had grown from a mere annoyance to a dull throb. The last time she'd had a baby, she'd been in the hospital with her own doctor, Joey, and lots of drugs. She dropped into the water with a splash. "This feels great!" She stayed around the shallow area, then moved waist deep, finally sinking in up to her neck. "I think I'll stay here a while."

Rebecca moved closer. "You *can* swim, can't you?" Tiny lines creased her brow with worry.

Laughing, Melinda dog-paddled in her direction. "Of course."

"Thank God!" Rebecca swam to the wide steps just beneath the water's surface against the wall. There, the warm bubbling liquid was only knee deep. "Come here and I'll rub your back. I remember some things from my training that might relieve some of the discomfort."

Melinda joined her one step below, where the

water met her distended belly. "It's okay to call a spade a spade. It's not discomfort, it's pain. Believe me, I ought to know."

Firmly pressing the small of Melinda's back, Rebecca moved in a pattern down to her buttocks, then up to the sacrum, where the spine and pelvis met—up and down, up and down.

Melinda moaned in obvious relief. "Thanks, that helps. Have you ever done this before?"

Rebecca hesitated. "We had to practice on other firefighters when we took the course, but that's all."

"That must have been a sight." She hunched her shoulders forward so Rebecca could better reach her lower back. "Was Mitch your partner?"

"Yeah. And *was* he a sight!"

Melinda turned her head to look at Rebecca, who continued the counter-pressure to relieve the pain. "Why didn't you and Mitch ever get together before he got married? You two have a lot in common—spend a lot of time together."

"Mitch?" Rebecca chuckled. "He's way too young for me. He'd get a kick out of you suggesting that he and I could have been anything but friends, though." Rebecca shook her head. "I do love him as a friend, but I've never been 'in love' with him. He just wasn't the one."

"And my father is?"

Rebecca stopped rubbing Melinda's back. "Yes." Her voice was thoughtful, yet strong and clear.

Stretching her arms in front of her, Melinda dipped both hands into the warm water, letting it flow through her fingers. When the last trickle had vanished into the clear green pond, she turned again, staring into Rebecca's face. "Do you love Dad?"

A silence stretched between them like a heavy mist over a river at dawn. Finally, Rebecca answered. "Yes. I love Steve more than I've ever loved anyone in my life."

"Have you told him? Does he know how you feel about him?"

"Yes. He knows."

Suddenly, Melinda felt the need to hear it all. She needed to know how this woman felt about her father and how he felt about her. She couldn't ask her father. He would try to spare her feelings, but Rebecca would be honest. "And he told you he loved you back . . . didn't he?"

"Yes, he did. How do you feel about that?"

Melinda could feel the color drain from her face, the flickering shadows hiding her reaction. "How can I feel? I want my father happy, but . . ." her voice trailed off into the silent darkness of the cave. . . . but . . . but . . . but . . .

"But nothing." Rebecca sighed loudly. "There's no reason to look back. The future is what's important. I want a life with your dad . . . and I want to be accepted by his family, by you and your children . . . and by Joey, if he's in your life."

Aware of the anger she'd harbored toward Rebecca, Melinda knew it was time to let go—time to wash away the jealousy and the fears. She swallowed with difficulty and found her voice. "I'd like to try to make things work out between us . . . for Dad's sake."

"That's all I ask." Rebecca got up and retrieved the empty soda bottle she and Steve had used for "spin the bottle" when they'd been there last. "See if this feels good." She wrapped the bottle in one of Lyle's T-shirts, then rolled it up and down Melinda's back.

"Ummm. The pressure helps." The pain was starting up again. Melinda took a couple of cleansing breaths. Stress was bad for the baby and the delivery—stress and panic, the two things that had gotten her into this predicament in the first place. The labor probably wouldn't have started if she hadn't been so petrified about the boys and Joey. Her thoughts returned to the fire and the danger they had been in. How long *had* it been since the crash? "Do you know what time it is?"

Rebecca glanced at her empty arm. "Sorry. I forgot my watch. My guess is we've been down a couple of hours. How are you doing?"

"I've been better. The contractions are getting worse. I'd like to get out of the water now."

Melinda took Rebecca's arm as she stepped from the water. She felt a sinking sensation and a trickle of water down her leg. The baby was dropping. It wouldn't be long now. She eased down onto the quilt, her legs bent at the knees and spread apart.

"Shouldn't we be breathing?" Rebecca pulled out a couple more of the T-shirts retrieved from the plane.

"Don't worry. The worse the contractions get, the more I'll breathe. I never did get the hang of all that he-he-he, blow, stuff."

Rebecca wiped herself dry with a T-shirt, then pulled a second one over her head. "They told us in class to let you position yourself any way you were comfortable, as long as you didn't close your legs and try to stop the baby from coming."

"I couldn't stop this baby from coming if I tried."

"What did they recommend in your birthing classes?"

Melinda shifted her legs. "Since I've had two pregnancies already, I only had to take a refresher course." She gave a ragged laugh and exhaled a long, deep breath. "That didn't start until this week and I hardly remember a thing they told me when Jake was born." She counted back in her head. "That was nearly eight years ago."

Rebecca wiped the perspiration from Melinda's brow with a folded T-shirt. "I guess you can get your money back."

Together they laughed nervously. The sound was hollow, ringing against the cave's moist walls. Melinda felt another sinking sensation. This time it wasn't the baby—it was deep within her heart. "Joey and I were going to go to the classes together. I thought it would bring us closer."

"How are things with Joey?"

The question hammered at Melinda as the pain started again. "Bad time to ask." She grabbed the quilt with clenched fists and panted through another contraction. "He got me into this, and he's not even here for the grand finale." When the pain began to subside, her mind turned back to her husband and the progress they'd made in working out their problems. "Joey is a good father. He was really looking forward to having the baby."

"He won't be disappointed after he sees the two of you. I promise."

A tear slid from the corner of Melinda's eye.

"You still care, don't you?" Rebecca touched her cheek, then pushed Melinda's damp hair behind her ear. "You were bound and determined to get to him when you thought he was in danger. That tells me you still have feelings for him. You do, don't you?"

"I love Joey. We just let our jobs get in the way.

Too much to do and not enough time for each other."

"What's stopping you now?"

"My pride." At last, she could admit it.

"I've got a cure for that." Rebecca dipped a shirt into the water and wiped Melinda's forehead with it. "There. It's as simple as that. Too much pride never made anyone happy. Wash it away and start over."

"I'll take that under advisement when I see Joey again." She laughed, then instantly grew serious again. "I hope he and the boys are all right."

"I know they are." Rebecca put a reassuring hand on her arm. "They'll be waiting for you as soon as we get home."

Melinda couldn't rest in the prone position. Her back ached, and the labor pains were coming faster. "I can't get comfortable."

"If you're up to it, let's try moving around. Some doctors think it eases your back labor, and gravity helps push the baby out. What do you say?"

Leaning up on her elbows, Melinda agreed. "I say this isn't working, so let's do something else."

Rebecca positioned herself behind Melinda. Putting her arms around her as if they were dancing, she rested her hands on Melinda's stomach. It felt strange at first, but Melinda finally allowed her muscles to relax, and leaned back into Rebecca for support. They danced a slow, halting shuffle, stopping only for the grinding pressure of the contractions.

The pains were getting worse and closer together. Melinda clenched her teeth, riding the swelling waves. "I think the water might help. Will you get in with me again?" She gripped Rebecca's hand, reassured by its firmness. "I don't want to do it alone."

Rebecca tried to swallow the lump in her throat. "You're not alone." She swayed another couple of feet until they reached a safe spot to get into the warmth of the pool. "I'm right here with you." Melinda winced as her whole body tightened with the onset of another contraction.

When the contraction eased, Rebecca got one of the sodas she'd saved from the airplane and set it on the pool's edge, then got into the water with Melinda. Exhausted from the painful waiting, the poor girl slumped on the steps, barely able to swallow the warm, sweet liquid. "You need to keep up your strength, honey. Sorry it's hot, but this is all we have."

Rebecca helped Melinda slip her wet panties off. They both knew it wouldn't be much longer.

Melinda reached for Rebecca's hand, squeezing it tightly as the pain engulfed her again. When she went limp, Rebecca started talking—about her father and what a good man he was, about the boys and all the crazy things they'd done, about Joey and how much he'd wanted to be with her during delivery—anything to distract her.

After a particularly bad contraction, Rebecca hesitantly asked, "What about a shot of that whiskey?" When Melinda protested, she added, "A little one . . . mixed into your soda."

Melinda shook her head with little conviction. "I can't. Liquor is bad for unborn babies."

"You're right, honey, during the pregnancy. But now that the baby is on its way, a small amount of alcohol will relax your muscles and take the edge off the pain. I wouldn't suggest it if I thought it would hurt you or the baby."

"Did you learn this in your training?"

"There, and from the books I've been reading lately."

"Reading? Now? Why?" She detected a thawing in Melinda's surprised tone.

"You were pregnant with Steve's grandchild, and I wanted to understand what you were going through," Rebecca explained. "For Steve . . . and because I care about you."

"I never knew."

Before Rebecca could respond, a contraction gripped Melinda, its unrelenting pain evident in her grimacing features. When it was over, she quickly fixed Melinda the "tonic" of whisky and soda and held it for her.

"That smells awful!" Melinda wrinkled her nose and pressed her lips to the can. "Tastes awful, too. I usually drink daiquiris."

Rebecca smiled, knowing full well Melinda hadn't swallowed a thing. She wouldn't push. It was her decision. But Rebecca could use a stiff shot herself. If she didn't need all her faculties about her, she'd take a shot straight from the bottle. That would have to wait until later.

Between contractions, Melinda surprised her by asking, "Why didn't you have children?"

Rebecca smoothed her hair away from her face. "My husband didn't want children until it was too late for me to have them." She clamped her lips shut as if the act would hold her raw emotion in check.

Her eyes filled with tears, Melinda softly whispered, "I'm sorry. I didn't know."

Another wracking contraction hit and Rebecca felt her confidence begin to slip away. What made her think she could do this? She'd had no experience with childbirth, and the training had done her little good. The books and videos in class hadn't done justice to what Melinda was going through to have this baby.

"Listen to my voice." She talked her through to the end, with Melinda squeezing her hand tighter and tighter, almost crushing Rebecca's fingers as her body tightened in labor.

"Did you ever bring Dad here?"

Before she answered, Rebecca offered her another swig, but she shook her head. "Once . . . a few weeks ago. We came here after his first flight in the hot-air balloon."

Melinda balanced her weight against Rebecca's as they left the steps and moved around in the water. "Tell me about it."

Gladly, Rebecca recounted the events—the flight, the picnic, the hike, the swim—leaving out the parts about the skinny-dipping and the snake. Her face burned as she remembered being held in Steve's strong arms, being kissed by his warm lips, being loved by the man she loved in return.

Another labor pain ripped Rebecca into the present. "That's it. Hang in there. You're doing great." She soothed Melinda with calming words until the pain subsided. Rebecca tensed with every contraction. By now, she was exhausted. It must be so much worse for Melinda.

"I'm getting close." Melinda's body sagged, her head leaning on Rebecca's chest.

"Do you want to get out now?"

"I think so." The two almost made it across the pool before Melinda slumped onto the first step. "I can't. It's too late."

"What do you mean it's too late?"

"The baby . . ." she gasped. "It's coming."

"What do you mean? It's been coming for hours."

"No! The head. I feel the head."

Rebecca reached down. The baby's head was crowning. They'd have to deliver it under water.

"Don't worry! People in other countries have babies under water all the time."

"They do?"

She sure as hell hoped so. That's what the books had said anyway. "Yes. Listen to me, Melinda." She took her by the shoulders. "I want you to stop pushing."

"Stop!" she cried. "Have you lost your mind?"

"Do not push. I want you to *breathe* the baby out. Breathe with me now." In unison they exhaled, long and loudly. "Again." They repeated the process as Rebecca checked their progress with her hand.

"The head's out." Melinda screamed, grabbing the edge of the step with her fingers. "I can feel it."

"You're right." With great effort, Rebecca kept her tone calm. "I'm going to line up the head with the shoulders, then I want you to push the shoulders through." She gently guided the head into place then strongly commanded, "Melinda, push—now!"

Rebecca eased the baby's head down so the shoulder nearest her slid out first, then lifted the head so the other shoulder was released. After both shoulders were clear, the body slithered out, then the legs. Still attached, she pulled baby and cord out of the water. The slightly pink, sticky infant began to cry when Rebecca placed her in Melinda's arms. "It's a girl!" Rebecca hugged both mother and daughter, an overwhelming relief flowing through her. "She's beautiful, Melinda . . . and so is her mother."

A smile trembled over Melinda's lips as her eyes darkened with emotion. "How can I ever thank you?"

For a long moment, Rebecca looked back at her, then answered in a hushed voice, "Be my friend."

Melinda's mouth parted into a smile as she looked from her new daughter's face to Rebecca's. "We passed into friendship hours ago . . ." She paused, her eyes glistening with tears. "Now we're family."

Twenty-four

The noise of the chopper was so deafening, Steve could barely think. Even though he looked out the window as little as possible, the charred remnants of the fire were impossible to miss.

This Christmas Eve nightmare had been the worst he could remember—worse than the year he'd been alone, stationed overseas . . . even worse than the year Melinda had gotten the measles and given them to him. Ever since he'd put his daughter and Rebecca on that damnable airplane, his mind had clicked from one image to the next as though a slide projector was playing in his head.

Steve and the three Red Cross volunteers quickly got out and ran toward the grounded plane. Steve breathed a sigh of relief to be on land again, and out of that tiny, claustrophobic copter. Yet he would have tried to pilot the thing himself to get to Rebecca and Melinda . . . fear or no fear.

Approaching the plane, he broke into a clammy sweat. At least they'd landed! A wave of anguish swept over him as he peered into the empty aircraft, shattering the last shred of his veiled control. Were they hurt? Was the baby okay?

The paramedic in charge, Ted, patted him on the back. "From the look of the plane, Steve, the landing went well. Good thing they weren't overloaded." The man gave him a sympathetic smile. "Ready to lead us to the cave?"

Steve nodded, wrenching his emotions back into submission. His brain told him he *had* done the right thing. Staying behind had been the only possible solution. His heart echoed tons of doubts. Couldn't he have anticipated the problem? Why wasn't he there for Rebecca and Melinda when they went down? Why had he allowed Melinda to fly in her condition? Why had he argued with Rebecca?

"Ready?" Ted asked again.

"Sure. You guys follow me." The volunteers, loaded with medical supplies and equipment, started across the clearing. He broke into a run when he saw the cave. "Rebecca! Melinda! We're here." He burst through the opening, totally unprepared for what he saw. Lying on the ledge, wrapped in a quilt, was his daughter with a beautiful, tiny baby in her arms. Of all the scenarios that had run through his mind, this wasn't one of them. He'd never imagined Melinda would have given birth this early.

The smothering heat in the cave added to his breathlessness, while his eyes adjusted to the dim light of the candle. He squinted into the flickering candlelight, trying to focus on the scene laid out beyond the misty pool.

"Hi, Granddad!" The sound of Rebecca's voice helped calm his heart, as he impatiently waited for the medics who were a few paces behind him. Steve resisted the urge to fling himself into the water and swim to them.

Before he could speak, the three men rushed into the cave. "What happened here?" Ted cried. The trio stopped dead in their tracks. Steve half expected them to bump into each other like the Three Stooges—sending supplies flying over the cave's damp floor.

Steve grinned broadly. "It seems my daughter has had her baby."

Ted's assistant pushed past him and asked Rebecca, "Do either of you need immediate medical assistance, ma'am?"

"No. Mama and baby are fine. We're all fine," Rebecca answered. "You've just got to get them out."

"Oh, that's all," Ted mumbled.

The young pilot yelled across, "Is there a way over to that ledge, ma'am?"

Rebecca chuckled, then motioned to the pool. "I'm afraid you're looking at it, boys."

The men groaned almost in unison as they set about unloading the equipment they would need to retrieve the new mother and child.

Steve couldn't wait any longer to make sure his daughter was okay . . . get his hands on his new grandbaby . . . and get his hands on Rebecca . . . maybe, not in that particular order. "I'm swimming over." He sat down on a rock and started to strip off his clothes. This was no time for formalities, and he had no intention of flying back soaked. He didn't care how big an audience he had . . . he would walk buck naked through Braves Stadium on game night if that's what it took to get to his family.

Ted noticed Steve taking off his clothes. He reached down and touched the water, then started undressing himself. "I think I'm gonna get rid of some of my clothes, too. No sense in getting everything wet." He yanked off his coat, then started to unbutton his shirt.

"This is a rescue, sir, we can't take our clothes off. It's not proper," the pilot complained while Ted shucked his high-top boots and socks, then stood to unzip his pants.

"In case you haven't noticed, we're going swimming. I checked and the water's warm, so we're in no danger of hypothermia." He finished undressing down to his long underwear.

"I'm not gonna do it," the pilot declared.

"You will if you know what's good for you. It's getting dark out there and we're in the mountains. Once the sun sets that spells c-o-l-d, cold. You'll freeze your . . . uh, your favorite friend off if you head down that path dripping wet in the wind. *You'll* be the one we'll have to take to the hospital, not these good people. Besides, you've got to fly this plane out of here, unless you want her," he pointed to Rebecca, "to do it."

That was all it took. The threat of turning his chopper over to another pilot—a female pilot— forced the young man to comply.

While the men finished their preparations, Steve entered the water in his Christmas boxer shorts. A flashback to the snake fiasco entered his mind as he swam across the pool. He cut his eyes to where it had been, then swiftly paddled to the ledge. He pulled himself up, plopped onto the rim, and grinned. At least Rebecca and Melinda hadn't killed each other. That was a good sign. Now that he was closer he could see they were both smiling and cooing at the baby.

"Daddy, I'm glad you're here." Melinda was leaning on a rock with his new grandchild nestled against her breast. "Come meet your granddaughter." Melinda looked tired, but happy, as the new little life nuzzled closer to her.

With a smile, Rebecca squeezed Steve's hand, then stepped back so he could sit next to Melinda.

"A daughter?" The joy Steve felt was so strong, a hot tear rolled down his cheek. When he touched the baby's face, he nearly broke down. The tiny infant clutched his outstretched finger and waves of love for both mother and baby passed over him. "She's the most beautiful little girl I've ever seen . . . she'll have Joey wrapped around her little finger before the end of the week."

With fear in her voice, Melinda asked, "Joey and the boys . . . are they all right?"

"They flew them out safe and sound. Rebecca was right. They hadn't even seen the fire—couldn't from where they'd camped—so they were fishing when the rescue team found them." Steve chuckled. "Joey wanted to be sure you got plenty of rest before he brought the boys home."

He cupped Melinda's chin with his hand. "This tiny one reminds me of another little baby I held not so many years ago." He hesitated, his voice a hoarse whisper. "The day that little girl was born, she became the apple of her father's eye . . . and she still is."

Melinda pulled Steve down with her free hand hugging him with the baby between them. "Oh Daddy, I love you."

"I love you, too, honey."

Ted loudly cleared his throat. "Sorry, sir, we're ready to move your daughter now." The man tugged a small knit cap onto the baby's head. "Fo warmth," he explained. After a quick check of their vital signs, the three men tediously moved mother and child safely to the opposite side with Steve's help.

While the others were busy with Melinda, Rebecca slid off the socks, shoes, and jeans she'd put back on after the baby's birth. She wrapped them in her shirt, then waded across in her T-shirt with the bundle held high. On the other side, she moved into the shadows and dressed again.

Steve noticed as Rebecca inconspicuously dried with one of the rescue blankets. Glancing over at the other men to see if they, too, were watching, he was pleased to find that they were taking care of his daughter's needs. When he turned his attention back to Rebecca, she'd dropped the blanket.

Rebecca looked up. He was caught. Steve couldn't have felt any more embarrassed if he had been peering through a hole into the girl's locker room. Then her gaze deliberately lowered to the darkened area of his wet boxers. Rebecca smiled that warm, easy smile of hers, and Steve relaxed. He left her alone and went to find his own clothes.

After the rescue team dressed and packed up, Ted pulled Steve aside. When they finished conferring, Ted returned to supervising Melinda, and Steve walked over to Rebecca. "There's a slight problem."

"If I hear that one more time today, I think I'll—"

Steve took her in his arms and kissed her fully on the mouth. "We can come up with something better than screaming."

"You were saying something about a problem?" Her eyes looked tired.

"That depends on how you look at it . . ." He kissed her again. "Melinda and the baby need more room in the helicopter than originally was planned. It would have been tight before, but we could have managed. Now, Ted doesn't want to try it."

"What does *Ted* plan to do?" Her voice was strained as she placed her head against his chest.

"I volunteered to stay behind . . . with you."

Rebecca pulled back and stared into Steve's face. "With me?"

He grinned and whispered, "You wouldn't want me to stay here in this big ol' cave alone, now would you?" He bent down and nuzzled her ear.

"I wouldn't dream of it."

Steve lifted her face, then kissed the tip of her nose. "I was hoping you'd say that."

"They will come back for us, won't they?"

"Eventually." Steve laughed, then turned serious. "Because of the fire, they've got a whole bunch of folks they need to airlift out from the far side of the park."

"Couldn't that take several hours?"

"Or all night."

Rebecca smiled and the tiredness in her eyes diminished, replaced by a gleam Steve hadn't seen all night. "Well, we'll just have to make the best of it here . . . alone . . . in the dark."

"You can count on me."

"Ump-uh. If everything's all settled, then we're heading out." Ted handed Steve one of the supply bags. "Here are some provisions to hold you until we get back—a few cans of orange juice and some nutrition bars we keep handy for diabetics, a thermal blanket, and a battery-operated emergency lantern. When we extinguished the candle and brought it over to this side, it was getting kind of low."

Rebecca and Steve walked over to say goodbye to Melinda, who was now lying on a stretcher near the entrance. The exhausting delivery had finally taken its toll, and Melinda could hardly keep her eyes open. "They are flying you and the baby out first, honey." Steve wasn't sure Melinda was awake enough to understand. "Rebecca and I will see you later."

"Okay, Daddy," she murmured, straining to stay awake.

Ted and his assistant hoisted the stretcher up. "We'll radio the fire station on the way. They'll locate her husband so he can meet her at the hospital."

"Hospital?" Steve asked, startled. Melinda looked tired, not sick.

"It's routine." Ted eased the stretcher past a boulder. "To be on the safe side, a doctor just needs to look Melinda and her baby over."

As much as Steve wanted to be alone with Rebecca, he hated to see his own baby girl carried out on a stretcher. A lump filled his throat.

"We'll be back for you as soon as we can. You two gonna be all right?" Ted yelled over his shoulder as they headed into the clearing.

Rebecca patted Steve's arm. "We'll be better than all right."

"Are you sure you don't want me to help get Melinda to the helicopter?" Steve took a step after them.

"We'll manage," Ted said. "It's cold and getting colder. You two are better off up here in the cave. Keep warm."

Warming up with Rebecca would be Steve's pleasure.

Taking his hand, she led him back to the cave. They turned on the white part of the three-sided emergency lantern, then spread out the blanket.

"Sit down and let me take care of *you* for a change. How about a snack? You've got to be famished."

Rebecca leaned against a rock with her legs stretched out in front of her. "I guess I am." It had been hours since she'd eaten, but it seemed like days since she'd slept. She nibbled one of the nutrition bars Steve opened for her and drank a can of orange juice. He sat down next to her and watched.

She seemed ready to drop from fatigue.

Taking the juice can from her hand, he put it aside, then pulled Rebecca toward him. Her head fit snugly in the hollow between his shoulder and neck. Steve rocked her gently in his arms until he felt her body relax. He knew she needed some sleep. She'd earned it after her ordeal. The woman he loved had delivered his grandchild. He was dying to hear all about it, but not now. That would come later.

There would also be other nights for what he'd had in mind earlier. As badly as he wanted her, he wanted their union to be right. And this wasn't. "Why don't you take a nap?"

With only a murmur, Rebecca lowered her head into his lap and curled up on her side. He ran his hand under her flannel shirt and rubbed her back. She was wearing no bra or undershirt, and all he touched was smooth, silky skin.

Rebecca didn't say anything, but shifted so he could get to her back better. When her breathing evened out, he knew she was asleep. He ran his fingers through the curls along the nape of her neck. Steve realized how much he owed this woman—not only for what she'd done tonight for Melinda, but for all the happiness she'd brought back into his life. He remembered all the months after his wife's death, the pain, the agony, the feeling that he'd never enjoy another day as long as he lived.

Then a miracle happened. A miracle named Rebecca came into his life and nothing would ever be the same again.

Rebecca turned and he could see her sleeping face. He'd grown to love that face . . . every curve, every feature. She had the kind of face any man would want to wake up next to in the morning—especially this man. Steve watched her sleep for nearly an hour before drifting off himself.

Momentarily disoriented when she woke up, Rebecca stretched her legs. Her back was stiff and sore from sleeping on the hard rock surface—plus all the other abuses she'd put her body through the past twenty-four hours. By now it was well past midnight—Christmas Day! And she was in the arms of the man she loved. They might not have a tree or eggnog or presents by the fire, but they had each other. Rebecca had a gift in mind for Steve . . . or actually, a gift they could give each other.

She sat up, slid her hand over his shoulder, and cupped the back of his neck. She coaxed him awake with delicate kisses that quickly turned into one slow, lingering embrace. "Merry Christmas!" she whispered, teasing his ear with the tip of her tongue.

Steve's hands caressed the length of her back as he gathered her in a warm, sensuous hug. "You feel so good." His lips brushed against hers as he groaned, "So-o-o good." Raising his mouth from hers, he gazed into her eyes.

Rebecca couldn't speak . . . the emotion was too great. There was no need for spoken words— the loving look that passed between them was enough. She buried her face against his throat, as a delicious shiver of desire flowed through her.

"I've been dreaming about this moment forever," Steve's voice was husky with excitement. His hand rested on her outer thigh. Even through heavy jeans, her skin prickled with the heat of his touch. Steve eased away from her arms, stood, then walked to the supply bag. Fumbling through it, he found whatever he was looking for and returned. He lit what was left of the candle before switching off the bright, offensive flashlight. "There. Isn't that better?"

"Umm. Much." She pulled him down to the blanket and planted a tantalizing kiss on his mouth, his musky smell mixed with the aroma of burning wick and citronella.

Steve traced his fingertips down to the last exposed inch of skin at her collar. With one hand, he unbuttoned her blouse, then gently outlined her sensitive, swollen nipples. She gasped as he tantalized them with his tongue, licking and nipping until they throbbed with pleasure.

Rebecca wanted to return his delicious torment. With both hands, she grasped the bottom of his sweater and slid it over Steve's head, then undid his shirt. Roughly pushing it aside, she teased his nipples with her lips. When she lifted her head, she knew it was time.

She stood, pulling Steve up with her. Together they undressed, throwing each piece of clothing aside with abandon until they were completely nude. Rebecca had caught glimpses of his naked body before, but always on the sly, mostly underwater. She'd never had the chance to study him— really look at, and enjoy, his commanding male physique—from his broad shoulders to his long, muscular legs, not to mention the part in-between.

Inches apart, the only barrier between them was the mounting heat of growing passion. She drew his head down, and kissed him gently. "I . . . love . . . you," she told him slowly. "I . . . want . . . you," she whispered, kissing his mouth, his eyes, and his chin, between each word.

Steve put his hand on her bottom and pulled her close against him. "Oh, love, I want you, too," he murmured into her hair. The mere warmth of his hand against her bare skin caused her to tremble.

Rebecca felt the hard strength of his masculinity as he pressed his body to hers. She'd been waiting for this moment for weeks . . . wanting him near her . . . inside her.

He began kissing her shoulders, tasting them lovingly, then her breasts, before bending down on both knees. Holding her close, he continued his tantalizing journey across her stomach, all the while exploring her thighs and bottom with his expert hands. When she thought her knees would buckle under the strain of delight, he slowed and waited.

She ran her fingers through his hair and moaned, as he caressed her private patch of curls with tender touches. He entered, first with his fingers, then with his tongue—exploring and stroking until she moved in response, lifting closer and closer, asking for more and more. She gasped for breath as the sensations continued to build and build until she thought she would explode into a thousand sparks of ecstasy.

"Wait." Her desire was almost unbearable, but she wanted the first time . . . *their* first time . . . to be together. Rebecca lowered herself to face him.

"Do you want to stop?" he managed to say through ragged breaths, the pain of the question in his voice.

Rebecca clasped his head to her breasts. "Oh, no. I want you now . . . inside me."

When Steve raised his head, she could see the flames of desire in his eyes, feel the passion in his masterful seduction. He lowered her back onto the blanket, then stroked her body until she writhed beside him.

Feeling as if she were going to die if he waited much longer, Rebecca took matters into her own hands. She reached down between their bodies and caught his throbbing shaft in her hands. Wrapping her fingers around him, she felt the heat in every swollen inch as she rubbed and caressed until Steve moaned in pleasure. "Come inside me," she pleaded. "Now." She knew he was close . . . and so was she.

Rebecca reclined on the blanket and Steve straddled her with one knee on each side of her hips. His gaze smoldered in the flickering candlelight, the hot depths of his eyes setting her aflame as she slid her hands up his thighs. She guided him over her, then pressed him down until once again she could feel his rigid tenseness.

"You're beautiful," he whispered. In one tender motion he gently eased inside her. She desperately wanted—needed—to move. Lifting to meet his tentative rhythm, she wasn't surprised when they quickly reached a frenzied tempo. With a hunger she didn't know she possessed, she met him thrust for thrust, feeling the heat of unbridled desire as her body clenched around his.

In the final glorious moment, as she exploded into a spasm of ecstasy, she cried, "I love you, I love you," over and over until she shuddered and clung to his chest. When she opened her eyes to see him smiling, the realization hit to her very core. "I . . . uh, left you, didn't I?"

Steve placed her hand over his rigid member. "Only for a little while."

She guided him inside again, then rolled over on top before beginning to move again. As they stared into each other's eyes, Rebecca felt a new wave of desire as she began to respond, knowing that this time would be faster, more intense. Steve placed his hands on her swelling nipples, and she groaned as the wild, hot ache shivered inside her a second time. Within moments, Steve's body trembled and bucked in a shattering release. Soft moans emerged from his lips as Rebecca collapsed on top of him.

In the quiet afterward, she lay in his arms, still craving the touch of his reassuring hands on her body as the dim candlelight flickered shadows on the cave's walls. They hugged and kissed in that intimate way reserved only for people in love, their bodies still moist from their passionate embrace.

"I love you, Rebecca, with all my heart and soul." He pushed a stray curl away from her face as they lay together with the blanket pulled around them. In the husky voice she had come to adore, he added, "I just wanted to say that . . . wanted you to hear the words from me."

A deep feeling of love swept over Rebecca—not the burning kind she'd had before, but the rock-solid assurance she knew would last forever. "I'm glad," she whispered. "I love you, too." He kissed her with so much feeling that she thought she'd cry from the sheer tenderness of it.

After a while, they decided to take a swim in the warm, bubbling water. They played and splashed and enjoyed the kind of secret moments two new lovers share until finally, Steve leaned on the edge to rest. "I've got an idea." He turned his head toward her and smiled. She recognized the gleam in his eyes and knew that he had something planned. "You've been stuck in this cave for hours on end. What do you say we get dressed and go for a short walk in the moonlight?"

Her first reaction was that it was cold and dark outside, but she had to admit she did have "cave fever," so she agreed. "Sounds great!" Together they got out, dried, then dressed. A bright flush crept up her neck as she gathered her clothes, remembering the passionate reason they were scattered all over the cave's floor.

Steve had been wonderful . . . but that wasn't a surprise. Her surprise was at herself and the depth of her response. It wasn't that she'd forgotten how . . . it was that she'd never reacted that way before.

When they left the warmth of the cave, the cold winter air sent shivers down Steve's spine he couldn't contain. "Just last week it was hot . . . now it's freezing up here in the mountains." He snapped on the flashlight as they walked into the clearing.

Rebecca shoved her hands in her pockets. "It had to turn cold. It's Christmas, remember?"

He remembered, all right. "I believe I was greeted with a 'Merry Christmas' before . . ." his voice trailed off. A tiny sliver of moon peeked out from the clouds, lighting her beautiful face with its hazy glow.

"You heard?" she asked, surprise in her voice.

He linked his arm in hers, his pulse racing from the touch of her fingers curled around his forearm. "Of course I heard, but my mind was on more important things at that moment."

She laughed—the low, throaty laugh he found so sexy. "Why, you—" she threatened in a playful tone.

He couldn't resist teasing. "Is that a complaint?"

"Not a chance." The satisfaction in her voice made his heart lurch madly. It confirmed that she'd enjoyed it as much as he. And oh, how he had enjoyed making love to Rebecca. He paused. "It—" he started, but stopped.

"It what?"

"Oh, nothing."

"Don't nothing me. Go ahead," she prodded. "It . . . what?"

He hesitated, then decided to be open about his feelings, not to hold back. "I've wanted you for so long . . . I just wanted it to be 'right' . . . to be perfect."

In the middle of the clearing, Rebecca stopped abruptly. "You listen here, Steve Jordan. It might not have been the perfect place or the perfect time . . . but it *was* perfect."

"Have I told you how much I love you?"

"You can always tell me again."

Steve switched off the flashlight, placing it by his feet. He gathered Rebecca in his arms and crushed her lips in a soul-searching kiss. "I love you." He turned her around so that her back pressed against him, keeping one arm snaked around her waist. Broadly he motioned to the sky twinkling with stars. "Since it's Christmas, I want to give you your present."

"I think you already have," she laughed, a warmth flooding her senses as she remembered his passion . . . their passion.

With a small nervous cough, he said, "I know you never believed in the 'man take care of woman' theory, so I gave up the notion of giving you the *moon*."

Rebecca chuckled and tilted her head so she

could see his face. "Yeah, I got over the moon stuff a long time ago."

"I know." Just the sound of his strong, affectionate voice made her feel glad to be near him. "Besides, you proved you could do it *all* on your own." He ran his hand down her arm. "That's one of the things I love about you."

When he kissed the back of her neck, she groaned, "Oh, Steve." The very touch of his lips on her skin kindled feelings as wild and intense as the forest fire that had changed her life forever.

"I wanted to give you something that showed you the depth of my feelings—something that would live on for eternity . . . like our love." He cupped her face and stared into her eyes. "You put the sparkle back into my life at a time when I thought my life was over . . . you *are* my life." With a deep sigh, he motioned to the sky. "One of those is named for you, Rebecca—brightening the night just the way you brighten my world."

She looked to the heavens in amazement. "A star?" When he nodded, she kissed his palm and held it to her heart, unable to speak. She stroked his hand in silence until she could suppress the deluge of tears threatening the dam of her emotions. "That's one of the sweetest, most romantic gifts I've ever received."

She felt the movement of his breathing against the back of her neck. "You really like it?"

"I *love* it."

Grabbing her by the shoulders, Steve swung her around to face him. "Rebecca, I have to ask you something . . . very important . . . it can't wait any longer."

"Steve—" she tried to break in, but he wouldn't let her. She knew what he was trying to say . . . at least she thought she knew. She let him continue . . . needing to hear the words.

"Rebecca, marry me. I want us to have everything . . . a home . . . family . . . love . . . everything."

He had stoked the gentle fire growing inside, then fanned the flames to a roaring blaze. "A family?" She smiled—half-amused, half-sad that she never could have children with this wonderful man. "You know I'm way past that stage of my life."

He chuckled. "How do you feel about a ready-made family? My family will be *your* family . . . Melinda, Joey, the boys."

As he gripped her waist with his hands, she felt an eagerness from him. Rebecca leaned forward and whispered in his ear, "How do you feel about making love to a grandmother? That's what I'd be, right?"

"Uh . . . well . . . do you want to be?"

Snuggling close, she put her arms around his neck. "I can't wait."

A soft gasp escaped Steve's lips. "Does this mean . . . ?"

"Yes, Steve. You've got yourself a partner."

He caught her face tenderly between his hands. "For life?"

In a hushed whisper, she promised, "Forever."

About the Author

Betty Cothran lives and works in beautiful Flowery Branch, Georgia, on the shores of Lake Lanier. When not writing, she enjoys boating with her husband, reading, and pampering her Welsh Corgi, Skipper, the only dog on the lake who hates water. *Over the Moon* is her first novel.

IT'S NEVER TOO LATE
TO FALL IN LOVE!

MAYBE LATER, LOVE   (3903, $4.50/$5.50)
by Claire Bocardo
Dorrie Greene was astonished! After thirty-five years of being
"George Greene's lovely wife" she was now a whole new person. She
could take things at her own pace, and she could choose the man she
wanted. Life and love were better than ever!

MRS. PERFECT   (3789, $4.50/$5.50)
by Peggy Roberts
Devastated by the loss of her husband and son, Ginny Logan worked
longer and longer hours at her job in an ad agency. Just when she had
decided she could live without love, a warm, wonderful man noticed
her and brought love back into her life.

OUT OF THE BLUE   (3798, $4.50/$5.50)
by Garda Parker
Recently widowed, besieged by debt, and stuck in a dead-end job,
Majesty Wilde was taking life one day at a time. Then fate stepped in,
and the opportunity to restore a small hotel seemed like a dream come
true . . . especially when a rugged pilot offered to help!

THE TIME OF HER LIFE   (3739, $4.50/$5.50)
by Marjorie Eatock
Evelyn Cass's old friends whispered about her behind her back. They
felt sorry for poor Evelyn—alone at fifty-five, having to sell her
house, and go to work! Funny how she was looking ten years younger
and for the first time in years, Evelyn was having the time of her life!

TOMORROW'S PROMISE   (3894, $4.50/$5.50)
by Clara Wimberly
It takes a lot of courage for a woman to leave a thirty-three year marriage. But when Margaret Avery's aged father died and left her a
small house in Florida, she knew that the moment had come. The
change was far more difficult than she had anticipated. Then things
started looking up. Happiness had been there all the time, just waiting for her.

*Available wherever paperbacks are sold, or order direct from the
Publisher. Send cover price plus 50¢ per copy for mailing and
handling to Penguin USA, P.O. Box 999, c/o Dept. 17109,
Bergenfield, NJ 07621. Residents of New York and Tennessee
must include sales tax. DO NOT SEND CASH.*

WATCH AS THESE WOMEN LEARN
TO LOVE AGAIN

HELLO LOVE   (4094, $4.50/$5.50)
by Joan Shapiro

Family tragedy leaves Barbara Sinclair alone with her success. The fight to gain custody of her young granddaughter brings a confrontation with the determined rancher Sam Douglass. Also widowed, Sam has been caring for Emily alone, guided by his own ideas of childrearing. Barbara challenges his ideas. And that's not all she challenges . . . Long-buried desires surface, then gentle affection. Sam and Barbara cannot ignore the chance to love again.

THE BEST MEDICINE   (4220, $4.50/$5.50)
by Janet Lane Walters

Her late husband's expenses push Maggie Carr back to nursing, the career she left almost thirty years ago. The night shift is difficult, but it's harder still to ignore the way handsome Dr. Jason Knight soothes his patients. When she lends a hand to help his daughter, Jason and Maggie grow closer than simply doctor and nurse. Obstacles to romance seem insurmountable, but Maggie knows that love is always the best medicine.

AND BE MY LOVE   (4291, $4.50/$5.50)
by Joyce C. Ware

Selflessly catering first to husband, then children, grandchildren, and her aging, though imperious mother, leaves Beth Volmar little time for her own adventures or passions. Then, the handsome archaeologist Karim Donovan arrives and campaigns to widen the boundaries of her narrow life. Beth finds new freedom when Karim insists that she accompany him to Turkey on an archaeological dig . . . and a journey towards loving again.

OVER THE RAINBOW   (4032, $4.50/$5.50)
by Marjorie Eatock

Fifty-something, divorced for years, courted by more than one attractive man, and thoroughly enjoying her job with a large insurance company, Marian's sudden restlessness confuses her. She welcomes the chance to travel on business to a small Mississippi town. Full of good humor and words of love, Don Worth makes her feel needed, and not just to assess property damage. Marian takes the risk.

A KISS AT SUNRISE   (4260, $4.50/$5.50)
by Charlotte Sherman

Beginning widowhood and retirement, Ruth Nichols has her first taste of freedom. Against the advice of her mother and daughter, Ruth heads for an adventure in the motor home that has sat unused since her husband's death. Long days and lonely campgrounds start to dampen the excitement of traveling alone. That is, until a dapper widower named Jack parks next door and invites her for dinner. On the road, Ruth and Jack find the chance to love again.

Available wherever paperbacks are sold, or order direct from the Publisher. Send cover price plus 50¢ per copy for mailing and handling to Penguin USA, P.O. Box 999, c/o Dept. 17109, Bergenfield, NJ 07621. Residents of New York and Tennessee must include sales tax. DO NOT SEND CASH.

MAKE THE
ROMANCE CONNECTION

Z-TALK
Online

Come talk to your favorite authors and get the inside scoop on everything that's going on in the world of romance publishing, from the only online service that's designed exclusively for the publishing industry.

With Z-Talk Online Information Service, the most innovative and exciting computer bulletin board around, you can:

- ♥ CHAT "LIVE" WITH AUTHORS, FELLOW ROMANCE READERS, AND OTHER MEMBERS OF THE ROMANCE PUBLISHING COMMUNITY.

- ♥ FIND OUT ABOUT UPCOMING TITLES BEFORE THEY'RE RELEASED.

- ♥ DOWNLOAD THOUSANDS OF FILES AND GAMES.

- ♥ READ REVIEWS OF ROMANCE TITLES.

- ♥ HAVE UNLIMITED USE OF E-MAIL.

- ♥ POST MESSAGES ON OUR DOZENS OF TOPIC BOARDS.

All it takes is a computer and a modem to get online with Z-Talk. Set your modem to 8/N/1, and dial 212-545-1120. If you need help, call the System Operator, at 212-889-2299, ext. 260. There's a two week free trial period. After that, annual membership is only $ 60.00.

See you online!

KENSINGTON PUBLISHING CORP.